Vanessa Gordon lives in Surrey and studied English and Irish literature before having a career in the music industry. She has travelled all over Greece, and enjoys learning about the country, its language and its history.

The Naxos Mysteries are set on the largest island in the Cyclades. Inhabited since the time of the Neanderthals, Naxos was an important site during the archaic Cycladic period, thrived in the Classical era, and was in the control of the Venetians for over three hundred years.

Today it is an island of contrasts. The main town is crowned by a Venetian kastro and surrounded by an interesting old town. Inland you can find uninhabited hills, the highest mountain in the Cyclades, attractive villages, quiet beaches and archaeological sites. There are historic towers and welcoming tavernas, collectable art and ceramics, and Naxos has produced some of the finest marble in Greece since ancient times.

This is where Martin Day has chosen to live, and for good reason.

BY THE SAME AUTHOR

The Naxos Mysteries

The Meaning of Friday

The Search for Artemis

Black Acorns

The Disappearance of Ophelia Blue

The Reach of the Past

The Reach
of the Past

A Naxos mystery *with Martin Day*

Vanessa Gordon

Published by Pomeg Books 2023

PoD - ISBN: 978-1-7393053-0-7
eBook - ISBN: 978-1-7393053-1-4

Pomeg Books is an imprint of
Dolman Scott Ltd
www.dolmanscott.co.uk

To James and Alastair

I am very grateful to my invaluable readers, Kay Elliott, Alan Gordon and Maroula Kondyli; to publisher Richard Chalmers and his team at Dolman Scott; and to proofreader Phil Clinker. I would like also to thank Professor Panayiotis Liaropoulos (Berklee College of Music and The Fulbright Foundation), for sharing his enthusiasm for and knowledge of the music of the Cycladic Islands; Marios Bazeos (Bazeos Tower, Naxos); Jean Polyzoides (Paros); Suzanne Hay (Naxos); and Lena Yacoumopoulou (Paros).

I am specially indebted to the friend who told me her own story, which was the basis for that of Paraskevi in *The Reach of the Past*. I am so happy that the outcome for her turned out so much better than it did for my characters.

Thank you, finally, to Robert Pitt, through whose friendship I have been able to explore the historic sites and collections of Greece in intelligent company, and who has kindled my love for the country, its islands and its antiquities.

Selected Further Reading

McGilchrist's Greek Islands Nigel McGilchrist
The Wines of Greece Konstantinos Lazarakis
Loot, Legitimacy and Ownership Colin Renfrew
Athenian Black Figure Vases John Boardman

More suggestions on www.thenaxosmysteries.co.uk

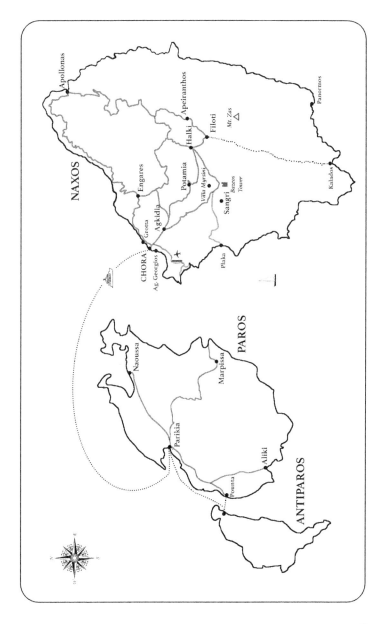

A NOTE ABOUT GREEK WORDS

MEN'S NAMES
When the man is spoken to directly, or as a close friend, the ending of his name can change, often dropping the final s.
Andreas/Andrea.
Irregular cases include *Alexandros/Alexandre.*

PLACE NAMES
Chora and *Halki* begin with the same sound as in the Scottish 'loch' (*x* in Greek).
Agios/agia means saint. *Agios Georgios* St George; *Agia Triada* Holy Trinity

GREETINGS & EXPRESSIONS
Kyrie (plural *Kyrioi*) and *Kyria* are forms of address like Monsieur and Madame
Kyrios is the word for Mr when not addressing him directly
Mou means 'my' and is often used after a name as a term of affection, as in
Agapi mou - my dear, my love
Kalimera - Hello, Good morning (*Kalimera sas* - formal or plural)
Kalispera - Good evening (*Kalispera sas* - formal or plural)
Yeia sou - Hello (*Yeia sas* - formal or plural; *Yeia* - Hi)
Ti kaneis - How are you? (*Ti kanete* - formal or plural)
Pos paei - How are things? *(poss-PIE)*
Etsi ki etsi - So-so
Kala - Fine, well
Kala, eseis? - Fine, and you?
Tha peite kafe? - You want a coffee? (lit. You drink coffee?)

Efharisto - Thank you
Hairo poli - Pleased to meet you
Kalos irthate - Welcome
Kali orexi - Bon appétit
Stin ygeia mas/Yeia mas - good health, cheers
Elate! - Enter!
Parakalo - Please. Also used as a way to answer the phone.
Physica - Of course, naturally
Panagia mou! - an explanation of shock, Holy Mary!
Lipon - Now, well, let's see
Adio - Goodbye
Polla - a lot (of things)

GENERAL

estiatorio - restaurant
zacharoplasteio - confectionery shop
kafeneio - traditional cafe
plateia - town square
paralia - beach, seafront
limani - port
kastro - castle
bourgos - area beneath the castle
fournos - bakery
tavernaki - little taverna (-aki is diminutive)
komboloi - popular string of beads
filoxenia - hospitality
meltemi - prevailing wind in the Cyclades
katharevousa - more formal modern Greek language
alkyoni - kingfisher
helithoni - swallow
myrsini - myrtle (plant)
sigma - Greek letter s

rho - Greek letter r
omicron - Greek letter o
archygos - commander, leader
anakritis - investigating judge
kefi - good mood, high spirits

FOOD & DRINK

kafes - coffee
Kitron - a liqueur made from kitron fruit on Naxos
tsipouro - distilled spirit (ts-EE-puro), not to be confused with
tsipoura - sea bream (tsi-PUR-a)
misokilo - half kilo: wine is measured by weight in Greece
kokkino - red
koulouraki(a) - Greek biscuit(s) (from *kouloura,* a coil)
horiatiki (salata) - the traditional Greek salad
kritharaki - small pasta like Italian orzo
dakos - rusk used in a salad
fava - yellow split-pea dip
meze/ mezedes - small savoury plate(s) of food
hortopites - vegetable pies
barbounia - red mullet
boureki - in this case, a baked vegetable dish with potatoes,
aubergines and cheese
kritamo - sea fennel, rock samphire
revithada - chickpea stew
marathokeftédes - fennel patties
kalogeros - veal or beef speciality dish of Naxos
patatato - meat and potato stew
baklavas - honey and nut slice
methismena - tipsy
amygdalota - marzipan specialities
raki - clear liquor made from grapes

rigani - Greek for oregano
patates tyganites - fried potatoes, chips
giouvetsi - lamb cooked in a clay pot (yu-VET-si)
saganaki - small frying pan
shrimp saganaki - cooked in the saganaki with tomato sauce and feta cheese
briam - roasted vegetables, Greek ratatouille

CHEESES

graviera - similar to Gruyere, made on Naxos (cow/sheep)
arseniko - hard cheese, made on Naxos, becomes spicy as it ages (goat)
x*ynomyzithra* - soft, white, creamy, sour cheese (sheep/goat)
xynotyri - hard, flaky, pungent sour cheese. (sheep/goat) (*xyno* sour, *tyri* cheese)

1

In the glow of the early evening, the speedboat in the bay appeared black against the shining surface of the sea. It was going fast, turning sharply, making another pass and turning again. The young man at the wheel was only a silhouette to anyone watching from the shore, yet his every movement was graceful. Using one hand to steer and the other to point towards the land, he was expertly balancing his body as the boat lurched and bounced in the turmoil of its own making. His passenger was a girl, but the details of her dark hair and pale face were similarly invisible in the gauzy late-afternoon light.

The small town of Koroni in the western Peloponnese, off whose shore the speedboat was playing, was undeniably a beautiful place. White houses with terracotta tiles sprawled alongside the serene waters of the Messenian Gulf, and palm trees abounded in its streets. The hill behind the town was crowned with a large Venetian castle that extended along its ridge. The couple in the speedboat could have chosen to holiday in Koroni for its beauty alone, but of more importance to them was its location: an hour by road from Kalamata.

It was, therefore, an ideal distance from home. Here at Koroni they could do exactly as they wished; here they need not hide their love.

This was, unfortunately, the last day of their visit; tomorrow they would have to return to work, to the need for pretence. To make the most of the day, the young lovers had not hesitated when told of a local man with a fast boat for hire. They had taken it down the coast to the uninhabited island of Venetiko, where they had spent many blissful hours together before returning to Koroni for their last night of freedom.

Now, as the sun began to sink behind the castle, they were forced at last to return to port. They sat close together in the boat, his arm round her waist, her head on his shoulder.

The entertaining display out in the bay had attracted the attention of the people taking the evening *volta* along the shore and those in the bars that lined the water's edge. The subdued homecoming of the couple was remarked upon, as was their romantic appearance in the mellow light of the setting sun. At the Taverna Byzantino, one of the older men looked up from his game of backgammon and murmured something to his neighbour.

'Those two will have fine, brave children - if they survive!' he said.

His friend smiled and nodded in agreement, and after a moment of reflection they resumed their game.

2

Archaeologist and TV presenter Martin Day had come to regard Andreas Nomikos as a good friend. They shared a passionate dislike of the lucrative illegal trade in Greek cultural heritage: the looting, smuggling and selling of ancient artefacts. That alone was a reasonable basis for a friendship of otherwise strongly contrasting personalities.

Despite being Greek by birth, Andreas had a mane of fair hair and the light blue eyes of his Norwegian mother that contrasted alarmingly with his Mediterranean complexion. His colleagues in the Helladic Police called him the Viking Policeman, though never to his face. He was broad and stocky, carried himself with authority, and had about him a professional air of Viking power and Spartan determination. He had recently been promoted to the rank of chief inspector.

Day, the classicist who had chosen life in the Cyclades over the rigours of academia, was tall, lean, and took things at an easy pace. When Andreas had invited him to Paros, Day had accepted immediately, telling himself that the review he was writing for a professional journal, already late, could wait a little longer.

He accepted a cold beer from his friend and chose a chair on Andreas's terrace with a good view across Paros to the sea. He placed his sunglasses on his face but wore no hat against the July sun. His light hair and complexion were occasionally an inconvenience to him when exploring shadeless ancient sites in his adopted Greece, but in general he tried to ignore it.

'This place was a great investment, Andrea,' he said, comfortably stretching out his legs.

'Thanks, I'm pleased with it. Paros is still a refuge of peace and quiet once you get away from the port.'

Day agreed completely; it was, after all, the reason he himself had bought a place on nearby Naxos. Paros had always struck him as a more gentle island than Naxos, but away from the coast both retained their rural character. Unlike Athens, where he owned a small apartment, the islands were still serene and largely unspoilt, except on those where tourism had begun to take over. Here, on a hill above Parikia, you could still hear a car door closing from half a mile away. Sparrows chattered in the low vegetation of the nearby field as they darted from one seed-head to another. A pair of collared doves in amorous pursuit made a wheezing noise with their wings, and the bleating of a sheep carried up to them from a smallholding in the valley. The heat of the summer sun seemed to make the reversing warning of a lorry a mile away seem just another element of the idyll. He took a deep swallow of his beer with satisfaction.

It would be good for Andreas to come here at times from Athens, where his job kept him tied to a rented apartment in Koukaki. The place he had bought was a modern version of the traditional Cycladic house: square, white and flat-roofed. It even had a distant view of the sea. The main town, Parikia, lay to the west, clearly visible but far enough away to appear to be sleeping in the sun. To the north, the land dropped away into a tranquil valley, then rose again to the hills at the tip of the island. You could see yellow fields of desiccated grass, dark patches of woodland, swathes of tall bamboo, and telegraph poles from which the wires hung low in the heat. What a contrast to the log-jam of traffic in the city.

'How much time will you be able to spend here?' Day asked, making himself comfortable with his feet on the rung of an adjacent chair.

'Less than I'd like. The job will keep me in Athens most of the time. I can only stay for a few more weeks before I'll need to get back.'

'How have you managed that? Seems a lot of leave for a policeman. Has crime in Athens dried up? It will do you good, though. You work too hard, you know.'

Andreas smiled and drank the last of his beer. He envied Day his casual attitude to life, only accepting work that interested him, doing just enough to fund his lifestyle in Greece. With an effort, he changed the subject to avoid speaking about the case which would allow him several more weeks here in the Cyclades.

'When are you expecting Helen to return?' he asked.

'There's no date yet. She's still busy in London. We talk on the phone, though; she's well.'

'Just not here with you,' murmured Andreas sympathetically.

Day smiled but said no more. He would prefer not to discuss his concerns about Helen with Andreas, even though he knew he was being unreasonable. There had been a time, a few years ago, when Andreas had been attracted to Helen himself and had begun to take her out; this was when Day had regarded her simply as a friend. Andreas's interest in her been a wake-up call for him, and it still shocked him to think how close he had been to losing her.

He was, however, more worried by her long absence than he liked to admit. He went over it every night in his mind. Yes, the reason for her trip to London had been work-related, but that gave him little comfort; she should have been back by now. He had no idea what he had done wrong, though he was quite willing to accept that he had said or done something insensitive. He was equally surprised that she had not simply told him about it, in her usual direct way. In his more reflective moments he had been wondering whether he had simply been a bachelor too long. Perhaps Helen had come to regret the relationship that brought him such happiness. The worst thing was that he had absolutely no idea.

Andreas had moved on.

'I've found a rather special woman myself, here on Paros,' Andreas said, interrupting his thoughts. 'We met when I came to view this house.'

Day was intrigued and saved from the gloom of his introspection. It seemed impossible that Andreas Nomikos had time for a relationship. The man never seemed to be off-duty, yet somehow always managed to have a personal life. He asked for details.

'She's an artist. She rents a small apartment behind the church of Agios Konstantinos. Do you know it?'

'Isn't that the church in the *kastro* of Parikia, overlooking the sea? The one built on ancient foundations?'

'Yes, that's it. She lives just behind it.'

'I'm jealous. That area must be really expensive, too.'

'Yes, it's not cheap, but the apartment is quite small. When she first arrived, she was supported by a charitable foundation for the arts, and now she can afford the keep the place. Her work sells well.'

'Is she from the islands?'

'No, from Karditsa in Thessaly.'

'Ah, the land of sausages and bicycles, which she has wisely exchanged for grilled *barbounia* and the glittering Aegean.'

'Indeed, she made the right decision. Life as an artist in the Cyclades is a good life.'

'What's her name? And how did you meet?'

'Fotini. We actually met in the street. She was coming out of the *fournos* next to the land agency that was selling this house. We bumped into each other - that's the English expression, isn't it?'

Day smiled; he enjoyed it when Andreas ventured to use colloquial expressions.

'I hope she didn't drop her shopping in the collision,' he joked. 'By the way, congratulations on your promotion. Chief inspector now, very impressive. New rank, new house and new lady.'

Andreas smiled vaguely towards the distant town, pulling on his beer. Day realised he had moved on from the subject of Fotini too soon.

'Tell me more about her.'

'We went for coffee right after we met, then for dinner the next evening. She invited me to her studio and showed me her paintings. She paints large seascapes, but also likes to do a few portraits, mostly of friends. She asked me to sit for her, actually, and she's doing one of me. She's very easy to talk to, it's a joy to be with her.' He nodded reflectively. 'I hope I can stay in touch with her when I go back to Athens. Only time will tell, I suppose.'

'I'd like to meet her,' said Day. 'Perhaps we can fix up something when Helen is back.'

Andreas agreed and went inside to fetch more beer, leaving Day looking across to the sea. The ferry *Blue Star Delos* glided round the headland and began its approach to Parikia port, sounding its horn before turning and reversing to the quay. From his viewpoint up on the hillside, Day heard its warning notes only distantly, and nothing of the clamour and frenetic meet-and-greet that would be taking place at the port. He raised his eyes to the horizon where, beyond the open sea, the island of Sifnos appeared to be no more than a slightly darker version of the sky, its high outline made insubstantial by the mist of distance.

He wondered what Helen was doing in England at that moment. London seemed impossibly far away. He wished she was here with him. Andreas's story of Fotini, his wistful tone and cheerful patience, had done nothing to assuage Day's own pangs of longing. He would ring her tomorrow. Would morning be best? Or evening? He didn't know. That was part of the problem.

An oddly insistent noise made him look round. A disorganised group of colourful birds, about eight of them, were flying at speed in the air to his right. Their flight was dazzling, chaotic, anarchic, and their screaming seemed without purpose. Bee-eaters, one of the few birds in Greece that he recognised. They appeared to be looking for the right direction to go before making a group decision. Their unmelodious calls became ever more strident, then rilled into a single knuckle of sound, and suddenly they were gone.

They must be in transit, he thought. Spring migration, perhaps. They might not know where they are going, but at least they know with whom.

Andreas returned with two more bottles of cold Mythos just in time to pluck him from his melancholy.

'Sorry, I had to take a call,' he said. 'Do you have any work on at the moment?'

'Actually, yes, something rather unusual. I picked up a nice job only last week. It's for a Greek-American who owns a private villa in a remote spot on Naxos. He booked me to give a couple of talks on archaeology to some important guests who'll be arriving soon to stay with him. It pays extremely well, I could hardly turn it down, and it sounds fun. I have to talk for an hour on a subject of my choice and join the guests for lunch afterwards.'

'That sounds perfect for you, and you for the job.'

'Yes, I thought so too. I did a little investigating online. The villa looks a stunning place, up in the hills near Sangri. The owner was born on Naxos but spent all his life in New York, where he made a fortune in top-end interior design, married well, and retired early back to Naxos. He had the old family home converted, complete with swimming pool and landscaped garden. It's called the Villa Myrsini.'

Andreas turned to him with interest. 'I seem to know that name.'

'Myrsini was the name of his design brand in the USA. It's the Greek for the myrtle bush, of course, and the flower was the company logo. The owner's name is Stelios Ioannides.'

'Have you been told who the guests will be?'

'I only know they'll be arriving on a yacht in time for the wine festival.'

'And when is your first talk at the Villa Myrsini?'

'A week on Tuesday. The second one is the following Tuesday, after the end of the wine festival. Why? You're sounding like a policeman, Andrea.'

'That's what I am, my friend.'

'Is something the matter? Are you going to tell me what this is about?'

'I'm sorry, I can't. Official business. What subject will you talk about to these important guests?'

'Oh, I don't know yet. I'm going to the villa next week, I should get a better sense of what they want then. Come on, you can trust me.'

'I'm sorry, I really can't discuss it. But I will say one thing, Martin: be on your guard. Take my advice, and don't get too involved with the people at the Villa Myrsini.'

3

On his way to the Villa Myrsini the following week, Day drove faster than usual, enjoying the fresh air through his open window. He had rolled up his shirt sleeves and the sun was already pricking his left forearm. It was no surprise that July on Naxos was remorselessly hot; all Europe was having a heatwave. No rain had fallen on the island in the last few weeks, and none was forecast till November. The farmers were worried, but the tourist industry had no complaints.

From his house in Filoti to the Villa Myrsini was only eight kilometres. He passed through the central village of Halki and followed the old road south-west towards Sangri. It was late morning and there was very little traffic. He had been told that the Ioannides family estate was set in a sparsely-inhabited area of undulating hills to the south of the restored Paleologos Tower, and was accessed by its own private drive. The directions mentioned a small, unnamed road leading uphill which he was to follow for about a kilometre, and the entrance to the Villa Myrsini would be on his left.

There were so few turnings off the road that he managed to find the entrance without a problem. The Ioannides estate was announced by a pair of tall white pillars supporting imposing cast-iron gates which were wide open and were probably never closed, to judge by the grass and scrub that grew through them at the base. The drive was rutted and gritty, but once he saw the house he paid the track no attention.

The Villa Myrsini clearly had its own water source, for it stood within a garden of conifers, pines and olives. He passed a small grove of fruit trees, oranges or lemons perhaps. Helen would have known which they were. Even at first glance, the work of the landscapers was evident. The house, too, bore all the hallmarks of professional restoration and considerable investment. It was in the Cycladic style, with white walls and a flat roof, but on a scale that elevated the tradition to new levels. Two slender towers with decorative perforations rose several metres above the building at the back, reminding Day fleetingly of the dovecotes of Tinos, and a low white wall encircled the property but for an elegant flight of white marble steps leading up to the main door.

As he parked the car in the shade and got out to stretch his legs gratefully, a slim woman in her early thirties opened the front door. She managed to look cool in light blue trousers and a white shirt, her dark hair tied back. He acknowledged her wave of welcome and began to climb the magnificent marble steps.

'Hello, I'm Maria Ioannides,' said the woman with a slight American accent, shaking hands. 'You're Martin Day? Thank you so much for coming. I hope you found us easily? Come inside and meet my father.'

She turned away and he followed her into the house.

This must be Stelios Ioannides's daughter, he thought. Her upbringing in New York accounted for her accent and explained why her surname had no feminine ending, as was the more usual custom in Greece. An air of competence and responsibility about her contrasted pleasingly with a certain innocence. Day found her immediately attractive, and it took the cool air of the interior of the house to divert his attention back to his surroundings.

The Villa Myrsini welcomed its visitors through a pair of arched, glazed doors into a dining room that would accommodate at least ten people. To Day's surprise, the furnishings were simple, almost modest, with a hint of traditional Mediterranean style. The modern glass dining table was surrounded by wooden chairs in the Greek fashion, painted olive green. Large ornate mirrors, their frames white or silver, reflected the light from the windows. The walls and the marble-tiled floor were white, and a black chandelier hung over the table. It was simple, in keeping with its Cycladic home, and it was perfect.

Maria led him through another arch to the next room, the living room. Arranged around a central glass coffee table in an informal circle was a collection of sofas and small chairs, all upholstered in matching cinnamon-coloured material that gave the room a decidedly non-Greek appearance, but a sense of calm. The paintings on the walls were unmistakably valuable.

'Please take a seat, Martin,' said Maria. 'My father will be with you in a moment. Would you excuse me?'

She turned her back on him again and left through a door at the far end of the room. Day sat down in an armchair and looked round. Another arched opening led into a marbled hall from which a staircase rose to an upper floor. A stairlift was fitted to this flight of stairs, and a pair of wooden sticks were propped against the rail. On a console table were some family photographs in a variety of frames, and there were more on a dresser by the wall. There were no books to be seen and very few ornaments, but on a marble plinth in the corner of the room stood a modern sculpture, a bronze bird in flight, maybe a kingfisher, larger than life-size and intricately worked.

The sound of a walking stick and the clearing of a throat announced the arrival of Stelios Ioannides. A small man in a suit, he appeared in the doorway through which Maria had gone. Day stood up. The Greek squinted at him through the rectangular lenses of his glasses, nodded, smiled, and came further into the room.

'I see you have noticed my *alkyoni*, Mr Day.'

With the tip of his walking stick the old man gestured towards the bronze sculpture of the kingfisher, before lowering himself into his seat.

'The kingfisher is the emblem of my family,' he continued. 'That model was made for me by a friend in New York. Now then, I really am delighted to meet you at last. I hope you can stay and talk to me for a while?'

'Of course, I'd be delighted,' said Day. That, indeed, was the reason he had come, but Stelios Ioannides seemed to imply the desire for company. 'I'm curious to know how you found me, Kyrie Ioannide.'

'That was not difficult, in fact. A small matter of lunch with an acquaintance of mine, the curator of the local museum. He was quick to recommend you as somebody both knowledgeable about Greek antiquity and blessed with a certain flair with words. Would you agree with that description of you, Mr Day? You've made a number of broadcasts on subjects covering Greek history, I believe?'

'I'm extremely grateful to the curator,' said Day politely, making a mental note to buy his friend Aristos a drink. 'Yes, I enjoy the filming side of my work. My last job was a series for the BBC on Greek marble from Classical times to the present day.'

'Yes, the curator told me of that. An enormous project. Will you stay for lunch, Mr Day? It would be pleasant to talk longer, wouldn't it?'

The old man used the end of his stick to press a small button set into the wall near his chair, and they sat in silence waiting for the outcome. Day guessed the button was a bell to summon somebody. Maria, perhaps.

'I shall call you Martin. You will call me Stelio,' said the old man firmly, then he shot Day a broad smile that deepened the lines round his cheeks and pulled apart his generous lips. 'Good, that's agreed. I don't like formality.'

Day took in the well-cut grey suit, pink shirt and striped tie, the gold pin on the lapel, the heavy gold watch, and the polished leather shoes, all of which were surprising in a Cycladic setting in July on a retired man who struggled with mobility. They were not indicative of informality. He was saved the need to comment by the arrival of Maria.

'Maria *mou*, our friend Martin is staying for lunch. Oh dear, of course, Yianni's still in town …'

'I can sort out the lunch, Papa. Perhaps Martin would like me to show him round the villa later?'

'Excellent idea, *agapi mou*. You must particularly show him my library; he'll be interested to see it.'

Maria smiled at them both and returned the way she had come.

'I'm so lucky in my children, Martin. When I lost my wife five years ago, my health took a bad turn. Maria looked after her mother until she died, and now she has to take care of her old father. It isn't much of a life for her. My son Yianni - Maria's twin brother - he takes care of all our meals. He trained as a chef in New York. Am I not blessed?'

'In your children, certainly. I'm sorry to hear of your loss.'

'Thank you, that's very kind. Now, Martin, let's talk about you. Far more interesting.'

Stelios struggled to remove something from the bag that hung over the back of his chair. It turned out to be a copy of the biography of Nikos Elias, the historian from Naxos, which Day had written a few years before.

'Your book on Elias,' said Stelios, waving it in front of him. 'Excellent, very insightful. Would you look at the paragraph I've marked?'

Day took the book from him and opened it at the bookmark. Some lines had been bracketed in pencil. He read them aloud.

'*As a young man, Elias was involved in the recovery of several vases of considerable historical value from the excavation at Pavos in Attica. These were presented to the National Archaeological Museum in Athens, where they are on permanent display. There is in the group a beautifully painted kalpis vase of some importance which Elias draws and describes in his papers.*'

He stopped reading and looked up.

'Why this particular section, Stelio?'

'I was thinking that your first lecture might touch on the painted vases of the Classical period in Greece. What do you think of that? I think it would go down very well with our guests.'

Day had always had a passion for Greek pottery, and the idea of preparing the subject for a specific event, at an accessible rather than scholarly level, certainly appealed. He would even be well paid for it. He said he would be delighted to accommodate the request.

'Very good. Your second talk can be on any subject you choose. Once you've met your audience, I'm sure you'll know what to select. Now, we have enough time before lunch, I think, for me to tell you what this is all about. Shall we sit outside? It might be more agreeable than indoors.'

He got to his feet carefully, appearing to be in some pain, and walked slowly to the door at the back of the house and onto the terrace. Day followed, unsure whether to offer his help. Once the old man had sunk onto a cushioned wicker sofa in the shade of a white awning, Day took a chair nearby and looked out across the garden. At the foot of a descending flight of marble steps was a deep turquoise swimming pool, its irregular, curvaceous shape reminiscent of a cloud. It was framed by cream paving-stones, low-planted flowerbeds, and tall palms with orange fruits high in their branches.

'It's beautiful here, Stelio,' said Day.

'Thank you. I've always thought so myself. The Villa has been in my family for generations. When my parents died, it lay empty for many years, as I had settled in New York by then. My business was interior design and I had a certain amount of success; I was able to sell the business and retire reasonably early. I had always dreamed of returning to the island of my birth, restoring the old family home, and bringing my dear wife to the Villa Myrsini. I imagined we had many good years ahead of us. I told Maria and Yianni they could do as they preferred, stay in America or come here to Naxos, and they chose Greece.'

He sighed.

'Caroline and I had such plans for this place and, as you see, they are complete. Sadly, she is not here to enjoy it with me.'

'I'm sorry. Was your wife American?'

'She was. A New England girl. When her cancer was diagnosed, everything changed. Without Maria, I don't know how I would have managed. That is still true today.'

Day turned his eyes from Stelios, who needed a moment to collect himself. He looked back to the pool. Something had just passed low across its surface at speed and risen again into the air, banked steeply and returned for another pass. Stelios smiled with delight and pointed to it with a crooked finger.

'There goes my swallow, Martin, my *helithoni*. He drinks from the pool, you know. Like on the Thira fresco. You know it?'

'The fresco from Akrotiri on Santorini? Yes, of course, a remarkable thing. Did you know, Stelio, that the swallows on the fresco were painted by one artist and the lilies by another?

The two painters can be distinguished from one another by their styles.'

'Ah, that's very interesting. So it's possible to identify a specific ancient painter, is it?'

'Sometimes. We'll never know their real names, of course, but some master painters can be identified from their technique.'

The real swallow made a third pass over the bright water of the pool, this time succeeding in scooping up a drink from its surface without slowing down or leaving a ripple. As the bird vanished from the garden, thirst quenched, Stelios Ioannides changed the subject.

'Now, about your talk next Tuesday, Martin. I'd like you to begin at about half past twelve, if you would, and join us afterwards for lunch so we can ask you questions informally. Now, let me tell you about about your audience. Maria and Yianni will be there, and my good friend Vassos, who lives here with us. Also my niece, Christina, who's staying for the summer. She's the daughter of my younger sister in Kalamata. That's five including myself so far, isn't it? I've also invited my friend Stefanos and his wife. He's a wine producer with a big place on Santorini called Ambrosia Wine. Yianni buys all our wine from there.

'That just leaves my four visitors, the ones I spoke about on the telephone: my elder sister, Eleftheria, her husband Theodoros, and the couple who are holidaying with them on their yacht. Theo and Eleftheria have come to stay with me every summer since I lost Caroline. You might actually have heard of my brother-in-law, Theodoros Kakouris? He's one of our nation's shipping magnates. You may be more interested in the fact that he owns a private art collection. I'm afraid I don't actually know what he collects, but rarity and value will be high on his list of priorities. To be fair, he knows a great deal about the subject. You'll see, he'll be very attentive to what you say; he's a clever man.'

Stelios shifted his position in the chair to make himself more comfortable, and wiped his forehead with a handkerchief. Day was not surprised that he felt the heat, in his suit and tie and leather shoes.

'My brother-in-law is also a lover of Greek wine, and the forthcoming Naxos Festival of Cycladic Wine is his creation. He has funded it and made it happen. He is going to open the festival himself on the first night.'

'I see,' said Day, adding philanthropy to his picture of Theodoros Kakouris.

'That brings me to the last two guests, Theo's friends. The man is an international art dealer and his wife is French. I think I was told he's Anglo-French; perhaps you know what that means? Now, I personally don't know these people at all. Unfortunately, I think the wife speaks very little English, so she may not understand a great deal of what you say.'

Day acknowledged the possibility of this with a slight movement of his head.

'The art dealer himself is another matter. I'm told he's a proficient linguist, with clients all over Europe and the USA. Theo values him very highly. He's a specialist in artefacts from Greece with clients among the rich and famous. I'm told he's very knowledgeable and interesting on the subject.'

'I see,' said Day again. 'Then I shall prepare my talk with great care.'

'I have no doubt of that, Martin,' smiled Stelios, his gaze drifting across the garden.

Lunch was a modest affair, eaten on the terrace. There were just the three of them. Maria told Day how much there was still to do before her uncle and aunt's visit, which would last the duration of the wine festival. It sounded as if the guests had given no clear departure date. Yianni was still in Chora, sourcing the ingredients he needed for his meals, and it was not the first such trip he had made. There were butchers to deal with, local artisan cheese-makers, fishermen, bakers and many more. The wine merchant, Stefanos, was expected later in the afternoon to speak to Stelios. It was clear that the arrival of the party from the yacht would be a major event at the Villa Myrsini.

'You'll meet my cousin Christina in a little while,' Maria said, as she took Day into the house later to show him round. 'She doesn't eat lunch and goes out for a walk about this time. She comes from Kalamata, where her family have an olive farm. Kalamata's famous for its olives. Oh, sorry, I guess you know that, Martin.'

She chatted lightly and continuously as she showed him round the house, describing every room in detail as if to a potential buyer. Her pride in the place was clear, yet he enjoyed the modesty with which she spoke. They lingered in the well-stocked library which Stelios used as his study and where the reason for the absence of books elsewhere in the house became obvious.

In the corner of the room, Day noticed a wall safe. It reminded him that the brother-in-law, Theodoros Kakouris, was not the only wealthy man he would meet at the Villa Myrsini.

They went up the internal marble staircase. It was hung with modern American artworks, and in the upstairs hall there was a modern bronze that reminded Day of the ancient statue of Antinous in the museum at Delphi.

'This is my room,' laughed Maria, opening the door to a neat upstairs bedroom. 'I tidied it especially for you. I thought you should see the view from our upstairs windows; all the main bedrooms look out this way.'

She proudly opened the shutters and windows which were closed against the heat. Beyond the encircling wall of the villa lay another area of citrus trees, and beyond them a building Day recognised:

the seventeenth-century Paleologos Tower, its buff-coloured stone walls and castellated roof glowing in the sun. Beyond it lay an even older building, the small, white Byzantine church of Panagia Orfani, which Day had only seen in photographs.

'You must have one of the best views on Naxos, Maria. I thought I noticed a painting of the Paleologos Tower downstairs.'

'That's right, in the library. That picture belonged to my grandparents. When we came here from the US after the house had been restored, a neighbour brought that picture to my father, saying he'd taken it away for safety when my grandparents died. The damp in winter can be very bad on the islands. He wanted it to hang again in its old home.'

'Nice story. And the pictures in the living room?'

'Ah, you noticed them. Two of them are by John Craxton, they're my father's pride and joy. He has a small collection of art, mostly modern American things, but he wants the Craxtons to be always where he can see them.'

'*Craxton*?'

Day could hardly believe it, and promised himself a closer look when he could manage one. He had assumed that all John Craxton's work was now in international galleries. It was like finding a Picasso in your mother-in-law's lounge. Maria smiled at his astonishment and led the way out of her bedroom. As he followed her, he noticed a single photograph on the bedside table. It showed a young woman that was not Maria and which he assumed to be her mother Caroline. There was no time to ask because Maria was heading towards the stairs.

'Ah, Christina's back. Come and meet her, Martin!'

The two young women embraced warmly in the hall. Maria kept hold of her cousin's hand when she introduced her to Day. Christina had Maria's warm, brown eyes and heart-shaped face, but where Maria's long hair was straight, Christina's was a huge mass of curls, tightly permed to make a bouncing frame for her face. On one side the curls had been artfully dyed a silvery colour to complement or disguise the touches of early grey at her temples. Her eyes were heavily made up and were the first thing you noticed after the hair. It all managed to distract the attention, albeit temporarily, from the vivid scar that ran the length of her right cheek.

Still holding hands, the cousins chatted constantly as they all went to rejoin Stelios on the terrace. The old man welcomed Christina with avuncular warmth.

Day was now struck by the differences in the speech and accents round the table. Maria's New York accent was gentle, and Greek phrases punctuated her speech occasionally. Christina, whose first language was Greek, spoke quietly in a mixture of Greek and English. Stelios, most curiously of all, sounded like an English gentleman, despite having spent a lifetime in the States. Day could not resist asking him about it.

'Sure, I can turn on an American accent when I want to, Martin,' he drawled with a smile, before changing effortlessly into Received English as if a switch had been flicked. 'I spoke almost nothing but Greek when I reached America, just a little English I'd learned at school, and I wasn't a natural linguist, I'm afraid. Then I studied English at high school in New York with a teacher who came from Bristol, England. I remember her to this day: her name was Mrs Jane Challenger. She was a very hard taskmaster. Caroline never succeeded in changing the accent that Mrs Challenger drummed into me.'

'Papa spoke to us in Greek from the start,' added Maria, 'because he never wanted to forget his homeland.'

'You spoke Greek as soon as you could talk, which in your case, Maria, was before you could walk. She liked to sit and give us instructions, you see, Martin.'

Day laughed with them, enjoying the family harmony that had been so noticeably absent from his own youth. After a minute or two, though, he decided to make a move. He placed a regretful expression on his face and said it was time he should go.

'Is there anything more you want to tell me about next Tuesday? I'll prepare something to last about an hour, keep it interesting but informal, and on the subject you suggested. I'll arrive at midday.'

'Thank you, Martin, I look forward to it very much.'

'I'll show you out, Martin,' said Maria.

Day shook hands with Stelios and Christina and followed Maria.

'I'm sorry you haven't met my brother or Vasso today,' she said, as they lingered by his car.

'Your father mentioned Vassos. Is he a relative?' asked Day, more to prolong the conversation with her than out of interest in the unknown Vassos.

'Ah, dear Vasso. He came to live with us shortly after my mother's death. Losing her broke my father's heart; he was devastated. His arthritis was already bad, and the combination of the pain and the grief seemed to break him. I really didn't know what to do for him. I was exhausted myself, and I just couldn't bear to see what was happening to Papa. I thought we'd lose him too. My brother came to the rescue. He found a health spa in the Peloponnese that offered thalassotherapy and specialised in arthritis. Not only that, but they encouraged meditation and welcomed people who'd been recently bereaved or suffered some personal loss. Papa eventually agreed to go, and that's where he met Vasso. They immediately got on well together. Towards the end of his stay, Papa happened to ask Vasso what had made him book the spa. Vasso confessed that his successful business in Athens had folded during the global financial crisis, and he had decided to spend the last of his money on his own happiness. He really had nothing left, and at his age the future looked bleak. Papa offered him a home with us.'

Day shook his head in surprise. 'How generous.'

'Not at all; he's a good friend to Papa,' she said. 'When you meet him, you'll understand.'

'Well, I'd better go home and start doing some preparation. I'm looking forward to next Tuesday very much.'

'Me too,' she said, and kissed him suddenly on the cheek. He got into the car to return to a less extraordinary world.

4

When Day arrived at Diogenes, his favourite bar near the port of Naxos, the waiter grinned and waved as he took his usual table.

'*Kalimera*, Alexandre! *Ti kaneis*? *Kala*?'

'*Yeia sas*, Kyrie Martin. *Kala, eseis*? *Tha peite kafe*?'

When his coffee arrived, Day stirred it absent-mindedly, watching the constant passing of people along the nearby pavement. One of the many things he liked about Diogenes was its location on the popular Protopapathaki, the wide pedestrian walkway parallel to the shore. It made the perfect place to watch passers-by as they sought the café of their choice or visited the iconic Portara. Day's preferred seat was a table with cushioned benches nearest this entertainment.

After several days at his desk, Day had been looking forward to this morning. He was due to meet an old friend from the Italian School of Archaeology in Athens. They had not seen each other for a long time, and Day had been delighted when Fabrizio messaged to say he was planning a few days on Naxos on his way back to his excavation site on Crete. Fabrizio, however, was always late, and today was no exception.

Day had just taken his first sip of coffee when his phone rang and he pulled it from his pocket. Helen. A huge smile spread across his face.

'Darling! Good morning,' he said, rather too loudly in his excitement, causing the woman at the next table to glance across at him. 'How are you?'

'Hi, Martin, I'm fine. I'm back in Hampstead. The event in Cardiff finished yesterday.'

'Did it go well?'

'Yes, I suppose so. How are you?'

'I'm okay. I'm in Diogenes waiting for a friend. It's Fabrizio, you remember him? He's on his way to Crete but stopping off on Naxos for a few days.'

'That will be nice for you. Have you seen anyone else?'

'None of our usual people. Aristos and Rania are still in Athens, and Nick and Deppi's baby is due any time. It's so hot here! I went to see a man who owns a beautiful villa yesterday, you'd love it, it's in the hills near Sangri. I'm going to give a couple of talks there to some rich visitors.'

He paused, the flow of news drying up.

'I miss you,' he added.

The woman at the next table opened a newspaper and pretended not to be listening.

'Shall I just come back?'

'No,' he said reluctantly, 'you mustn't miss any good opportunities now that you're there.'

'Mmm. You're not involved in anything risky again, are you, Martin? I feel a bit twitchy not being there to keep an eye on you.'

Day laughed.

'Of course not; there's absolutely nothing going on here. This is the most peaceful island in the Aegean. You know that! Even Andreas has moved to the Cyclades to escape from the world of crime.'

'Oh, has he? He bought that place he saw on Paros?'

'Yes, and I went to see him a few days ago, and … Oh, sorry, darling, but Fabrizio has just arrived …'

'Okay. Ring me when you can.'

Day watched the screen darken after the call ended, then put the phone on the table.

A short Italian of about forty, similar in age to Day if not in appearance, walked up to the table.

'*Ciao*, Martin Day. It's been a long time, my friend. How are you?'

'*Ciao*, Brizio,' said Day, submitting to an Italian-style man-hug. 'Good to see you.'

Fabrizio Mirano grinned and slapped Day's arm, before sinking into the seat opposite him. They had met for the first time completely by chance about twenty years ago, in the Mycenaean Epigraphy Room in Cambridge University. They had discovered they were there to look at the same collection of letters, and this had led to a conversation. On finding that they both worked in Athens, they had gone for a drink on the strength of it.

Alexandros took Fabrizio's order for an espresso and offered the lunch menu, which they both declined. Day drank from his glass of water, appraising his old friend over the brim. It was surprising how little he had changed in the last two or three years. He still looked young for his age, but only because he was clean-shaven, short-haired, had big eyes and a very white smile. It also helped that he was dressed in jeans and a white T-shirt, and favoured sandals.

'So, how's life in Athens? Changed much? I haven't been back this year.'

'Plaka's completely crammed with tourists, Martin. There are more than ever before, you can't believe it. All the sites are far too busy, especially the Acropolis, which is out of the question for anyone serious till five in the afternoon, when they all go back to their hotels. Apart from that, I guess nothing has changed much, except that there isn't anybody who makes a good gin and tonic since you left. The Italian School still funds my research, that's the main thing.'

'Still working on the Phaistos Disk?'

Day knew no-one else who had Fabrizio's tenacity and dedication. Since the discovery of the famous inscribed disk in Phaistos on Crete in 1908, its signs and symbols had defied successful decipherment. From a non-academic family in Bologna, Fabrizio had shown a natural ability in both maths and languages as a boy and become determined to be the one who solved the puzzle of the Disk.

'Of course. There's big news, Martin. The next few weeks are going to be important. I tell you, we're very close! It's a bit of a race, in fact, to complete the decipherment. I'm not the one whose name will go down in history, unfortunately, but at least I'll be there at the end.'

'The decipherment's close?'

'Yes, really. Our group are going to excavate a completely new area between Kamilari and Agia Triada. If it turns up some new examples of the script, as we hope it will, that might be conclusive. In fact, that's one of my reasons for coming here to see you. Now that there's a chance of a real breakthrough, I have a proposal. We might be able to help each other.'

'Really? How?'

'I heard you're planning a TV series next year about excavation sites in Greece, no? Sites that are currently being worked, interesting digs. I thought you might like to include mine, at Kamilari.'

'You're inviting me to Crete? Do you really want a film crew getting in your way?'

'That would be unavoidable, but no more than an inconvenience. The thing is, if we find something important, I want the moment to be recorded. It would be good for me, it would be good for you. What do you think?'

Day shook his head doubtfully. He had been trying not to think about that particular film contract, which posed considerable challenges and would involve a great deal of work, all of which would fall to him.

'Thanks for the suggestion, but …'

He heard the negativity in his own voice and started again.

'Sorry, I'm sure we can do something. I've been a bit distracted recently and rather lost the momentum with that job. We were originally going to start filming next month, but that boat has sailed. London seems prepared to wait. I could get a cameraman out to you, though, and I'll come at short notice.'

'Good, do think about it. What are you working on at the moment, if you're not starting that series?'

'I've got a couple of talks to give, very lucrative and frankly a lot more fun than filming in this heat. The man who booked me is expecting influential guests.'

'Nice work. Good for you,' said the Italian, then looked at him appraisingly.

'Is something the matter, Martin?' he asked.

Fabrizio had always been rather observant; Day decided there was no point in prevaricating.

'Do you remember Helen?'

'The writer? The woman you've known a long time?'

'Yes. Since you met her we've started living together. Unfortunately, we're spending some time apart at the moment. I hope it will only be a temporary separation, but I don't know.'

'*Mi dispiace*. I feel for you, my friend. It's a strange coincidence, in fact. I have a similar problem: *una donna*.'

'Really? I thought you were unattached. Perpetual bachelor.'

'You're right, there has been nothing but work in my life until two years ago.' He shrugged. 'Things change. I met a beautiful woman and we were together for a few months. She moved away, but we kept in touch and I always thought we had an understanding. I thought that one day we'd get together again. Perhaps I was naïve, and I know I shouldn't have left it this long. I've made up my mind to find her now and put it right. I'm going to surprise her - turn up unannounced and, as you say in England, sweep her off her feet!'

Day looked at him thoughtfully.

'Are you sure that's a good idea, Brizio? Not a bit sudden, after all this time? You could call her first …'

'Don't worry, Martin. We Italians know how to be romantic, you know. And it has to work. She's the one for me.'

'You may say it's romantic, and I'm certainly no expert, but I think you may be making a mistake,' said Day. 'You're really going to turn up at her door without warning after two years?'

Fabrizio pulled a face and Day backed off.

'Fair enough, you do as you like and the best of luck. Do you need somewhere to stay? There's a spare room in Filoti if you want.'

'Thanks, but I booked into a guesthouse down in Agios Georgios. I won't be around much, either. I want to go back to Delos to check out a few things, and I'll visit some other places.'

'Will you be here for the wine festival? It starts next Thursday and goes on till Saturday, from six each evening, here in Chora. The first night will be the best. I plan to sample pretty much everything. Do you want to do the same and then have dinner in a taverna somewhere?'

'*Perfetto*!' said the Italian, offering his boyish smile. 'Perhaps by then I'll be able to bring a friend…'

'Are you telling me that this woman of yours is here on Naxos?'
'I'm afraid you'll just have to wait and see, Martin!'

5

Day was not a natural early riser, so he woke only when a slight breeze, no more than a whisper, moved the fly-curtain on his window. The single sheet that covered him was already making him too warm. He reached out to his mobile to check the time and see whether there was a message from Helen. He discovered only that it was just past eight.

He swung himself out of bed and stood up. He was tired of seeing the other side of the bed empty and knowing that Helen was not sitting with a cup of tea somewhere in the house. He went sadly to the bathroom, where the meagre water from the shower, in which the pressure was never strong, did little to improve his mood. Only afterwards, with his face buried in the towel, did he make a decision to pull himself together and use the coming morning to get some work done. He would begin, naturally, with a coffee.

He found a clean shirt, dressed and went to the kitchen. As he waited for his coffee to be ready, he opened the glass door and went out onto the balcony. The hill across the valley was still patchy with the shadows of early morning, and the air carried the aromas of the parched Greek land, its grasses and dry soil stressed by summer. He thought he could smell the sea in the gentle breeze. He leaned against the railing, breathing deeply, and looked in vain for the mule that was often tethered in the shade of a solitary tree.

Once again, he reflected how much he loved this house, which he had bought several years ago after the death of his father. Originally, he had planned to spend only the summers here on Naxos, and use his small flat in Athens for the rest of the year. From Athens it was easy to fly to London to see his agent; he had access to the museums and libraries, and colleagues from all over the world passed through the capital of Greece. How easily he had changed that plan. The Athens apartment was now in the capable hands of Irini, his occasional cleaner and housekeeper, and the Filoti house had become his home. His and Helen's. It was perfect: the last house on a village road, it was quiet yet convenient, and it overlooked a valley in which little moved apart from the birds.

He was soon established at the balcony table, a power cable connected to the socket in the house and his coffee at hand, but the laptop remained unopened. The smell of the coffee made him smile, and he held the cup to his face to enjoy it. The morning sun was rising over the hills with the promise of another hot day, banishing the last shadows from the valley. In what remained of the coolness of morning, a pair of doves flirted together in the neighbour's plane tree, before settling on the bamboo canopy over his head.

When he could procrastinate no longer, he checked his emails and answered two of them briefly. He even wrote a message to Maurice Atkinson, his London agent, about Fabrizio's invitation to Crete. The next hour and a half were devoted to Attic vases of the Early Classical Period, around 480 BCE, in happy contemplation of some of the most accomplished vase painters of Ancient Greece.

He wished he knew more about the members of his audience at the Villa Myrsini, who seemed to be a very mixed group. He was used to talking about his subject, but he usually knew whether to pitch it for experts or general interest. How much background information did he need to give to keep his listeners involved? He would prefer not to bore the more knowledgeable among them. He decided to limit himself to explaining the decorative vase-painting techniques known as Black Figure and Red Figure styles, showing illustrations of some of the best examples of both. The pictures would make it interesting enough for everyone, and he could go into detail for the two men from the yacht if they seemed to want it.

Having made this plan, he lost himself in the subject, and only just heard the heavy knock at the front door. Emerging from somewhere in the distant past with the vase painters of antiquity, he stepped over the laptop cable and went to answer the door.

A familiar figure with blue eyes and a mane of light hair stood there; behind him on the road was a white police car that had already attracted the curiosity of a neighbour. Andreas had clearly borrowed a vehicle from the local station.

'You could at least have parked down the road,' Day joked, letting Andreas into the small front room, wood-floored and all but empty of furniture. 'Come in. Coffee?'

'No thanks, but some water would be good. Sorry I didn't call first. I got the early Sea Jet and went straight to the police station to call on Kyriakos Tsountas. He sends his regards.'

Day felt sure that Inspector Tsountas, the relatively new chief of police, had said no such thing, but that Andreas felt he should have. He poured two glasses of cold water and followed Andreas onto the balcony.

'What are you working on?' asked the chief inspector, peering at Day's laptop and settling himself into Helen's usual chair. 'Your talk for the Villa Myrsini?'

'Yes. It's tomorrow.'

'I know. I hope you'll forgive my discourtesy, but that's the reason I've come to see you.'

'Discourtesy?'

'I … It's not a social call, Martin. It's police business.'

'No problem. Tell me about it.'

'I was obliged by professional courtesy to speak to Inspector Tsountas before coming to see you, which I've just done. The Villa Myrsini has a direct bearing on my current case.'

'What *case*, Andrea?'

'I'll explain. I'll start with what I've been doing recently. As you know, for some time I've wanted to specialise in antiquity crime. My promotion to chief inspector wasn't actually with the regular Athens force, but came with my move to the International Antiquities Fraud Agency, known as the IAFA. I'm still based in Athens, and my house purchase on Paros was coincidental to my changed role, but as it happens, it's convenient. I'm working on a serious case of suspected antiquity fraud which appears to involve your new acquaintances at the Villa Myrsini.'

'Not old Stelios?'

Andreas acknowledged this admission of Day's involvement with the family at the villa with a slight tilt of the head.

'Possibly not Ioannides himself, although that remains to be seen. I'm investigating his brother-in-law, Theodoros Kakouris, the shipping magnate.'

'Right. My God. Can you tell me about it?'

'That's why I'm here. Every summer for the last few years, ostensibly on vacation, Kakouris's yacht, the *Alkyoni*, has sailed round the Aegean, loading and unloading small amounts of freight at various ports. That's what attracted our attention. We now have an undercover officer on board posing as Head of Security for Kakouris. This year, I intend to discover exactly what, if anything, is happening on these summer cruises. The *Alkyoni* has already stopped at Crete, where we suspect illegally acquired, possibly illegally excavated artefacts were taken on board, and a small secure package left the boat. After Crete, the yacht moored at Santorini, at Mykonos and at Folegandros, and more activity was observed; but, frustratingly, we still have no incontrovertible evidence of illegal trading. Kakouris's high profile makes this a particularly sensitive matter. Which brings us to Naxos. This weekend, as you know, Kakouris and his little party will arrive here and stay at the Villa Myrsini.'

'In time for the wine festival.'

'Yes, for the great new Naxos Festival of Cycladic Wine, the brain-child of Theodoros Kakouris himself. Martin, I don't need to tell you that there have been wine festivals in the Cyclades before, and a few are annual events on some of the islands. I ask myself why Kakouris needed to instigate a new one.'

'I'd assumed it was a combination of vanity and too much money,' said Day. 'Did you know that Kakouris and his wife, who is Stelios Ioannides's sister, have visited him every summer for the past few years?'

'I did, but this year is a little different. There's the new wine festival, and the fact that Kakouris has brought someone else on the trip.'

'You mean, the art dealer?'

'Yes. Pierre Ridgeway is his name. Works out of London and Paris, fluent in both languages. Ridgeway acts as Kakouris's acquisitions agent. Kakouris is said to own the largest collection of Ancient Greek artefacts in Greece, outside the museums. When a desirable object comes on the market, Kakouris gets Ridgeway to buy it for him. The transactions that hit the press are legal, and they're high-value. It's the things that don't appear in the news that I'm interested in. Ridgeway's private clients are some of the wealthiest of Europe's elite, and he keeps them happy with antiquities from Greece and Italy. He also sells to the major museums of Europe and America. He's kept himself well within the law so far. However, a word in the wind told me he also sells things which have not come to him from a *bona fide* source. His clients, for the most part, wouldn't particularly care. In the case of the museums, he probably persuades them to 'rescue' the objects to prevent them from disappearing underground.'

'Yes, still common practice. Even if the museum suspects illegal excavation or outright theft, they feel a responsibility to save the artefact, which might be completely unique and otherwise be lost. In reality, if they turn it down a rival museum would buy it. Either way, it's tempting to accept the object. What about your man on the yacht? Can't he find some evidence, if there's any to find?'

Andreas smiled sadly.

'You would think so, but it's not that simple. His job as security officer is to protect Kakouris and his wife, not to interfere with their business. He has to tread carefully. He's told us that Ridgeway sends sealed crates to Paris or London from every port, which we suspect are acquisitions that he doesn't want to keep on the yacht for long. He has a storeroom in the hold to which he alone has access. We're tracking the crates that leave the boat, of course, but it takes time, and nothing must be done to give away the identity of our man or alert the suspects.'

'Is it Theodoros Kakouris you're interested in, or Ridgeway?'

'If both are involved in illegal trading, then I want both of them. Pierre Ridgeway has the best cover in the world: his legal antiquities business. As a renowned dealer, he's working in full sight of the authorities, and he's clever; it will be hard to find the evidence, but we should be able to do it. I really need to know more about the millionaire. He might simply be shutting his eyes to where his antiquities have come from, or he may be more deeply involved, using his yacht, and possibly the festival, to buy or trade in artefacts.

'Things are coming to a head, Martin. My man tells me the atmosphere on the *Alkyoni* has become poisonous. Kakouris is desperate to please his dealer and ignores everything else, especially his wife Eleftheria. Elodie Ridgeway is a silent and sulky woman, and the two wives don't speak to each other. The party is going to break up soon. After the wine festival, the yacht will leave Naxos for Sicily, where Ridgeway and his wife will disembark and disappear. If we haven't found some strong evidence by then, the opportunity will be lost.'

'What are you going to do?'

'First, I'll tell you what I'm *not* going to do. Kyriakos Tsountas knows as little as I could reasonably tell him, Martin. I have no time for the man, and the fewer people who know about my investigation the better; that includes the local police.'

Day, who knew the new chief of police slightly, was not really surprised.

'Okay, that's your decision. I'm sure you'd prefer not to tell me too much either. Why are you telling me anything?'

'Obviously, Martin, because you have a unique connection with the Villa Myrsini. And therefore with Kakouris and Ridgeway. I want you to be on the inside for me with the group at the villa, just for a couple of weeks.'

'You want me to *work* for you?'

Andreas hesitated. Though it was true, he was still uncomfortable about it.

'You're about to give two lectures at the Villa Myrsini. The first, tomorrow, will be an opportunity for you to meet and assess the suspects and the family. I just want you to observe them carefully and report to me. Trust your instincts. Be vigilant, and don't draw attention to yourself. I need them to accept you and have no suspicions regarding you, which will place you ideally for what I have in mind later. Report only to me. You must say nothing, under any circumstances, to the Naxos police.'

Day gave a sniff and nodded, filing that last comment away for consideration later.

'Go on.'

'The important thing is to keep it very light with Kakouris and Ridgeway. Things could get complicated. Desperate people facing the end of a lucrative trade and the probability of imprisonment can be as unpredictable as cornered animals.'

Helen's words on the phone that morning came back to Day: *You're not involved in anything risky again, are you, Martin?* He assumed that if he did what Andreas wanted he would not be allowed to tell her, and would therefore be forced to be dishonest with her. It was not ideal.

Andreas was watching him shrewdly.

'I must know that I can trust you, Martin. No, no, I don't doubt your integrity in the least. What I mean is, I must be able to rely on you doing *exactly* what I ask of you and no more. I've seen in the past how you like to take things into your own hands. Your hallmarks are guesswork, intuition and risk; and, of course, they're what has often made you extremely useful to me. Frankly, they make you invaluable. My officers, even the best of them, don't work like you do, because they've been properly trained. But, as I've told you before, when you act on your own you can be something of a liability.'

Day asked for a little time to think. He excused himself and went to his room, where he sat at the small desk by the window. He was hesitating because he was uncomfortable with the idea of being dishonest with Helen. The notion of risk that Andreas had implied was not the problem, as he saw no reason to be concerned; but the effect on his beleaguered relationship was something else.

On the other hand, the trade in Greek antiquities was something he deplored. Irreplaceable evidence of past lives were ripped from their context, their place in the levels of history destroyed, rendering them meaningless to historians, mere trophy items on a shelf. Once an ancient site had been robbed of what it contained, there was no chance, ever again, to retrieve the knowledge that could have been gleaned from it. Nothing less than our human heritage was ultimately at stake if this trade could not be halted. Day had bored people about it for many years.

Those who spent their lives trying to stop this trade had a difficult task. One way was to discover the source, where the illegal excavation of antiquities, the thefts from collections, or the looting of ancient sites took place. Another was to find the buyers; and then there were all the dealers and handlers. It frustrated him that there was nothing he personally could do apart from educating the few people he could reach through his TV work or his writing. Today, if he accepted Andreas's proposal, there was a chance to make a real difference.

Guesswork, intuition and risk. He rather liked Andreas's assessment of him. That was it, decision made. He smiled and returned to Andreas.

'All right, I'll do it,' he said. 'You've done me enough favours in the past.'

'Thank you, Martin. For now, all you have to do is get to know the people at the Villa Myrsini.'

'Why don't you come to the wine festival with me on Thursday and meet these people yourself? I'm already going with a friend from Athens and it will be busy. Nobody would notice you if you joined us.'

'Thanks, but I'd rather stay away from the festival.'

He got up and gave a wistful look at the peaceful valley beyond the balcony.

'If I go now I'll get the afternoon ferry back to Paros. Would you mind coming over at the weekend? Come for Sunday lunch; that should give me enough time. You can bring your friend with you if you want. We'll eat at the local taverna and I'll introduce you to Fotini, but I'll make sure we have an opportunity to talk in private.'

6

Day was not due at the Villa Myrsini until noon, so he drove to Chora first to spend some time watching the world go by from a pavement café.

He parked in a place he knew near the police station and sat down outside the Café Seferis in the shade of the awning. The *plateia* was busy with traffic, being on a popular route between the villages and the port, and the heat was already significant. He ordered a coffee and an omelette and settled down in good spirits to wait for his breakfast. His mind was embedded in the subject of his lecture. The previous evening he had gone through his library and chosen a selection of his own books on ceramics to show his audience. They were beside him now, treasured possessions in a beautiful old leather briefcase that had belonged to his father.

It was then that he picked up the newspaper that had been left on the seat next to him.

ASSAULT BY INTRUDER THREATENS WINE FESTIVAL

Naxos police are appealing for witnesses to a break-in that occurred at approximately 23:15 on Sunday 10th July at the Ambrosia Wine office on the Naxos-Engares road.

Mitsos Lamptis (27), the assistant manager, noticed a vehicle outside Ambrosia Wine as he was driving home to Galini after an evening with friends. He discovered the warehouse door unlocked and found the intruder in the process of searching the office. He tackled the man, who pushed him to the floor and escaped. Kyrios Lamptis was not seriously hurt and called the police, but was unable to give a clear description of either the intruder or the vehicle.

Ambrosia Wine is owned by Stefanos Patelis from Santorini, who is the Director of the Naxos Festival of Cycladic Wine. This major event in our summer calendar begins on Thursday of this week, thanks to the generous initiative of philanthropist Theodoros Kakouris. Over forty stalls will be set up along the *paralia* of Chora, offering information and the chance to taste wine from across the Cyclades. Representatives from our own wineries on Naxos, and others from Paros, Santorini and neighbouring islands, will be taking part. In addition, some stalls will offer speciality Cycladic delicacies, and many restaurants on the island will showcase traditional products.

Stefanos Patelis, who opened the office of Ambrosia Wine on Naxos five years ago, said that nothing was taken or damaged in the break-in. He expressed relief that his assistant manager had not been hurt, and believed that this unpleasant incident was entirely unconnected with the forthcoming festival.

The Naxos police are investigating.

Day skimmed the rest of the article. The journalist returned to the subject of the wine festival, and indeed seemed more interested in it than in the assault on the young manager. There was nothing more about Theodoros Kakouris and no mention of the Villa Myrsini.

He closed the paper, put it down and looked up, his attention drawn by two police cars which had just passed the Café Seferis and stopped in front of the police station. This was causing a certain amount of traffic congestion in the *plateia*. The door of the leading car opened and Inspector Kyriakos Tsountas got out. In defiance of the July heat, he was wearing black civilian clothing to which he had added a short leather jacket, also black, which perhaps lent him the authority he desired. His preference for black was one of the things Day recalled most clearly about the chief of police. Only a year ago, shortly after Tsountas had taken up his post, they had been forced to work together in connection with an important archaeological find, but the collaboration had not been a happy one. Tsountas had struck Day as a difficult man, one driven by ambition.

The young inspector scanned the *plateia* as if to ensure everything was secure, while his officers brought a man in handcuffs from the back of the vehicle and took him into the station. Noticing Day at the café table, the inspector gave him a look of abstracted displeasure and a curt nod before turning away. The duty officer on the main door visibly relaxed once his superior had gone inside.

Day was not alone in finding the incident curious; the people around him in the café were already discussing it. Was it connected to the break-in at Ambrosia Wine? Was the handcuffed man suspected of something more serious? This kind of thing was unprecedented on the peaceful streets of law-abiding Naxos.

Day lifted his bill from the metal cup in which it was curled and left the correct money on the table. Picking up his briefcase, he walked thoughtfully across the *plateia* to his car and headed for the Villa Myrsini.

Stelios Ioannides's son was waiting for him when he arrived. In looks, he closely resembled his sister Maria, from the innocent eyes to the straight dark hair, and his smile, like hers, was welcoming. Unlike his sister, Yianni had an air of reserve, but his greeting was warm enough. His accent was pure New York, but his looks were Greek, from the thick eyebrows to the long, straight nose. His words came out in a rush.

'Let me take you to meet everyone. Can I call you Martin? Yianni, Maria's brother. I'm afraid I won't be able to take in your talk, I need to finish up making the lunch, but I'll catch you later, okay? I wish you luck with those two guys from the yacht. My father's really pleased you agreed to come and help entertain them.'

Day thanked him, noting the warning about his audience. He found the challenge exciting, however, and felt more than capable of winning over these people. The prospect completely banished the memory of Kyriakos Tsountas and his entourage.

He followed Yianni to the living room. A large group of people was seated round the low table, some lounging on sofas, others less relaxed on upright chairs, talking and drinking coffee. From his high-backed chair, Stelios saw him arrive and gave a little wave, a large smile transforming his face. Day waved back. Yianni laid a hand briefly on his shoulder as if in solidarity before disappearing into the house, leaving Maria to announce him.

'This is Martin Day, everyone.'

Conversation stopped and the millionaire brother-in-law, Theodoros Kakouris, came over to shake Day's hand and introduce himself. He added how pleased he was to meet the man whose informative programmes on Ancient Greece he had so greatly enjoyed. Kakouris was clearly identifiable from the images on the internet which Day had explored since speaking to Andreas, but what had not been apparent was his size. He was a very large man, a man who had lost his figure long ago, though clearly he did not greatly care. From his open-necked shirt to his elegant leather shoes, he was expensively dressed. He had small eyes behind tinted glasses and a prominent bulbous nose, but also a ready smile, and he exuded bonhomie. Day sensed a certain vanity about him, but heaven knows he had made a success of himself.

Kakouris introduced his wife, Eleftheria, who offered her hand without getting up, but gave Day a polite smile. She too was immaculately dressed, the epitome of a wealthy Athenian lady. Day guessed that her clothes were from some international fashion house, and her hands were heavy with gold rings and chain bracelets; her nails were ostentatiously manicured. Like her husband, she must have been in her late sixties or possibly older, but her hair was glossily black and neatly arranged. Her left hand was at rest on her brother's arm, which she would occasionally pat gently as you would an anxious child.

Insisting on the use of first names, Theodoros Kakouris moved on to introduce the Ridgeways.

'This is my good friend Pierre and his wife Elodie. They have joined us on the yacht this summer as our guests. I owe Pierre much more than a holiday in the Cyclades, of course: he has been of invaluable help to me in the past few years. So, we're all looking forward to your talk today, Martin, and I know we'll learn a great deal. What is to be your subject?'

'I'll be talking about vase painting during the Early Classical period in Greece,' said Day, placing his briefcase on the coffee table, having shaken hands with the Ridgeways. 'I hope there'll be one or two things that will surprise you, though I know you have a great deal of knowledge yourselves.'

'We're always learning,' said the art dealer as he sat down again.

A short Greek who had been sitting on the sofa next to Elodie Ridgeway came forward to introduce himself.

'*Kalimera, ti kanete*? I am Vassos. *Hairo poli*,' he said. 'I live here as the guest of my generous friend Stelios. I'm of very little use, Martin, and I'm certainly not decorative, and yet he makes me welcome.'

So, this was the man Stelios had rescued. Day found him immediately likeable.

'May I introduce Christina Vassilaki?' Vassos continued.

'We've already met,' she murmured. '*Yeia sas*.'

'And lastly,' said Vassos, 'this is Stefanos Patelis and Klairi his wife.'

The wine producer from Santorini and the director of the Naxos Wine Festival. The man who, in the newspaper article, had expressed concern for his staff. Day shook hands amicably, but reminded himself that, as he worked with Theodoros Kakouris, Stefanos Patelis himself was not above suspicion. Still, he liked the look of him; he had a capable but amiable manner. In his early fifties, he was still a good-looking man. What was more, he was sitting next to his wife and introduced her to Day with pride, which was in notable contrast to the other two couples in the room, who sat apart.

'I'm a great admirer of your wine, Kyrie Pateli,' said Day truthfully.

'Stefano, please. You know our wines? You must visit our display at the festival and allow me to offer you a taste of one or two which you may not have tried before.' The wine producer creased his eyes into a smile. 'It will be a pleasure.'

'I will, thank you. I'll look forward to it.' Day looked round the room and noticed that Maria had sat down. 'Well, would you like me to make a start?'

After fifty minutes, Day had delivered most of his prepared talk and was reasonably happy with how it had been received. It only remained to sum up the main points, which he had found was the best way to leave an audience with a clear memory of what they had heard, and it made for fewer questions.

'So, while you're still looking through the illustrations in the books, let me summarise these two styles of vase decoration, the Black Figure and the Red Figure.

'Black Figure vase painting is the older of the two styles and originated in Corinth and Athens, but then became popular across the Mediterranean. The design was applied to the vase using a layer of slip made from thin clay, which would darken during firing. This left the figures and decoration standing in black against the natural terracotta colour of the pot. A sharp tool was used to incise decorative lines and lettering, and details like the eyes, the spear and the clothing were added this way. Dark red and white colours could be used for additional details. On the amphora in that picture you can see how the woman's face is white, which was a common treatment of female figures.

'Black Figure technique remained popular for a long time, and very high levels of artistry were achieved by some painters. Art historians have even been able to attribute some vases to a specific master, who would have been a leading practitioner of his time.

'These vases continued to be made as the new Red Figure style became more popular. The trends overlapped, as trends in fashion do today. Red Figure vase painting began in Athens later, around 530 BCE, and took the art to a still higher level. It's the background now that is black, rather than the design elements.'

He lifted one of his favourite books and offered the open page to Theodoros.

'The woman in this illustration is an excellent example of Red Figure work. Details of the clothing and the face have been added with great skill. So, how was this level of accomplishment achieved?

'Once the pot had been made it was allowed to become dry and hard, then burnished using a stone to achieve a fine, smooth finish. A very dilute wash of pale red-ochre would then be painted all over it, which improved the natural colour of the clay. After this the pot was burnished again, and only then did the artist draw his design lightly onto it with charcoal. Black slip was applied around this design, creating the dark background.'

'Was the firing process any different between the two techniques?' asked Vassos.

'We think they both involved the same three-stage firing process. The first firing was done with a lot of oxygen in the kiln, which enhanced the delicate red colour of the clay. The second was hotter, with wet leaves or green wood added to give the distinctive black colour of the slip. The third stage was a repetition of the first, but this time the black areas were unaffected and the design was fixed.'

Eleftheria hesitated before asking her question.

'I've always wondered why people think that Red Figure vases are better than Black Figure. I really like them both. The earlier ones are simpler, and the black design is very dramatic.'

'That's true,' said Day, 'and everyone's entitled to their own feelings about a work of art. The reason that Red Figure vases are so admired is to do with the rapid changes that were taking place in Greek art at that time. The human form was beginning to be shown more realistically. It happened in Classical sculpture as well; the figures appear to be putting their weight on one leg, or to be caught in the act of stepping out or extending an arm. The vase painters began to use delicate brushwork to show garments and anatomy in more detail, and suggest emotions like anger, fear and grief. They could produce very sophisticated work.

Only the absolute masters of Black Figure, in my opinion, can rival it.'

Eleftheria nodded and looked down at the open book in her lap, where she had been comparing the illustrations. Day hoped that hers was going to be the last question: his brief summary had become more detailed than he had intended, and Ridgeway and Kakouris were looking rather bored.

'Well, unless you have more questions for Martin, lunch will be on the terrace shortly,' said Maria.

Stelios Ioannides cleared his throat apologetically.

'I have one question, if I may, Martin. Can you explain why some ancient vases have a *white* background? Is there a style called White Figure?'

'Not exactly. It's called White Ground, and we find it on both Black Figure and Red Figure vases. The vase was coated in a white slip and the decoration drawn on with a brush. They can then be painted in either black or red, or left as delicate outlines. It's a very varied style used by many outstanding painters. Some White Ground vases have been found here in the Cyclades, by the way, though most come from Athens. It was a popular style for funerary offerings, such as vases that would be buried with the dead. When the practice of leaving precious items in the grave fell out of fashion, so did the White Ground style.'

Stelios nodded and thanked him, and Day turned to Maria, smiling in a way he hoped suggested he was finished.

'Lunch on the terrace in fifteen minutes,' she announced obligingly. 'Do go on out. Yianni and I'll bring everything from the kitchen.'

Day watched her as she retreated gracefully to the hall and disappeared towards the kitchen; the sound of plates and cutlery could be heard when she pushed open the door. Then he found himself surrounded by people as they all made their way outside.

Only the French woman, Elodie Ridgeway, hung back, looking at him in a way that made him feel utterly exposed.

7

Day had been looking forward to the possibility of an excellent glass of wine with lunch, and was not disappointed.

Once everyone was seated at the long table on the terrace under its white, sail-like canopy, and Yianni had been complimented on the array of dishes in front of them, Stefanos stood up to introduce the wine.

'First, Klairi and I would like to thank our generous host, Stelio, for his wonderful generosity and hospitality. Then, on behalf of us all, may I propose a vote of thanks to our excellent speaker?' He raised his own glass and the others did the same. 'To Martin. Thank you so much.'

'*Stin ygeia mas*!' said Stelios, smiling happily. 'Good health to all, and thank you, Martin.'

'Now,' said Stefanos, holding up a wine bottle. 'This is one of my lightest, most delicate white wines, which I think is most suitable for this enjoyable occasion and particularly for such a hot day. I hope you all enjoy it.'

Round the table there were murmurs of approval, and conversations between neighbours began as soon as Stefanos sat down. The first exchange that Day tuned into was Vassos asking Eleftheria what had inspired her husband to inaugurate the new Naxos Festival of Cycladic Wine.

'Theo, you see, has two major passions in his life,' she said, 'and it may surprise you, Kyrie Vasso, that making a huge amount of money is not one of them, although it has certainly enabled the others. Now that he's retired, he can use his wealth to indulge his love of Greek wine. He always attends the 'Map of Flavours' wine exposition in Thessaloniki. You know it? Two years ago he conceived the idea of establishing a new wine festival in the Cyclades, and he chose Naxos. Ambrosia Wine being one of his favourite suppliers, he contacted Stefanos at once to discuss it. Theirs turned out to be a perfect partnership, Kyrie Vasso, and Theo has enjoyed every minute of planning the event.'

Day, who sat on the other side of Vassos, took the chance to join the conversation.

'The festival was an inspired and generous impulse, Kyria Eleftheria. Your husband is to be congratulated. Many people on Naxos and the neighbouring islands will be able to promote their businesses: small growers, restaurant owners, the local hotels. Tourism will benefit hugely. I'm looking forward to it myself, very much!'

Eleftheria gave a small smile and took a sip of water. She seemed already to have lost interest in the festival, or perhaps in Day.

'Until I met your brother Stelio recently, I was unaware of your husband's reputation as a collector of antiquities,' Day continued, undeterred. 'It's been a life-long interest of his, I understand?'

'Since before we married, yes.'

'Has he ever exhibited his collection?'

'No, it's a private pleasure.'

'No doubt greatly supported by your friend Pierre.'

Day glanced across the table to where Ridgeway was now talking with Stefanos, and was relieved to see he was paying them no attention. Vassos had dropped out of the conversation and was helping himself to salad.

'That is correct,' conceded the magnate's wife.

'Someone with Pierre's expertise must be invaluable to your husband. A friend of mine has recently explained to me the benefit of knowing an eminent dealer with professional connections if you want to acquire specific artefacts. The top international collectors of antiquities use the very best experts, because such items are rare and much sought-after.'

'Yes, I suppose so,' said Eleftheria. 'I do not involve myself.'

'May I pour you a little more wine, Kyria Eleftheria?' asked Vassos politely. When she declined, he filled both Day's glass and his own, and raised his to Day.

'A very enjoyable and informative talk, Martin,' he said in a slightly lower tone. 'I thought it was particularly clever how you gave everybody in the room something interesting to think about, despite our different levels of expertise. Stelios is delighted. I expect he will want to ask you more questions privately when you have a little time. It's a subject close to his heart.'

'My pleasure,' said Day, thinking how generously he was being paid for his talks, not to mention an excellent lunch.

'Your background, Martin - what is it exactly?' Pierre Ridgeway asked from across the table, now giving Day his full attention. His accent, despite being highly educated and inflected with something French, betrayed him to Day's ear as coming from the English Midlands.

'University of Cambridge, Classics. I live here on Naxos now. I do research, mainly for documentaries, articles, projects for museums and so on.'

And what are you working on at the moment?'

Day gave it no thought. He simply lied. It was instinctive and inspired.

'It's a London-based project for a television series about illegal excavation and artefact trading across the world. You know, from Lord Elgin to Syria, Libya, Iraq, Egypt. There's no shortage of examples, we can make quite a few episodes.'

'I see. Who are you working with?'

'A guy who runs an independent film company and who does some work for the BBC. There's a group of academics and curators on board too. It's in the very early stages. You must know a bit about the subject yourself, Pierre. Maybe we should invite you to join us.'

'Oh, you can find much more knowledgeable people than me, Martin. Intriguing, though. I had no idea the subject was so mainstream.'

'Mmm, and hopefully will become even more so once the series is broadcast. So, have you come across the problem much in your line of work?'

'Illegal trading? From time to time one hears of it. I'm successful precisely because I keep well away from all that. You could say it would be career-limiting. Rather seriously so.'

'Your professional integrity is well-known,' Day hastened to reassure him, now enjoying himself considerably.

With a small smile, Ridgeway turned away to listen to what Christina was saying to Maria. He murmured something to them that made Maria laugh, though Christina appeared not to have heard. His glance rested on Day thoughtfully again, before he returned his attention to the young women.

Conversations of many kinds continued throughout lunch, and Day sat quietly, listening unobtrusively. The afternoon began to cool when a small breath of wind made the sail above them gently undulate. He looked round the table. Christina and Yianni, who sat close to each other, were talking of the family in Kalamata; Stefanos was speaking in French to Elodie Ridgeway about wine; and Stelios and Eleftheria were chatting with the fondness that Day had already noticed between the brother and sister, though they spoke too quietly for him to hear. There was nothing that would interest Andreas. He focused for a while on his lunch, therefore, and savoured the last of his wine. It was indeed delicious.

His gentle reverie was interrupted by a snatch of conversation at the top of the table. He tuned in to it. Theodoros and Stefanos were discussing the intruder at Ambrosia Wine in Chora.

'Have you heard that the police have already charged someone?' asked Stefanos. 'He's a Santorini man with a small vineyard not far from our terrain. I know him, he's part of the local co-operative. I can't believe he had anything to do with the break-in, and I'm sure he's incapable of hurting anyone. Apparently, the police only arrested him because he was in a bar the previous night complaining about me in a loud voice.'

'What on earth was he saying, Stefano?' interrupted his wife Klairi indignantly. 'How dare he?'

'He was just a bit angry, *agapi mou*. He thinks that, as the director of the festival, I'm getting favourable rates and preferential treatment over himself and the other Santorini producers. Not the case, of course. Our stall will not even be in a good location; I've deliberately chosen to be slightly out of the main area. He's also upset by the modernisations we've made at Ambrosia: he thinks I'm betraying the old Santorini traditions of wine-making. He's not the only one; quite a few of our colleagues agree with him. Don't worry, he was probably a little drunk, and everyone has their own problems. Unfortunately for him, it was enough to get him arrested.'

Day recalled the scene in the *plateia* and the handcuffed man brought from the police car. No doubt handcuffs could be used whenever physical violence was suspected, but it was unsettling all the same. He took a drink from his glass of water. Theodoros and Stefanos had moved on to a discussion of modern wine production methods, but he saw that Klairi was looking across at the garden thoughtfully.

'The break-in must have been a terrible shock for you,' he said to her sympathetically.

'Yes, it was. I'm so thankful that we decided to rent a house here for the festival. There are rooms above the office we could have used, but then it might have been Stefano who disturbed the intruder.'

Day nodded. 'What do you think the man was after?'

'Oh, I expect he just wanted a few crates of wine but was disturbed before he could get away with them. The building is mostly for administration, but we keep a little stock there. It's surprising it doesn't happen more often, I suppose.'

'I've heard a lot about Ambrosia Wine,' said Day. 'You have an impressive reputation. I'm not surprised that Theodoros chose your husband to help with his new festival.'

'Thank you. We've been supplying wine to Theodoros for several years.' She gave him a warm smile. 'Do you know how Ambrosia Wine came to be so successful, Martin? I think it's a rather nice story. My husband started working there when he was barely out of his teens. He arrived on Santorini with no money and no qualifications; he just wanted to join the wine business and was willing to start at the bottom. He worked really hard and would do everything that needed doing. Over the next few years he mastered every part of the business. I remember him clearly from those days. Eventually, he became the most useful man in the winery. My father promoted him on merit year after year, until eventually Stefano was in overall charge.'

'Your father?'

'Yes. My family have always owned the winery. When Stefano asked permission to marry me, my father realised he could retire and leave both the business and his daughter in good hands.' She laughed. 'He didn't hesitate to give his permission, and here we are.'

She smiled at her husband, who returned her smile and raised his eyebrows fractionally. Klairi nodded and folded her napkin.

'Excuse me, Martin, but Stefano and I need to return to work. There's still a great deal to do before the festival opens on Thursday.'

As Stefanos and his wife left, they were embraced with genuine affection by almost everyone.

'Klairi and Stefano are such good people,' said Maria when she returned from showing them out. 'Uncle Theo trusts Stefano completely with the arrangements for the festival, and my father loves having him visit. The Greeks like a self-made man, you know, Martin, nearly as much as the Americans do. Especially one as successful and modest as Stefano.'

Her eyes turned to her brother, and for a few moments she watched him collecting the plates. Day took the chance to admire her profile. Then she looked away from Yianni, not back to Day but to the person sitting on the other side of him. Vassos. It was a lingering look. Vassos, who had not a euro to his name. Vassos who was nearly as old as her father. Yet Day was sure he was not mistaken in interpreting Maria's expression. She was in love. It was equally obvious that Vassos was unaware of it. He was looking at Stelios Ioannides, not bothering to conceal his affection.

Day sighed and looked out across the low white wall and past the well-tended flowering shrubs to the immaculate turquoise swimming pool. The rustle of dry branches high in the palm trees betrayed the gentle breeze that still brought a little freshness to the terrace. Beyond the pool a small brick pathway opened into a gravelled area with Cretan pots of great size, which in turn led the eye to the more distant view. The garden of the Villa Myrsini was expertly laid out. On the left, a spiny thicket of the indigenous juniper trees of Naxos gave the impression of guarding the villa from the outside world. In the other direction lay the grey mountains, flecked with green where the native vegetation refused to give up the struggle against the drought.

Only when Theodoros Kakouris tried to attract his attention did Day realise he had been lost in thought. The magnate had been conversing with the French woman, Elodie, but it seemed it was now Day's turn.

'Martin, you clearly know a great deal about ancient vases. Is this your academic specialism?'

Day hardly knew where to start. Impossible to explain his ambivalent attitude to academia and almost promiscuous love of ancient Greek history.

'It's not my period, but I've been interested in Greek pottery since I was a student. I suspect it's also something of a passion of yours?'

'Yes, you're right. I've been collecting vases for the last forty years, among other things of course. Now that I'm retired, I have plenty of time to focus on my collection. It's hard work, believe me!'

He smiled down the table towards Pierre Ridgeway, and Day followed his glance. Ridgeway had not heard. He was staring at Christina. Day was struck by something unpleasant in his look, and noted how uncomfortable Maria's cousin appeared to be as the object of it.

'Are there any active excavations taking place on Naxos at the moment, Martin?' continued Theodoros. 'I expect you're the man who would know. Any interesting new discoveries being unearthed?'

A fleeting image of a lot of people with trowels and brushes labouring in the soil of peaceful Naxos flashed before Day's inner eye. Perhaps it was the wine.

'Nothing of that kind. The preservation of a circular Hellenistic tower is a particularly fine project here, but not one to excite a collector, I'm afraid. It must be challenging these days, collecting antiquities? So hard to be certain of the legality of the source, I would think. Do you know, I even heard a rumour about certain corrupt archaeologists removing objects surreptitiously from the dig they're working on, objects which then completely disappear. Sold on the black market, of course. Disgraceful, in someone of my profession especially. Have you come across such a practice in your travels, Theodoros?'

'I'm happy to say I have not. If I heard so much as a whisper of that kind of illegality, I would have no more to do with the opportunity.'

Day nodded. He found it impossible to resist poking the wasps' nest still further, and decided to resume his assault on Ridgeway.

'Pierre, I expect it makes your job very much harder, ensuring the objects you're offered have legal provenance?'

He took a deep swallow of water to cover his impulsiveness. He had just contravened Andreas's most adamant instruction with particular recklessness, but he would defend himself if necessary. These two men were not going to make any unforced errors, and he felt a compulsion to upset their well-established complacency.

'Illegal trading, you mean? Look, Martin, one whiff of that and my career would be at an end. I told you that already. It even makes me nervous to hear you speak of it like this. Of course I deplore the practice; it's becoming a kind of unseen pandemic and it will continue to flourish unless the laws are changed and the authorities everywhere get a grip on the problem. But what can we do? We are little people in the large machine of the antiquities scandal.'

Day nodded. He could not have put it better himself.

'A shocking, most shameless form of crime, I agree,' added Stelios. 'It should be a serious concern for any of us who love art, and Greek antiquity in particular. I was told by your friend the curator that you succeeded in recovering some stolen objects yourself a few years ago, Martin. Is that true? Please tell us all about it.'

Day composed his thoughts and gave them a carefully edited account of his discovery of the ancient artefacts stolen from an American who had retired to the Peloponnese. It was part of his job as a presenter to create and tell a good story, and he held everyone's attention while managing not to give away any details of the police operation. He particularly minimised his own role in it, for the benefit of anyone at the table who might be listening rather carefully. He now suspected that they were.

'Well,' said Theodoros, 'that's fascinating, Martin. Luck was definitely on the side of the virtuous.'

'Indeed. I was just in the right place at the right time.'

Yianni and Christina had completed clearing the table and the party seemed to be about to break up, so Day thought it was time to make his excuses and leave. He thanked Stelios and promised to be in touch soon, to which Stelios replied that he would call Day in due course. Shaking hands all round, and urging Maria not to see him out, Day walked back into the villa to collect his briefcase and jacket.

The cool of the interior was delightful after the heat of the garden. Having retrieved his things, he paused in the hall. Raised voices were coming from the direction of the kitchen. He heard Christina say the name Ridgeway and Yianni react angrily, but other than that he could hear nothing clearly. Christina's tone then became conciliatory, and gradually the argument quietened until all that remained was the gentle sound of crockery.

He left the villa and opened the door of the Fiat to let out some of the accumulated heat. He wanted very much to speak to Helen, and promised himself he would call her as soon as he reached home. After that, of course, there was only one thing to do. It was the hour when Greeks retire into the cool to enjoy the siesta. It would be a chance for him to mull over everything he had heard, before inevitably being claimed by sleep.

8

Thursday 14th July had been eagerly anticipated by everyone on the island, resident and visitor alike. For the last few weeks, posters everywhere in Chora had advertised the new Naxos Festival of Cycladic Wine, and the first day had finally arrived. The event would be opened by Theodoros Kakouris at six in the evening, and festivities would continue late into the night.

Unsurprisingly for July, the morning had dawned fine and clear, the rising sun dazzling the east coast of the island from Apollonas in the north to Panormos in the south. It warmed the white houses of Apeiranthos that clung to their marble hillside, and eventually woke Day in his bedroom in Filoti. Before long, the whole of Naxos was busy, none more so than those whose job was to erect the stalls and performance platforms along the shore road, Papavasileou.

Day faced a familiar choice. Either he could set up his computer and put in several hours of work for his London agent, the main benefit of which would be to keep Maurice happy, or he could go and enjoy a coffee. Convincing himself that Maurice would understand his need for caffeine, he stepped out of the shower pondering which café would offer the best view of the festival preparations. He decided on the Café Kitron.

He hummed a snatch of song as he drove towards the coast. The Fiat was very small, especially for a man of his height, but at least its air conditioning was effective. He felt cheerful because the call with Helen last night had been good, despite there being no suggestion that she intended to return. When he reached Chora, he parked behind the Kastro and wandered through the shady lanes until he emerged on the *paralia* close to Diogenes bar. Tempting though it was to stop there, he kept to his plan and began the long walk to the Café Kitron.

It quickly became clear that no expense had been spared by the festival organisers. Several raised platforms were being erected for the use of musicians, many of whom would play with their backs to the sea and the sunset. The stalls themselves were being placed at intervals along the road wherever there was space. They were solidly-built wooden cabins of quality, thanks, no doubt, to the generosity of Theodoros.

He had nearly reached the Café Kitron when the phone in his pocket rang: a number he did not recognise. It turned out to be Theodoros Kakouris himself. With a lack of preamble that seemed typical of the man, Day was invited for drinks on the luxury yacht *Alkyoni* the following evening at seven. No time was wasted on niceties. They both knew he would accept, so the call was short. Day closed his phone and sank into a chair at the café.

He ordered an espresso and put his feet on the bottom rung of the next chair. The invitation to the millionaire's yacht was an interesting one, not least because he had never before been aboard one of the enormous sleek boats that increasingly graced the harbours of the Greek islands. It would also give him an excellent opportunity to continue his work for Andreas, and the more he thought about it the better it seemed. He would be able to report his findings when he saw Andreas on Sunday. He might even spot the undercover policeman, about whom he felt curious. There was only one small concern at the back of his mind: what had prompted the invitation? Had it simply been a hospitable impulse, or had Day's probing questions at the Villa Myrsini aroused suspicion? If so, all well and good, he thought. It had been his intention to rattle their cages.

His coffee was brought to him by a particularly good-looking waiter who seemed in some haste to move on to a group of laughing girls at the next table. For a while Day sat staring thoughtfully at the boats that were moored on the other side of the shore road. Their flags drooped in the morning sun. He wondered whether to tell Andreas now about his invitation to the yacht. He was still considering this when his phone rang again.

'Martin? This is Nick.'

'Hey, Nick! Is the baby born?'

'No way, mate, not time yet,' laughed his friend, bringing a smile to Day's face with his Aussie accent. 'I'm just calling to tell you we're leaving for Syros today. They want Deppi under observation in the hospital; nothing seriously wrong, just the best place for her to be right now. Okay? Nesto and I will stay with her parents. I thought you might be thinking of popping over to see us, and I didn't want you to find the place deserted.'

'Mmm, right. Thanks. So you'll be over there for the birth?'

'I reckon so; only a couple of weeks to go. You'll be hearing from me when there's some news!'

'Give my love to Deppi, and may all go well,' said Day. 'Let me know.'

'Yep, will do.'

Day put the mobile on the table feeling guilty. He had not once considered going over to Plaka to visit Nick and Deppi, his best friends on Naxos, but in his defence he really had no idea of what to do in the face of imminent birth, especially without Helen around. His instinct had been to leave them in peace. Two weeks till the new baby. This business with Theodoros Kakouris would all be over by then, one way or another. Perhaps Helen would be back too.

He drank his coffee and left some coins on the table. Turning up his shirt collar to protect his neck from the sun, he continued his walk along the *paralia*. He passed Nick and Deppi's pretty boat, the *Zephyro*, at its mooring. The sign that would normally have stood beside its gangway advertising boat trips for visitors was nowhere to be seen, and the yacht's covers were firmly closed. In a normal summer, when no new baby was expected, Nick and Deppi would be taking tourists for sightseeing, swimming and sunset trips, as much for their own pleasure as for the extra income. Nick really did have an enviable life. As the owner of a restoration company specialising in historical buildings, he had a good and interesting living. He had returned to the Cyclades from Australia to marry the beautiful Deppi, and now lived permanently on Naxos. On top of that, he owned the *Zephyro*. It was just as well he was also an extremely likeable guy.

After a good walk and a certain amount of pleasant time-wasting watching the activity along the shore, Day reached his hot car and braced himself to get inside. This time, heading home, he put the windows down and allowed the rush of air to dry the sweat on his face. His route took him past Agkidia, where his friend Aristos, the curator of the Naxos Museum, lived when he wasn't visiting Athens, then out towards the rural centre of the island where the land rose in gentle peaks and Cycladic traditions remained largely unchanged. He followed the road to Potamia, a village made up of three small communities, blessed by ancient springs and a river which gave it its name. The white houses decorated a hillside rich in trees and surrounded by fertile fields. The contrast between this area and the coast could hardly be more marked.

Halki was the next place he passed through, a small town that could boast it had once been the capital of Naxos, and was all the more peaceful now for having lost that honour. As he approached Filoti, he was already looking forward to the cool interior of his own house. Something small to eat, a few hours of work, a call to Helen perhaps, and then a siesta. He was due to meet Fabrizio at the Naxos Festival of Cycladic Wine at half past seven. Fabrizio, of course, would be late. He always was.

Chora was buzzing with people by seven in the evening when Day returned. All the best restaurants and tavernas on Naxos were advertising local specialities and Cycladic wines, but it was still early and people were focused on the stalls. There were tastings and good prices to be enjoyed.

The platform where, an hour ago, Theodoros Kakouris must have declared the festival open, was now a stage for traditional music. A violinist, a guitarist and a bouzouki player were surrounded by a crowd who had gathered to listen and seemed likely to remain there for some time. As Day reached them the song changed and the violinist put down his instrument to become a singer, his clear voice as rhythmic as it was melodic. The bouzouki player led the melody and sang quietly too, while the guitarist improvised round the notes of the bouzouki with a practised skill. At the end of each verse, the singer would pick up a tambourine-like drum and enthusiastically mark the rhythm of the chorus. The young couple next to Day were clapping with him, moving with the music, miming the words. Day asked them what the song was called.

'*Yia sena, mavromata mou*,' the girl told him. 'It means *For you, my dark-eyed girl*. It's very old. Everyone knows it.'

He thanked her and stayed to listen for a while. The song for the dark-eyed girl ended to great applause and cries of 'Bravo!', and the singer grinned as he picked up his violin again. A new tune began, the folk-violin soaring over the bouzouki and guitar, floating on the slight breeze from the sea that would die down as suddenly as it arose. With some reluctance, Day walked on in the direction he expected to meet Fabrizio.

A walking band was coming towards him, working its way along the bars, playing and asking for contributions from the tables, just as they did in the streets of central Athens. In fact, he suspected this group of having come from the city just for the three days of the festival, because he had never seen this before on Naxos. There were six of them, and there was something appealing about their music in this party setting: the enthusiasm of the two accordion players, the unstoppable tambourine and the virtuoso saxophone. A big man played guitar, and a thin man at the back played a double bass which he whisked along with him as he walked. No tune was ever finished; each just moved seamlessly into the next. Day called it street jazz, but perhaps it had a proper name. He heard a tune he recognised from the years he had lived in Athens, then another, and thought that the standard repertoire of groups like this might never vary greatly.

He looked around for Fabrizio and spotted him in a flamboyant green shirt striding from the direction of Agios Georgios. He seemed in high spirits.

'*Kalispera*, Martin! Sorry I'm late. Isn't this great? All the buzz of Athens without the heat and the fumes, just sea air and Cycladic charm. What's the plan?'

'I think we should start one end and work our way to the other,' said Day happily. 'We stop at every stall and allow them to tempt us with their wares. What could go wrong?'

'You haven't changed. Right, what's that one over there? The Floga Winery of Tinos. Never heard of them. Let's put that right.'

They wandered from stall to stall, tasting wines and local produce whenever they felt like it. Most exhibitors in this part of the *paralia* seemed to be from smaller establishments, such as organic family farms and producers with a limited range of wines. Some people added to their income by offering tours of their vineyard, others by producing delicious roasted nuts and other handmade food. There were a few local co-operatives working together in the inhospitable conditions of the Cycladic islands to produce wine from some of the oldest vine-stock in Greece. Everyone was friendly.

Several times, Fabrizio and Day heard about the problems arising from the recent boom in tourism in the Cyclades. Many local people had found they could make a better living from the hospitality industry in the four summer months than they could by labouring year-round at their vines. This had led to a serious decline in wine production on several of the islands. The problem was, they said, that the busiest season on a vineyard coincided with the most lucrative months of the tourist season. More than one wine producer complained that the production of local wine seemed destined to become a thing of the past. The older people bemoaned the golden era of Greek wine, the 1980s, when to be a wine producer was both profitable and prestigious.

Yet here they all were, celebrating the tradition of Cycladic wine. Despite the difficult climate of these islands, with almost no summer rainfall and relentless winds, the wine producers insisted that by growing the right vines, those historically known to be best suited to the terrain and the weather, it was possible to produce truly exceptional results. Most of those who said this, of course, added that theirs were among the most exceptional. Day and Fabrizio were happy to put it to the test.

Not all the stalls were taken by wine producers. There were suppliers who provided hotels and restaurants in bulk, and even a cruise company offering wine-themed trips round the Cyclades. These were of less interest to Day. He was more inclined to tease his tastebuds with varieties he knew well, like Assyrtiko, Mavrotragano and Mandilaria, and compare them with ones he knew less well, the delightfully-named Potamisi, Malagousia and Mavro Athiri. He tasted grape varieties whose names he did not even recognise. He listened to stories of poor yields, cool planting spots, and vines trained into a basket shape called a *kouloura*. It was all as fascinating as it was tasty.

He and Fabrizio wandered the length of the shore, listening to these stories. Everywhere he found enthusiasm and expertise. Among the stalls of the larger wineries, such as those from Santorini and Paros, Day expected to find Ambrosia Wine, but as Stefanos had said, his stand was not in a prime position. Santorini wines generally, though, were well represented. Day drew the line at sampling the rich Vinsanto, but fell in love afresh with the Nykteri, the fine white wine for which the grapes are traditionally picked at night, the growers working through the hours of darkness. He could taste jasmine behind its delicate and teasing flavour. He must remember to ask Stefanos about it.

'Have you noticed,' he said thoughtfully, as he turned away with great satisfaction from his most recent sampling, 'there's a sense that the man on the next stall, or the next hillside or the next island, is not so much a competitor as a colleague? I get a feeling of mutual support within the wine industry, here at least, rather than old-fashioned rivalry. Maybe it's something to do with the global financial crisis, making everyone pull together.'

'Yes, I think you're right about that atmosphere, although very soon I won't have an opinion worth mentioning. When shall we get some food?'

Fabrizio was fond of his food, but it was also true that even Day was experiencing a certain headiness from sampling the wines.

'Let's just get to the end of the *paralia*. I want to speak to the wine producer I met at Villa Myrsini. His stall will be called Ambrosia Wine. I think I'll order a few cases.'

'Santorini produces some of the best wines not only in Greece, but in the world,' began Stefanos Patelis in reply to a question from Fabrizio, whom Day had told about his modern wine-growing methods. The story was clearly not going to be a short one.

'Traditionally, our vines were always grown low to the ground in the shape of a basket, as I'm sure you know. This lessens wind damage, but it means everyone has to work on their hands and knees, which is hard, slow and labour-intensive. When I began work at Ambrosia, the owner, Klairi's father, was starting to think that the pioneers in wine production, people who wanted to try new methods, might have a good point. We installed pneumatic presses and stainless steel fermentation vats, and today we grow the majority of our vines along a wire in the modern way. Timing and planning are the key.'

'And you've kept developing your methods since you inherited the estate?' asked Fabrizio.

'Of course. Change or die, my friend. In the last ten years we have bought five hectares of mixed-level land in the west of the island and planted older varieties there as an experiment, as well as two of the tried and tested ones, Assyrtiko and Mandilaria. Every season brings a fresh excitement!'

'And the other wine estates? Are they doing the same kind of thing?'

Stefanos gave a smile of regret and a sideways shake of the head as he carefully formed his reply.

'It's fair to say that there's still a certain amount of resistance to the new methods. There are some signs of change. Even the age-old argument surrounding the use of oak barrels is calming down. We know we need to support each other these days more than ever.'

'I enjoyed the wine you brought to Villa Myrsini, Stefano,' said Day. 'I'm afraid I don't remember the label …'

'Ah yes, it was the 2017 Nykteri. It's Stelio's favourite, and with good reason. I have a joke with him that those vines are older than he is.'

'How old can your vines be, then?' asked Fabrizio.

'I'm not sure there's an answer to that, my friend. You see, if a vine is fifteen years old above the surface, it may have a root system as much as four hundred years old. This is the result of the traditional Santorini cultivation method we were talking about. The *kouloura* 'basket' was a living thing woven from the stems of the vine. When it stopped being productive, the stems of the vine were cut away and a new *kouloura* was woven using the fresh growth from the rootstock. This way there was no need to replace the plant.'

'*Bellissimo!*' murmured Fabrizio, and accepted a small plastic tasting glass from Stefanos's young assistant.

'That, my friend, is the Nykteri that Martin likes so much,' Stefanos told him. 'Martin, you should try something else. This is an Assyrtiko, which, as you know, is a variety for which Santorini is famous; but this particular one is very special. It is a wine I designed myself when I took over Ambrosia. It is 90% Assyrtiko and 10% secret ingredient. I rarely make it now, but this bottle is from last year, and I would be delighted to open it for you.'

He reached behind him and pulled a bottle from the fridge, smiling as he removed the foil with a professional-looking tool, pulled out the cork and poured a little for Day.

'I keep it for family and friends, so I'm afraid it is not available for sale, but I would like to hear your opinion.'

'I like that very much,' said Day. 'Clean, light and refreshing.'

'That's right, and not very high in alcohol. Greeks prefer not to become intoxicated.'

Fabrizio shot Day a meaningful look.

'I could stay here for hours, Stefano, but I'm afraid we really must go and get some food before we have anything more to drink. I'll come back tomorrow evening and place my order with you.'

'You want to buy? Don't make a rushed choice, Martin. I'll be here after the festival ends, we have plenty of time. I'm busy on Sunday night, but please come for coffee with Klairi and me on Monday morning. We can talk properly and get to know one another.'

The arrangement was confirmed and Day noted down the directions to the house where the Patelises were staying. They left Stefanos dealing with another customer, and finally Fabrizio could focus on his dinner.

9

Taverna O Glaros, 'The Seagull', was on the first floor of a building on the edge of the *bourgos*, and was extremely busy when they arrived. It was already nine o'clock, the time when Greeks like to begin their evening meal, and having spent time at the festival the summer visitors were eating later too. Day and Fabrizio were shown to one of the few remaining tables.

O Glaros had only opened that summer, and Day had been looking forward to trying it. It overlooked the sea, and one entire wall was open to the air like a huge balcony. Seagulls being few on Naxos, he was hopeful that the restaurant was not named after unwanted feathered visitors.

The proprietor was a moustachioed older Greek whose brown suit added an air of respectability and even venerability to the place. He brought the menus to their table in person, as he seemed to do for all the customers before his staff took over the ordering and serving of the food.

'*Kalispera sas. Kalos irthate!*' he said, handing them each a printed sheet of paper. 'Tonight we have special dishes for the Naxos Wine

Festival, with wines from our Naxos producers and our friends on Paros. The wine list is on the back, Kyrioi.'

With a hint of a bow he returned sedately to his stool at the back of the taverna to continue his iced coffee. Day studied the menu and his appetite awoke; the chef of O Glaros had been busy. There were regional dishes from most of the islands of the Cyclades, each with a short, mouthwatering description. He looked across at Fabrizio and saw a man who appeared to be in a small, personal heaven.

'Some of these Cycladic specialities look amazing,' he said, without taking his eyes from the list. 'I've not even heard of most of them. Shall we order to share?'

'Best way. Choose whatever you like, as long as it includes the local potatoes. They're the pride of the island. What do you see that takes your fancy?'

'*Polla, polla,*' laughed Fabrizio, making the Greek sound curiously Italian in only four syllables. 'I'd like to try some local cheese.'

'What about the salad with *xynomizithra*? That's very traditional here. What else? We could try the *revithada*, the chickpea stew from Siphnos. There are lots of unusual little fritters that look interesting: there are *marathokeftedes* from Tinos, which are made with fennel. Tomato balls from Santorini … I really could eat any of this. The fava would probably be excellent. Helen loves fava.'

'Have you spoken to her recently?'

'Yes, we had a long talk last night.'

Fabrizio nodded and returned his attention to the menu.

'So, I like the sound of *kalogeros*. It says here it's a traditional Naxian dish of meat with eggplant and the local *graviera* cheese melted on the top. Do you know it?'

'Yes, let's have some of that. Although there's also an interesting meat and potato dish from Amorgos called *patatato*. I've never tried that.'

'Oh, would you please just order, Martin? I'm starving.'

Day waved to the waiter and lost no time. He ordered a portion of *kalogeros*, a salad with *xynomizithra* cheese, some fennel fritters and a plate of fried potatoes, all for them to share. He praised the menu enthusiastically to the waiter in his best Greek, ensuring that his voice reached the proprietor. It never hurt to make a good impression on a local restaurateur. Sure enough, the old man in the suit inclined his head and raised his hand slightly in thanks.

'And a *misokilo* of your red wine, please.'

Fabrizio smiled, shaking his head. Even after all the unique wines they had sampled that evening, his friend still ordered the local red from the barrel. He had missed Martin Day in the last year or two.

'So,' he said as the jug was placed in front of them with two small glasses, a basket of bread and a bottle of water. 'I've spent three days on Delos since I last saw you. I went on the boat every morning from Mykonos and came back each night to a cheap room in the town. Delos was pretty crowded, but I had a good hunt around and an interesting meeting with the woman in charge of the museum. It was three days well spent. Tomorrow I'm off on another trip.'

'Not contacted your friend yet?'

'Not yet.'

'Where to next, then?'

'I'll just roam around,' said Fabrizio vaguely, 'staying away from the crowds, if I can.'

'Good luck with that. Just avoid all the towns and beaches, you'll be fine.'

'How was your talk to the millionaire? Last Tuesday, wasn't it?'

'It went down well, thanks, and the lunch was excellent.'

At this moment the first plates of food arrived. The salad was topped with a mountain of crumbly white cheese, drizzled with rich olive oil and sprinkled with oregano. The other plate contained the small, crispy fritters, the speciality of Tinos island. The sight alone was enough to make Day's mouth water.

'I think I told you that the man we just spoke to, Stefanos Patelis, was at my talk on Tuesday?' he said. 'He was saying that his office here on Naxos had been broken into, and the intruder escaped after assaulting the manager. Nothing was stolen.'

Fabrizio paused in the middle of placing some salad onto his plate.

'I heard about that from the people who run the hotel where I'm staying.'

'Anyway, no real harm was done; nobody was badly hurt. The police have arrested a man, but possibly not the right one. Let me tell you about the rest of my little audience. It's quite entertaining.'

Once again, he was interrupted in the best possible way. A dish containing steaming meat and glistening aubergines covered in melted cheese was placed in the centre of the table, and, as if by magic, the fried potatoes were set down at Day's right hand. Fabrizio laughed.

'You look as happy as I've ever seen you, Martin. Do you still not eat much during the day?'

'I had a bit of salad and some cheese at lunchtime,' he recalled vaguely.

'No wonder you don't put on weight. *Buon appetito*! *Kali orexi*!'

They began to talk of old colleagues, of life among the Schools of Archaeology in Athens, of the latest so-called discoveries to hit the press, and various rumours and scandals among members of their profession. Only when they had done justice to their meal did a minor disagreement about the honesty or otherwise of a certain politician bring to Day's mind again the questionable honesty of Theodoros Kakouris. He decided impulsively to take

Fabrizio into his confidence, as his friend could be trusted and had no connection with the case.

'You must keep what I'm going to tell you completely between ourselves, okay? The millionaire guest at the Villa Myrsini is Theodoros Kakouris, the shipping magnate who has sponsored this wine festival. He has a private collection of Greek artefacts which must be jaw-droppingly interesting, and nobody has seen any of it. The antiquities police have asked me to see what I can find out about it.'

Fabrizio stopped eating and reached unthinkingly towards his glass.

'Really? The police? Why you? That sounds completely *pazzo*!'

'And that means what?'

'It's Italian for mad, Martin.'

'Ah, I see.'

'You don't work for the Greek police now, do you? Did you discover anything?'

'Not yet.'

'Of course not; you were there to talk about Greek history, I imagine.'

'Vases, actually,' said Day.

'Ah, and while doing so you tried to get them to tell you how they smuggle them out of Greece? Really, you are sometimes completely *pazzo*, Martin!'

Day laughed.

'Kakouris called today and invited me onto his luxury yacht for drinks tomorrow evening. If nothing else, I'll see the inside of one of those yachts for the first time in my life. I just hope the police don't raid the boat before I've had a chance to enjoy it.'

Fabrizio said nothing, shaking his head and returning his attention to his food. Day let the word *pazzo* hang between them for a while before trying to move on.

'I've just remembered, Brizio, a friend of mine has invited us to lunch on Sunday at his place on Paros. Can you squeeze it into your island-hopping schedule? It'll be good fun; he's an interesting guy, and he's going to introduce me to his new girlfriend, a beautiful artist called Fotini. How about it?'

Fabrizio closed his cutlery on his empty plate and shook his head firmly, his eyes focused somewhere over Day's shoulder.

'I can't, I'm afraid, not this time. Not possible. Thanks for the thought.'

He covered his glass with his hand, so Day poured the last of the little pitcher of wine into his own glass and waved to the waiter for the bill.

They said goodbye outside the restaurant and Fabrizio went off to find a taxi to take him to his hotel. Day headed back alone towards the *paralia* to enjoy the buzzing late-night atmosphere of the festival and sober up a little before driving home.

There seemed to be people and music everywhere. The biggest crowd sat facing inwards on the outdoor terrace of one of the cafés, and more people stood behind them looking over their heads. Day found a place where he could see what they were watching. A violinist and a man playing the Greek lute, the *laouto*, sat in the centre of the space. Day listened for several minutes, admiring them. He had heard about the traditional music of these islands, but it was probably the first time in his life that he had genuinely understood the brilliance and beauty of it in the hands of expert performers.

After the spontaneous applause at the end of the song, the violinist started a new melody, his eyes focused inside his mind, a very slight smile on his face. Day continued to watch and listen. Without warning, an old man in the audience began to sing. No word had passed between them, yet the players showed no surprise. The strong, reedy voice of the singer cut through the violin, and every eye was on the old man. White-haired, with a bushy moustache and wrinkles round his eyes, he sang without self-consciousness, without a care, and with a compelling power. The words he sang were immaterial for Day, as for him the Greek was hard to understand, yet every note carried straight to his soul. This was a traditional performance as good as any he had heard before, despite all his years in Greece.

It was with reluctance that he finally decided to move away. He walked through the stalls in the direction of the Portara; most of the vendors were clearing up and closing down, loading stock into vans to take away until the next evening. As he approached Diogenes bar, he heard more music coming from the small square nearby and saw that the inevitable had happened. Groups of people were dancing the *syrtaki*, holding hands and slowly progressing in a circle, performing the traditional steps as had generations before them. There were small lines of three or four dancers and a larger circle of more people moving gently round. A man would separate from the rest occasionally to execute some fancy footwork, to the delight of the crowd. People were clapping, and the three string players and the singer performed tirelessly. Alexandros, the waiter from Diogenes, was exchanging full glasses of *raki* for the empty ones at the musicians' feet.

The party was certainly not finished yet in Chora, although for Day the time had come to drive carefully home to Filoti.

10

Theodoros Kakouris, one of the most private but most successful figures in Greece's prestigious shipping industry, regarded Day affably over the rim of his cocktail glass. The lights of the bridge deck occasionally reflected off his pink-tinted glasses as he turned his head to include everyone in his remarks.

Day was the only guest that evening. He had been collected from Chora port by the yacht's tender, a twelve-foot black and white miracle of speed and comfort. As they bumped across the bay towards the *Alkyoni*, Day had watched the crewman in his white uniform and cap, clearly loving every moment. The man's bearing suggested he was living some kind of dream, one in which he drove the sleek vessel across the warm Aegean sea in the starlight, and was even paid to do so.

Climbing onto the beautiful *Alkyoni*, Day had been welcomed aboard by a man who introduced himself as Captain John and appeared to be as English as Day himself. He was led to the upper bridge deck, where a loose arrangement of comfortable chairs upholstered in white were ranged round two glass tables under square white parasols. The varnished wood of the deck shone in the discreet lighting, and candles in amber jars on the tables lent the area a feeling of sensuousness. Theodoros and Ridgeway had stood to greet him, while their wives remained seated, comfortably sipping their drinks.

Afterwards Day had little recollection of the initial small-talk. A waiter brought him a decorative bottle of cold water with slices of strawberry floating in it, and a frosted glass straight from the freezer. He was offered his choice of cocktail and requested a gin and tonic. Theodoros began telling him about the yacht.

'The hull and superstructure are aluminium. She was built in 1987, but refitted to my own specification in 2017. She cruises at sixteen knots, but can go at nineteen if we feel like a bit of fun. Greek made, of course. Perama.'

He had named a famous shipyard in Piraeus about which Day knew very little. The others looked like they had heard all this before.

'What size of crew do you need on the *Alkyoni*?' he asked, while his mind played with the idea of the English captain and the undercover policeman.

'There are seven permanent crew members plus Captain John. John came with the *Alkyoni*, and I'm the envy of all my friends because I have him. In addition, I've taken on a security man and a PA - she takes care of shore liaison for me, especially in connection with the Naxos Festival. It's a bit of a squeeze in the staff quarters on this trip, I'm afraid.'

Eleftheria paused in the act of sipping her Martini.

'The *Alky* is forty metres long, Martin. That's a hundred and thirty feet in English. That's right, Theo, isn't it?'

Day was pleased at this point to receive his gin and tonic. The atmosphere in the little group was awkward in a way he found hard to explain. Theodoros excused himself for a moment to fetch something, and Day turned to Ridgeway.

'Should I call the *Alkyoni* a 'super yacht'?' he asked in a confidential tone. 'What's the right term? I'm not well-versed in this kind of thing.'

'Best to say luxury yacht, I understand. It's quite something, isn't it? We've lived like kings on her for three weeks. I could get used to this life.'

'How much longer will you be on board?'

He remembered that the plan was to head for Sicily once the wine festival was over, but Andreas would appreciate precise information. Day was disappointed by the vagueness of Ridgeway's reply.

'Only another week, perhaps less. Then we sail to Sicily and say farewell to all this. Next stop Paris for Elodie and me.'

'Do you have such a thing as a busy season, or is business much the same throughout the year?'

'Always busy,' Ridgeway laughed. 'You?'

'I'm not a typical archaeologist. I spend the summer researching and writing; sometimes I have a brief period doing a bit of filming. Winter is usually spent in London, finishing work and talking to my agent about contracts for the next year. A real field archaeologist would normally excavate in the height of the summer. Did you know that?'

'What, in the Greek sun?' said Eleftheria, stirring from her reverie. 'It can be over forty degrees here, you know!'

'Very true, and the sites are usually in exposed places where there's no shade. People work under makeshift canopies if possible, but that's mostly for the sake of the excavation rather than themselves.'

'That's true dedication,' murmured Ridgeway, distracted by the sight of Theodoros returning, followed by a Greek man in a kind of uniform who was carrying a small but sturdy box. Theodoros sat down heavily in his chair.

'*Lipon*! You probably wondered why I invited you here this evening, Martin. For the pleasure of your company, naturally, but also I have something to show you. Aki, if you would.' He beckoned to the uniformed man and gestured that the box should be placed on the glass table.

Theodoros bent over and opened it carefully. Day glanced at the man called Akis. He was about thirty-five, bearded and sharp-eyed. He held Day's eyes for a fraction too long.

'This will interest you, Martin. I plan to give it to the Municipality of Naxos to be awarded annually at the Festival for the best contribution to the event. Each recipient will hold it for one year. A prize, you see. I'm a believer in competition.'

He lifted out a small object and passed it to Day. It was a drinking cup in the Ancient Greek shape known as a kylix, shallow-bowled like a champagne glass, with two loop handles and a small pedestal.

'You know what it is? What do you think?' asked Theodoros, and he fixed his eyes on Day. Ridgeway was smiling in a way that Day disliked. From a respectful distance, Captain John was taking an interest.

The kylix was a modern reproduction. Day placed a polite expression on his face, remembering the originals he had held in his hands in Athens and New York, pieces painted by named artists whose skill was still admired thousands of years after their deaths. He wondered what he was expected to say.

'Well, it's a cup of the kind used at symposia, the drinking parties for the privileged men of Ancient Greek society. The stem is held between the index finger and the other fingers, while the thumb slips through one of the handles, like this. The idea was that nothing is spilled, no matter how inebriated the drinker. Rather an apt choice of prize for a wine festival, and an interesting design: this pair of eyes painted inside the bowl watches the drinker every time he takes a sip. This figure here is a typical representation of Dionysos, god of the good grape, and of special importance on Naxos.'

'Very good, Martin,' said Theodoros with a smile at Ridgeway. 'What else can you tell us about the cup?'

The two men seemed to be enjoying his discomfort, and the man called Akis was looking at him suspiciously. Annoyance was beginning to get the better of Day, and he no longer cared whether he was being rude.

'The shape and images are Archaic. The cup, of course, is modern.'

He caught a confused look on the face of the security man. In his position it must be a problem to be certain of anything. It was not the job of a policeman to know one kylix from another.

'Who made it?' Day asked, though he had no further interest in the object.

'A craftsman in Athens,' said Theodoros offhandedly. 'I think it's entirely fit for purpose, don't you?' He handed the cup back to Akis and waved him away. Day swallowed some gin and tonic and gave up on caution.

'The world is full of reproductions these days, some better than others. That one's good, but surely you didn't think I'd mistake it for genuine?'

'You're the expert, Martin, of course. Just a bit of fun. Would you like to see round the yacht now?'

Day said he would, and Captain John was summoned over to be his guide. Before they left, Theodoros added a request for more drinks. The captain said he would send the barman out to them, and invited Day into the gleaming interior of the *Alkyoni*.

'Fourteen years!' said John in answer to Day's first question. 'Best job in the world. What skipper wouldn't want to sail this thing round the Aegean?'

He was about Day's age but a great deal more tanned and muscular, both of which were shown to advantage by the white polo shirt that bore the silver logo of Kakouris Industries S.A.. Short light brown hair and clear green eyes, white teeth that had seen a good dentist.

'You're married I see, John,' remarked Day on noticing the ring. 'How does that work in your job?'

'Yes. My wife and I live in Provence. I'm only needed on the *Alkyoni* for a few months in the summer and some short trips during the rest of the year. Alyson and I have a couple of places near Aix that we hire out, so she has plenty to do and some company while I'm away, and the rest of the year we take it easy. It's a hard life!'

Day found him likeable and wondered how much he knew about whatever might be taking place on the *Alkyoni*'s summer cruises. They passed through a sumptuous private lounge with blue-tinted windows through which glinted the lights of the shore, then through a dining room which could be transformed into a cinema, and even onto the bridge itself. John was still telling him in great detail about the yacht's impressive marine radar and navigation system as they arrived back at the upper bridge deck. Day had tried to follow the captain's technical explanations, but as they passed through a spacious cocktail bar he saw something which distracted him considerably.

Back on the deck they found that Elodie Ridgeway had gone to her cabin to change for dinner at the Villa Myrsini later that evening, and Eleftheria was engrossed in a magazine. Theodoros and Ridgeway were silently looking at their phones with fresh drinks in front of them. It was time to leave, and Captain John went to summon the tender for him. The farewells were courteous but brief, leaving Day as puzzled as before about the reason for his invitation.

'Well, Martin, we look forward to seeing you on Tuesday,' said Theodoros, shaking hands. 'Have a good weekend.'

11

The following afternoon, Saturday, Day finished a little work on the possibility of filming Fabrizio's excavation on Crete, and then drove to Chora to buy a small gift for Andreas and Fotini. It was an excellent tradition in Greece that a guest invited for Sunday lunch arrived with a present, usually confectionery or some special kind of food.

The *zacharoplasteio* was one which Day had used before for this purpose. It was just off one of the older squares of the town and was the best confectionery shop on the island. This, at least, was the verdict of Helen, who knew about these things. Despite having no liking for sweet food himself, he would have to make the purchase without her this time.

The girl behind the desk looked at him curiously, perhaps confused by his serious expression; a broad smile usually lit up the faces of customers who saw the delicacies in her glass cabinets. There were small treats of every colour: miniature macaroons, traditional biscuits, generously-sized *baklavas*, handmade chocolates, green pistachio bites, crystallised orange segments dipped in dark chocolate, and a great deal more. The sweet smell of the shop was almost overwhelming.

The assistant offered to help.

'I need a gift for friends on Paros,' he said. 'Something that will survive the journey. What do you suggest?'

'*Lipon*,' she said, scanning the counters. 'Anything with chocolate will spoil in this heat.'

She reached beneath the counter and brought out a silver cardboard box into which she placed a piece of white tissue paper.

'Perhaps some of these *koulourakia*? They're flavoured with orange, cinnamon and a little *raki*. We call them *methismena*. I don't know the English.'

'Tipsy,' supplied Day, who unsurprisingly was not bad when it came to Greek words relating to alcohol. 'Yes, good idea. Some of those, and something else to go with them?'

'*Amygdalota!*' the girl declared with conviction, pointing to the other end of the shelf. 'They're really delicious marzipan specialities with a delicate flavour. Very popular.'

Day agreed they would do well. The girl arranged the items in the gift box and folded the tissue over the top before closing the lid. She completed the effect with silver ribbons, curling the ends with scissors, applied an attractive sticker bearing the name of the *zacharoplasteio,* and placed the result on the glass counter. Day reached gratefully for his wallet.

Having accomplished this important task, he decided to visit Diogenes.

The afternoon was warm and pleasant, the July heat moderated by a light wind from the sea that gently moved the awnings of the shops. He lengthened his walk by going through the back streets of the town, enjoying the relative quietness away from the tourist areas and the wine festival. At a turn in the road he came across a small *kafeneio*, the kind of traditional café beloved of the older

Greek generation, and sure enough outside it sat two men and a woman of similar age. The woman wore a comfortable floral dress and grey cardigan, with canvas shoes on her feet. She sat at a table without a coffee or even a glass of water, listening and observing. At one point she reached over to the Greek basil that grew in a metal pot behind her, pinched its leaves and carried the smell to her nose.

The two men, meanwhile, chatted and laughed as the mood took them. The older of the two sat squarely on his chair, feet solidly on the floor in front of him, holding his walking stick upright between his open knees. His hands rested on each other over the rounded head of the stick, and he regarded the street steadily over the top of them. He had receding hair and a generous grey moustache, an open-necked short-sleeved shirt and the shapeless black trousers of an earlier era. His younger companion, who was probably in his seventies, wore faded jeans and a maroon shirt. He had bright eyes and watched the world go by as he played abstractedly with his *komboloi* beads. His left foot rested on the brace of the blue metal table in front of him, on which empty coffee cups sat next to small glasses of ouzo.

The sight of them reminded Day of the Greece he had known twenty years ago when he had first travelled there as a student. In this nostalgic mood he emerged onto Protopapathaki, where he saw Yianni Ioannides sitting at a table at Diogenes with an empty beer glass.

'Martin! Good to see you. Join me?'

Day sat down opposite the American, giving Alexandros an order for two beers. Drawing deeply on his cigarette, Yianni then extinguished it in the ashtray as if it was no longer required, and seemed keen to make the most of the unexpected companionship.

'I'm in Chora to pick up a meat order,' he explained. 'I thought I deserved a beer.'

'It's a busy time at the villa. You do all the cooking yourself?'

'That's right. I trained as a chef in the States.'

He was interrupted by the return of Alexandros with their drinks. Another bill was added to the existing roll of paper in the small glass on the table.

'With that kind of qualification, wouldn't you rather work in one of the restaurants on the island? Your food's great, from what I've seen.'

'One day, maybe,' said Yianni, lifting his glass and swallowing his beer with something like relief. 'When we first moved to Greece, our parents needed Maria and me at the villa. Our mother became very ill; I think you heard?'

'Yes. I'm sorry.'

Yianni nodded. His dark eyes had saddened and he focused for a moment on his beer.

'So you understand that initially there was no question of looking for work in a restaurant. Now … well, now it would be possible, but there's no need. I work for my father.'

Day asked what had made Yianni choose to become a chef.

'Maria did well at school; she had all the brains. I found out that cooking was the one thing I was good at. That's all there is to it.'

He laughed and took another drink.

'After I finished training, Dad suggested getting some experience of Greek cuisine, which was great, because I wasn't keen on the idea of working in a big professional kitchen. Not then, anyway. So I came to Greece and worked in a small restaurant with a really well-known chef called Panos Zamanis. He taught me all sorts of new stuff. He wanted me to stay and work with him, but we were still living in the States at the time. It was a great year, though.'

'I suppose you choose all the menus and arrange the wine at the villa, that kind of thing?'

'Yes, it's what I'm trained to do. Even though he's not well, my father still likes having people to visit, so sometimes the villa feels more like a hotel. I've found the best butchers and fishermen, I buy from the local farmers, and the supermarket in Chora gives me a special price on the big orders.'

'Does all the wine come from Ambrosia?'

'Most of it, certainly recently. I used to get our wine from Panayiotis in the *plateia*. Now Dad only wants us to use Stefanos.'

He was silent for a moment.

'I went to Santorini recently, actually. I thought I'd see the Ambrosia vineyard for myself. Call it professional research.'

Yianni applied himself again to his beer. Day prompted him for details.

'It's very impressive. Modern, with a great visitor centre and sales outlet. They even have a wine club. I didn't want a fuss so I just took a look round. You've got to hand it to Stefanos, he's done well.'

'He seems a really nice guy,' agreed Day, which Yianni acknowledged with a nod.

'So, what did you think of Uncle Theo?'

'He's certainly hospitable. Last night I went on board his yacht for drinks. I've not been on a boat like that before; it was quite an experience. Are he and your father close?'

'Oh, Dad's close to Eleftheria rather than Theo, but he likes it that they visit every summer to keep an eye on him. Since Caroline's death, you know.'

'Caroline? Your mother?'

'Yes, sorry. We called her Caroline. Do you want another drink?'

Yianni had drained his Mythos and looked at him hopefully.

'No time, I'm afraid, I've got a call with England,' he lied. 'I'll see you at the villa on Tuesday.'

Yianni said he was looking forward to it and insisted on paying for the drinks. As he walked away, Day saw the young man wave towards Alexandros, whether to pay or to ask for another beer he didn't wait to see.

He drove slowly through the Naxos countryside towards Filoti, skilfully guiding the Fiat round the uphill hairpin bends. The terrain grew wilder as he drove further into the centre of the island. He came up behind a small truck carrying animals, so fell back, opened the window and enjoyed the scenery. The land was parched, but Naxos was used to this, and the vegetation across the hillsides, in the valleys and in the upland meadows had been surviving for thousands of years in the dry Aegean summers. There were rugged wild fig trees, bent bushes stunted by the hard conditions, and the maquis vegetation that could cope with almost any drought. The grass, of course, was long, exhausted and almost white, and would not recover until the rains of winter and the eventual regeneration of spring. In a steep-sided valley he was forced to stop when a herd of goats decided to cross the road in search of more palatable food. When at last he could drive on again, the truck had disappeared.

He decided to make good his lie to Yianni and call Helen once he reached home, but getting there had become frustratingly difficult. A coach was trying to negotiate the narrow turn into the main street of Filoti, and traffic from both directions clogged the road through the village. Only past Thanasis's taverna was his way clear, and he drew up in front of his house with relief.

It was pleasantly cool inside and smelled of his library of books. He opened the balcony doors to let in the sweet, warm air of the valley, and sat there for a while watching the minimal movements of the Cycladic countryside. On the opposite hillside the blue beehives were just catching the sun, and the familiar mule was motionless beneath the tree that offered the only available shade. As he watched it, the animal's prolonged, high-pitched cry carried to his ears, an insistent combination of defiance and complaint. Otherwise the only sound was of doves on the roof; even the sparrows seemed to be taking a rest. Nothing moved along the mountain road that was just visible in the distance, the difficult road from Filoti to Kalados. Behind it, Mount Zas silently challenged all comers to climb to its peak.

He took out his mobile and checked the time. In England it would be just after four o'clock, and if Helen was working she might welcome an interruption. She might even be having a cup of tea. That was all the excuse he needed.

When the moment came and she answered the phone, Day was inexplicably unable to utter any normal greeting. Instead, his eyes fixed on the valley, he described what he saw.

'The mule is under the tree and the beehives are shining in the sun. Everything else appears to be having a siesta.'

'And you aren't? Is something the matter?' she asked kindly.

'I'm fine. You?'

'Fine too. London is muggy and airless, and I'd give anything for a Cycladic breeze. I went for a walk this morning, and there seemed to be dirt and graffiti everywhere, even here in Hampstead. The park was a bit better, except for the parched flowerbeds and the students lying on the grass who had probably been there all night. Forgive me if I sound cynical.'

'You sound fed up. You're not far from Heathrow. Can I persuade you?'

She hesitated for a second, and his hopes rose.

'Suzanne's coming to stay on Tuesday. You know, my old school friend. Her husband died last year and she's been finding life really difficult. I said she could stay with me as long as she wanted.'

'Of course. Well, her need is greater than mine. It's the right thing to do. I just rang to say that I miss you.'

12

'I'm at the port now, Andrea. I'm going to be on the *Blue Star Patmos* that gets to Paros at ten twenty,' said Day into his phone from the ferry passenger waiting area, raising his voice above the tumult. He was leaving a voice message, as Andreas had not picked up. 'I'll get a taxi up to your house. I should be there by eleven.'

The crossing from Naxos to Paros could take as little as half an hour on a speedy Sea Jet, but it was considerably cheaper to use the big ferry of the Blue Star line. He would still reach Paros in fifty minutes at most, and it was enjoyable to stand on deck and watch the wake churned up by the ship's propellers. Sometimes the fresh air helped him to control his seasickness, an inconvenience to a man living on an island, but one which he had not managed to overcome.

In the ferry office, as he was buying his ticket, he had seen a poster advertising trips to Santorini, the unmistakable blue domes and white houses catching his attention. He had asked the young lady for details and she had given him a leaflet, as a queue had formed behind him. Now, standing in the crush of the departure shed, he looked at the leaflet while waiting for the *Patmos* to appear round the headland. He read the schedule with interest.

Given the sailing times between Naxos and Santorini, it did not seem possible for Yianni to have travelled there and back in a single day and still to have had any time to visit Ambrosia Wine. Surely he must have stayed overnight. Moreover, his return ticket would have cost him almost four times what Day had paid to go to Paros.

He quickly put Yianni out of his mind and dreamed instead of taking Helen to Santorini. The *Patmos* soon emerged from behind the promontory and neared the port. It sounded its horn, executed its customary turn accompanied by the insistent warning of the alarm, and put its massive engine into reverse thrust to approach the jetty with its car deck already open. Black smoke billowed as the white-shirted crew manned the ropes and shouted instructions. The ramp touched land and almost at once the first car took its chance to leave the ship, accompanied by waving and shouting and the whistle of the policeman on the quay. Foot passengers dragging luggage streamed down either side of the ramp, struggling to maintain control of wheeled suitcases, dogs and small children as they did so. The first car was soon followed by others, and impatient trucks, vans and motorbikes.

Day fought his way on board with the other travellers, and made the crossing to Paros standing at the stern rail of the *Patmos*, controlling his inevitable slight nausea. He watched as they headed away from Naxos and the Portara disappeared behind them. The deck was windy and he could feel the effect of both the wind and the sun on his skin, and taste salt on his lips. The ferry headed north-west, skirted the tip of Paros, and then turned south towards the port of Parikia.

As they entered the bay and prepared to make the turn at the dock, the public address system advised passengers with vehicles to make their way to the disembarkation deck. Day remained at the rail to enjoy the familiar sight of Parikia's windmill, its old town above with its castle and church, and the wide bay into which the ship was sailing at a remarkably fast rate of knots. He lingered as long as possible before making his way downstairs to the car deck with the other foot passengers. Carrying his small holdall containing the gift from the *zacharoplastia*, he was among the last to leave the boat. There must be plenty of time, he thought, as there were so many cars and trucks to disembark, and more foot passengers than he had imagined possible. Only when he turned to look back from the road did he realise that the ferry had already drawn up its ramp and was urgently heading back to sea.

Having deliberately avoided the taxis who were waiting on the quay to meet the boat, he walked to the regular rank on the main road and took the car at the head of the queue, a smart black Mercedes among many identical smart black Mercedes. He explained to the driver where he wanted to go, and the man, who introduced himself as Savvas, said he knew the place. They drove along the Limani Parou, the shore road, before turning inland through a residential area and steadily forging uphill. Savvas delivered him to Andreas's door without any trouble at all, which was impressive as addresses on the islands were casually used if they existed at all. Taxi drivers needed very particular skills in the Cyclades. Day took Savvas's card and said he would call whenever he needed transport on Paros in future.

Andreas was ready for him. Two bottles of beer were waiting on the balcony table. It was like *déjà vu*.

Andreas wasted no time in asking for a complete update. His light blue Nordic eyes, which contrasted so impressively with his Greek features, were full of anticipation.

'Right, so I turned up at Villa Myrsini last Tuesday to give my first talk and was introduced to everyone. Both the men you're interested in were there, Ridgeway and Kakouris, with their wives. Stelios Ioannides, of course, and his son and daughter, and his niece, who's having a holiday at the villa. And there's also a single man living there, some kind of permanent guest or live-in friend, name of Vassos.'

'Is that his first or second name?'

'Sorry, I didn't ask. There was also a couple from Santorini, the wine producer who supplies Stelios and his nice wife Klairi. Stefanos Patelis is his name, owns Ambrosia Wine.'

'The place that was broken into last week?'

'That's right.'

Andreas nodded and held up his hand briefly to ask for a small pause. He pulled a notebook and pen towards him and wrote for a moment.

'Okay. Anyone else?'

'No. Theodoros Kakouris took charge, socially and in every other way, as you might expect. He made a point of insisting on informality and introduced everyone as if it was his party. I suppose in a way it was. Stelios is not a well man. He has problems with mobility and I wouldn't be surprised if he's in pain a lot of the time.

'I talked about Early Classical painted vases, as Stelios had requested. It was a good choice, because I wanted to get Kakouris talking about Greek antiquities, and I guessed he was likely to collect either terracotta vases or, heaven help us, Cycladic figurines. Showy, expensive, rare things, anyway, rather than tiny bronzes or gold hairpins.'

'I agree,' said Andreas, and clamped his mouth shut again to allow Day to continue.

'They all listened politely while I told them what some of them already knew on the subject of vases. Ridgeway's wife didn't understand much of it, I'm sure: her knowledge of any language but French seems to be limited. If she has any involvement in illicit deals, I'd be surprised. The others showed a fair degree of interest in my talk but gave very little away. I didn't expect anything else, but it was still pretty frustrating, so when I'd finished I thought I'd try to provoke them a bit.'

Andreas had been listening with his eyes unfocused and resting on the distant sea. Now he turned them back to Day.

'I told Ridgeway that I was making a series in London for the BBC about the looting and sale of antiquities from Elgin to Egypt. I thought it was a good touch to mention Elgin. Everyone loves to hate old Elgin, don't they? In fact, it really would make rather a good series. I suggested he might be a good person to advise the directors, as he must know a lot about the subject.'

'For God's sake, Martin! I specifically told you to be careful.'

'Yes, I know, but no harm done. Ridgeway insisted on his professional integrity, and said it would be disastrous for his business if he were to be mentioned in connection with the illegal antiquities market. Something like that. Kakouris's wife backed him up, saying that her husband was extremely grateful for the help of someone as respected as Ridgeway.'

'Naturally,' said Andreas. 'Did you really expect anything else? Anyway, carry on. Don't omit anything, anything at all.'

Day thought.

'It was clear that Ridgeway takes no notice of his wife and pays a great deal too much attention to Stelios's niece Christina,' he remarked with a look of disapproval, and took a swallow from his bottle of Mythos. 'Stelios's daughter Maria is infatuated with the house guest Vassos, who in turn is probably attracted to Stelios himself.'

'I'm frankly more interested in their financial dealings than their sexual ones,' Andreas muttered. 'Nobody said anything about buying items during the current trip?'

'No, but Kakouris did ask if there were any current excavations in the area likely to turn up interesting finds. I told him there weren't. Perhaps I should have strung him along a bit.'

Andreas threw him an unreadable look.

'What else? Yes. I spoke a bit to the wine producer's wife at the lunch. She told me about the break-in, and how they were relieved that she and her husband had decided not to stay in the flat above the office but in a rented house in Chora. She was worried her husband might have been hurt in the break-in. The local police have arrested someone for it, they said.'

Andreas grunted, stopped writing, and said he was going to get more beer. He was gone a long time and when he returned Day had remembered more to tell him.

'Kakouris boasted he'd been picking up Greek vases for the last forty years, and was obviously proud of his collection. I learned from his wife that he never exhibits them. I asked if he'd ever been offered illegal artefacts. I implied, of course, that he would have turned them down and reported them to the authorities. I made up a story about an archaeologist who stole from his own excavation and the objects never being seen again. It was a bit of fiction, but it got a reaction out of Kakouris. He absolutely denied ever being offered anything like that and said he would never touch anything illegal anyway. Ridgeway gave a very pretty speech about how he was on the side of the angels.'

'Of course he did,' muttered Andreas, dragging on his beer bottle moodily.

'The thing is, Andrea, I definitely made them both uncomfortable. Perhaps what I said touched a nerve. They might have thought I was just rude, of course, but the result was I was invited for drinks on Kakouris's swanky yacht.'

'*Swanky?*' For once, Andreas had met an English word that was new to him; he almost spat it out.

'Luxurious, expensive, big and shiny.'

'Mmm. And you didn't think to tell me about that before?'

'I thought I knew what you'd say. Nothing ventured, nothing gained.'

Andreas bowed his leonine head thoughtfully.

'They've been sailing round the Aegean for three weeks,' continued Day, 'and there's one more week to go till they head to Sicily. I expect you know that from your man on board. I saw him, by the way.'

'He saw you too.'

'Something odd happened, actually. Kakouris showed me a modern replica of a Red Figure drinking cup which he'd commissioned as an award for the Wine Festival. It was quite good, but wouldn't fool anyone. He asked what I thought of it, as if he was testing me. Why do you think he did that? I told him it wasn't a bad bit of work, for a replica.'

'That's the most interesting thing you've told me so far,' said Andreas. 'Nothing Kakouris does is likely to be without purpose.'

'Well, I certainly don't understand it,' said Day. 'I met the ship's captain, by the way. He's English. I got no sense of where he stands in all this.'

'It's being investigated. What else?'

'That's all, I think. I'm due back to Villa Myrsini on Tuesday to give the second talk. I haven't written it yet. I want to be controversial, stir them up a bit, or there won't have been any point in any of this.'

He expected an argument from Andreas, but the professional policeman was keeping his thoughts to himself and still making notes. Day sat quietly with his beer and gave him time. He had chosen not to mention the only interesting object he had noticed on the *Alkyoni*; he needed to make a few enquiries first.

He looked around. Below Andreas's terrace, partially concealed by an old wall, was a smaller house whose garden consisted of a drought-ravaged plot, a hard-standing for cars, and an old well with a circular wooden cover. Across the road from it, a mule was tied to a post in the centre of a hot, empty field, which reminded him of the one in Filoti. Just as he was wondering whether mules suffered in the midday heat, this one raised its head and let out a strident cry that carried forcefully over the distance between them. It was hard to tell whether it was a demand for food, a complaint at spending the day in the sun, or an expression of defiant joy.

After a few minutes he grew tired of waiting.

'Andrea, I have to ask you: has anything I've told you been of any use to you at all?'

Andreas almost shrugged and closed his notebook firmly.

'We'll see. This has only just started. I've told Inspector Tsountas that it will be necessary to make a simultaneous raid on the yacht and the villa, in which I need him to play a part. Co-ordination will be vital, and I'll make the arrangements myself when the time comes. Until that time I still need you, Martin. You'll be my eyes inside the villa. Just be prudent and do nothing else without consulting me. With luck, we'll be successful on several fronts.'

'Okay. I'll do my best.'

'You know Kyriakos Tsountas, don't you?'

'A little. We worked together a year or so ago. He's not the easiest of men.'

'That's true of many people,' said Andreas with a tight smile. 'Now, I suggest we make a move. We have enough time to walk into Parikia and work up an appetite for lunch.'

The sun beat down on them with a fierce, dry heat as they left the house. Day turned up his collar and put on his sunglasses. At first there was no pavement and the road downhill was narrow.

They walked in single file past houses that were still being built, and an unwary driver came round a blind corner narrowly missing Andreas.

'That was close!' he muttered, staring after the car.

When the road levelled out they were able to walk in relative safety and soon reached the sea. The long road round the bay offered the welcome shade of the beach bars, and their path continued towards the town under the tamarisk trees. The storm gullies were bone dry.

'Have you heard from Helen?' Andreas asked.

'Yes, we've spoken a few times.'

'Good. Don't lose her, Martin. I speak as your friend.'

'She'll be back soon,' he said. 'I hope.'

When they passed the quay where the fishing boats were moored, men were mending their nets in the glare of the sun. The small tourist boat to Antiparos was about to sail, tickets only two euros; it was already full. At the windmill by the port, taxis were jostling for position to meet the next ferry from Piraeus. This was the hub of activity that had been so remote from Andreas's terrace.

Then, with the ferry port and bus station behind them, they left the tourist season behind again. On the clifftop high above the road was the old Kastro of Paros, and in front of it was Agios Konstantinos, the church of St Constantine. With mounting pleasure Day followed Andreas up the steep steps cut into the rock.

Agios Konstantinos, in the traditional livery of white paint, had an octagonal tower topped with an azure dome, a lofty arched bell-tower, and a view across the sea to Sifnos and Antiparos. It was actually two churches in one, being connected to a little eighteenth-century Chapel of the Annunciation whose arcaded entrance porch offered welcome shade to those who came to admire the view. Beautiful though it was, it was the history that lay beneath the churches that most excited Day's imagination.

The past revealed itself to him as a series of levels, and this was a good example. This was the original acropolis of Paros, and there had been settlements here since the Middle Bronze Age or before. Much later, in about 520 BCE, an imposing temple to Athena had been built here at the command of the tyrant Lygdamis, the same ruler who had ordered the construction of the Temple of Apollo on Naxos. Its columns of white Parian marble, topped by a vast pitched roof, would have been visible from far out to sea, designed to impress and give pause to any approaching navy.

But this was Greece. Seismic activity and erosion had brought the structure down, ripping the ground from beneath Athena's house and sending most of it into the sea. Centuries later, Agios Konstantinos had been built on the mighty slabs of rock that had formed the platform of the ancient temple.

Day rested his hand on one now, and imagined the marble columns that might still have stood here if history had played out differently. When he roused himself from his thoughts, he found Andreas waiting for him in the shade of the portico, looking out across the sea.

'Sorry, I was distracted. Stunning, isn't it? This is a perfect place for an artist to live. Bright, light and full of history.'

Andreas grinned and suggested they get going. He set off along a pathway of grey paving stones outlined with white paint in the traditional style of the Cyclades; they were quickly in the narrow lanes of the Kastro of Paros, but heading away from the old castle itself. There were no names on the narrow streets here, and few numbers on the houses, and one or two buildings were in a state of critical but beautiful ruination.

The path began to rise and widen as they approached a pair of restored, white-painted houses with first-floor balconies of dark blue wood. A woman in a short yellow dress stood on one of them, and waved when she saw them.

Fotini Peraki may have been as much as ten years younger than Andreas, but in self-assurance she matched him. That in itself made her remarkable. Day liked her frank, unpretentious warmth, her immediate statement that a friend of Andreas was a friend of hers, and the double kiss with which she greeted him. She gracefully accepted the gift from the *zacharoplasteio*, and on the way up to her apartment gave him the choice whether they would talk in English or Greek.

'The balcony will be too hot just now,' she then declared, accepting a kiss from Andreas. 'Let's sit in here. I'll bring something to drink.'

Day chose a seat from which he had a good view of the apartment. A gauzy curtain was drawn across the large balcony window, filtering the light and keeping out much of the heat. The living area consisted of a kitchen and dining table, and a closed door probably concealed the bedroom and bathroom. In the studio at the far end, an artist's easel stood near another tall window which gave good light for working. A table of heavy, old-fashioned design against the wall was laden with paints, brushes, cloths and canvases.

Fotini returned with a tray of glasses, wine and mineral water. There was also a plate of hard cheese, olives and squares of spinach pie. The wine was in a former lemonade bottle with the label removed. Day smiled happily.

'Now, Martin, before you ask, the wine comes from the local store and costs five euros, but wait and see!' she said. 'It's good. I hope you like it.'

'I will, I promise you,' he said. '*Yeia mas!*'

They raised their glasses to each other and drank. The wine was gentle and satisfying, with a light, fresh flavour. Day caught a passionate look pass between Fotini and Andreas, and experienced both vicarious pleasure and a twinge of envy.

'Excellent wine! Full of Parian sunshine!' he said, taking a small piece of pie. 'I think this is the first time I've been in an artist's studio, Fotini.'

'You never forget the smell,' said Andreas. 'Oil paint and thinner. I remember how strong it seemed at first, but now I don't notice it much at all. How's my portrait coming along, Fotini *mou*? Have you done anything to it since I last saw it?'

'A little,' she said. 'Come and see. You too, Martin! I'll show you round.'

Beyond the part of the studio that he had seen from the living room, the area opened out into a spacious workspace. Here the walls were covered from floor to ceiling with paintings, the majority of which seemed to be finished. Fotini smiled at Day's interest.

'There is never enough space, Martin, so I attach the paintings to the walls with velcro.'

She demonstrated by ripping a small seascape off the wall and turning it over to reveal a strip of the material that matched the one glued to the wall.

'Ingenious!'

'Some of these will soon go to the two galleries which take my paintings, one in Naoussa and one here in Parikia. Then I'll have more space for new work. This is my portrait of Andreas. It's not finished, of course. Oil paint takes weeks to dry before the next layer can be applied.'

She pulled down a small canvas on which Andreas's generous features, light hair and blue eyes were skilfully caught. Day wondered why the portrait seemed subtly unlike the man he knew, until he realised that the face bore a gentle expression which he had only seen a few times before: here today at Fotini's apartment, and when Andreas had occasionally looked at Helen in the same way.

'Do you prefer to paint from life?'

'Of course. I always want to have the sitter in front of me, if possible. When I work from a photograph, it's far more difficult and less satisfying. Take a look around, Martin, if you like.'

She put the portrait of Andreas back in its place and Day accepted her invitation to wander round the studio. All her work caught the special light of the Cyclades. There were a number of seascapes showing headlands, beaches and boats, and several of fishermen mending their nets with wooden shuttles, the broken net spread over their legs and held in place by their toes. He could well understand that there was a market for these pictures. He particularly liked two large canvases which showed wild seas driven into foam by the Meltemi wind, which could turn the Aegean into a fury. These paintings would have stood out in any international gallery.

Andreas and Fotini had returned to the main room and he could hear them laughing together. In the far corner of the studio was one more picture that caught Day's eye, a head and shoulders lightly sketched in sandy brushstrokes, the early stages of a portrait in oils. It was intriguing that so few marks could make him feel that he knew the sitter. He went to ask Fotini about it and she explained that she was unhappy with that particular picture. It was, she said, something she had started many months ago and doubted she would finish. She disliked working from photographs, she repeated. Her tone dissuaded Day from asking more.

'We should probably be going to the taverna now,' said Andreas with a glance at his watch. It was mid-afternoon. Sunday lunch was a relaxed affair on Paros.

So it proved. They lingered over their meal because Day was not due to leave Paros until the last ferry at eleven o'clock, and afterwards they watched the sun set with a glass or two of *raki* at a quiet bar tucked into the side of the cliff below Agios Konstantinos.

Day was extremely content.

13

The following morning, having not reached Naxos until midnight, Day slept in. He woke with a sense of well-being, and after freshening up in the shower and choosing his lightest shirt and trousers, he made coffee and took it to the balcony. The morning air was particularly sweet after the *raki* on Paros with Fotini and Andreas, and he realised he had a slight hangover. The coffee made him feel much better. This afternoon he planned to write his talk, but first he would take up Stefanos's offer to visit him in Chora, and he would buy some wine. He was looking forward to it. It should only take him forty minutes to reach the place from Filoti, so he could take his time and enjoy the drive.

Not even the hot air trapped inside his Fiat 500 could affect Day's good spirits as he set off. He had just called Helen, having overlooked the time difference between Greece and the UK, and had spoken to her while she was still in bed. It had been a good conversation and he was optimistic that she might be sharing the new wine with him before too long.

He parked on the single-track road outside a white Cycladic country house which matched the description Stefanos had given him. A huge bougainvillea grew over the porch, its long, thorny branches heavily laden with purple flowers. The blue gate that led to the front door stood open, and a sign gave the name of the villa, indicating it was available as a holiday let. Day locked the car, tucked his sunglasses into his shirt pocket and walked up to the house. He knocked on the door and called to Stefanos.

The door swung inwards and there was no reply. He noticed a dark smear on the white paint near the light switch, and his next call stuck in his throat. He pushed the door fully open and took a step inside.

The body of a man lay face down on the white-tiled floor, its legs trapped beneath an overturned chair. It was Stefanos. From beneath him came a black pool of blood.

For a moment Day could not move, barely managing to breathe, caught somewhere between freezing and falling. Sweat tickled on his forehead and he wiped it away from his eyes mechanically. His hand was trembling as he lowered it again.

The house was silent.

'Klairi?'

The sound of his voice seemed too loud in the presence of Stefanos's body, and again there was no reply. Another spit of alarm constricted his chest. He called her name again as he slowly moved towards the middle of the room and knelt down by the wine producer. He placed his forefinger gently on the cold neck and stood up, stepped back, and looked round the room.

Where was Klairi?

There was a small kitchen through an arched doorway, but no sign of her there. He turned to the stairs and took them two at a time. There was another smear of black blood near the bedroom door, which was open, and inside he found her. It looked as if she had been trying to open the window before she had fallen at the side of the bed. There could be no doubt that she was beyond help.

Day's voice shook as he let out an involuntary cry of pity and protest. He had never made a sound like it before. Then came a prolonged scream which he realised only existed inside his head. He leaned against the side of the door and reached into his pocket for his phone. Mechanically he called the police.

There was nothing more he could do, so he went downstairs and sat on a hard chair at the side of the room to wait for them to arrive. How long would that be? Fifteen minutes? He stared at Stefanos until he felt he had to look away. He had shaken that hand only a few days before. He looked round the room. It contained almost no personal touches, like any rental place, but a bottle of wine and three glasses stood on a tray on a low table. Day thought he recognised the Assyrtiko that Stefanos kept for special guests. Only one item seemed out of place: a small piece of paper which lay face up on the floor. He got up and went over to look at it, and picked it up. It was a photograph of a young woman in the clothes of many decades ago. He took it back to his chair and sat down again with it.

He was still looking at it when he heard the police arrive, the slamming of car doors and the issuing of instructions.

Acting completely without thought, Day folded the little picture and slipped it into his shirt pocket. Afterwards he wondered what had made him do it. Did he believe it was unimportant, that removing it was therefore less blameworthy? If that was the case, it had not been worth taking. No, at some level it must have seemed relevant, in which case he should have left it where it was, or given it at once to the police.

Inspector Tsountas, chief of Naxos police, darkened the doorway, closely followed by a number of uniformed officers.

'Martin,' he said. Nothing more.

The inspector's use of his first name after so long was slightly unnerving, especially given the guilt Day felt at concealing the photograph.

'You reported this? Two victims, I believe. Where's the other body?'

'She's upstairs.'

'Remain exactly where you are, please. Stay with him, Karra. You men, secure the building. Skouro, come with me.'

Day was thus placed in the charge of Karras, an officer whose face he didn't recognise, while Tsountas and the one called Skouros, whom Day remembered was the second-in-command, examined Stefanos's body and the ground floor of the house. Day slumped back onto the hard chair and watched the Helladic Police take control of the crime scene.

It was many months since he and Kyriakos Tsountas had worked together on a case involving a newly-discovered antiquity. Tsountas seemed to have put on a little muscle since then, as if he had been working out. He cut a commanding figure with his black leather jacket and carefully trimmed black beard and moustache, a powerfully-built man who could give the impression of being over-bearing.

Tsountas and his deputy went upstairs to the room where Klairi lay. Through the open front door, Day watched more cars arrive. Men in white dungarees assembled outside, putting on blue gloves and covering their hair with paper caps. Photographs were taken and the ground floor was checked meticulously. Tsountas came downstairs and gave orders in rapid Greek. The young officer, Karras, took Day outside to the waiting police cars. He gathered they were going to the police station, but nothing at all had been said directly to him. Within a few minutes he was back on the road to Chora, leaving the Fiat behind.

He was left to wait in an airless ground-floor interview room that contained only a table and four chairs. Inspector Tsountas, he was told, was completing his examination of the crime scene and would speak to him when he returned. After about an hour, the inspector's strident voice, carrying easily through the building, raised his hopes, but Tsountas himself did not appear. Another half an hour passed. He could hear some of the orders that were issued in the main room of the station, one of which concerned the man who had previously been arrested for the break-in at Ambrosia Wine and since been released. He was to be brought in for further questioning. The inspector also demanded the names of all the wine producers registered at the festival and ordered that those who had not yet left the island should be questioned. The airport and ferries were to be alerted accordingly.

Finally, Tsountas came in. There was an excitement in his bearing now. Day had seen it before: Tsountas was a man who revelled in action and was transformed by it. His dark eyes shone with the urgency of his task. He took the seat across the table from Day and stared at him. He appeared to see no need for preliminary courtesies.

'Why were you there? Why did you go to that house?'

Day had already prepared his answer.

'Stefanos Patelis invited me because I wanted to order some wine. We agreed this on Thursday night at the festival. When I arrived this morning the door was already open.'

'Did you see anyone when you arrived? Any other cars?'

'No. I went in and found him on the floor.'

'The white Fiat belongs to you?'

'Yes.'

'Did you move anything in the house or touch anything?'

'No.'

'And the woman upstairs. Do you know who she was?'

'Yes, it's Klairi Patelis.'

A policeman knocked on the door of the interview room and the inspector left to speak to him. When he returned, he said that Captain Skouros would take Day's statement and fingerprints in due course. His tone was more civil, as if he had remembered that he and Day actually knew each other, that they had drunk together, that their partners had chatted with each other.

'I'm leaving now,' he said. 'I have an appointment with Kyrios Kakouris. It's my duty to inform him of what has happened. You can go when Skouros has finished with you.'

'Thank you, Kyriako. Do you have any idea who did this?'

Kyriakos just gave him a condescending smile and left the room. Day sat back in the chair and crossed his arms. He spent the next half hour waiting alone.

Captain Skouros was a wiry man who was no rival for Kyriakos when it came to natural intelligence, but he was nothing if not diligent; his examination of Day was thorough, if not imaginative. Day found it possible to avoid any mention of the Villa Myrsini, where he had met Stefanos and Klairi for the first time, and made no reference to the photograph in his pocket. Skouros asked no difficult questions and said that, once fingerprints had been taken and Day's statement written up and signed, he would be free to leave.

'My car is still at the house,' said Day, without much hope.

Skouros shrugged. 'We have no need of it,' he replied.

From this Day understood that he would have to make his own arrangements to retrieve his vehicle.

It was the middle of the afternoon by the time he was allowed to go. The young officer who had dealt with his statement seemed slightly embarrassed as he escorted him from the building. Day had once been a familiar face at the Naxos police station, a trusted civilian working with them on certain investigations. A new era had been ushered in with the arrival of the inspector from Volos; city policing methods had reached Naxos, and Day thought it rather a shame.

He headed towards the port, taking his time. He badly needed some exercise to clear his head. He would walk to the taxi rank near the bus terminal, take a taxi to his car and drive home; only then would he worry about what to do next.

After leaving the small *plateia* near the police station, he joined the throng of people in the shopping streets and was swept along by couples in sandals and children in sun-hats. To his relief, the wide view of the sea rescued him from their company. He sauntered along the pavement where the motor boats and fishing caiques were moored, registering only the names: *Ag. Nikolaos*, *Kapetan Georgios*, *Sofia*. There was even a caique called *Kyriakos*, but it failed to raise a smile. When he reached Diogenes he sat and ordered an espresso. There was no sign of Alexandros and he recognised nobody among the customers, but it was comforting to sit at his favourite table in his favourite bar, alone and undisturbed among the many tourists. He ordered a toasted sandwich and ate it mechanically.

After fifteen minutes he began to feel better. He texted Andreas, asking him to call, and left another message for Fabrizio. Leaving money on the table, he waved to the waiter and walked to the taxi rank. An hour and a quarter later, home in Filoti, he had just settled himself gloomily on the balcony when his phone rang. Andreas's name showed on the screen. Day hesitated, as if confronting the reality of what had happened could somehow be deferred. It could not.

'Hi,' he said. 'Thanks for calling me back.'

'No problem. Are you okay?'

'I'm all right, thanks. You know what's happened?'

'Yes, I spoke to Tsountas just now. A tragedy. It's regrettable that you were the one to find them. Are you home now?'

'Yes. What's happening at the station?'

'Tsountas has just taken into custody the man from Santorini who was suspected of the break-in at Ambrosia Wine. The supposed motive for the double murder is a resentment of the modern wine-production methods used by Patelis. I doubt it will convince the public prosecutor.'

'Unlikely,' agreed Day. 'Have you told the local police about my connection with your investigation? I avoided mentioning the villa at all when they questioned me this morning.'

'Thank you for that. No, I've not told them.'

'May I ask why not?'

'The answer may not help you very much. It might be useful to have a card up my sleeve. That's the English expression, isn't it?'

'It is. And I'm the card?'

'Ha! Leave that to me, Martin. Just keep out of Tsountas's way.'

'You can't be serious!' Day snapped. 'I felt he even suspected that *I'd* killed them! And I want the real killer found. I'm not going to walk away from this!'

'Calm down. You can tell Tsountas that your connection with the villa is to give your talks on ancient history and that you first met the Patelises at one of them. Stelios Ioannides may cancel your talk tomorrow, given what's happened to his friends, but if it does go ahead just do what you're paid to do and don't try to push anyone into betraying themselves, or whatever you were planning. Just watch and listen.'

Day discarded many of the things he was tempted to say.

'Wouldn't it be better to work with Kyriakos, Andrea?' he asked instead.

'That's my business.'

'I see. In that case, since I'm not allowed to communicate with the Naxos police, can I tell you my theory?'

'If you want.'

'I think the murder weapon was one of those expensive professional bottle-openers, the kind that have a wooden body, a corkscrew and a long blade. I saw Stefanos using one at the festival.'

'What makes you think this?'

'There was a tray in the room with a bottle of wine and three glasses on it, but no kind of opener. It was a white wine, so they would have left it in the fridge and only brought it out when they were ready to serve it. The bottle still had its foil and cork intact when I saw it, so they hadn't had time to open it before they were killed. It was a wine that Stefanos showed me a few days ago; he told me he saves it for very special occasions. So, the killer was somebody important to Stefanos and used the blade on the tray on him and Klairi just as the wine was about to be opened.'

'You deduced all this from a bottle? And you didn't say anything to Tsountas?'

'No. I wasn't asked for my opinion on the wine.'

Andreas failed to conceal his amusement.

'If I'm right, the murders were committed on impulse,' Day went on. 'The killer used what was to hand, the sommelier's blade.'

'Let's not jump to any more conclusions,' said Andreas.

'It was a bloodbath, Andrea. Why kill Klairi too?'

'I expect she witnessed the murder of her husband. It looks like she ran upstairs, the killer caught up with her, she had nowhere to go.'

'My God.'

'Now listen to me, Martin. Keep your head down. Someone out there is unpredictable and dangerous, and it's possible they know who you are. Admittedly, neither of our two suspects seem the murderous kind, but there's no such thing as a typical killer. Do you understand?'

'Yes. Have you decided when you're going to make a move on Kakouris and Ridgeway?'

'Not yet. Look, Martin, did you hear me just now? For your own sake, just give your talk, don't draw attention to yourself, and leave the rest to me.'

Day rang off feeling frustrated and annoyed. He was appallingly hot and the sweat was trickling down his spine. He went inside where it was cooler and called Fabrizio's number. It rang out until the answerphone kicked in, so he left another message.

Then he reluctantly accepted that it was time to begin preparing his next talk for the Villa Myrsini. Maria had messaged to confirm that they would like him to be there as planned the next morning, as it might help to distract her father. He sighed. Perhaps working would calm his nerves too. His laptop was on the dining table; he needed only to choose a few books from his library and settle down.

For some reason, he didn't act on this sensible resolve. He thought of Maria, and old Stelios, and the beautiful but scarred Christina. Inevitably then he remembered Klairi exchanging a private look with her husband and sharing a moment of mutual understanding. He took the little photograph from his jacket pocket and looked at it carefully. He was sure the young lady in the picture was not Klairi; not only was the face pear-shaped where hers had been round, and the brows delicate where hers were pronounced, but there was something vulnerable about the girl in the photograph that did not match the confident doyenne of Ambrosia Wine. Yet somehow he knew the face. And what was it doing in Stefanos's living room, if it was not a picture of his wife?

He placed the photograph under the generous weight of Renfrew's *The Emergence of Civilisation* to flatten it out, and got up to get a drink. After all that had happened today, it was not too early for a gin.

14

He drove to the Villa Myrsini the next morning ill-prepared for his lecture and increasingly concerned about Fabrizio, from whom there was still no word. He barely noticed the state of the landscape, which was even more parched than the previous week. The heatwave that was crushing Europe and causing wildfires in France, Spain and other parts of Greece was breaking all records. There was a sense of doom in the news, the reality of climate change hitting home at last. The eight-kilometre route from Filoti to Villa Myrsini, passing through the normally fertile growing area of the Tragea, would have underlined the problem to Day if only he had been paying it attention. The drooping leaves of the fig trees, the silent stoicism of the silver olives, made no impact on his thoughts. He was not even thinking about his talk, which he had decided to improvise. The memory of Stefanos and Klairi lying dead in their house would not give him any peace.

On top of that, he was becoming concerned about the lack of response from Fabrizio. Whatever the problem with him was, it had begun during the meal at O Glaros, when Fabrizio's mood had changed. He knew it had been a mistake to tell Fabrizio that he was helping the police, but why should that cause his friend to disappear? He could only find one explanation that fitted the facts. Incredible though it was, he wondered whether Fabrizio might have something to hide.

In view of these preoccupations, it was surprising that he took no wrong turns on the way to the villa. The Fiat's hot tyres threw up small stones and dust as he turned into the drive between the proud old gateposts. As the house came into view, he was once again struck by its beauty, surrounded by palms and thick junipers like a stately oasis. Maria must have heard the car, because the front door opened before he reached it and she came out, shielding her eyes from the sun. She looked particularly American in her jeans shorts and a tailored blouse, white canvas shoes on her feet, and no less attractive.

She gave him a hug of welcome and a kiss on each cheek. He was no longer inclined to worry about Fabrizio, and followed her into the cool interior of the house.

'Papa would like to be in the garden today. Is that okay with you, Martin *mou*?' she said, turning to him in the hall. 'There's plenty of shade under the awning. I'll go and help him from his study. Why don't you go ahead? We'll be with you in a few minutes.'

He agreed, and she disappeared in the direction of the library. He hesitated. He could hear nobody in the house and only the distant sound of voices from the garden at the back. He put his briefcase on the marble-tiled floor of the hall and bent to examine the framed family photographs that were arranged on the table by the staircase. One after another he looked at them carefully. There was a wedding picture of Stelios and Caroline, but nowhere did he see the pretty young girl in the mottled image.

He found the others in the garden under the white canopy, sitting round the table on which lunch had been served the previous week. While far from cool, it was as airy and pleasant as possible, and Day was content that his listeners would have the view of the garden to distract them if his inventiveness failed. The wives of Theodoros and Ridgeway were absent, which he found less than surprising, but everyone else was there. The absence of Stefanos and Klairi was the elephant in the room.

Vassos got up to welcome him, and Christina once again gave him her thoughtful, trusting smile as she pushed back her abundant curly hair. Yianni said cheerfully that he was looking forward to hearing Day's talk this time, at which Pierre Ridgeway remarked that a good lunch would not cook itself. If this was intended to be funny, it failed. Yianni got up crossly and strode off towards the house.

The arrival of Maria and Stelios prevented anyone from remarking on Yianni's departure. The old man, who looked smaller than before, walked carefully with his eyes on the ground in front of him, his stick in one hand and Maria on his other side. He sank with relief into the chair Vassos pulled out for him.

'Ah, well, here we are,' he said when he had caught his breath. 'We meet again, though in sad circumstances. We have lost our dear friends, Stefano and Klairi. Such a terrible tragedy. I know you all feel as I do. Stefano was a dear, dear man.' He looked round for Day. 'Thank you for coming, Martin. Stefano would have approved, I'm sure.'

'It's unbelievable that anybody would hurt such a good man,' added Vassos quietly, rubbing his eye with his index finger. 'And the gentle lady, his wife, who did nothing to deserve such a thing. She reminded me always of my little sister, may she rest in peace.'

'Papa, should we ask Martin to begin?' said Maria.

'By all means, *agapi mou*, by all means. If that's okay with you, Martin?'

'Of course,' said Day, and braced himself against the arms of his comfortable chair.

'I'm going to make my talk a little shorter today, and tell you of a myth which has a strong connection with Naxos. It's the myth of Ariadne, which is one of love and lust, devotion and betrayal, and has inspired many of the vase painters we spoke about last week. As we shall see.

'Ariadne was the daughter of King Minos of Crete. I'm sure you all know the story. She falls in love with Theseus, the son of the King of Athens, when he comes to Crete to kill the Minotaur and rescue the young hostages who have been sent with him to be sacrificed. She says she'll help him to find the monster and escape the labyrinth after he has killed it, if in return he will marry her and take her safely away from Crete. Theseus, as we know, agrees.

'Here we discover the magic of the ancient myths, because there have been many different endings to the story of Ariadne. All of them take place here on Naxos. As well as considering the various versions, we'll look at how they're depicted on ancient vases.'

He brought several of his precious books from his briefcase and opened them on the table where the bookmarks indicated, revealing colour plates showing vases decorated with mythical figures. The guests reached for them with interest and browsed as he talked. All was going well.

'After killing the Minotaur, Theseus sails away from Crete with Ariadne. The ship makes landfall on Naxos near where the Portara stands today. This area was associated with, and possibly sacred to, Dionysos, the god of wine. Some versions of the myth say that Theseus and Ariadne make love in the sacred grove before he leaves her asleep there and returns to his ship.

'Excuse me,' said Christina. 'I noticed a modern sculpture on the causeway near the Portara. Is that Ariadne?'

'Yes. She's been celebrated on Naxos for hundreds of years, sometimes as a heart-broken and abandoned woman, sometimes as a goddess. I'll come to the goddess part in a moment.

'In most versions of the story, Ariadne is a woman treacherously betrayed by the man she loves and who owes her his life; she dies of grief, or kills herself, when she wakes to find Theseus gone. This is the most well-known myth of Ariadne on Naxos. However, there are quite a few others.

'In Homer, for example, it's the goddess Artemis who slays Ariadne in a fury, because she and Theseus made profane love in the sacred grove of Palatia. In Plutarch's version, Ariadne is already pregnant on board the ship and suffering terrible morning-sickness; Theseus takes pity on her and lets her rest on Naxos, tragically finding her dead when he comes back later to get her.'

'Goodness, the ancient myths are very complicated,' murmured Stelios.

'My favourite version,' continued Day, 'is where the god of wine, Dionysos, who lives on Naxos, discovers the heart-broken Ariadne and falls in love with her. He marries her and she becomes fully immortal, unlike most humans who marry a god in the Greek myths. Dionysos and Ariadne are the joint deities of Naxos from then on, according to local folklore.

'So, shall we look at a few examples of the myth as represented on ancient vases? Let's start with this one. It's a hydria, which is a pot for carrying water, in the Red Figure style, painted by one of the artists who has been identified as a master.'

He handed the open book on his knee to Theodoros.

'The tall, striking figure here, who is commanding Theseus to abandon Ariadne, is the goddess Athena. This is yet another version of the story, as told this time by the dramatist Euripides. Why is Athena involved? Well, Theseus was on his way home to Athens. He was the son of the king, and would in time become king himself. Athena, the goddess of the city-state of Athens, didn't consider Ariadne fit to be his queen because she was a foreigner. It seems odd to us today that being Cretan would make

Ariadne a foreigner to the Athenians, but historically Crete and Athens were rival states. In fairness to Theseus, he isn't going to argue with the goddess.'

Day pointed to the figures of Athena and Theseus in the illustration.

'Theseus's smaller size suggests his lack of significance or heroic status. The artist is belittling him. Athena is shown as tall and regal, dominating the picture. Now look at this: on the back of the same vase the lovely Ariadne is walking with bearded Dionysos. She already wears a crown and is clearly leaving with him, having forgotten Theseus already, by the look of it. In her hair she's wearing the love token given to her by Dionysos, a gold circlet set with precious stones. This circlet eventually becomes the constellation Corona Borealis, the Northern Crown.'

'How can you tell who the figures are meant to be when you look at a vase?' asked Maria. 'For instance, how would I know this is Athena?'

Day gave her a look of approval.

'That's a good question. Sometimes the painter inscribes the figure's name close to it, which makes things a lot easier, but not always. Instead, the most important mythical characters are often drawn with specific features which show who they're meant to be. Athena's identifying features are a shawl of live snakes and a war-like helmet, as we see here. The hero Heracles is another one that's easy to identify: he slew the Nemean lion, you remember, and he's shown with a lion skin round his shoulders, complete with the head. These were accepted conventions.'

They went through all the illustrations that Day had brought with him, passing round the books and talking about the vases. The conversation ranged from myths and terracotta pottery to the artistry of the painters of the Classical period. Day, who had nothing else planned to say, began to relax. With luck nobody would ask him anything that, with his general knowledge of Attic vases and Greek myths, he would find too hard to answer. He allowed himself a couple of minutes in which to sit and look round the table as they chatted among themselves. He tried to imagine which of them might be corrupt, who might have a secret to hide, and, above all, who might be a killer. He found his failure to do so extremely frustrating.

'Love, lust and betrayal,' said Theodoros lightly. 'The myth-makers chose interesting subjects.'

'I feel Theseus didn't have much choice,' said Maria sadly. 'It seems to me that he might not have wanted to abandon Ariadne, but he could hardly defy both Dionysos and Athena, could he? Mortals can't always help acting as they do.'

Stelios smiled kindly and lifted his arthritic hand.

'Shall we stop for lunch, before we all get upset over Theseus and Ariadne and the unfairness of life?'

Day gladly took his cue and began to put his books back into his briefcase. The talk had lasted barely an hour, and he had achieved nothing for Andreas, but he had done nothing to draw the wrong kind of attention to himself either, and perhaps he had succeeded in distracting the family for a little while. He was now keen to go home.

Just then, Stelios beckoned him with a gentle wave of his stick and a sideways tilt of his chin. His smile suggested he wanted to say something confidential. Day obediently went over and bent down to him.

'Perhaps you and I could go into the house, Martin? Just for a few minutes.'

'Certainly. Then I think I'll leave you all to your lunch; I have some work to do.'

'Whatever you please.'

He pushed himself up from his chair and took Day's arm.

'Let's go to the library,' he said. 'I'd like to ask you about something.'

They progressed through the villa, saying little except when Stelios apologised for his slowness. Maria passed them heading back towards the terrace with a tray. She gave Day a smile that left him glowing, and he briefly regretted his decision to leave.

The library, when they reached it, was a haven of coolness and peace. Stelios sank with obvious relief into the chair behind his desk.

'I'm sorry, Martin. Some days I'm more mobile than others.'

Day took a nearby chair and expressed his sympathy. At that moment there was a small knock at the door and Vassos came in, locking the door behind him.

'Ah, Vasso,' said Stelios. 'Thank you for coming.'

To Day's surprise, Vassos moved over to the safe.

'I'm very pleased with my safe,' said Stelios, looking at it appraisingly. 'It has both an electronic combination lock and a biometric fingerprint scanner. Double-walled steel door, very heavy, American-made. Thank you, Vasso.'

Vassos opened the safe with practised ease. Not only did he know the lengthy combination, but his fingerprints must have been programmed in. He opened an inner compartment and brought something out with particular care.

'Now, Martin,' said Stelios, 'I hope you'll forgive me, but I'd like to ask your opinion. This lovely thing doesn't belong to me, and I don't know anything about its history, but I hope you can tell me more about it.'

Vassos handed Day a clay vase and went to sit by Stelios, who patted him on the arm affectionately. They sat together in silence, waiting for Day to speak.

The vase in his hands was of the type called a lekythos, a container for scented oil, made for a funerary ceremony. It was a tall and elegant example with a black design painted on a white background. It had a black foot, a slender body and an elongated neck topped by a flared spout. A single handle looped from the spout to the shoulder, which was decorated with elaborate lines and intricate patterns. These included the traditional meander, the symbol of unity and infinity.

'It's a White Ground vase, isn't it, Martin?' asked Stelios, unable to be patient.

'That's right. Is that why you asked a question about White Ground last week?'

'Yes. Beautiful, isn't it?'

Day turned the lekythos over in his hands. There was no sign of any breakage, nor of a repair. He looked at the images carefully, a funerary scene typical of the period.

A woman in a graceful garment was sitting in a high-backed chair with one arm gently outstretched, as if she was lovingly addressing the two small figures in front of her, children perhaps, who had the appearance of warriors. One was armed with a spear and a shield, the other with a stick or sword. Something in the way they were standing suggested sorrow: one looked up at the woman's face, the other looked down to the ground. Day thought they seemed rather alike, like a pair of brothers, but reminded himself that the characters on ancient Greek vases were representative not realistic figures.

Near the woman were some inscribed letters which he guessed might be her name, but with the passing of the centuries they had become difficult to read. There were also marks that Day knew to be 'nonsense inscriptions', lettering that was not intended to make sense, a feature of some Attic vases. On the reverse side of the lekythos the decoration had worn away completely except for a few unintelligible marks.

'Well? What do you think?'

'It's a lekythos, an oil flask. This type of vase dates from the time when precious items were left in the tomb with the body of the deceased. The seated woman is the person who has died, and these figures are saying goodbye to her. A lekythos like this would have been commissioned by a wealthy family. Usually the design would have been a mythical scene of some kind. Sometimes it might depict something specific to the individual for whose tomb it was made. These particularly unique vases would have been made for high-ranking families.'

His listeners nodded and left him to continue.

'You've noticed the wear here on the back? The decoration has all but disappeared. That's the kind of damage that can result from being buried in the tomb; this surface would have been in contact with the earth, while the rest of the lekythos remained dry. It's a sign that we might be looking at a genuine vase from some time around the start of the fifth century BCE. I'm rather concerned, though, that the overall condition is so good. It's almost too good to be true. Hard to believe an ancient artefact could avoid more damage than this. What's the story, Stelio?'

'I'm very sorry, but I cannot tell you at present. I'm only its guardian, you might say. I know this is asking a lot, Martin, but I'd be very grateful if you would give it some more thought.'

'I doubt I'll be able to do much else,' murmured Day. 'I'll need to take some pictures.'

Stelios agreed, and Day placed the lekythos on the desk so he could take photographs with his phone from every angle. When he had finished, Vassos returned it to the safe.

Day watched wistfully as the massive door closed on it.

'I'll try to discover more about your lekythos, but on one condition. When I come back you must tell me everything you know about it. That's all I ask.'

'Agreed, and thank you, Martin.'

'Meanwhile, I strongly advise that you don't bring it out of your safe again, not for anybody. Preferably don't tell anyone that you have it.'

'That sounds very sensible,' said the old man. 'I knew you were the right person to ask.'

15

Day lost no time in investigating the lekythos when he got home.

Against his better judgement, and despite all the caution habitual to his profession, he could not rid himself of the idea that it might be a genuine piece of Black Figure, White Ground pottery. Apart from anything else, the quality of the painting on it was outstanding. He even toyed with the idea that it was the work of a master vase painter, because the figures were so finely drawn and conveyed such emotion.

Some two and a half thousand Ancient Greek vase painters had so far been 'identified', a random fact that Day remembered from his student days. Many of these were the so-called masters. The scholar who had first worked on this had become one of his heroes, the twentieth-century British classicist and art historian, Sir John Beazley. Beazley had begun to notice certain features that appeared to link some vases together stylistically. Having formed a theory that they had been painted by the same hand, he gave a meaningful name to each such painter he singled out. The Edinburgh Painter, for example, he named after a work held in the National Museum of Scotland. Subsequent scholars then built on Beazley's groundwork. The possibility that Day had just held such an object in his hands was intoxicating, but he would never be certain unless he managed to get expert help.

This posed several problems. Nobody of standing in his profession would venture an opinion without seeing and examining the object themselves, and even then the process would be long and painstaking. It would also be hard to prevent talk getting round the archaeological community if this vase turned out to be exciting, and Day's first duty was to Andreas's investigation.

Then Day remembered the Stilgoes. Two of the top authorities on Ancient Greek vases, they were also personal friends and he might be able to persuade them to help him. They could definitely be trusted to say nothing to anyone if he asked them. Best of all, they were married to each other, so he would get two opinions rather than just one.

Harold and Jennifer Stilgoe were in their seventies now, both emeritus staff of the University of Oxford. Day remembered meeting them once in a mountainous part of northern Greece where they were hiking across difficult terrain. They were past normal retirement age even then. They believed that archaeologists never retired, and they were still proving it.

Day found Jenny's number in his phone list and called it.

'Hello, Martin! What a surprise! We couldn't believe it when your name appeared.'

'Hi, Jenny, how are you? How's Harold?'

'We're both very well, thank you. How are you?'

'All's well, thanks. I'm in Greece, on Naxos. I live here now.'

'Excellent,' she said, showing no surprise. 'We're down the road from you in Athens, just passing through on the way to Boeotia. So, to what do we owe this delightful call?'

Day could easily imagine them in a house in Athens belonging to one of their many Greek friends. Jenny, who was extremely thin, would be sitting with perfect posture at a table, while Harold would be bent over a book.

'I'd like to ask your opinion about a lekythos,' he said. 'Really beautiful example. I was shown it today, and the owner asked me if it was the real thing.'

'And you think it is? You wouldn't have called us otherwise. What else can you tell us about it, Martin?'

'Well, it's Black Figure, White Ground. On one side it shows a woman being mourned by two small figures who look rather like warriors. I think the name inscribed next to the woman might be Antiope. The other side is worn, probably through long contact with bare earth, very little left, possibly a bit of lettering. Apart from that there's no apparent damage to the vase. The decorative banding is very fine, and the figures convey emotion in a way that I think is pretty interesting.' He paused, feeling rather uncertain. 'I took a few photographs. Could I send them to you? I know you'd prefer to examine the vase yourselves, but I'd be really grateful for your first impressions.'

'Happy to help,' said Jenny. 'Off the record, of course, until we can see the vase itself. What's the mystery?'

'I'm sorry, I can't tell you at the moment. I'll give you the whole story as soon as I can. I also need this to remain between ourselves for now, Jenny.'

There was a fractional pause before Jenny agreed. Day suspected she had quickly consulted Harold, that he was listening to the conversation.

After closing the call, Day transferred his pictures of the lekythos from his phone to his laptop and sent them to Jenny, including some measurements and a few notes of his own.

He smiled to himself and followed up his success with a short email to his art historian friend, Jacques Avian, who had an unusual sideline to his academic post at the Sorbonne: a considerable knowledge of the murky underworld of the black market. If the lekythos had appeared for sale in the last twenty years, Jacques would know about it. How exactly he came to have this expertise, and how he had found his dubious contacts in the underbelly of the antiquities trade, were questions that Day had never asked. It was enough for him to believe, beyond doubt, in his integrity.

Having sent the question and photographs to Jacques, he took his laptop out to the balcony. He was not going to be able to leave this to the Stilgoes, it was far too exciting. Using his membership of various institutions, which gave him access to resources not available to the general public, he searched for anything he could find that might throw some light on the lekythos.

He found absolutely nothing. There was no record of any such item with that design and decoration in any of the museum records or auction house catalogues, nor was it mentioned in scholarly articles, in the annual reports of the Schools of Archaeology, or in the summaries of recent excavations. Even before he heard back from Jacques, he was tempted to guess that the lekythos had not been bought, sold or stolen in the past few decades. Indeed, it may not even have been seen.

He turned his attention, then, to the master painters of Black Figure vases. As he worked, he felt a pleasant wave of nostalgia for the passion that had gripped him at university. He examined all the images of White Ground vases he could find, on the web and in his own library, looking for anything that resembled the style of Stelios's lekythos. This was a level of artistic appreciation for which he was untrained and lacked the necessary skills, but he could not remember the last time he had enjoyed himself so profoundly.

When, at last, he turned off the computer and went to his room, he lay on the bed and closed his eyes. Images from Greek mythology filled his mind, racing shapes that ran and jumped, quarrelled and loved. As he dozed off into a well-earned siesta, he toyed again with the question of how Stelios Ioannides had come to have this particular treasure, this possibly priceless object of great beauty, in his possession.

When he woke, he had an extraordinary appetite; he could not even remember the last time he had eaten properly. He needed a substantial meal and knew exactly where to go. It felt strange, an hour later, to walk into Thanasis's taverna on his own. The warm-hearted Greek proprietor looked round for Helen.

'*Kalispera*, Martin. You want a table for one? La Belle Hélène, where is she?'

'She's in London.'

'I see,' said Thanasis gravely, as if he had just been told of a death in the family. 'Where will you sit? I will get you some ouzo.'

Day took a table in the corner where he had a long view across the restaurant. Everything about the place was designed to raise his spirits: the traditional decor, the blue and white covers, the sepia photographs, the wooden chairs with woven seats. Vangelis, Thanasis's son, waved from across the restaurant like an old friend and brought him a glass of ouzo. With the ouzo was a modest plate of *mezedes*: chunks of local sausage, small local olives and a few home-pickled vegetables. A bottle of water and a basket of bread also appeared, together with the menu. He took a piece of the bread and bit into it hungrily, before adding a little water to his ouzo and savouring its aniseed aroma and comforting smoothness.

He ordered lamb *giouvetsi* and a portion of chips. Chips were essential to Day whether he felt depressed or elated, and at the moment both seemed to apply. It was still only forty-eight hours since he had found Stefanos and Klairi murdered in their own home. He missed Helen. He felt like a suspect to the local police. However, this morning he had talked at length about the myth of Ariadne of Naxos, and, best of all, been shown the highly exciting lekythos.

He was debating whether to have any wine, a debate which he rarely held with himself, when Vangelis arrived with a jug of it. The debate had been concluded. Vangelis also brought a small *horiatiki* salad which Day had not ordered but which someone in the kitchen had apparently decided he needed. The crisp cucumber, tasty tomatoes and local white cheese, to which he added a generous application of olive oil, served only to increase his appetite for the meal. Even the onions that lay scattered in fine slices across the salad were mild and juicy, and he ate each piece with a little of the fresh bread. He left only the olives, to which he was not partial. When he had finished everything else, he put down his fork and sat back, glass in hand.

The main course arrived sooner than expected. The *giouvetsi* looked and smelled excellent; just the comfort food he needed. The small shank of tender lamb, traditionally cooked for a long time in the clay giouvetsi pot, rested on a bed of *kritharaki*, the rice-shaped pasta known in Italy as orzo. It was all softly wallowing in a light sauce of ripe tomatoes, garlic and a touch of lemon. The fact that he had no need of the additional chips would make no difference to his enjoyment of them, and it was with them that he started.

Having nobody to talk to, he focused exclusively on his meal. It really was astonishing how much better one felt on a full stomach, he thought. Living alone over the years, even though he was happy in his own company, had led him into bad habits, and missing meals was high on the list. He drank some water then pushed back his chair; it was time to do a little serious thinking.

He found it very hard to think about Stefanos and Klairi, and he would rather think of Helen in private. He therefore returned, inevitably, to the mystery of the lekythos.

He would swear that Stelios Ioannides was not knowingly involved in illegality, which meant that the old man was probably being used. By whom? The answer came straight away. Who was more likely to convince an amiable and frail old man to keep a valuable artefact in his safe than his own brother-in-law?

'Ah!' he said to himself in the privacy of his own thoughts. 'Perhaps this explains why Stelios invited me to the villa in the first place. It was all about the lekythos. He may even then have had some suspicions of Theodoros. Having found out about me from Aristos, he then read my book on Nikos Elias, being particularly interested in the sections about vases. He needed to find out exactly what it was that Theodoros had entrusted to him.'

His smile faded. It was an attractive idea, but he had to discard it. Stelios had called him *before* the *Alkyoni* had arrived on Naxos, *before* Theodoros could have brought him the lekythos.

This forced him to re-evaluate his assumption that Stelios was innocent. The lekythos might belong to him after all, and he wanted help in discovering its value. If this was so, how had the old man acquired it in the first place? If not from Theodoros, then from whom?

He waved to Vangelis to ask for the bill. Vangelis placed it on the furthest corner of the table and Day accordingly ignored it, consistent with their normal habit. He was, in fact, in no particular hurry to go home. He emptied the last of the wine into his glass and sat pondering what possible connection there might be between the lekythos, illegal trading, and the murders of Stefanos and Klairi.

Perhaps there was no connection at all. Perhaps, in some way that was not clear to him, the common factor was the Festival of Cycladic Wine, which at least linked Stefanos Patelis to Theodoros.

There was nothing so far, however, to prove that Theodoros was involved in any way with antiquity trading.

He was feeling in his pocket for his wallet when his mobile rang. It was an unknown number.

'Martin? This is Maria. I'm outside your house. Are you there?'

16

In the darkness of the late evening, Day was sitting with Maria on his balcony. She had turned down a glass of wine as she was driving. Day was relieved, having already drunk enough for one night.

'I'm sorry to come uninvited and so late,' she said. 'I meet a friend in Chora on Tuesday nights; we usually have ice cream after she finishes work. She runs a gift shop that stays open till nine. Papa won't expect me back for a while…'

'That's fine. Is anything wrong?'

'Yes and no.'

She fell silent and Day stared out into the dark night, waiting for her to choose what she would tell him. A single light shone like a firefly somewhere on the opposite hillside. He was resting his gaze on it, relaxing drowsily into the warmth of the evening, when he felt Maria's hand on his forearm. She ran her fingers down until they rested across his hand, and twined them through his.

'You're surprised, Martin?'

Of course he was, but he wondered whether he should be. He remembered the tour of the villa, the visit to her bedroom, her sudden kisses on the cheek.

'I saw how you looked at Vassos,' he protested.

'*Vasso?*' Her laugh was indulgent, embracing both Vassos and himself. 'He's the kindest, most wonderful man, and devoted to my father. Yes, I love him, but as a sort of uncle, I guess. What did you think?'

'Well, …'

'Silly man. Is that all you noticed?'

Day gently removed his hand from beneath hers.

'I'm afraid I've been a bit unobservant,' he said. The single light from the wall-lamp behind them threw shadows across her face that did nothing to conceal the expression in her eyes and the teasing twist of her mouth. He couldn't deny how attractive she was.

'It's been a difficult time,' she said. 'Poor Stefanos and Klairi.'

'Yes. Did you know that I found them?'

'No, I didn't! How awful. What happened?'

'Stefanos had invited me to visit him because I wanted to buy some wine. The door was open and I found him inside. Klairi was upstairs. I called the police and spent half the day at the station.'

Again she placed her hand on his arm, this time to express sympathy. He left it there.

'Is your father still very upset?' he asked.

'He is, deeply. I'll be glad when Uncle Theo's visit is over and things can get back to normal for Papa. Except that I won't see you again. That's why I came to see you tonight.'

Day said nothing. Now was the moment to tell her honestly about Helen, but she had already started to tell him a story, her voice soothing in the quiet of the Cycladic night.

'When we left the States it was very hard for me. I'd met someone there; we were dating and things were beginning to get serious. I knew there was no way our relationship would survive if I moved to the Cyclades. He had a career, family, friends - his whole life was in New York. The parting was, well, very hard. Since we came to Naxos I haven't met anyone else.'

'Couldn't you have stayed in New York with your boyfriend?'

'Not really. Papa was in relatively good health then, and we didn't know Caroline was going to get cancer; but it was for Yianni's sake that I came here. We're twins, you know, although we don't really look alike.'

'Oh, you do!' he murmured.

'Well, Yianni had no real choice about coming with Papa, so I came too. It's what twins do. Some of us, anyway.'

'I don't understand.'

Maria looked at him directly. Even in the soft light he could sense that she was deliberating whether or not to say any more.

'I'd like you to understand, Martin. It started a long time ago when Papa and Caroline got married. I've always called her Caroline, by the way, because she preferred it. Anyway, when she and Papa found they couldn't have children, they decided to adopt.'

'You and Yianni were adopted?'

'Yes. We were just babies. We were in Athens, but Papa persuaded the authorities to allow him to take us to the US. I expect money helped. He wanted little Greek kids, you see. He wasn't told anything about our background except that our natural parents were Greek. It must have seemed like a gift from God. So we grew up in New York, in the home of a prosperous businessman, with everything we could possibly need.'

'You were lucky.'

'Yes, very lucky. We were sent to a good school and I did well there. It wasn't the same for Yianni, though. He had a rough time.'

'Why? He seems bright and capable.'

She smiled and took his hand again.

'My brother was badly bullied at school. He had emotional problems that made him an easy victim. He couldn't bear school life and failed all his exams. Papa didn't know what to do to help him. Then Caroline got him cooking. He loved it, he was good at it, there were no exams involved and no competition. He never lost his temper or got upset in the kitchen, and we realised that this was what he could do in life that would make him happy.

'After his training, which went well, he got various dead-end jobs, so Papa sent him to stay with his younger sister, Aunt Marianna, in Kalamata. Christina's mother. Anyway, she had a friend who owned a top restaurant in Kalamata, and Yianni worked there for a year. He learned all about Greek cuisine, and when he came back to New York he was a changed person and got a job in a Greek restaurant in Manhattan.

'He did well in the Kalamata restaurant and they liked him, but despite his skill and flair in the kitchen he wasn't really coping with the busy workplace and started to get anxious again. It's all about Yianni's nature. No matter what he's doing, where he is, he can't handle too much of the real world.'

'I had no idea,' said Day. 'He always looks so relaxed.'

'He is, most of the time, when nothing happens to stress or upset him. Do you see now why I came to Naxos? He needed me.'

'Yes, I see,' said Day. 'When did you find out you were adopted?'

'We were told when we were fourteen. Papa and Caroline didn't know who our birth parents were, because that was the law in Greece at the time, but it didn't matter. They were our real parents.'

Somewhere in the darkness an owl hooted and another responded from still further away.

'I guess you don't know about adoption laws in Greece, Martin. I didn't either until after Caroline died, and then I did a bit of hunting on the internet. I found out that when we were born the law in Greece prevented adopted children from ever knowing the identity of their birth parents. In the 1990s, though, that had changed and there was nothing to prevent me now from finding out the truth. I began to look into it. I think perhaps that was a big mistake.'

'I suppose that depends on what you found.'

'You're right. Do you want to know what happened?'

'If you want to tell me.'

'I found her, I found my birth mother. She was living in Athens, out in the west of the city in a kind of hospice. I've never seen anywhere so sad and horrible. She, though, was wonderful. Her name was Paraskevi.'

Day watched the beautiful eyes glisten in the half-light of the balcony and wanted to comfort her. He confined himself to listening attentively.

'I went to see her in Athens as often as I could, but Yianni wouldn't come with me. He wanted to know all about her, but he didn't want to meet her. I understood; he was pretty upset. He was angry too, not *with* her but *for* her. Angry that she'd had such an awful life. I felt the same, and it got more difficult every time I went to see her. I also felt guilty knowing that we could have helped her if only we'd known, and instead we'd had a really easy childhood in America …'

'That's not your fault. Did she tell you why she'd given you and Yianni up for adoption?'

'Oh yes. It was a heartbreaking story. She'd fallen in love with a boy and got pregnant. They wanted to get married but they were still very young. They couldn't support a child on their own, they would need the help of both families, and that was the problem. Her family were religious and strict, as her name suggests - it means Friday, the preparation day for the Sabbath. They were appalled and ashamed, and gave her a choice. Either she agreed to go away and have the child in an institution of their choosing, and give it up for adoption, or they would disown her and she would be out on the street.

'She was sent to a place run by the Church to have the baby and return home without it. Of course, the baby turned out to be twins, Yianni and me. We were taken away from her straight away, she never even held us. She was told she would never see us again, and never know what had happened to us. Then, of all cruel things, her family still refused to have anything to do with her. She had to fend for herself, and it was difficult. The boy she loved had vanished.'

'Poor girl, abandoned when she most needed support,' murmured Day. 'Did she tell you who your father was?'

Maria shook her head.

'She didn't want to talk about him, but she didn't blame him and I'm sure she still loved him. After the birth she had looked for him, but his whole family had moved away. You know what she said, Martin? She said she was happy for him that he had got away. She never said a word against him all the time I knew her.

'She'd had a very sad life. She was always poor, living with what help she could get from the Church and the kindness of neighbours. She was in bad health when I found her, and eventually it turned to pneumonia and she died. At least we had some time together at the end.'

Maria wiped away a tear with a tissue from her bag and then took his hand again.

'I've never said anything about this to Papa. Please don't tell him.'

'Of course not.'

'I can talk to Christina about it, the three of us are very close. Nobody else knows.'

'Did Yianni see Paraskevi before she died?'

'No. He probably regrets that now, but as I told you, I'm not sure he could have handled it.'

She had come to the end of her story and it became clear that she was not going to say any more. She stood up and he stood with her.

'I should go home,' she said. 'Thank you for listening, and I'm sorry I intruded. Goodnight, Martin.'

She leaned up to him, wrapped her arms round his shoulders and kissed him fully on the mouth as if she wanted to remember it for a long time. She left him on the balcony in a daze.

17

Day slept badly.

The following morning he took his laptop and walked into Filoti, hoping that a few hours at Café Ta Xromata would enable him to do some proper work. It had been a long time since he had sent something to Maurice, and it might take his mind off everything.

Café Ta Xromata was aptly named the café of colours. The seats of the sofas and chairs were an eye-catching array of lime greens, yellows and blues, and the cushions were no less vivid. The place was quiet when he arrived and he sat down on a bright blue sofa with a scarlet cushion. The owner, who was doing her paperwork behind the bar inside, didn't notice him at first, but he was content to sit and watch Filoti going about its morning business. The women with shopping bags were probably heading for the small covered market at the other end of town, where traditional cheeses would be for sale. Men sped past on motorbikes, and delivery vans pulled up in the main street to unload fresh produce from the surrounding farms. The first bus arrived from Chora, and the priest ambled past towards the taverna where he would be given a thick Greek coffee to help him with his daily meditations.

After a few minutes the lady proprietor looked up and recognised Day as one of her regular customers. After a thorough enquiry into his health, she disappeared back into the café to prepare his coffee. He opened his laptop and stared at his inbox for a while, during which time his coffee arrived. He stirred it thoughtfully, then took out his mobile and sent a text to Helen.

Fancy a video call?

The only thing he wanted to do now, especially after what had happened last night, was to talk to Helen. After all, this was their favourite coffee place and he was sitting where they would usually sit together.

Yes. Now? Call me.

As he set up the call he made up his mind. He would not mention Maria; what would be the point? But he would tell Helen about working with Andreas, and the deaths of Stefanos and Klairi. He could not begin to imagine how angry she would be with him for not telling her before. He would tell her about the lekythos too.

To his surprise there was no anger in her voice when she asked him for details. Not only that, she did not even mention that he had once again become involved in exactly the kind of difficult and potentially risky situation that she always urged him to avoid.

'I'm sorry, darling,' he said, in no doubt of his culpability. 'When Andreas asked me to help him it didn't seem very much, I was just doing him a favour. And then the lekythos … I'm very excited about it.'

'Yes, I can tell that,' said Helen.

In the small rectangle of his screen her face betrayed the gentle, amused tolerance that he had often seen before. Was he imagining a touch of pride in her expression? On the other hand, she also had the look of a primary school teacher faced with a bright but exasperating five-year-old.

'How's Suzanne?' he asked, to change the subject.

'Don't change the subject, Martin. When are you going to tell Andreas about the lekythos?'

'Later this morning. I want to know what Jacques thinks first. I don't suppose Jenny and Harold will get back to me for a few days, so I won't wait to hear from them before I call Andreas.'

'Right. Well, Andreas knows what he's doing. Give him my love when you speak to him.'

Day sniffed. There was just the smallest suggestion that Andreas was the only one who knew what he was doing. He knew better than to ask.

'So, what about Suzanne?'

'I'm pleasantly surprised. We're having a good time, doing a lot of walking and talking. I think she's on her way to being in a far better place. She says she's happy to go home at the weekend. I think she'll be all right.'

'You must have been really good for her, darling. I wish her well. And what about you?'

'Actually, I'm thinking of booking myself a plane ticket soon. If you're happy with that.'

He noted the absence of a question mark as she announced that she would soon be coming home. They said goodbye not long afterwards.

Before his delighted smile had even begun to subside, he noticed a new email in his inbox from Jacques Avian. He was briefly interrupted by a small boy who was dawdling along the pavement with a child's tambourine turned upside down, asking people at the cafés for coins while his mother kept pace with him on the opposite pavement. Thanasis had mentioned that the family had arrived recently to try their luck on Naxos and had been working the Filoti cafés. Day broke the habit of a lifetime and gave the boy all the loose change he had in his pocket.

'Your timing was good,' he muttered in English, but the boy had already moved on.

Jacques's message was characteristically short.

Martin,

Thanks for your latest enquiry. Interesting about your lekythos. I can't find any trace of it in the Dark World, but I'm pretty certain that it's not been offered for sale in the last five years. It may have been in a private collection for a long time, or it may be a completely unrecorded piece. It could have been illegally acquired at some point in its history, simply lost to records. It's an impressive thing, isn't it? Good luck, and do let me know the outcome. Why don't you come to Paris? It's been years.

Yours ever, Jacques

That was quite a good result, he thought. He had never expected a black-market trail that led right to Kakouris, and now he could tell Andreas about the lekythos without implicating Stelios in a criminal transaction. The fact that Jacques had found no record at all of the lekythos was, in fact, very exciting: its provenance, if the thing was genuine, was now intriguing.

He decided to make one last attempt to locate Fabrizio before he phoned Andreas. He would call the hotel in Agios Georgios where Fabrizio was staying; he might even catch him there.

'*Parakalo.* Pelagos Suites, Naxos. How can I help you?'

'*Yeia sas.* I'd like to speak to a friend who's staying with you at the moment.'

'Certainly. The name of your friend?'

'Fabrizio Mirano, from Athens.'

'Ah, Kyrios Mirano. Yes. He checked out … let me see … last Friday.'

'Checked out?'

'That's right, Kyrie. The room was booked until next week, but your friend had to cut short his visit. Yes, on Friday morning he paid his account and left.'

So, Fabrizio had left Naxos without a word on the morning after their meal at O Glaros. This did not feel like the casual trip to one or two nearby islands that they had discussed. It was not the behaviour of a friend of many years.

'*Efharisto poli. Adio.*'

There was no more he could do now, he thought. He should probably share his suspicions with Andreas. He brought up Andreas's number.

'Martin. *Yeia!*'

'Hi. I have some information for you. Good time?'

'Yes. Give me a minute, I'll go indoors. Right. What is it?'

'For one thing, there's a large and very secure safe in the Villa Myrsini. I saw it yesterday. I was shown an object that Stelios keeps locked away in it. He wanted my opinion. I think you'll find it interesting.'

'Well, what is it?'

'A type of vase called a lekythos. Tall, cylindrical, single handle, made to contain scented oil. You know the kind of thing I mean?'

'I've heard of it. Stelios Ioannides has one?'

'Yes, and I have a feeling it's genuine. He told me that it doesn't belong to him, he's just looking after it for a friend, and he wouldn't say any more. I took some photographs and I've made some enquiries, including whether it's been seen recently on the black market. Don't worry, the people I've consulted are discreet. One is my friend Jacques in Paris, who takes an interest in the antiquities trade. He hasn't heard of it being for sale in the last five years or more. I've also asked two of the absolute experts in the field what they make of it. I'm waiting for them to get back to me.'

'Right, but what do you think of it yourself?'

'I would guess it's either the real thing or a very bold piece of forgery. The point is, Andrea, it's particularly good. Could be a very significant vase. I should be able to tell you more soon. It's a possible link to Theodoros Kakouris, don't you think? How else did it come to be in Stelios's safe?'

'It's a possibility.'

'Vassos Nikolopoulos, the live-in friend at Villa Myrsini, also knows about the lekythos, and he can open the safe. Stelios got him to bring the lekythos out to show me.'

'Interesting. Anything else?'

Day didn't give it a second thought. He simply changed his mind. He would say nothing to Andreas about Fabrizio after all. There was, however, one last thing he wanted to mention: the object he had spotted on his tour round the *Alkyoni*.

'I saw something curious on the *Alkyoni*. It took me a while to realise it might be important. Captain John took me into a big room with a glittering bar and a small stage. There, bold as brass, was a chunk of stone, might have been marble, just sitting there like a bit of classy decor. I'd almost swear there was an ancient inscription on it. I couldn't take a photo, of course, so I'll have to rely on memory. I want to follow it up, but it means going to Athens.'

'How might this inscription help us?'

'If it's ancient, and if we can prove it's been removed without proper permission, it should open the way for you to examine the rest of Kakouris's collection.'

'That would be the pot of gold at the end of the rainbow,' muttered Andreas, 'but I don't know how long I can wait, Martin. Things have started to move fast. The crates that Ridgeway shipped off the yacht have been intercepted and examined, and we now have all we need to arrest him. I'm only waiting because I'd love to find some evidence against Kakouris before the raids on the yacht and the villa.'

'You're going to raid the villa?'

'Of course, I said so before. The two raids must be simultaneous to benefit from the element of surprise and prevent the disposal of evidence. That's why I need Tsountas, reluctant though I am to have anything to do with him. I'm bringing my own team from Athens to search the yacht, but I don't have enough men to raid the villa at the same time. One way or another, Martin, I'm going to have to act in the next few days, before Kakouris sails for Sicily.'

'What if I go to Athens tomorrow? I could be back the next day.'

'If you think you might find something against Theodoros Kakouris, go as soon as you like.'

18

The wind had risen considerably by the time Day finished his calls and left Café Ta Xromata, having not started any work. The village of Filoti was in the relative shelter of the mountains, but at the coast now it would feel like a hair dryer turned in the face of Naxos. The strong Meltemi wind blew from the north-west, which might make the flight to Athens tomorrow exciting, but he had no choice: flying was by far the fastest way to get there, and time had become important. He put on his sunglasses to keep the dust from his eyes and headed home.

The house was full of new noises brought by the Meltemi. He listened to the shutters rattling like old people gossiping, the gusts buffeting the jutting walls of the balcony, the glass doors whistling as the wind found the gaps between them. The Meltemi could be a nuisance when it was in full swing, especially on Tinos and Andros islands, and on Mykonos, where the waves thrashed round the old port known as Little Venice. Here on Naxos, though, there was something enjoyable in a dry wind, especially when the sky remained bright and sunny.

He made himself a snack of cheese, bread and tomatoes and took it to his room to eat at his desk by the window. Outside in the wind-swept valley, a pair of the island's resident Bonelli's eagles, blown across from their home on Mount Zas, stooped and soared on the invisible waves of the wind, so low at times that he could see the turning of their white heads and the fanning of their wingtips.

It took him a matter of minutes to spend 180 euros on return flights from Naxos to Athens. He had a seat for the next morning at the astonishingly early hour of eight for a flight that would take only forty-five minutes. He would return on the last plane back to Naxos the following day, leaving Athens Venizelos Airport at about five in the afternoon. That should give him enough time in the city for what he needed to do, and he could spend the intervening night comfortably in his own bed in his apartment near Lykavittos. He called Irini, who kept an eye on his flat for him, to let her know his plans. With luck, he would be back on Naxos on Friday night with something to bring a smile to Andreas's face. If his guesswork was right, he would have an even bigger one on his own.

The phone rang on his mobile and his laptop simultaneously, and both offered the information that the caller was Professor Harold Stilgoe. In the time it took to stifle the noise by answering the call, Day experienced a range of sensations from excitement to apprehension. He would accept whatever Harold said about the lekythos, but there was only one thing he wanted to hear.

'Martin? Hi, Harold here. Well, you sent us an intriguing conundrum!'

'I do my best to please, Harold. What do you think?'

'Mmm, we think it's rather interesting. I haven't sought the opinion of any other colleagues, because you said it was a bit hush-hush. Respect that. Bound to be a good story. Tell me when you can. It means you have to do a bit of the leg-work yourself, but I expect you'll enjoy that, eh?'

He paused, chuckled, said something to Jenny in the background. Day ran out of patience.

'So, what do you think?'

'Yes, well, your lekythos is a nice piece. Please don't run away with the idea that this is more than a hunch, but it shows several significant similarities with the work of the Sappho Painter. Could be one of the other artists of the time, plenty of them were producing work of this kind, but yours is a fine little vase. Know much about all this?'

'No, not really. Go on.'

'The artist we call the Sappho Painter was given the name because of a beautiful vase showing the poet Sappho. Of course, we don't know what Sappho really looked like, but the figure is holding a lyre and the word Sappho is written next to her.

'So, the Sappho Painter produced many lekythoi, and I'd say half his output was in White Ground like yours. He specialised in these funerary scenes, had wealthy clients, and probably a number of other painters working for him.'

'You think there's a chance my lekythos was painted by the Sappho Painter?' Day insisted.

'It's possible. Something about the figures, the decoration on the shoulder of the vase, the nonsense inscriptions, and the … the *life* in the whole thing … I just have a gut feeling. Not the stuff of scholarship, obviously, more work to be done. Jenny isn't completely convinced, I have to say, but when do two academics ever agree, especially if they're married to each other?'

Harold laughed heartily at his own joke, and in the background Jenny was laughing too.

'Now, what are you going to do next?' said Harold.

'I can't do anything more on the lekythos for the moment. I'm going to Athens tomorrow because I have some other things to check, nothing to do with this. Thanks, Harold. What you've told me is brilliant.'

'Athens? Well, pity we're not there any more, could have met up. We're up in Boeotia now. But while you're there, do that leg-work I mentioned. Go to the Americans, compare your pictures with a lekythos they have in their Collection. I'll dig out the catalogue number for you, but you'll know which one when you see it. And then go to the Kerameikos. Ask for Achilles, get him to show you the things not on display in the museum. Tell him you want to see Stilgoe's Folly.'

Again the laughter. It was immensely infectious. Day chuckled.

'Will this Achilles explain why it's called your folly?'

'Try to stop him. Right, anything else?'

'The image on my lekythos. What do you make of the two little warriors?'

'Funerary scenes were very popular. This one, though, is intriguing. The lettering above the head of the woman, that's Antiope, as you thought. Could be that it's the name of the deceased, or that the Antiope myth was important to the family, but it's a traditional enough reference to the mythical character. Antiope was raped by Zeus and gave birth to twins, before being driven mad by Dionysos, poor woman. Look up the story if your Classics degree has faded from your memory, Martin. Now, the small figures look rather like twins, don't they? I think that's what it's about. This woman was the mother of twins.'

Day was lost for words. He should have seen that himself.

'Thing is,' went on Harold, 'with the Sappho Painter you have to look for sprightly figures - not my words, the great Boardman's - and a liking for lettering: he names his figures, litters nonsense inscriptions about, all that kind of thing. On your lekythos there are both lively figures and lettering. Look carefully at the worn side of it when you get a chance, there's definitely some more lettering there. Can't tell without seeing the vase myself. Over to you.'

'Right,' said Day. 'Thanks, Harold. I'll do what I can.'

'You're most welcome. Come and see us before we get too old.'

Day spent the rest of the afternoon reading everything he could about the Sappho Painter.

On the web, he found a few vases attributed to the master located in museums round the world, with informative descriptions and images, and from his shelves he took down the most expensive book he had bought as a student, a tatty first edition of *Attic Black-figure Vase-painters* by J D Beazley, published in 1956. He lost himself for a while in the world he loved almost more than the real one, the contemplation of the past. Only the stiffness of his neck finally made him stop. The wind was still clearing the Naxos air of the stifling heat of recent days, its music the powerful orchestra behind the gentle susurration of his computer. He drank a glass of cold water by the window, completely content, his earlier excitement grounded in constructive action. It was only natural, afterwards, that he found himself wandering to his room for a siesta. Even a text from Helen telling him she was postponing her return to Naxos did not really upset him. He stretched out, folded his hands and closed his eyes.

He woke again after a couple of hours when his phone rang in the other room. By the time he reached it, the ringing had stopped and no message had been left, but the caller had been Fabrizio. At last! He returned the call.

'Martin?'

Day swallowed the temptation to ask where the hell he'd been. Fabrizio's voice sounded unnatural, low-pitched, lacking in life.

'I was wondering about you. In fact, I called your hotel today and they said you'd checked out last Friday. Did something happen?'

'A lot of things have happened, Martin. Look, I only just got back to Naxos, and I've still got to find a room for the night. I go to Crete tomorrow morning at ten. Maybe we could meet up later for a drink? A taverna in the Chora maybe?'

'No, grab a taxi and come here. You can stay in the spare room. I've got food, and you can tell me what's been going on. I'll text you with directions for the taxi. Tomorrow I'll take you to the ferry on my way to the airport.'

'*Grazie mille*!' Fabrizio sounded relieved. 'I'll be there as soon as I can.'

Day went to the kitchen and opened the fridge. When he had said there was food, he had been rather over-confident. There was plenty to eat for himself alone, because he would have been content with a plate of left-overs, but now he would have to be creative. He had potatoes, so he would roast a lot of them. There were plenty of tomatoes, a cucumber and an onion, and he had oregano, olive oil, and black pepper. He was already happy with that; a salad would be easy. What else? There was no meat. A bag of dried split-peas caught his eye. Could he make a fava, Helen's favourite? He had once watched her make one using a recipe from an old Greek cookbook they had found in the house. He decided to give it a try. He reckoned Fabrizio would be there within the hour, but that gave him enough time to get the food going.

He peeled and cut far too many potatoes and put them in a baking tray with plenty of good Greek oil, lemon juice squeezed from one of his last precious lemons, oregano and salt. He switched on the oven and put the potatoes in to cook. Now for the fava, having found the old recipe. Rinse the split-peas, boil water, cook for half an hour. Grate an onion, cook it, add to the split-peas, season… With luck, they would have a meal of sorts. He could make the salad later. At least there was no shortage of drink in the house.

He managed a quick shower before Fabrizio arrived. He was just slicing up a lemon in preparation for the *aperitivi*, as his friend would call the gin and tonic, when he heard a knock on the front door, which he had left ajar.

'Come in! My god, Brizio, you look like you could do with a drink.'

'I knew you'd say that.'

The Italian threw his bag on the floor and straightened his hair with his hand. His taxi completed a turn in the road and sped off.

'Good to see you,' said Day.

'Thanks for offering me a bed for the night. I owe you an apology, Martin.'

'Beer or gin?'

Fabrizio shook his head. 'Gin. You're the gin expert.'

Day made the drinks while Fabrizio leaned against the kitchen counter, watching him. Ice into the glasses, gin to half way up, new bottle of tonic, lemon.

'Too windy outside,' said Day, looking regretfully at the balcony. 'We'll have to be in here.'

Fabrizio took his glass and went to sit on an upright chair, while Day chose the old armchair that had been in the house when he bought it. He raised his glass.

'Cheers,' he said. 'So, where have you been? You haven't been replying to my messages.'

'Paros,' said Fabrizio, and the word hung there as if Day should make something of it.

'Should I understand that?'

'Probably not. I'll explain. Remember our dinner on the night of the wine festival? You invited me to meet your friends on Paros for Sunday lunch. The lady artist?'

'Ah.'

And now Day did understand. Fotini. The unfinished portrait in her studio, the one that she was painting from a photograph, was of Fabrizio. He had recognised it at some level at the time. Fotini, therefore, was the woman he had come to the Cyclades to find. Fotini, who was in love with Andreas.

'You said that your friend was with a beautiful artist called Fotini,' confirmed Fabrizio. 'I checked out of my hotel the next morning and went straight to Paros. I knew where she lived, because I had an old letter from her. I didn't want to surprise her any more, there was no point, but I did want to talk to her. Perhaps I hoped it wasn't too late.'

'I'm guessing that it was,' said Day.

'She sent me away. She was kind, but very clear. I found somewhere to stay in Parikia and she agreed to see me. I never met your friend the policeman, the one she's so clearly in love with, but from what she said about him I have a good idea what he's like. We talked about old times in Athens, and about what has happened to each of us since then, and why I never contacted her. There always seemed to be a reason to wait; I always thought it would work out in the end. I was too absorbed in my work. *Colpa mia.*'

'I saw the paintings in her studio that Sunday,' said Day. 'There was an unfinished portrait. It was of you. From a photograph. That's something.'

'Yes, she told me about that. Something, as you say.'

Day left him staring into his gin while he finished making the food. They ate it at the table and Day opened a bottle of red wine. Fabrizio began to rally. When he spoke of his work in Crete, he became more like the man Day recognised, driven and enthusiastic. They even talked of filming the excavation at the new site near Phaistos as Fabrizio had suggested. Day moved the plates to the kitchen and poured more wine into Fabrizio's glass.

'I really am sorry, Martin,' he said. 'I should have been open with you about Fotini, and listened to you. I should have answered your calls.'

'Forget it. Actually, I should apologise too. I was starting to think that you'd run away because you had a guilty conscience.'

He described how he had misinterpreted Fabrizio's abrupt change of behaviour over the dinner table at O Glaros.

'I understand now, of course,' he said. 'I mentioned the antiquities investigation and Fotini at about the same time.'

'Well, you must admit it was complete madness on your part to involve yourself with the police …'

'I should never have suspected that you were mixed up in illegal activities. It was only because you arrived on Naxos without warning at the same time as the yacht, you seemed to disappear, and you're in the business.'

Fabrizio looked scandalised, having understood for the first time.

'Not *that* business, Martin. *Cazzo!*'

'And that means …?'

Fabrizio ignored him.

'I would *never* have anything to do with … ! *Merda!* How could you think that of me? This is what comes of too much contact with the police. You have clearly lost your mind!'

A great deal of indignation having been vented, and additional wine having been added to his glass, Fabrizio eventually fell silent, then even began to smile.

They talked into the small hours, confining themselves mostly to archaeology; those in the profession can speak endlessly on the subject. Then, both of them the better for sampling some of his 12-star Metaxa brandy, Day shared the story of Maria and Yianni. He was not surprised to find that Fabrizio was insightful when it came to the situation in which the brother and sister had found themselves, particularly their sadness, remorse and guilt about what had happened to their birth mother. Fabrizio also pointed out, with surprising perspicacity, that Day's own family history, particularly the early death of his mother, should help him to understand Maria and Yianni's conflicted feelings.

Having delivered himself of this wisdom, Fabrizio became thoughtful.

'If I was not so drunk, Martin, I'd think you were a great deal more attracted to this Maria than Helen would like you to be. No?'

'*In vino veritas?*' said Day. 'If you were not so drunk, my friend, we could have a very long conversation about unrealistic and hopeless relationships with women, no?'

He laughed to cover an inebriated awareness of his own guilt.

'Perhaps, as things are, it would be better to stick to the Metaxa,' he added. 'Shall we have another?'

When Fabrizio finally staggered off to the spare room, leaving him to finish what was left in his glass, Day was in no state to pack for Athens. Yet it had to be done. He threw his travel bag on the bed and found a change of clothes for two days. From under his heavy copy of *The Emergence of Civilisation* he retrieved the photograph and looked at it thoughtfully. Soon he would know what it meant. At least, he sincerely hoped so. He put it carefully into the pocket of his laptop case, finished his packing and set the alarm on his phone. Thinking of Athens, he sent three messages, despite the lateness of the hour and the state of his head, to the key people he needed to speak to while he was there.

The wind was still noisy when he lay down on his bed to sleep. The Meltemi usually lasted for several days, and he was worried that, if it grew stronger, his plane would be cancelled. He doubted that Athens would be affected by the wind, nestling in its circle of mountains, as long as he made it there. He closed his eyes, painfully aware of how few hours remained until his alarm would go off, but his mind refused to quieten. The last thing he thought about before eventually falling asleep was Antiope, unhappy Antiope, mother of twins.

19

Early the next morning, rather earlier than either of them would have wished, Day and Fabrizio abandoned the Fiat in a gravel car park on the outskirts of Chora. At the bus terminal by the Portara, where Day would get a taxi to the airport for his early flight, they parted ways.

'*Arrivederci!* See you in Crete,' said Fabrizio, clasping Day's hand and slapping him on the arm with his other hand.

'Safe trip. I hope you get your breakthrough.'

'Thanks. You'd better be there when I do. Look after yourself, and stay away from the police. They're bad for your health.'

Fabrizio wandered away towards Diogenes bar to apply soothing coffee to his hangover, and Day took the taxi at the head of the rank. In less than fifteen minutes he was dropped at the passenger terminal of Naxos International Airport.

Built in the 1990s over a wetland nature reserve near the coast, the runway was too short for large international aircraft, but ideal for smaller planes. The terminal was busy, buzzing with excited travellers, and Day began to enjoy himself. He took his seat on the

Aegean Airlines flight to Athens and watched from the window as the propeller began to turn. The plane taxied into the wind, the pitch of the engines rose, and the runway began to flash past. They lifted into the air just before the perimeter road. The plane climbed steeply before banking to the left and flying over the Bay of Naxos.

Only the sturdiest of ships were braving the rolling Aegean below, but both aircraft and pilot could handle these conditions, and for forty-five minutes the passengers had an impressive view of the Aegean islands between Naxos and the mainland.

Day's regular Athens taxi driver, Nasos, was waiting for him, paper coffee cup in hand. The genial Athenian waved using the mobile phone he had been holding against his ear. Day liked to use Nasos whenever he needed a taxi in the city, and in return for this loyalty he received reliable service and a good price. It had been a successful arrangement for many years, and Day now knew more about Nasos's family than he did about his own. He threw his holdall in the back, took the passenger seat beside Nasos, and repeated the plan that he had previously outlined over the phone.

'So, it's Palaio Faliro first,' he said, 'The address is in Artemidos; it's a photographer's studio. I need you to wait while I go inside, then take me to my apartment in Dinokratous, the usual drop-off place. Tomorrow, can you pick me up from there at three in the afternoon and get me back to the airport? My flight leaves at five. Okay?'

'*Physica!*' confirmed Nasos, and began to describe the wonders of his new satnav, a piece of modern technology that would surely make every schedule possible, even in the madness of the Athenian traffic.

He negotiated the airport roads and took the motorway towards Athens, updating Day with gusto on the latest transgressions of his disreputable cousin. This same cousin, whom Day had never met but felt he had, was an interesting subject of conversation that was extended on every trip. Nasos always pretended to be shocked by the cousin's escapades, but talked about him with huge enjoyment. Barely slowing for the toll station, where he took the taxi lane with a beep of the automatic counter, Nasos cut south on the peripheral road round Mount Hymettos, chatting all the way. As they passed through the parched land outside the city, Day sat calmly in the passenger seat, unconcerned that at times, through a need to gesticulate or adjust his rattling dashboard, Nasos was compelled to steer with his knees.

The serious congestion only began when they entered the southern suburbs of Athens. Palaio Faliro, once a home to fishermen, farmers and shepherds, had undergone a boom in the 1960s and further modernisation for the 2004 Olympics. It was now a popular destination in its own right and the gateway to the Athens Riviera. Nasos navigated its smart streets without need of his satnav before pulling up suddenly at the side of the road in a gap between parked cars. He pointed to the premises of Studio Anatoli opposite. It had taken just forty minutes to reach their destination, and Nasos looked pleased with himself. Day got out of the taxi and the heat of the city enveloped him like a greenhouse.

Studio Anatoli was upmarket, and images of wedding couples and smiling babies adorned the walls. The photographer was a woman called Elektra, who looked up in surprise when he entered as if it was unusual for a customer to arrive without appointment. Day introduced himself and they exchanged pleasantries. She pointed to the chair by her desk and invited him to sit down.

'How can I help you, Kyrie Day?'

'I have an unusual request,' Day began. 'I have a photograph that I need to ask you about. It has the name of your studio on the back.'

'How interesting,' she said politely. 'It's not your photograph, I understand?'

'No, it's not mine. I found it.'

The woman looked doubtful and he did not blame her. He opened his laptop case, brought out the photograph and handed it to her. She examined it carefully with a frown. When she said nothing, Day feared he would be leaving empty-handed and wondered whether he should have invented something more persuasive.

'What is your interest in this image, Kyrie?' she said, placing the picture on the desk. 'I have to consider the privacy of my clients.'

'Of course. I found it in a place where something terrible has recently happened. I'm trying to help the people connected with it who are facing a difficult situation at the moment.'

'And how do you know that, if you don't know who they are?'

He shook his head. 'It's guesswork. I believe the lady in the photograph has recently died, leaving a son and daughter.'

Elektra sat back and looked at him. He hoped he looked honest, because his explanation sounded suspect even to himself. He couldn't even force a smile, which may have been what ultimately convinced her that he could be trusted.

'I do remember this job,' she conceded. 'The client came to me about six months ago. She had an old and very damaged photograph and asked me to make two copies from it, enlarged and improved as much as possible. You're right, the lady in the picture had died. I did what I could on the image and was quite pleased with the result. It was a satisfying job.'

'Do you remember the client's name?'

'One moment. Excuse me.'

Elektra went into the room behind the studio and Day heard the sound of a filing cabinet drawer opening and closing.

'Maria Ioannides,' she read, and placed the sheet of paper in front of him. The address on the account was Villa Myrsini, Naxos, and it was dated the previous December, just over six months before.

'The client told me that the picture was of her late mother. I remember because the mother's name was quite unusual.'

'Paraskevi,' murmured Day, and Elektra nodded.

They left Palaio Falirou, and Nasos found every gap in the fast-moving traffic on the arterial road into the centre of Athens. It was still over half an hour before they reached Day's apartment. In the narrow street beneath the towering hill of Lykavittos, Nasos stopped in the road, there being nowhere to pull in, causing the cars behind to come to a halt. Day paid him and pulled his bag from the back seat. Nasos consulted his mobile calmly before driving away, his car just another yellow taxi among the fifteen thousand that serve the city of Athens.

Day found his keys and let himself into his apartment building. In the familiar dark hall he checked the uncollected post before pressing the brass button for the lift. It arrived with a thud and the interior light came on. Beyond the narrow door and the old-fashioned accordion gate there was barely room for two people. He juddered upwards.

As soon as he opened the door of his apartment he knew there was someone inside.

'Ah, Martin *mou*!' sang Irini. 'Here you are! I have finished, I will leave you. I just wanted to …'

She stopped, indeed perhaps had never intended to say more, enjoying the pleasure on his face. She had clearly been hard at work for a long time, airing and cleaning, rearranging and tidying, and the small apartment looked almost as good as a hotel room. He would not have thought it possible. Silk purses and sow's ears came to mind, though this translated poorly into Greek, so he just thanked her instead.

Irini was delighted by his obvious surprise. Assuring him she would continue to take good care of the place, and wishing him an enjoyable visit to Athens, she accepted the envelope into which he had put her payment and took the lift back down to the ground floor.

He dropped his bag in the bedroom, washed his hands and went to the kitchen. Irini had left him a small container of milk, so he boiled the kettle and made tea in the old teapot that he had brought from his father's house in Tunbridge Wells. Drinking it on the sofa with his feet up, he took stock of what he had to do. There really was little time to waste, now that he had Harold's extra instructions to include. Before leaving for the airport tomorrow afternoon, he needed to spend time at the library of the British School, meet a friend from the Epigraphic Museum, check out the collection in the Agora, and visit somebody called Achilles in the Museum of the Kerameikos.

He would start with the only thing on the list that could be done without leaving the apartment. Sandy McPherson of the Metropolitan Museum (retired) was worth asking about the lekythos. The Metropolitan owned eight vases attributed to the Sappho Painter, and Sandy had been in charge of the collection before his retirement. He was a man with a memory the size of Stirling Castle and would enjoy the challenge.

Sandy sounded the same as ever, his strong Scots accent occasionally overlaid by that of his adopted New York.

'You must know more about the Sappho Painter than most people alive, Sandy,' said Day, when asked the reason for his call.

Sandy laughed; even this seemed to carry a Scottish inflection.

'The question I have for you is this,' went on Day. 'Someone recently showed me a White Ground lekythos, and you can probably guess that I'm hoping it might be something very interesting. You know Harold and Jenny Stilgoe? I thought so. I sent Harold my photographs of it yesterday, and he hasn't discounted the possibility that it might be the work of the Sappho Painter. Unfortunately, the lekythos is in private ownership and we can't examine it for the moment. What do you think are the chances of another vase by the Sappho Painter showing up now, Sandy?'

'Where was it found?'

'Greece. The Cyclades. No known provenance.'

'Highly unlikely, but I don't need to tell you that. Nothing is impossible, however. Can you describe it to me?'

'It shows a seated woman being mourned by two small figures, boys in warrior-like garments. The woman is named on the vase as Antiope. The reverse is impossible to make out, consistent with damage sustained during burial, but there may be lettering on it.'

'Mmm. Other markings? Decoration?'

'The decoration round the shoulder consists of lines in black and red, a narrow meander, and above that an ornate organic pattern. There are some nonsense inscriptions around the smaller figures. I can't make them out.'

'Did you mention photographs? Could you send them to me?'

'Sure, I'll do that as soon as we finish. When you were at the Met, did anyone offer the museum a lekythos like that?'

'No, and I'm pretty sure I'd have heard of it if they had. You sound as if you're clutching at straws. What's the story?'

'At the moment there is no story. It's appeared as if from nowhere. I've seen it, I've held it, and I don't know the first thing about it.'

'Frustrating,' said Sandy with sympathy.

They chatted briefly, but it was clear that Sandy was keen to see the photographs, and Day sent them at once. He did not have long to wait. Despite the cautious choice of phrase, Day deduced that, though almost unprecedented in Sandy's experience, it was not impossible that only hours ago he had held a newly-discovered work by the Sappho Painter. He set off in good spirits to his first destination.

The British School at Athens, the main home of British archaeology in Greece, stood in a large and well-tended garden of palm trees, flowering shrubs, a British-style lawn and a spreading mulberry tree. It lay between Lykavittos Hill and busy Vasilissis Sofias Avenue, and had the feel of an oasis about it. Letting himself in at the top gate with his own key, he headed towards the staff entrance to the library. They heard his footsteps on the stone staircase.

'Martin Day! Stranger! Where have you been?'

The greetings of the library staff had temporarily interrupted the scholarly silence within the library. Several people at the wooden tables in the reading room looked round, and more than one acknowledged Day with a nod or wave before returning to their work. Lizzie, the head librarian, closed the interconnecting door to the office and the gentle sound of keyboards once again became the most violent noise in the sanctuary of books beyond.

He was made to swear that he would soon return and go for a meal with them, as he used to in the old days when he lived in Athens, before he was allowed to explain why he had come.

'I need your help again, of course,' he said. 'What would I do without you? Digital archives and library systems are a form of the occult to most of us, not to mention the new collections.'

Lizzie laughed. Martin Day could always twist them round his little finger. She wondered what he was up to this time.

'All right, what are you looking for?'

'Any reference to a White Ground lekythos depicting Antiope and her sons.'

'What's the history of this lekythos?'

Day shook his head. 'That's the problem. I have no idea. I've seen it and examined it, and I want to know if it's on record anywhere, because I know nothing about it. I wouldn't know where to start.'

'Can you leave it with us for a few days?'

'I'm afraid I need to know by tomorrow. Can you just point me in the right direction? I have a couple of hours now.'

'Oh God, Martin! A couple of hours is hopeless,' said Siobhan, Lizzie's deputy. 'There's the Digital Collection, the Papers Collection, the general catalogue that goes back for ever, and the new RDA. You know what, Lizzie, we need Tom. Is he in today?'

The Librarian shook her head and picked up the phone. As she was explaining to this Tom that she needed him to come and help someone with a bit of detective work, Siobhan explained that Tom was their current intern, and that he was a godsend.

'Completely amazing with the digital archives, doing wonders adding the collections to it. I can't believe he's going back to the UK at the end of the summer.'

Tom arrived wearing shorts and an old shirt with a Bath Rugby logo on it. He was taking a few years out before starting a Master's at Oxford, he said lightly. He had one of the widest grins Day had ever seen and asked no questions beyond the task in hand. He looked about twenty-four and made Day feel old. Athletic and energetic, Tom nevertheless sat at the computer in the Assistant Librarian's Office for the next three hours, patiently searching a succession of collections held by the BSA and other institutions for anything matching the description of Stelios's lekythos.

'Not finding anything doesn't mean there isn't anything to be found,' Tom said from time to time. 'It only means we haven't found it yet.'

'I know,' said Day, irritated each time Tom made this remark. He did not have Tom's skills with the new digital systems, but he was well aware of the basic principles. The library gradually emptied and Siobhan went home. Lizzie put her head in to ask how it was going.

'Tom's done a great job,' said Day. 'Let's finish up now, Tom. Thanks for your help.'

'I'll keep looking for a bit,' Tom offered with the enthusiasm Day remembered having at the same age. 'I'll let you know if I come up with anything.'

Day left the British School, once again using the back gate, reconciled to having come up with yet another blank. He walked through Kolonaki and joined Solonos, the road named after the ancient law-maker Solon. There seemed nothing now to connect the statesman and the twenty-first century street. The remains of old posters and the ubiquitous graffiti of the modern city decorated every flat surface between prosperous antique sellers, expensive opticians, bookshops, florists and jewellers. Everywhere there were cafés and juice bars spilling their tables across the pavement. People walked with an air of determination amid the noise of engines and the stifling heat of the afternoon. Apartment blocks rose many floors into the air, their balconies planted with greenery from which came the sound of caged birds.

As he neared Exarchia Square, the shops became less exclusive and the graffiti more dominant. The sky, what little you could see of it between the high buildings, was criss-crossed by countless cables. He passed the junctions of Mavromichalis Street and Zoodochou Pigis, and gratefully turned off into a peaceful, pedestrianised lane called Koletti. His feet seemed to know the way without much input from himself. This used to be his regular stomping ground. The noise of Solonos disappeared, replaced by taverna tables that filled the lane. He continued on Soultani to avoid Exarchia Square, and turned into Tositsa.

It was almost exactly seven o'clock when he reached the Epigraphic Museum, home of the world's largest collection of ancient Greek stone inscriptions. Efi Charalambou, the daughter of the man who had first introduced Day to Greek epigraphy, was standing there waiting for him. She opened her arms and he bent down for the inevitable double kiss. When he stood back and looked at her, he realised how long it must have been since they last met. Efi had lost weight, there was grey at her temples and new lines on her face. It was seven years, she told him, and her sigh conveyed even more than her words.

'Let's go for a drink,' he said. 'And we'll get something to eat. We have a lot to catch up on.'

'You wanted to talk about an inscription?'

'That can wait,' he said.

She suggested a Cretan restaurant not far from the museum, a place she went to often and could recommend. She reminded him that she did not eat meat or fish, and he shrugged.

'Great. You can order for both of us.'

A glance at the menu told him the place was inexpensive, and the portions were generous when they came. Efi ordered Cretan *dakos*, the rusk that resembled a bruschetta, topped with tomato and a crumbled Cretan cheese; a *boureki*, which was a gratin made from courgettes, potatoes and cheese; a salad with cold potato, tomatoes, boiled egg and something called *kritamo*; and little *hortopites*, which were miniature pies containing wild greens and herbs.

'And we must have the fries,' she said. 'They're really good here. They come with a special sauce.'

Day watched the arrival of the food with pleasure, realising how hungry he was. They drank water and ate with relish. The *kritamo*, which Day had never tried before, turned out to be like samphire, a branched and shiny wild plant from the coasts of Crete. Efi informed him that its health properties had been well known since the time of the Ancient Greeks. It was not unpleasant, reminding him of seaweed. She regaled him with a list of the vitamins in the plant, and told him it provided quantities of omega 3, iodine, and antioxidants. The list went on and on.

'They say it's good for the libido also,' she concluded with a chuckle.

'I'm just happy that it's good for the liver,' murmured Day, recalling his evening with Fabrizio and helping himself to the chips.

As they ate, they talked about what had happened since they had last seen each other. Efi's father, Panayiotis Charalambos, had died recently, leaving her to continue the family tradition in Greek epigraphy. The news saddened Day, who had good memories of the sharp-eyed old epigraphist, and he listened sympathetically as Efi spoke about her feelings of grief and lack of direction.

'You've lost your father too, Martin, I think?' she added. 'It made you leave Athens. I'm sorry for your loss.'

'Thank you,' said Day. 'I'm surprised you heard about it. The archaeology grapevine, I expect. Yes, he died a few years ago. We were very different people, but since moving to Naxos I've come to understand him better than when he was alive. I'm ashamed to say we weren't very close then, not like you and Panayiotis. Your father was a wonderful human being. You must miss him.'

She laughed indulgently, as if he had accidentally said something clever.

'I do, but I don't think I'll be moving to an island like you. I'd like to make some epigraphic discovery or other, some improbable identification that would have made him proud. At least, that's the idea.'

She said it lightly, and while appreciative of Day's sympathy, she seemed to want to change the subject. It might be the moment to introduce the puzzle of the inscription he had seen on the *Alkyoni*. He told her about it diffidently, bearing in mind the need for circumspection and also aware that he was groping in the dark. When he had finished, Efi summarised neatly for him.

'You saw a chunk of stone on public display on a private yacht where anyone can see it, and there was some kind of inscription on it. That's what you're saying? And you thought the inscription might be genuine, ancient, and illegally removed?'

'Perhaps I'm on the wrong track,' he said, surprised by her directness. 'The inscription probably has no great significance, but since the owner might possibly be involved in illegal trading - which must remain strictly between you and me - I decided to talk to you.'

'Did you take a photograph?'

'No, unfortunately not. I couldn't give away my interest in the inscription. Luckily, your father taught me a thing or two about epigraphy: I made a drawing of it from memory as soon as I was alone.'

He handed her the sheet of paper that had lain folded in his wallet since leaving Naxos. Efi took it from him, pressed flat the creases, and laid it on the table in front of her where she studied it carefully. After a while, she made a small noise of surprise and interest, but nothing strong enough to require the parting of her lips.

He had reproduced exactly what he had seen on the piece of stone. There was very little of it. As on the original, there were no spaces between the letters to show where words began or ended. A crooked line on the right indicated where part of the block had been broken off, leaving the inscription incomplete.

'What type of stone was it?' she asked, her eyes still on his drawing.

'It may have been unpolished marble, hard to tell; it may have been some other kind of fine-grained stone.'

'Hmm. I take it the placing of the symbols is exactly as you remember? What size were the letters? Have you copied them faithfully or written them as you were taught at school?'

He turned the paper round to face him and looked at it carefully.

'This is how it was on the stone,' he said. 'The *omicrons* were about half the size of the other letters. The *sigma* was four-barred like I've drawn here, and the *rho* had this kind of tail.'

Efi turned the paper back to herself and looked at it again in silence. Day thought he understood what was going on in her head: the possibilities and wild theories, the return of scepticism, the attempt to establish what could safely be assumed and how to proceed. He was encouraged that she had not already dismissed his inscription as worthless.

'How deeply would you say the letters were inscribed?' she asked.

'Quite deep,' he said vaguely, wondering how deep was deep.

Suddenly, Efi picked up the paper and gave it back to him. He tucked it into his wallet, smiling. She was about to tell him what she thought.

'You obviously know what it says, even though some of the letters haven't survived,' she said. '*Horos temenos Athenaies*. I'm sure you know what it means, too?'

'Boundary of a sacred place of the Athenians,' he admitted.

'Bravo. That much you learn in First Year. What about the shape of these letters?'

He was being put through his paces like a student, but played along with her.

'They suggest a specific period, but I can't remember which now. I just remember people disagree about it a great deal.'

She nodded and caught the eye of the waiter, summoning the bill.

'I don't need your piece of paper, you keep it,' she said. 'I'm not going to say any more now, because my idea could very easily be wrong. I'll think about it and let you know. I wish I could examine the real thing, or at least see a good photograph. You're sure your copy is accurate?'

'It's as accurate as any other observational record, I suppose. You might be able to examine the stone one day, if you can give me just enough to enable the police to confiscate it. What are the chances?'

'I don't give odds, Martin, I'm afraid,' she laughed.

She told him he would hear from her in a few days, perhaps sooner. The way she chose her words carefully, rather like a pathologist, surprised him. He almost dared to hope that she thought there was something of interest in his inscription. The waiter brought the bill to the table and pushed it beneath the condiments tray. Day grabbed it before she could.

'No way,' he said. 'This meal is most definitely on me.'

20

Friday was going to be as hot a day in Athens as the previous night had led Day to suspect. The air-conditioning unit in his apartment, which pre-dated his ownership of the flat, was at best temperamental and had now failed completely. At least when deprived of sleep there had been plenty to occupy his mind.

He dressed quickly and stepped out into Dinokratous. It was a quiet street, the traffic noise from Vasilissis Sofias Avenue no more than a gentle hum. Potted shrubs rejoiced in the morning sun on the balconies of the apartment blocks. The wealthier apartments were completely screened by foliage, but even the most modest veranda was home to containers of flowers. By contrast, the tiled pavement below was in need of repair and the storm gutter was disintegrating. There was never enough money in the city's coffers for the work that needed to be done. In the white morning light of mid-July, however, even the broken paving stones looked beautiful.

He set off at a good pace, heading downhill in the direction of Syntagma Square and Plaka. The going was steep in places, the narrow pavements regularly interspersed with the planting holes of leafy acacias through which the morning sun threw filigree shadows. The plate-glass windows of Kolonaki offered international designer clothing, jewellery, shoes, all types of luxury goods, interspersed with grab-and-go coffee bars. The pavements became wider here, pink-tiled and shiny.

His route to the ancient sites - the Acropolis, the Agora, the Pnyx, the Areopagus, the Kerameikos and the rest - was one of his favourite walks in Athens. He strode along with the affection born of long familiarity, crossing Syntagma Square and walking up Philhellene Street, grubby and functional though it was, for the pleasure of entering Plaka by the small road called Kidathineon.

His pace slowed as he entered the area that had once been Ancient Athens. The paving beneath his feet now changed from modern slabs to marble. At the Lysicrates Monument, where Byron once enjoyed the hospitality of the French Capuchin monks who used it as a library, he turned right onto Tripodon and skirted the Tower of the Winds in the Roman Agora to reach the street of Hadrian, or Adrianou. He was early for his appointment with 'the Americans', so he felt happy to indulge himself in this walk through history. By the time he sat down at his favourite café on Adrianou, he was emotionally and intellectually back in the heart of the ancient city.

He ordered a cold coffee and sat looking across the sun-drenched expanse of exposed antiquity that lay beyond the railings in front of him. This was the site of the Agora, possibly the most important meeting place and market of ancient Athens. A queue had formed at the ticket booth. Once inside, the visitors would be swallowed up by its vast area, their footsteps covering the same ground as that taken by the ancient processions to the Acropolis in honour of Athena.

Less than a hundred years ago, the Agora had been covered in small, local houses, four hundred of which had to be destroyed so that excavation could begin. Columns, drains, walls and inscriptions had then emerged, and in the 1950s, with the support of the Rockefeller Foundation, the Americans had ambitiously reconstructed one of the original buildings. Called the Stoa of Attalos, it had become the Museum of the Agora.

A visit to the Stoa was Day's first item of business that morning. In half an hour he was due to meet one of the real characters of the American School of Classical Studies at Athens, John Jacob Field. He and JJ had never actually met, but Day had no doubt at all that they would greet each other like old friends. They had collaborated on some work a few years ago while JJ was still in California.

The Stoa was a long, colonnaded building with a terracotta-tiled roof that formed one boundary of the Agora. White Doric columns shone in the sun along its whole length. The museum inside housed the discoveries made during the excavations. Or, more correctly, some of them. In the basement there were thousands upon thousands of sherds and fragments still waiting to be studied.

Day would see neither of these places today. Upstairs, at the back of the building, was a very special room that was not open to the public. In JJ's knowledgeable company, he was about to visit this unique if dusty hall, which was known informally as the Comparison Collection.

He left the money for his coffee, adding the usual tip, and, with a wave to the waiter, walked across to the entrance gates of the Agora. The woman in the ticket cabin glanced at his Ministry of Culture pass and let him through. The glare of the sun bounced off the pale surface of the path that led to the high steps of the Stoa.

He spotted JJ at once. Small but imposing, he had a grey beard and long hair tied back in a bun. His keen brown eyes and generous smile competed for dominance of his face, and he wore the uniform of the American School: a white T-shirt and loose summer trousers with trainers. The photograph on the dust jackets of his publications failed to convey his impressiveness.

JJ's handshake was as generous as the man himself. There was no unnecessary chit-chat; it was as if they had only spoken last week. He waved Day ahead of him up the steps to the first floor and unlocked a door at the back. A couple of visitors watched them curiously as they went through, and JJ gave them a kind smile as he closed and locked the door against them.

'Inner sanctum,' he drawled, using a syllable more than Day thought necessary. 'Your message was a whole lot more interesting than anything I've heard in the last few months, Martin. Nothing here but summer school groups from the US. Kids, but one or two bright ones this year. So, it's a lekythos you've come to investigate?'

'That's right. You know Harold and Jenny Stilgoe, I think?'

'Sure. Great people.'

'Harold suggested I check out your samples. The one on Naxos has no known provenance and I'm trying to place it. The Stilgoes are my go-to experts for vases, and they're quietly confident that my lekythos is interesting. Well, Jenny has her doubts, but Harold told me to come here first and then go to the Kerameikos.'

'Okay, well, let's get on with it, then. I'll get you to the right place, then you tell me what we're looking for.'

They entered a long room that smelled of old wood, dust and age. Its size was hard to guess because it was filled with tall wooden shelving units with sliding glass doors. The units may have dated from the 1950s, like the Stoa itself. Crammed inside them was the Comparison Collection: pots, sherds and objects of every kind, meticulously labelled with their date and the location where they were found. It was a reference library of excavated remains for archaeologists to refer to when trying to identify any historical object from Greece. For Day, this was one of the most exciting collections he had ever known, although also the most dusty. JJ walked ahead towards the far end of the room and stopped by a cabinet containing fragments of lekythoi. Day bent closer to examine the samples, as far as he could in the poor light.

The example that most reminded him of the lekythos on Naxos was a broken but interesting fragment. It was in the White Ground style, with a busy and detailed pattern round the shoulder and a mourning scene depicted on the body. A woman wearing a shawl-like garment round her shoulders, her hair gathered at the top of her head and hanging down her back, sat facing a man in a cloak and helmet, his hand outstretched towards her in a traditional gesture of sorrow. A dead woman and a warrior. It was frustrating that the rest of the lekythos was missing. Then Day noticed, just on the jagged edge of the fragment, a second outstretched hand. Another warrior, perhaps? On this vase, though, the figures were full size and lacked the detail of the ones on the Naxos example.

He looked along the shelves until he realised he had no idea what he should be looking for. JJ caught a sense of his exasperation.

'I can open the cabinet if that would help,' he offered.

'Thanks, but I don't think it would. Harold gave me a catalogue number. Could you tell me which object it refers to?'

JJ took the number and went away, leaving him pondering the display cabinet. The men who had painted these funerary vases would have done so believing that their work would be buried in the ground for ever. They would have put their heart, soul and skill into each one, never imagining that a tiny proportion of their work would end up here, in the Comparison Collection, behind dusty glass.

'It's that one,' announced JJ on his return, 'the one you were looking at a minute ago. The catalogue entry says the painter is thought to have been working for a single family whose two sons were lost in battle. Philip Carey has suggested that this means we can date this particular lekythos, and therefore the artist, with some accuracy, though not everyone agrees with him.'

'Naturally, when do we ever agree?' said Day, taking a photograph of the fragment with his phone. 'Unfortunately, I don't understand what Harold wanted me to see in this. The decoration round the shoulder is quite similar to that on the Naxos lekythos, and it shows the usual elements of the traditional funerary scene, but that's all.'

'Sounds like no great break-through, then. What next?'

'Following Harold's instructions, I'll go to the Kerameikos to speak to a man called Achilles. I don't suppose you want to come?'

'Sure,' said JJ. 'I know Achilles. Give me five minutes.'

When Achilles, correctly known as Dr Achilles Kefis, heard that John Jacob Field and Martin Day had arrived, he felt sufficiently entitled to abandon his paperwork for the Ephorate of Antiquities. He was overjoyed when he was told that the reason for their visit, about which the message from Day had been vague, was to ask about something called Stilgoe's Folly.

'So, what the hell *is* Stilgoe's Folly, Achille?' asked JJ.

'Well, the story goes back many years. My good friend Harold has a theory. It's more of an obsession, in truth. First, let me show you the object, and I'll tell you about Stilgoe's Folly. Then you'll know as much as I do. Follow me.'

He led them into the Kerameikos Museum's inner recesses through a discreet locked door. He walked softly, with a care born of years spent curating a museum. His movements were minimal, his pace measured. It was impossible, Day thought, to tell his age. A man of slight build and gentle bearing, Achilles Kefis was not best named after the hero of *The Iliad*. He took them into a secure room with a heavy door and a single, barred window.

'This is where we store objects that are in poor condition or of dubious authenticity. In the case of Stilgoe's Folly, it's a fragment, a broken lekythos.'

He unlocked a reinforced cabinet and handed Day a partial vase, one of several that were languishing in its dark interior. Day held it in his hands, but it told him little and he felt even less. Achilles sensed his reaction and nodded.

'Harold would not disagree that this vase was painted by an unexceptional artist,' he conceded. 'He believes, however, that the painter might have been trying to copy the work of someone much more skilful. Someone who produced fine, energetic work, full of life and passion, expressive of the grief it was designed to depict. Frankly, I don't see any evidence of it when I look at this poor piece. That's why I call it Stilgoe's Folly.'

'I don't suppose Harold told you whether he was thinking of any particular master painter?'

'Yes, he did. He thinks the artist was emulating the Sappho Painter.'

Day took the fragment to the light. He turned it round in his hands, trying to think like Harold. This was a larger fragment than the one in the Stoa; the spout and foot were still present, but there was no sign of the seated woman here. It did not, in fact, show a traditional funerary scene at all. Two figures in black were all that remained on the White Ground, except for vestiges of elaborate patterning near the spout. The two figures wore helmets, carried weapons, and appeared to be running from left to right across the vase. One of them carried a bow. Faint markings suggested that some lettering may have been lost when the object was broken. He felt completely at a loss. He handed the sherd to JJ.

'Is anything known about this fragment, Achille?' Day asked. 'Do you have records for it?'

'I looked up the records when you messaged me, but I'm not sure they'll be of much help to you. We're going back a long time. This piece was found here in the Kerameikos in the nineteenth century, along with most of the sherds in the museum's possession, but no exact date is given. The Athens Archaeological Society began work on the Kerameikos in 1870, and the Germans took over in about 1913. A great deal of material was brought out from the very start, and the early record-keeping is quite unreliable. Some finds even seem to be missing. For example, a complete lekythos from the same area seems to have disappeared almost at once. All that is given in the report is that it entered a private collection in Athens around 1879. It's never been seen again, and we don't even have a description of it. This is the kind of problem we're up against.'

'Antiquities were vulnerable to thieves even then,' muttered Day. Achilles nodded sadly.

'This design on the shoulder,' said JJ. 'Rather ambitious compared to the rest of it, don't you think? Harold could be right. It could be an attempt to copy a superior work.'

Day took the fragment back from him and examined the faint markings that leaked across its fractured edge.

'What do you make of these letters? This looks like the name Apollo. If so, the other figure, the one with the bow, could be Artemis.'

'Possibly. It's hard to tell,' said JJ cautiously. 'The lettering's very damaged, and the figures have no identifying features except that bow.'

He was right. Nothing about the two figures identified them as specific mythical characters. No lyre or laurel wreath adorned the figure that might be Apollo, and only the bow suggested that the one in front could be his sister Artemis.

Day photographed the disappointing fragment and Achilles replaced it in the dark cabinet. They thanked him for his time and wandered back through the museum, exchanging the cool of the building for the hot July sunshine. JJ spotted a friend and went over to speak to her, leaving Day alone. He was glad of the chance to deal with his frustration and disappointment.

He walked away from the museum to a place where he could look out across the entire site of the ancient Kerameikos and collect his thoughts. The Kerameikos was an expanse of lumpy land with countless low walls, ditches, and replicas of important monuments, but he loved it. Dry paths meandered through the parched grasses, and what remained of the historic river Eridanos bisected the site, now only the dry bed of a once important torrent. A few wild tortoises lived here, and small brown birds flitted from stone to stone among the ruins. The Kerameikos offered a place of contemplation and quietness, despite the presence of tour groups and the urgent whistling of the site guard when someone unwarily climbed on a section of ancient wall.

The Kerameikos was so called because it had once been where the potters and vase painters of Athens had worked and sold their wares, giving us today the word ceramics. It was also where many of the Red and Black Figure vases in the world's museums were originally created. Later, it became the most famous cemetery of ancient Athens, where its heroes and victories were commemorated, and brought the modern visitor into a strange and intimate relationship with the distant past. Its use as a cemetery also explained why so many fine lekythoi had been found here.

Day wandered into the museum's small, colonnaded garden. Several large urns were displayed here, huge memorials that had once stood over a family tomb. Between these were a number of *stele*, the headstones of the ancient world, on which were carved the same kind of funerary scene as on the Naxos lekythos. There was one here which drew Day to look at it every time he came to the Kerameikos. It showed a seated woman saying goodbye to her husband and her little boy. A puppy was jumping up at the heels of the child, who leaned into his mother's knee with a little rag dangling from his hand. The pathos of the scene, the touches of human detail in the child with his puppy and blanket, never failed to move him. He lost all sense of where he was as he stood in front of it.

He turned abruptly when he realised that JJ had rejoined him.

'I need to get back to the office,' said JJ without visible regret. 'I have some young minds to fill with an appetite for the Hellenistic Period. Let's fix lunch when you're back in Athens?'

'Sounds good,' said Day, who was now pressed for time himself. Nasos was due to take him to the airport within the hour.

They left the Kerameikos and said goodbye in Monastiraki Square. Day then strode up Mitropoleos to Syntagma, where he took the metro to Evangelismos, a ride of two-minutes which saved him twenty, which left only a short uphill walk to the apartment. That much exercise would be good for him, he thought. Packing would be easy, at least. He smiled to himself that he was once again going to avoid a six-hour sea crossing on his way back to Naxos.

21

The air in Filoti was a great deal fresher and cleaner than in Athens, and Day woke up feeling invigorated after a long and restorative sleep. The trip to Athens had not been a complete waste of time, and he hoped that Efi would get back to him soon with something Andreas could use. He would call him in a few hours to bring him up to date on the trip, but first he would go to the Villa Myrsini. He would make Stelios tell him the story of the lekythos, and accept no excuses. He would also make him aware of the trouble he would bring on himself if he failed to disclose it to the appropriate authorities. The law concerning antiquities was strict, and concealing an object pre-dating the fifteenth century without proper permission was illegal.

He drove towards the coast, wary of the possibility of rockslides and oncoming motorbikes, which was second nature to users of the steep and winding roads in the mountainous interior of the island. He was held up in Halki by a lively performance between two drivers exchanging accusations with a certain amount of good humour, before finally being able to continue south towards

Sangri and the villa. There was no sign now of the Meltemi wind, which had been replaced by a dry, still, searing heat. Enjoying the movement of air through the open car window, Day smiled at the prospect of hearing more about the lekythos.

The nearer he came to the Villa Myrsini, the more relaxed he felt. He took the turning onto the unmade road through the estate and drove up to the house. The palm trees near where he parked had dropped some branches in the recent wind, and a few unripe olives had fallen from the young potted trees on either side of the front door. He stood for a few moments waiting for his knock to be answered.

Then he heard a woman scream.

She screamed again, and it sounded like Maria. Voices were raised and somebody else called for help. He pushed the door, found it locked, and began to run towards the noise. Climbing over the waist-high stone wall that ringed the property, he pushed through the deep group of junipers that guarded the garden. People were shouting now, and he heard the sound of splashing. He forced his way with difficulty out of the conifers and saw people running towards the swimming pool: Yianni, then Theodoros, and Christina.

The pool was in shade, the morning sun still hidden behind the taller trees, but the scene could not have been more vivid. Despite being out of breath and scratched from his scramble through the junipers, he was aware of nothing beyond the sight of Maria in the middle of the pool, her brother wading towards her fast. She was trying unsuccessfully to lift the unmistakable shape of a man's body from beneath the water.

Yianni submerged, brought the body with difficulty to the surface, and struggled with it towards the side. He lifted the dead weight so that Theodoros and Ridgeway could pull it onto the paving stones. Ridgeway began to give CPR as Yianni helped his sister from the pool. Christina had brought towels, one of which

Yianni wrapped round Maria. In the strange silence that followed the drama, the sound of Ridgeway's fruitless efforts to revive the dead man had a sinister resonance.

Nobody had acknowledged Day yet, so absorbed were they by the nightmare at the pool. He reached into his trouser pocket for his mobile just as Theodoros patted his clothes, as if searching for something.

'Anyone have a phone? Martin? We need to call the police.'

Day had already pressed 112 for the emergency services. He gave the details and looked up again to find Maria staring helplessly at Ridgeway, who had given up his attempt to bring life back to the drowned man. She began to cry uncontrollably.

'Poor, poor Vasso!' she sobbed.

Nobody moved. Not even Theodoros had anything to say. Eleftheria and Elodie stood a little distance away with horror on their faces. Christina was trying in vain to distract Maria from the lifeless body. Ridgeway was drying his hands on a towel, shaking his head, staring at Day uncomprehendingly. Then from the house a voice broke the spell that had paralysed the group round the pool.

'What's happened? Yianni? Who is it?'

It was Stelios, supporting himself with two walking sticks, his head straining forward like a lizard's. He had reached the upper terrace and was trying to understand what he was seeing. Then he recognised the figure on the ground behind Ridgeway, his mouth opened, and his face lowered. He seemed about to fall.

His sister Eleftheria was nearest and reached him first, but now everyone was moving. Day watched as they went to support Stelios; everyone except Ridgeway and Theodoros, who remained by the body as if on guard. Christina sent Yianni and Maria to change into dry clothes, told Eleftheria and Elodie to take Stelios inside, and told Day to make sure nobody touched anything. She gave him a meaningful look and nodded towards Ridgeway and Theodoros before hurrying away in the direction of the kitchen.

Day understood, and moved closer to the side of the pool, where he found Theodoros and Ridgeway speculating on the tragedy.

'I think he must have been dead a while,' Ridgeway muttered. 'There was no sign of life …'

'You did your best.'

'Whatever was he doing out here? Was he drunk last night?'

'No more than the rest of us. Tragic accident, I expect.'

Day's first question seemed to surprise both men.

'Is that what Vassos was wearing at dinner last night?'

'Yes, I think so,' said Theodoros. 'What are you doing here, Martin?'

'I came to see Stelios. I was at the front door when I heard Maria call for help.'

'I'm going into the house,' said Ridgeway, indicating his wet clothes. 'I'll check on the others.'

The millionaire nodded, losing interest in them both and staring again at the body on the ground. He rubbed his eyes with both hands, then stared into the swimming pool as if revisiting the events of the last twenty minutes.

'Did you tell the police to get here quickly?' he muttered.

'I don't think that was necessary, was it?' said Day. 'It won't be long now.'

Inspector Kyriakos Tsountas took charge of the situation and deployed his team effectively to ensure that nobody left the grounds of the villa. Having taken careful note of the body, he placed a guard on it and ordered everyone to assemble in the living room. Captain Skouros was told to identify two rooms that would be suitable for holding interviews, and to take the details of everyone on the premises.

Kyriakos then turned his attention to Day with suspicion.

'You appear to be bleeding,' he said.

Day glanced down at his hands; they were badly scratched and a cut had opened up on one of them. He explained the circumstances of his arrival and the density of the junipers through which he had fought his way. He registered the coldness in the inspector's monosyllabic reply, and it occurred to him, as he watched Kyriakos stride purposefully away, that he needed to be very careful about how he handled himself. He must not give away that he had come to see Stelios about the lekythos, because if he mentioned the vase at all it would impact on Andreas's investigation. That meant he could not say truthfully that the last time he had seen Vassos alive was with Stelios in his study. It would be hard to account for himself with any semblance of honesty.

He could think of only one excuse for being at the villa. He would have to tell the police that he had come to see Maria, and that he had lied when he told Theodoros that he had come to speak to Stelios. After that, he would have to rely on his powers of improvisation.

He joined the others in the living room and took a chair by the wall. There was an uncomfortable silence in the room. Stelios was white with shock, tapping his stick on the floor repeatedly. The only conversation in the room came when a young policeman asked for their names and details, speaking to each person in turn. Christina had prepared coffee and was quietly handing out cups. They all looked round when Kyriakos strode in from the library, glanced at the paper given to him by the young officer, and looked round the room.

'*Kalimera.* I'm Inspector Kyriakos Tsountas, Chief of Police. I'm afraid we must ask all of you some questions right away. We need to know everything you can tell us regarding the victim, and exactly where each of you were last night, what you saw, what you heard. It's important you answer these questions accurately, and I urge you not to hold anything back.' He looked round grimly. 'Until I have more information from my forensic team, I must keep an open mind regarding the cause of death. There may have been an accident, but we cannot yet discount the possibility that the victim may have taken his own life. We could even, I'm afraid, be dealing with a deliberate assault.'

'Assault?' Stelios could barely speak. 'Who would want to hurt Vasso?'

The inspector seemed not to have heard him.

'My officers will bring you in turn to speak to myself or to Captain Skouros. Meanwhile, please do not discuss the matter amongst yourselves, and do not make any calls, use social media or any other form of communication. You are not to leave this room unless given permission. My men will be here to assist if anyone has a problem. Kyrie Kakouris, I'd like to begin with you, please. This way, sir. Kyria Kakouris, would you kindly accompany Captain Skouros?'

Theodoros and Eleftheria went out and the rest were left looking silently at each other, aware of the two policemen observing them from the side of the room. Day caught a desperate look from Maria which she made no attempt to conceal. Christina moved over to Stelios, sat on the arm of his chair and took his hand. The silence now seemed fraught with more than grief and shock; now there was the first hint of disquiet, doubt, suspicion. More vehicles drew up on the drive outside, voices and slammed doors indicating the arrival of a further contingent of police. Faces turned apprehensively towards the door.

Eleftheria was the first to return and sit down. Her hand shook slightly as she reached out for her coffee cup. Such was her shock that she looked across at Elodie and smiled at her reassuringly, the first communication between them that Day had seen. She then spluttered slightly, having sipped her coffee carelessly, and murmured apologetically to the room. Her polite words, though brief, resonated in the awkward silence.

'Madame Ridgeway now, please,' said Skouros from the door to the hall. Elodie went with him and everyone waited once more. Theodoros strode back from the library and told Yianni that the inspector wanted to see him next. Yianni left immediately.

When all but Stelios and Day had been interviewed, Captain Skouros made an announcement.

'The inspector would like to speak to you now, Mr Day, in the library. Kyrie Ioannides and I can talk in here. The rest of you, please go to your rooms, but remain in the house. Thank you for your co-operation.'

Day opened the library door and found Kyriakos seated at Stelios's impressive desk, a junior officer taking notes on an upright chair at his side.

'Well, Martin,' said the inspector, 'this is the second time I find you at the scene of a violent death. Let's begin with when and why you came to the Villa Myrsini today.'

'It must have been just before ten o'clock this morning that I arrived.'

'And for what reason did you come?'

'To speak to Maria.'

'I see. Why was that?'

'It's a private matter.'

Kyriakos stared at him, his eyes devoid of expression. This was even more disconcerting than malevolence.

'Nothing is private in the investigation of a suspicious death, Martin. Moreover, the young lady herself said nothing of the kind when I spoke to her a few minutes ago, so I would be grateful for your co-operation.'

'I'm sorry, but I promise you it has no bearing on this tragedy.'

'Indeed? It's customary to leave that kind of judgement to the police. Once again, to what matter does your presence here refer?'

'Maria and I have formed an attachment. I wanted to talk to her about it. It's something she would probably have preferred not to tell you.'

Kyriakos glanced at his stenographer to confirm that this had been taken down, and when assured that it had, he moved to his next question.

'I see. When did you last see the victim, Kyrie Nikolopoulos?'

Day sighed and pretended to dredge his memory. He felt himself sinking ever further into a mire of his own making.

'Stelios asked me some time ago to give a couple of talks on Greek antiquity to his guests, Theodoros Kakouris and Pierre Ridgeway, who are both very interested in the subject. Vassos attended both talks.'

'I see. So your connection to the Villa Myrsini is that you were employed here?'

'Correct.'

'Stefanos Patelis and his wife were at one of your informative events, I believe?'

'Yes, the first one.'

'Naturally. By the second they were dead. You were the one who found them.'

Day covered the jolt it gave him to see the way Kyriakos was thinking; there was no ignoring the insinuation.

'Look, I've made a statement about that,' he said as calmly as possible. 'And I didn't find Vassos today; I arrived as he was being brought from the pool.'

Kyriakos left a short pause before he responded, and when he did his words were anything but reassuring. He ran his fingertips appreciatively across his tidy black beard.

'Don't get excited, Martin. I'm simply noting that you were at the scene of the double murder, and here you are again now, where a suspicious death has taken place, with damage to your hands and arms.'

'I explained that.'

'Indeed you did. And where were you between ten o'clock last night and your arrival here this morning?'

'I was at home in Filoti.'

'Completely alone?'

'Yes. I arrived back from Athens on an afternoon flight yesterday.'

Kyriakos nodded, his tight smile laden with unspoken meaning, and Day felt increasingly uncomfortable.

Asked to describe what he saw when he reached the poolside, he felt on firmer ground. He had a good memory and found it easy to account for the positions, movements and reactions of every individual as Vassos was brought from the water. The inspector praised the accuracy of his recall.

'And lastly, please tell me about your interest in the yacht *Alkyoni*.'

'What do you mean, my interest in it?'

'Perhaps you would rather I asked about your relationship with Theodoros Kakouris?'

'I have no relationship with him.'

'Yet you were invited to visit the yacht recently. You were the only guest on that occasion, in fact.'

'Yes, I was invited for a drink one evening after meeting Theodoros for the first time here at Villa Myrsini. We mostly talked about the wine festival.'

'I see. And before you were hired by Kyrie Ioannides, had you known or heard of Vassos Nikolopoulos?'

'No.'

'Very well, Martin, you can go, but please remain on Naxos. I expect I'll want to speak to you again.'

When Day reached the living room, it was empty. There was no sign of Stelios and little to hear from elsewhere in the house. The empty cups were still on the coffee table, and one of Stelios's walking sticks was propped against the wall near his bronze sculpture of a kingfisher.

While he was hesitating, Kyriakos and his officer appeared from the library, walked through the room and left the villa without even acknowledging Day's presence. When they had gone, Day looked down at his hands, spread the fingers, and watched a drop of blood darken the end of a particularly deep scratch.

He was about to leave when from the window he noticed Maria outside, hugging herself with her crossed arms, watching the police conclude their preparations for the removal of Vassos's body. The stretcher was carried past her towards a waiting ambulance by two men in white overalls, who slid it expertly into place. The vehicle's doors slammed shut.

Maria's rigid posture crumpled then, and he heard her going rapidly upstairs.

22

The police left shortly after the ambulance. Day was thinking of doing the same, when he heard Stelios call out to him. It was like a muted cry for help. The old man had appeared in the doorway from the hall and was leaning unsteadily on his stick. Day reached him quickly and helped him to a chair.

'Thank you, Martin. I'm sorry. He meant so much to me, you know.' There were tears on his cheek. 'I should have told him, but I never did. Too late now.'

Day murmured the conventional words of sympathy, wishing there was something better to say. Stelios spoke with affection and sorrow of those he had lost, until at last his words ran out and he simply sat quietly, holding Day's arm. When he had recovered a little, he softened his grip without actually letting go.

'Do *you* have any idea what can have happened to Vasso?' asked Stelios. 'The police were very unhelpful. I don't understand. Where's Maria? And what brought you here this morning, Martin?'

'I came to see her. I think she's in her room,' said Day.

Stelios released his arm and patted it abstractedly.

He reached for the reassurance of his stick, but accidentally knocked it to the floor, and Day picked it up.

'You're always welcome here. So much has happened, Martin, terrible things, but I believe that in you we've found a good friend. There's something I'd like to tell you.'

He removed his glasses and cleaned them on a small cloth from his breast pocket. Placing them on his face again, he regarded Day steadily.

'It is this. Maria and Yianni are adopted. The bonds between us are loving and strong, and in terms of their legal rights they are, of course, my joint heirs. This is what I want you to know.'

Day stared at him. Was the old man telling him that Maria would inherit on his death? There could only be one reason for him to do so. This was going to be even more difficult than he had imagined.

'Maria is a wonderful young woman,' Stelios continued, 'and whoever marries her will be a very lucky man indeed. I want her to be cared for by a loyal and considerate partner, as she deserves. Martin, she needs your support. I'm worried about her.'

He lifted his stick and pressed the bell on the wall that summoned his daughter.

'I'll leave you to talk to her and go to my study. If you would just help me up?'

Day did so, and Stelios moved slowly into the library. Maria arrived just as the door closed after him. Day went across to her, shocked at her pallor and the sign of recent tears, and hugged her.

'Are you all right?'

'Yes,' she said, then leant into him with a sigh. 'Actually no, I'm not all right at all. It's the most horrible thing. Poor Vasso. None of us will ever be the same again, Martin. Everything is broken.'

He steered her to the sofa and sat down with her. It was true, nothing would be the same again. He wondered whether she really knew quite how much worse the situation was about to become.

'Look, there's something we must talk about,' he said, coming to a decision. 'It would be better to do it now.'

She smiled and moved closer to him, which made it so much more difficult.

'What do you want to tell me, Martin *mou*?'

'It's about the photograph on your bedside table.'

She looked surprised, disappointed, and her face filled with anxiety. Over her shoulder, Day could see that the door to the library was slightly ajar, and knew that Stelios was probably listening to everything they said. He had just heard that Day was familiar with his daughter's bedroom, but he was about to hear far more shocking things. Day was filled with pain at the thought.

'What about it?'

'It's an enhanced copy of an old photo, isn't it? The young woman in the picture is Paraskevi, your birth mother.'

She drew back from him just enough to stare at him.

'How on earth did you know that?'

'I came across an identical picture somewhere else and took it to the photographer whose details were on the back. She told me that a client had ordered two copies of an older original.'

Maria said nothing. He wondered about that. She should be surprised that he had bothered to find out about the photograph, and she had not asked where he had found the other copy. She was gripping her hands tightly together in her lap and avoiding his eyes.

'The client was you, of course.'

Maria replied crossly, 'You're right, it's a picture of her when she was young. I just asked the photographer to improve it as much as possible.'

'And to make copies for yourself and Yianni.'

'I thought it would help Yianni. It shows her when she was happy. I like to think it was taken by the man she loved, when they were young and full of hope.'

'How did your brother react when you gave it to him?'

'He was upset, because I had to tell him she was dead. What else could I do? He had to know. He looked at the photograph for a long time without saying a word. Then he wanted to know absolutely everything I could remember about her. After that, he never spoke of her again.'

She looked up at him with eyes round and unblinking.

'The last time I went to see her, she was very close to death. She was fully aware of what was happening. She said goodbye to me and told me how much I meant to her. She asked me to tell Yianni that she loved him, and that she'd never stopped thinking about us, not in thirty-three years. The photograph was her most treasured possession, and she wanted Yianni to have it.'

The tears that had never been far from Maria's eyes now fell down her cheeks.

'She also told you about your father, didn't she?' said Day gently. 'You had a right to know his name.'

'Yes. She hadn't tried to find him, and was sure he didn't know what had happened to her. She said it was up to me to decide whether to contact him.'

'And did you contact him?'

'No. I wanted to, but Yianni wouldn't hear of it. To be honest, Martin, I was tired of doing everything on my own. I wanted us to do that together, Yianni and I.'

'It must have been very hard for you, seeing him so often and saying nothing to him.'

Maria looked up sharply.

'Yianni told you!'

'No, nobody told me, I worked it out for myself. I wish I could have thought of some other explanation.'

Behind them, the door of the library opened and Stelios appeared. Maria stared at him open-mouthed. The old man came a little way into the room and then straightened, smiling sadly at his daughter.

'My poor girl,' he said. 'My poor Maraki. That was your name when you were little, you remember? Please forgive me, Maraki *mou*.'

He sank into a chair. Maria went to him, protesting that none of it was his fault in any way.

'I'm afraid I heard what you and Martin were saying,' her father confessed. 'I couldn't help myself. But I didn't hear the name … the name of the man who …'

'Please, Papa, it's not important …'

She sat down with her arm round him and looked beseechingly at Day.

'Why don't you tell your father, Maria? He can't be the only member of the family not to know the truth. You won't be able to protect him for much longer anyway.'

'What are you talking about? Protect me from what?'

Day sighed. They must speak now, or Stelios would hear everything from the police. It was then that Maria gave him permission.

'You can tell him,' she said quietly. 'Everything.'

Day braced himself; he could think of nothing worse that he could tell the old man.

'Maria was told that her birth father was Stefanos Patelis. Stefanos never tried to deceive you, Stelio; he was as unaware as you were of his relationship to your family. I'll tell you what I think happened; Maria has already told me some of it.

'When his young girlfriend was sent away to give birth to her illegitimate child, Stefanos had no way to find her. I imagine neither of the families wanted the young couple to see each other again, and refused to help him. Stefanos eventually had to give up and wanted to get as far away from Athens as possible. He made a new life for himself on Santorini, having begged Ambrosia Wine to take him on and train him in the business. All his life since then he has remained completely unaware of Paraskevi's situation and knew nothing about the twins.

'A few years ago, Stelio, you discovered Ambrosia Wine and began to buy your wine from them. Stefanos visited the villa more and more frequently, you became friends. I don't know exactly when it was that Maria and Yianni learned that he was their biological father, but they decided to hide it from you. It must have been difficult for Maria because she wanted to be open about it, but for Yianni the situation was even harder: a fuse had been lit that he could do nothing to control.

'I can only imagine how he must have struggled. He couldn't escape from Stefanos, whose visits became a torment to him. He had to be affable and welcoming to the man he believed had abandoned his mother, his sister and himself. His anger was probably compounded by his own guilt at having refused to see his mother before she died. Anger turned to obsession. He went in secret to spy on Ambrosia Wine; he told me so himself.'

'Stefanos never knew any of this?' said Stelios.

'I think he found out just before he died. Yianni told him. When I discovered Stefanos's body, there was a copy of the photograph of Paraskevi on the floor next to it.'

Father and daughter were frozen, unable to say a word. Both were transfixed; only one of them was surprised.

Maria stood up, placed her hand briefly on her father's shoulder and left the room. Day let her go.

'You think … my *son* killed Stefano and Klairi?' The old man's voice was shaking. 'Vasso, too?'

'I don't know. The police …'

'It can't be!'

A car started up outside, turned and drove away. Maria came back into the room.

'There! Do whatever you think is right, Martin, which will be to call the police, I guess. But I've just done what *I* think is right. He's my brother.'

Day nodded. He had expected her to warn him and had made no attempt to stop her. He could have gone to the police before now, he could have given them the photograph instead of hiding it in his pocket, but he had chosen to do neither of those things. He had protected Yianni as surely as Maria had, and without her excuse, yet he would do the same again. He would do the right thing, he would call Andreas in a few hours and the law would take its course, but he was in no rush.

'Where will he go?' he asked her.

'What are you going to do? Send the police after him?'

'No. The police will find him, but not for a while. I'd like to speak to him.'

'Come outside.'

Maria turned away, leaving him to follow her. They left Stelios staring at the bronze kingfisher as if somehow it might comfort him. Outside, she gently touched Day's cheek before urging him to leave.

'I trust you, Martin. Find Yianni for me. There's a place he goes to when he's not feeling well, I think he'll be there: the Bazeos Tower. It's not far. Please be quick, *agapi mou*. The tower is high and open at the top. Yianni's broken.'

Day nodded and got into his car at once. In his mirror he saw her looking after him as he drove down the drive at speed, scattering grit onto the verge.

His mind was racing. The Bazeos Tower was less than two kilometres from the Villa Myrsini. It was a popular visitor attraction and might be full of people, making an encounter with a killer irresponsible. He had little time to decide. He toyed with the idea of calling Andreas rather than going on by himself, but his foot never moved from the accelerator except to negotiate the road as he headed south towards the tower.

The midday sun shone gold on the mellow stone of the four-storey stronghold. Day crossed the courtyard and took the steps up to the low entrance door in a single stride. He headed straight to the roof, but there was no sign of Yianni, only a couple sitting quietly on the ledge of the parapet. The old tower overlooked fields and hills as far as the horizon, everything drenched in peaceful sunshine, but the sheer drop to the hard earth below sent a chill through him.

The internal staircase was narrow and built for people shorter than him, forcing Day to descend more slowly than he wanted. Light from outside filtered through each narrow window as he searched every small room on the way down, stooping to avoid hitting his head on the low Venetian lintels. When at last he reached the ground floor, he thought Yianni could not have come here after all. Then he heard faint music from somewhere nearby, recorded church music sung by a woman with a high, ethereal voice. It was coming from the tower's private chapel, about which he had forgotten.

That was where he found Yianni.

The face that looked up when Day walked into the chapel was ashen. It was somehow the face of a man ten years older than the one with whom Day had sat with a beer at Diogenes. There was resignation in his eyes as he looked round, as if for the last time, at the uneven stone walls, the old iron candle-holders and the icons. These, and the beautiful singing most of all, infused the small chamber with a feeling of unworldliness.

'Maria thought you might be here. I'm alone, Yianni, and I think I know what happened. I'd like to hear it from your side.'

For a moment, Yianni seemed not to have heard, his eyes fixed on the embroidered cloth over the small altar table.

'Hi there, Martin,' he murmured. 'My side? I don't know where to start.'

Day sat on one of the short pews and attempted to look relaxed.

'Then why don't I tell you what I think happened?'

Yianni nodded absent-mindedly.

'Maria told you that Stefanos Patelis was your natural father. You refused to talk to him, but as Stelios made you buy his wine and Stefanos visited the villa whenever he came to Naxos, you were forced into contact with him repeatedly. He became a close friend of your father; you even found yourself liking him. You became rather obsessed with him, even went to Santorini to see where he lived. Did you really not speak to him when you got there?'

'No, I just wanted to see the place.'

'And it was you who broke into Ambrosia Wine's office on Naxos, I guess?'

'Yeah. I thought there might be some private papers there. I never meant to steal anything or hurt the young guy.'

'This was your father, Yianni. Why not just talk to him?'

Yianni had no reply. He seemed to be drifting away from Day with each passing moment. Day felt as if he was reaching out and grabbing a drowning man.

'So what happened when you went to his house on the last night of the wine festival?'

Yianni raised his hands in despair, shrugged, and dropped them again onto his knees. He looked directly at Day for the first time, his big brown eyes expressionless.

'Maria wanted us to talk to him together, and I should have listened to her. I was so confused. So angry. I couldn't just let it go, wanted to make him admit his guilt. You do see, don't you, Martin? He left his girlfriend pregnant and went off to start a new life, made a success of himself, married the boss's daughter, inherited the lot, lived happy ever after. Gee, what a bastard, I thought. It seemed to be up to me, her son, to avenge our mother. It seemed to be my duty.

'But I did *nothing*. He would come to the villa, I ordered wine from him, he talked to my father, I even grew to like the guy a bit. Klairi - Klairi was one of the kindest women I ever met.'

'So what happened?'

Yianni pinched the bridge of his nose and wiped his hand across his face.

'I finally found the nerve to call him. It was on the day of your first talk, Martin, in the evening. I told him that Maria and I were his children. I told him that Paraskevi was dead. He was very shocked, very upset. He begged me to go and talk to him.'

'Did he ask you to take Maria with you?'

'Yes, but I said it would be better if I went alone, the first time.'

'So, you arranged to go, on your own, to their rented house on that Sunday evening. Had you decided to kill him?'

'No.'

'I expect they welcomed you like the proverbial long-lost son. They'd chilled a special bottle of wine for the celebration, maybe made some food. Stefanos would have been excited. He could not have known how deeply conflicted you felt.'

'No,' Yianni said quietly. 'He had no idea.'

'Was it really so impossible to accept the affection of two kind-hearted people and put the past behind you? Revenge is no solution. You could have thought of a reconciliation as redeeming Paraskevi's suffering by reuniting her children and the man she loved.'

'I tried. I thought perhaps I could, but …'

Day waited while Yianni searched for words.

'Ever since that trip to Santorini, for weeks and weeks without a break I'd felt as though my heart was going to explode in my chest. I had the feeling my hands were shaking all the time, but when I looked at them they were steady. I had the kind of palpitations in my stomach you get before an exam, but they didn't stop, night or day. My heartbeat seemed to be racing. I started to sneak into Papa's bathroom at night and take one of his beta-blockers, just to get a few hours of relief; but when that wore off, the problems started up again. On the Sunday evening when I went to see Stefano, I could barely drive the car. I stood at their front door feeling like I might fall over.'

Yianni paused, hearing footsteps outside the chapel door. They both listened as the unseen visitors passed by the chapel and went out into the courtyard.

'Go on,' said Day quietly.

'The three of us talked. I asked Stefano to tell me the truth about what happened. He said they had always wanted to get married, but neither family would hear of it, and when they discovered she was expecting a child, that was the end of everything. One day she simply disappeared and nobody would tell him where she was. He wasn't even allowed to write to her.

'He just wanted to get as far from his family as he could. It was unbearable, he said. He was twenty but still living at home, and that had to change. He had enough money for a ferry, no more. He went to Santorini and worked in a bar before he got his first job at Ambrosia Wine.'

'So you knew Stefanos had done all he could at the time to find your mother. Didn't you believe him?'

'Yes, I believed him.' Yianni swallowed noisily. 'But then he said that he'd always meant to go back and find her, but he just hadn't ever done it. "That's life, I suppose," were his exact words.

'I was sitting next to the tray with the wine and the glasses on it. Stefanos was smiling, saying we should share a glass, how it would be the start of putting it all in the past and moving on as a family. There was one of those fancy wine-waiter's tools lying on the tray. French-style thing; I've seen them in some of the places

I've worked. The blade was already open. It was about six inches long, wicked-looking. Stefanos was about to use it to remove the foil on his bottle. I picked it up. I don't remember the rest.'

'You must have stabbed him repeatedly, then chased Klairi upstairs and done the same to her.'

Yianni covered his face and shook his head, as if the idea was new and appalling to him.

'I would do anything, *anything*, to change what I did, if only I could.'

'What about the photograph of Paraskevi? The one I found on the floor?'

Yianni dropped his hands and answered with a hint of defiance.

'I did it for her. So I left her with him.'

Day was too full of dismay to speak. In the incongruously uplifting atmosphere of the little chapel, the only sound was the sacred motet sung by a soloist in the echoing acoustic of some lofty cathedral.

Yianni stood up slowly.

'Will you do me a favour, Martin? It will be the last I ask of anyone. Take me to the police. I don't think I can drive, and I'd appreciate your company.'

23

Neither of them said much as Day drove from the grassy car park of the Bazeos Tower to the police station in Chora, where a policeman stood outside on the pavement with slumped shoulders, enjoying a cigarette. Day pulled in on the other side of the *plateia* and switched off the engine. Neither of them made a move. When Yianni finally released his seatbelt, the sound of the retracting strap seemed unusually loud.

'Thanks,' he said.

He gave Day a strange smile, got out and walked away.

Day watched him enter the police station and waited for a few minutes, imagining what was happening inside. He switched on the engine again but sat there a little longer, not even finding the will to decide where to go. Without reaching a decision, he released the handbrake and slowly pulled out into the traffic.

The clock in the car told him it was after midday. He drove without purpose through the busy streets of Chora towards the sea. Only when he saw a parking space did he decide to get out and take a walk. His head ached, he felt unwell and was desperate for fresh air. There was a slight swell on the water, and the masts of the yachts moored along the shoreline rattled and clinked.

After ten minutes contemplating the bay, he turned his back on the sea and strolled inland until he reached a quiet part of Agios Georgios and found a small corner café with three empty tables outside. The decision practically made itself. He asked for a double espresso, and when his order arrived with a glass of cold water, he drank most of the water at once.

Snippets of normal conversation reached him from time to time as people passed the café, but he sat like an automaton. An old woman with a heavy carrier bag of groceries paused near his table to rest for a moment before continuing her slow walk up the street; he felt he was invisible to her. He reached for the coffee cup and put his feet on the rungs of the chair opposite. The coffee was hot and strong, immediately waking that part of his mind that would almost rather remain dormant. He imagined Yianni now, confessing to murder. Six or seven years younger than me, he thought, and his life is over.

He watched his memory replay the succession of occasions when he had spoken with Yianni in the past three weeks or so, a young Greek-American with a cheerful face and friendly chat, a man with a passion for Greek cuisine, a welcoming, accommodating person who gave no outward sign of the demons that afflicted him. A man whose shadowy alter ego was being relentlessly driven to an act of violence that would change the lives of his family as much as his own, and end the life of someone whose genes he carried.

His mobile phone dragged him away from his thoughts with its strident ringtone. He pulled it from his pocket and saw that the caller was Andreas.

'Andrea! *Pos paie*?' he said, forcing his voice to sound normal.

'*Etsi ki etsi*. You're back from Athens, then. Was it worth the trip?'

'I need to talk to you.'

'I'm on Naxos, so we could meet now if it suits you,' said Andreas. Day guessed this had been the purpose of his call. 'Are you at home?'

'No, I'm at a café in Agios Georgios called … Café Gonia. It's a bit out of the way. I could meet you somewhere else.'

'Out of the way is good,' said Andreas. 'Share the location to my phone and I'll join you. I'll be coming from the police station.'

Day did so and settled down to wait; he did not have to wait long.

There was no way Andreas Nomikos could blend into a crowd, even if he had wanted to. Day saw him from a distance. His leonine head and the assurance of his stride marked him out. The chief inspector was a figure of authority, a man with opinions and objectives, not to be confused with anyone on vacation or buying their bread and milk.

Throwing himself into a chair at Day's table, Andreas shook his hand with a friendly but short-lived smile.

'You were at the police station, you said?'

'Yes. Tsountas is hyper-ventilating,' said Andreas, not even trying to conceal his antipathy. 'In fairness to him, it isn't every day a man hands himself in and confesses to murder.'

'I imagine not.'

Andreas frowned. 'You already knew, didn't you?'

'I took him to the police station myself.'

'Wait! I need a coffee for this. Another one for you?'

Andreas waved to the proprietor and ordered two double espressos. Day let it happen, mostly because it was easier than explaining that any more coffee would probably make him sick. Given the events of the morning, a caffeine overdose was all but insignificant.

'Right. Start at the beginning.'

Like flicking through the pages of a novel trying to recapture the thread of the plot, Day wondered where to start. With Yianni?

With Maria? No, it was necessary to admit that it had all begun with an impulsive and blameworthy act of his own.

'On Monday, when I found Stefanos and Klairi, there was a small photograph lying on the floor near Stefanos's body. There were no other personal possessions around, it was a rental place, and I didn't think it was a picture of Klairi. When the police arrived, I put it in my pocket.'

'You did *what*? You tampered with a crime scene? You removed evidence?'

'Yes, but let me tell you the rest, because that's how I worked it out.'

Andreas said nothing. It appeared to be costing him a considerable effort. When the coffee arrived, he applied it directly to his irritation and recovered his composure to some extent.

'On the back of the photograph was the address of a studio in Athens, so I took it to them. I found out that the woman in the picture was Maria and Yianni's birth mother; they were adopted, I already knew that, and I'd seen the same picture in Maria's bedroom without knowing what I was looking at. Two copies of the photograph had been made, making it likely that the one I took from Stefanos's living room had belonged to Yianni. It looked possible that Yianni had left it there.

'This morning, I went back to the villa because I had some idea of speaking to Maria about the photograph, and I also wanted to see Stelios. I arrived just as they found Vassos in the pool. You probably heard this part from Kyriakos. The police were called, we were all questioned, everybody was badly shaken.

'Afterwards, when Maria and I were alone, I told her what I've told you about the photograph. Her father heard. I tried to explain to him as best I could, and while I was doing that, Maria went to warn her brother. He drove away.

'I didn't call the police; another sin, I'm afraid. Maria told me that her brother goes to the Bazeos Tower when he's upset, and she was worried he might do something desperate to himself, so I went after him. I found him, we talked. In the end I drove him to the police station.'

'I'm afraid I still don't understand,' said Andreas, the exasperation evident in his voice. 'Are you saying that Yianni Ioannides confessed to you that he killed Stefanos and Klairi Patelis? Why?'

'Why did he confess, why to me, or why did he do it?'

'Just tell me the story, Martin.'

'After Maria told him that Paraskevi was dead and that Stefanos Patelis was their father, Yianni blamed Stefanos for everything: for abandoning Maria and himself, and above all for leaving Paraskevi to suffer. He began to feel it was his duty to avenge his mother. He has long-term mental difficulties and copes badly with any kind of stress, which was why the family brought him to Naxos from New York.'

'So the killings were premeditated?'

'Wait a bit, I'll tell you the rest. Yianni called Stefanos and told him that Paraskevi was dead and that he and Maria were his children. Stefanos was very emotional, naturally, and asked to see both Yianni and Maria. Yianni arranged to go alone and took his copy of the photograph with him.'

Day's head was ringing from the combination of caffeine and tension. He continued wearily, no longer sure whether he was making sense.

'At this point, I think, Yianni had no intention of killing anybody. When Stefanos said he wanted to build bridges and get to know Yianni and Maria properly, I think Yianni believed him and would have gone along with it. Stefanos convinced him that he had tried to find Paraskevi at the time, but nobody would tell him where she was, and he had left Athens not knowing what had happened to her.

'Things went wrong when Stefanos tried to make light of it and spoke of moving on. Yianni snapped. He told me there was a sommelier's knife next to the bottle of wine and he used it on Stefanos in the heat of the moment. He killed his own father.'

Day's voice drifted to nothing. Andreas sat back in his chair and crossed his arms in front of him. After a while, the policeman in him could restrain himself no longer.

'I can't say it comes as any surprise to me that you got so involved, Martin, and you've handled it as I've come to expect. You took evidence from a murder scene, you failed to tell the police of your suspicions, and you approached a dangerous man alone in a public place with no consideration of the risk, to yourself and to others. It's no thanks to you that there wasn't an incident; people could have been hurt. A murderer could easily have escaped justice.'

Day regarded him sulkily, too tired to bother to adjust his expression. Andreas visibly controlled himself.

'You know this confession puts you in the clear?'

'Me?'

'Maybe your fabled intuition hasn't served you as well as you think, Martin. Kyriakos Tsountas dislikes and distrusts you. Can't blame him, really, can we? He finds you at the scene of the Patelis murders with no alibi; your ferry from Paros that night would have got you to Chora in time to commit the crime. Then it happens again: you're on the spot when a dead body is pulled out of a swimming pool, and again you have no alibi. It's easy to see why he has his eye on you. I realise you and Tsountas know each other from the past, but I don't think you have the true measure of him.'

'I can't believe he's that stupid, Andrea. What motive could I have had? And are you telling me that Vassos's death was definitely murder?'

'I'm afraid so. Someone dealt him a severe blow to the head with a sharp-edged solid object which hasn't yet been found. Whether that caused his death or he drowned will be decided at the post mortem, but it was no accident. It happened between midnight and two o'clock on Friday night. The flight back from Athens that afternoon would have given you plenty of time to commit the murder. Of everyone connected to the villa, you alone haven't provided an alibi.'

'What? Do you think I did it?'

'I know you didn't.'

Day expelled his breath slowly. Kyriakos's manner towards him during questioning was starting to take on a new significance. Andreas, however, had already moved on.

'I need to tell you something else,' he said. 'The raids are scheduled for noon tomorrow.'

'*Tomorrow?*'

'Yes. The *Alkyoni* could sail for Sicily any time in the next few days. At the moment the yacht isn't allowed to leave Naxos because of the murder of Nikolopoulos, but when Tsountas is satisfied that none of the people on board are responsible, he will have to lift the restriction. The wives have sworn that Ridgeway and Kakouris were with them all night, and the crew were on the boat. I'm not going to let Ridgeway slip out of my hands, Martin.'

'And what about Theodoros? Have you found anything on him?'

'I have nothing, nothing at all, except association with Ridgeway. It won't be enough. What about the things you were looking into? The inscription and the lekythos?'

'I need a bit longer.'

'For what? You said you'd get me something in Athens.'

'I need longer to make sure you don't lose him,' said Day patiently, 'or end up with an angry millionaire on your case. All right, I'll call my epigraphist friend and get her answer on the inscription. As for the lekythos, how much time do I have?'

'As I said, the raids take place at midday tomorrow. I'll tell Tsountas to secure the contents of the safe at the Villa Myrsini, but we have nothing to connect the lekythos to Kakouris. For God's sake, Martin, get me something I can use.'

Day nodded and picked up his mobile phone. His message to Efi Charalambou was succinct: *Any news? Now urgent.*

'What do you want me to do tomorrow?' he asked when he'd finished. 'Can I help?'

Andreas shook his head firmly. He signalled to the proprietor that he was ready to pay and reached in his jacket for his wallet.

'Better you're not involved. The police will be armed, and Tsountas still has no idea that you're working with me. Let's keep it that way. Stay away from the Villa Myrsini tomorrow.'

Day shrugged. Andreas appeared satisfied and searched in his wallet for the right change.

'Why don't you find a way to work with Kyriakos, Andrea? You outrank him. You could get him to do what you want with no trouble. What's going on?'

Andreas pushed back his chair and stood up with a grunt.

'Let's take a walk. It's probably time you knew more about your current chief of police.'

24

After a day that had begun with a dead body in a swimming pool and continued with a murder confession, it was no surprise that he felt terrible. He turned the key in his front door and went into the house with no clearer plan than to lie flat on his bed.

As he pushed the door open, however, a flashback to the safety of his childhood home in Tunbridge Wells brought with it a wave of relief. He breathed in the consolation of his Greek house with its familiar smells: wood, old books, the lingering suggestion of coffee. Opening the shutters, he went out onto the balcony. The delicate aroma of the sun-parched slopes of Mount Zas, whether real or in his imagination, soothed him even more.

He stood and gazed at the mountain, suddenly reminded of the time when, as a student, he had climbed to the summit and seen the legendary view for himself. The highest peak in the Cyclades, he had already known that Mount Zas was about as high as Mount Snowdon in Wales. On its western slope was a cave where, according to myth, Zeus had spent his childhood. Day was more excited by the fact that Neolithic and Bronze Age remains had been found in this cave, including a thin strip of beaten gold with perforations in the corners, an item of Mycenaean jewellery. All of these factors had played a part in making up his mind. He had decided on impulse to get to the top.

The memories were flooding back now. Leaving his student friends to sleep off their hangovers, he had taken the bus to Filoti and set off alone to climb the mountain. At first, it had been easy. He remembered a shaded area with an ancient spring known as the Aria Spring, which trickled in a pleasant, tree-filled clearing.

After that, however, the ascent had become more challenging. The upward path became ever more narrow and precarious as he followed the steep trail indicated by the rock cairns that served as route markers. The peak of Zas began to look very high and very close, so he knew the final climb would be precipitous. Three-quarters of the way to the summit, he had nearly given up: the trail had become no more than a rocky scramble with low, thorny bushes as the only hand-holds. To admit defeat so near the top, however, had been unacceptable.

His reward had been immense. Standing by the rock that marked the highest point, overlooking the unfolding island below and the surrounding sea, had been one of the best moments of his life. He had been completely alone, and yet somehow he had brought the human race with him. Perhaps he had been light-headed, but it made no difference. He would never forget that climb, nor the sweetness of the mountain air, up there where he had felt close to the stretch of history.

The memory had cheered him, and he went to the kitchen to see what there was to eat. It would be easy to go to a taverna, but he wanted to stay at home. There was frozen chicken in the freezer, a box of dried pasta in the cupboard, there was gin, there was wine. He drank a glass of water and took the chicken out to thaw.

In his bedroom, he opened the window, lay on the bed and folded his hands, closing his eyes and emptying his mind. Thoughts of Yianni, of Andreas, of Helen were looked at in turn and placed in safe corners of an imaginary room where he could re-examine them another time. He gradually drifted into unconsciousness and slept for no more than an hour, probably less, but it was enough. He woke feeling calmer and headed to the shower, where he refused to connect with the subjects he needed to resolve. Not yet.

In fresh clothes, he emerged back into the main room and set about preparing his dinner. Once the chicken was cooking in the pan, he wandered back to the balcony where the air was warm, almost motionless, and the late afternoon light flooded the hills and the valley. For once, there was no sound from the doves or the small birds that enjoyed his neighbour's garden. There was barely any noise to be heard. Although quite peaceful, it was also rather like having lost his hearing. He thought of Helen in Hampstead, a quiet suburb, but never free from the constant hum of the city. A feeling of loss grew inside him as he thought of her, like stepping onto soft, wet sand on a tidal beach, knowing the ground would hold, but feeling as vulnerable as if there was an actual possibility of quicksand.

With a sigh he returned to his cooking. Onions and garlic went in with the chicken, followed by a couple of tomatoes that were on the turn and needed to be used. The flavoursome Greek *rigani*, roughly milled salt and ground black pepper - what else could he add? The meal was smelling good. He found a vegetable stock cube and some paprika which he added sparingly, put a lid on the pan, and turned down the heat. He opened a bottle of Nemean red and took it back to the balcony to wait for his dinner to be ready. With the bottle and the glass within reach, he sank into his usual chair.

He was about to pour himself a drink when his mobile rang. The number was a landline that he did not recognise.

219

'*Parakalo?*'

'Martin? It's Efi here.'

'Oh, Efi, hello. *Ti kaneis*? I didn't recognise your number.'

'I'm at the museum. I got your message. You need to know right now?'

'Sorry, I really didn't want to rush you.'

'As long as you understand that I'm guessing until I see the inscription myself, I can give you my thinking up to this point. You want that?'

'Absolutely.'

There was a pause, during which Day wondered whether he could actually hear Efi's indrawn breath.

'What do you know about the fifth-century horos inscriptions on Aegina?'

Day shrugged in the privacy of his own balcony.

'I've read about them.'

'So you don't know much, I take it. Okay. They're inscribed boundary stones. There's still a lot of academic dispute about their importance, their date and so on, but people seem to agree that they're in Attic dialect and script, and therefore Athenian in origin. They marked off areas of agricultural land owned by the city-state of Athens itself or by individual Athenians. They were probably created during the Peloponnesian War, when Athens occupied Aegina. Fourteen of these boundary markers have been found on the island, and they vary considerably in most respects. Some are on marble - nothing elaborate, just whatever odd chunk was to hand. At least one is not on marble at all, but a rock called trachyte. Then the inscriptions. There are endless debates about the variations in lettering on the stones, especially the shape of the *sigma* and *rho* that you cleverly noticed. Anyway, you don't need to know the details of it all, you can leave that to the epigraphists, but what you do need to know is that it's possible that the block you saw on the yacht is one of these horos stones.

'Now, these objects are not immensely exciting in themselves, Martin, except to people like me, and then not greatly! However, if your inscription is a horos from Aegina, then it's interesting precisely because it's not on Aegina. The island is so close to the mainland that it could have been removed from there by boat, but why would anyone bother? The removal would have been difficult to accomplish and undoubtedly attracted attention, although once upon a time nobody would have cared. The Greeks used to move and re-use blocks of stone all the time, as you know. Things are very different today. As what we call an Ancient Immovable Monument, an ancient inscription is protected by law. If, as in this case, it's in private ownership without the necessary permission being obtained, there may be a case to be answered.'

Day grinned. This should give Andreas just enough to enable him to take possession of the inscription and submit it for evaluation by the authorities. Should it be found that Kakouris had not obtained permission to own it, it would lead, at the very least, to an investigation into him and his collection.

'Efi, I really owe you for this.'

'You do not. You really do not. Just make it happen that your inscription ends up in the hands of the Ephorate, preferably with my name on it so I can examine it. I'd like to see it.'

'I'll do what I can. Thank you.'

He decided to eat his dinner before calling Andreas with the good news. The food was hot, it was plentiful, and it was exactly what he needed. When his plate was empty he poured a little more wine into his glass and sat back, resting his feet on the balcony rail. As the flush of warmth created by the meal began to fade, a pleasant coolness came over him. His breathing deepened and he closed his eyes. Extraordinary though it was, he felt really clear-headed.

His mind drifted across the reach of the past. In the twenty-first century, people like Efi and her father lived and breathed the inscriptions left by men who died many, many hundreds of years ago. Harold and Jenny Stilgoe devoted their lives to the study of the masters of Greek vase-painting in the fifth and sixth centuries BCE. There were many others, including Fabrizio and himself, whose careers were focused on the past. Archaeologists apart, millions of visitors travelled to the Acropolis of Athens every year to wonder at the achievements of Classical Greece.

It was when he was thinking about Athens that the idea occurred to him.

He opened his eyes, brought his chair abruptly from its tilted position and stared into the twilight that had enveloped the valley. It was as clear and obvious with his eyes open as it had been with them closed. Where on earth did these flashes of intuition come from? If only he knew. He gave himself time, nearly half an hour, going over the implications of it in his head, looking for the inevitable flaws. It was impossible to prove, of course, but that was true of many a supposition that had resulted in a significant discovery in archaeology. It would be enough if his idea started some ball rolling.

His next step must be to speak to Harold Stilgoe.

He finished the wine in his glass and refilled it from what remained in the bottle. His mind was hovering in the uncertain midpoint between clarity and fantasy. He had better act swiftly and then go to bed.

Harold, it seemed, had also been enjoying a little wine. It was Jenny who answered the call, and she sounded doubtful as to the wisdom of handing the phone to her husband. She may have expected a social call; her voice changed at the mention of Stilgoe's Folly.

'So, how was Athens?' asked Harold, taking the phone from his wife.

'Interesting,' said Day. 'I consulted a friend about an inscription, and it may turn out to be something. Not the most significant or unique of objects, but of some interest. A displaced Athenian horos from Aegina, actually.'

Epigraphy was not Harold's favourite topic. He merely grunted politely before changing the subject.

'Did you look at the lekythos fragments I sent you to examine? What did you make of them?'

What indeed? thought Day, and prepared to embark on his theory, feeling like a student giving his first important presentation.

'I went to the Stoa of Attalos and looked at the fragment in the collection with John Jacob Field of the American School. I'm afraid it didn't tell me anything, so we then went together to see your friend Achilles at the Kerameikos. He showed us the Stilgoe's Folly fragment, but I wasn't particularly impressed by it either. Not at the time.'

'Ah. And what do you think now?'

'I thought at first that Stilgoe's Folly referred to the piece of vase in the Kerameikos museum, but I was wrong. Achilles explained that Stilgoe's Folly is a theory, not a sherd of pottery. It's your theory that the fragments in the Stoa and in the Kerameikos are connected with each other, and that both of them are connected to the Sappho Painter.'

'That's correct. What do you make of my theory?'

'On the face of it, it's unlikely that two rather average pots could be connected in any way to the Sappho master.'

'So? Do get on with it, Martin.'

'It was only this evening that I worked it out. Your theory couldn't be taken any further without the discovery of the Naxos lekythos. It's the missing piece of the puzzle, and I think you always believed it was out there to be found.'

'Aha! Now this is getting interesting. Wait while I put you on speaker so that Jenny can hear.'

'Hi, Jenny,' said Day.

'Hi, Martin, darling. Have you been up to your old tricks, then?'

'Old tricks? I'm not sure how to take that.'

'Being precocious as usual and leaping to wild conclusions.'

'Well, go on,' urged Harold.

Day stretched his neck to one side until it gave a satisfying little crack and the stiffness eased. He was sitting forward in the chair, his shoulders tensed. He imagined the Stilgoes round the phone somewhere in Greece, poised to pass judgement on his debut in their field of expertise.

'The fragments in the Kerameikos museum and the Stoa collection were probably painted about the same time by relatively unskilled craftsmen working in the Kerameikos itself. There are faint stylistic similarities between the two, particularly the attempt at the ambitious pattern round the neck. If Carey is right in identifying a wealthy Athenian family who commissioned the Stoa fragment, we can even take a guess that both fragments were painted around the same time.'

'Conjecture, but entertaining,' said Harold, but there was encouragement in his voice. Day carried on.

'According to Stilgoe's Folly, both fragments were attempts to copy a vase of greater complexity and excellence. I would add that it's possible both inferior works were made in the same workshop according to the master's instructions by his apprentice painters. Either way, the reason Stilgoe's Folly had to wait this long to be resolved is that no such masterly vase has ever been found. You had a good theory, Harold, but it couldn't be proved.

'Then I sent you my pictures of the Naxos lekythos. Perhaps you began to wonder whether you had just been shown the vase you'd been waiting for.'

He paused. There was the unmistakable sound of a wineglass being filled from Harold's end of the line. With a smile in her voice, Jenny asked Day to go on.

'I started to see if I could prove the theory that the Naxos lekythos was the original model for the fragments. It was not unreasonable to assume that the Naxos lekythos could have been made for the tomb of the woman from the family of the two fallen heroes, the family Carey mentioned in connection with the Stoa fragment. It honours a dead woman, the fallen warriors, and the patron who commissioned the vase. I'll return to that idea in a minute.

'A single warrior consoles the woman on the Stoa fragment, but behind him you can just make out the outstretched hand of another figure, which suggests that originally there were not one but two mourning figures facing the deceased woman. In other words, the same image as on the Naxos lekythos, except for the size of the figures. On the Naxos vase, the two warriors are very small by comparison to the woman, which could be a way to suggest that they're the dead woman's sons, or to indicate the relatively greater importance of the mother. Both would surely have gratified her grieving husband, the painter's patron. If I'm right, it was the inspired concept of a master painter, an idea lost on the less skilful one who made the Stoa fragment depicting adult warriors.

'There is another possible interpretation of the small figures on the Naxos vase. The young warriors of the family, who have already died in battle themselves, have presumably returned from the after-life at the death of their mother, perhaps to take her back with them. They might be smaller than life-size because they are no longer alive. Perhaps I'm getting carried away? All the same, there's enough that connects the two designs to open the door to Stilgoe's Folly, I think. Also, the organic and linear designs on the shoulders of both examples are strikingly similar, even though painted with different levels of skill.

'The name Antiope inscribed on the Naxos vase is interesting. It was traditional practice to introduce a mythical context to elevate the subject, and Antiope was herself a mother of twins. If the dead woman's warrior sons were twins, this would be an appropriate choice of designation.'

Day stopped, hoping for a comment from Harold or Jenny, but he was left to continue without one. He put that subject to one side for a while.

'I was quite happy with these apparent connections between the Naxos lekythos and the sherd in the Stoa, but that left the trickier question of the fragment in the Kerameikos. It doesn't depict a funerary scene at all, and on first impression there's little to connect it with the other two. Instead of showing a dead mother and warrior sons, it seems to show, unless I'm mistaken, the twin gods Apollo and Artemis, the children of Zeus and Leto, with Artemis's bow ready for the hunt. There are a few marks that could have been the names of the deities on the broken edges of the fragment. For a while, I couldn't see what you must have seen, Harold.'

The professor made no comment, forcing the student to carry on.

'The key to the whole thing, I think, is that *this is only a fragment*; the rest of it is broken away and lost. As I see it, the seated mother and the twin children shown on the Naxos vase (and possibly on the piece of vase in the Stoa) would have been on the *reverse* of the Kerameikos fragment, all of which has been lost. Conversely, the figures of Apollo and Artemis, mythical representations of the 'god-like' children of the wealthy Athenian family, would have been on the *reverse* of the Naxos vase, on the area that's now worn away, and on the piece in the Stoa. The original design of the Sappho Painter, therefore, would probably have shown the dead mother's heroic sons *both as mortals and as immortals*.

'In short, the painters of the Kerameikos and Stoa fragments were reproducing versions of the Naxos lekythos as best they could. The drew the figures of Apollo and Artemis on one side, both gods of hunting associated with death and prowess in battle; on the other, the dead mother (elevated as Antiope) with her dead warrior sons. In neither case, though, did a whole design survive. Today, we have two apparently very different fragments painted by quite ordinary vase painters, and now a complete, if slightly worn, lekythos painted by an artist of an altogether different kind.'

There was a full moment of silence from the Stilgoes, before Harold said something that Day thought sounded surprisingly like professorial approval.

'Wonderful!'

'Pardon?'

'I said, it's wonderful. The Sappho Painter's original design, I mean. So ground-breaking that at least two of the other artists in the workshop tried to reproduce it. I admit it used to bother me that Apollo and Artemis were chosen as the deities to represent the fallen warriors, Artemis being female, when there were various male sibling warriors he could have chosen instead, such as Castor and Polydeuces. But by using Apollo and Artemis, the Divine Twins, he was complimenting his wealthy patron in the highest way possible. He was linking *him* to Zeus, the father of Apollo and Artemis and greatest of the Olympian gods, and therefore his *wife* to Leto, who gave birth to the twins on the sacred island of Delos. This would have pleased the wealthy patron a great deal. I'm sure the painter was richly rewarded. Wonderful!'

'I thought for a moment it was my argument that had impressed you, Harold,' chuckled Day, sitting back in his chair and picking up his glass. 'You think I'm on the right track, then?'

'You've done well. Bravo!'

Day was grateful that there was nobody to see his smile of satisfaction. The only living creature nearby was a solitary bat, attracted by the dim wall-light behind him, and the bat was not interested in his theory.

'The Naxos lekythos will be confiscated by the police tomorrow,' he told the Stilgoes, 'and we'll do everything we can to persuade the Ephorate to let you examine it. I'm sure the wheels will turn slowly, but in the fullness of time you may be able to resolve Stilgoe's Folly.'

Jenny's voice: 'Heaven be praised!'

'Then it will just remain a mystery that the Naxos lekythos, as we seem now to be calling it, turned up in Naxos,' said Harold.

'I've made a start on that,' said Day. 'Achilles said something else that I found intriguing. The records of the nineteenth-century excavations of the Kerameikos mention the discovery of another lekythos, a complete one, of which there is no drawing or description. It seems to have been lost almost as soon as it was unearthed. It's rumoured to have entered a private collection in Athens in about 1879, the year that the area was excavated.'

'In those days, they were finding so much, and so many people were involved, it was chaotic,' murmured Jenny. 'And money talked then, just as it does these days.'

'I see where you're going with this,' Harold put in, ignoring her in his excitement. 'Day's Folly?'

'Perhaps. What if this complete, highly desirable lekythos from a tomb in the Kerameikos Cemetery made its way to the Cyclades? Who knows how complex its journey, who handled it, traded it, hid it? Has the Sappho Painter's Apollo and Artemis Lekythos ended up, so long after having been brought out of the ground, in a twenty-first century villa on Naxos?'

Lying in bed hours later, his mind still racing and conflicted, Day wrote an email to Helen. He would rather have talked to her, but it was well past midnight in England. Besides, writing it down would help him to get his thinking straight, to understand where he was and what was about to happen. He was still elated by his theory of the lekythos, but Yianni's confession, Andreas's dark warnings and the expected challenges of the following day would not let him rest. He wrote about it all, holding nothing back. He ended with a simple enough statement of his love for her, managing to say nothing of his overwhelming need for her. Of that he was quite proud. He could not have stopped himself if she had been on the other end of the phone.

He had completely forgotten to call Andreas.

25

By eight o'clock the following morning, Chief Inspector Andreas Nomikos was controlling the police operation from his rented room in Chora. It was Sunday 24th July, the day of the raids.

Everything was going according to plan. The police launch from Athens had almost reached the port of Paros, from where it would continue towards Naxos but remain round the headland, out of sight of the harbour, to avoid alerting the crew of the *Alkyoni*. Akis Lianos, the undercover detective on the yacht, had confirmed that the crew were going about their work as normal, and that Kakouris, Ridgeway and their wives were absent, having not spent the night on board. Andreas was satisfied: at noon his men from Athens would raid the yacht, and at the same time the Naxos police would raid the Villa Myrsini, where Theodoros Kakouris and his party were staying. There would be no time for any evidence to be destroyed or warnings given.

Andreas picked at the breakfast provided by the landlady, whose two young children he could hear in the little courtyard inside the building. There was a decent pot of coffee, bread, cheese, ham, and yogurt with honey. He ate for fuel rather than for pleasure.

When he finished, he paced the small bedroom wishing he could be doing something practical. He checked his watch. Nine forty-five. He could no longer hear the children. Outside in the street, the hum of voices and vehicles became the soundscape of his impatience. From his open window he watched a woman hanging out her washing on the balcony opposite. A taxi dropped a young couple with suitcases further down the road, and a man with a motorcycle helped his girlfriend to adjust her helmet before they rode away. With nothing more happening in the street to distract him, Andreas resumed his steady pacing.

The clamorous ringing of his mobile seemed unnaturally loud in the rented room, as if presaging an emergency. Andreas grabbed it and saw that the caller was Day.

'Andrea! I'm at the villa. Kyriakos is here. They're coming in.'

The phone went dead.

It was ten o'clock. Andreas leapt up, cursing. Two hours early. The *bloody* man!

He pressed the number for the officer in charge of the raiding party from Athens.

'Move as fast as you can on the yacht. Go now! Repeat, go now! The raid on the other target is already in progress.'

He received unquestioning confirmation. His men were professionals. Next, he called Akis Lianos.

'Liano! The local force has moved on the villa two hours early. Our launch is on its way to you now, should be there in fifteen to twenty minutes. I want you to close down the yacht. Make sure no papers are destroyed, nothing is touched, nobody leaves the boat, no calls are made. I'm on my way to the *limani*. Report to me when you can.'

He slammed the phone into his pocket and vented his frustration with a shout and some cursing as he ran down the stairs towards his car. It was about a ten-minute drive to the spot where the *Alkyoni* was moored, and he was planning to shave a few minutes off that.

Day had woken with a sense of purpose at around eight o'clock. He was pleasantly surprised at the clearness of his head, and even happier when he saw the succinct reply from Helen to his late-night email.

I'll be there as soon as I can.

It was a considerably more cheerful man, therefore, who showered, dressed and swallowed a quick coffee, before setting off for the Villa Myrsini. He had decided to disobey Andreas's instructions and go there, and had formed a plan of action. His objective was to warn Stelios about the value of the lekythos, find out who had given it to him and get well away before midday. He was fairly sure that the answer would be that Theodoros Kakouris was behind the presence of the lekythos in Stelios's safe, and that the old man would admit it to him. Andreas would have his evidence in time to arrest Kakouris, and Stelios would see that the vase must be given up to the Ephorate of Antiquities.

As he drove through the agricultural plain towards the Villa Myrsini it was still quite early. The farming and tourist sectors had been at work for hours already, but that did not prevent the country roads from being busy. He was hopeful of a successful outcome, and an energetic piece of music played in his head.

He pulled up in front of the villa at half past nine, with his plan clear in his mind. He would be away from there by eleven o'clock, well before the raid at noon, having spoken to Stelios and Maria while avoiding contact with their house guests from the *Alkyoni*. He pressed the doorbell.

Maria opened the door rather more quickly than he expected. He guessed she had heard his car. Saying nothing, she stood back from the door and gestured him to come inside. He could tell from her expression that she wanted to know what had happened between him and her brother.

'I'm sorry, Maria,' he said when she closed the door behind him. He wanted to console her, but dared not reach out. 'I'll tell you as much as I can, but not now.'

'Maria? Who is it?' came Stelios's voice.

'It's Martin, Papa.'

'Bring him in!' commanded Stelios from within the house. The three words, despite being abrupt, seemed also to convey relief.

In a strange and very different replay of his initial visit to the villa, Day was taken through the mirrored dining room and into the living room, where Stelios sat in his usual chair, facing the bronze sculpture of the kingfisher. He still wore his formal suit, but now wore it carelessly.

'Do you know about Yianni?' asked the old man. 'He's been arrested for killing poor Stefano and his wife. I can only pray that there's been a mistake.'

'Yes, I know,' said Day. 'I wish there was something helpful I could say.'

Stelios waved his walking stick in front of him in time with the shaking of his head.

'Nothing you can say, nothing. So, why have you come?'

'I'd like to talk to you about the lekythos. I have some answers and we should have a serious conversation about it. It's important.'

He was invited to sit down, but Stelios remained guarded.

'What's more important than my son?' he muttered.

'Can we talk somewhere private?' said Day. 'In your study, perhaps?' He could hear voices from elsewhere in the house. 'Maria is welcome, of course, but I'd rather no-one else overheard us.'

Maria helped her father to the library and Day closed the door. He paused to listen, but nobody seemed about to follow them inside.

'I've done what you asked, and as far as we can be sure before the experts examine it, your lekythos is probably one of the most beautiful and valuable vases to come to light in recent years.'

He quickly explained how he and his colleagues had come to believe that it might have been painted by an ancient master, possibly the one known today as the Sappho Painter, and how two fragments in Athens might have been made by an apprentice or junior craftsman copying his superior craftsmanship.

For a while, Stelios seemed able to lose himself in this story of the ancient past. He was, in that respect, something of a kindred spirit, Day thought. Lodged on the arm of her father's chair, Maria listened quietly, her eyes never leaving Day's face.

'That's as much as I can tell you. We must wait for the experts, and it's important that you contact the authorities immediately and make arrangements to give them the lekythos. Now, will you honour our agreement? Who owns it, and why did they ask you to keep it in your safe?'

The old man passed his free hand over his eyes, the hand not holding the head of his walking stick as if it was a lifeline.

'Of course, Martin, of course. It belonged to my dear friend Stefano. He and Klairi found it among her father's things soon after he passed away. They had so much to do with settling her father's affairs and building up the wine business that they forgot all about it. A while ago, Stefano came and showed it to me. He knew I was interested in these things. I said he had to hand it over to the State, because it looked like a genuine ancient vase. I know the law and so did he, but he asked me to keep it for him for a short time until he had spoken to Klairi. I agreed; what else could I do? Time passed, and then … then they were killed.'

It was at that moment, before Day could reply, that the peace of the Villa Myrsini was shattered. It was ten o'clock.

Maria ran to the window and shouted that there were police everywhere. Day followed her and looked out. A van and four marked cars were drawn up outside the villa, and armed men, some carrying rifles, were running towards the house. He pulled out his phone and called Andreas, keeping the message short. He even had the presence of mind to erase the record of the call before dropping the phone back into his pocket. It was done within a minute, by which time they could hear shouting in the house and orders being issued in the living room beyond the library door. Maria screamed when the door crashed open, and Day put his arm round her shoulder.

Two men in police uniform wearing bullet-proof vests took command of the room. One of the men, a rifle in his hands, seemed to recognise Day and said something to his companion, who came purposefully across to him. Ordering Maria to sit down, the man told Day to put his hands behind his back, removing handcuffs from his belt as he did so. Too shocked to protest, Day did as he was told. The metal closed round his wrists and the mechanism tightened with a click.

Then Kyriakos strode into the library. His face glowed and a muscle twitched in his cheek. He checked the room, registered Stelios and Maria and then focused on Day. His expression was severe. He straightened, his black jacket creaking with the authoritative sound of expensive leather.

'Martin Day, I'm arresting you on suspicion of murder and the trafficking of antiquities.'

With that, he instructed his men to take Day to the car.

Still in shock, Day was escorted out between the two armed policemen.

In the living room, the Craxton paintings looked down on a scene of chaos. Everywhere there was noise and confusion as the raiding party searched the villa. He registered hysterical protests from Maria in the room behind him, and heard Kyriakos order Stelios to open the safe. From upstairs came the sound of doors slamming and the indignant protests of Eleftheria. The Villa Myrsini had been taken over.

The whole of the ground floor was crowded, and Day and his escort were forced to wait. Theodoros Kakouris, who was not under arrest, was making a fuss. The millionaire was threatening to protest to his friend the Minister, but allowed himself to be led outside by a notably civil police escort. Ridgeway was right behind him, also in handcuffs, protesting even more indignantly in a strident British accent that could be heard even when he was outside. His wife Elodie, her hair dishevelled, was being brought downstairs to wait while the first floor was searched. She looked across at Day, who felt flushed and wrong-footed with his hands behind his back, and gave him a smile that he remembered later, a smile that seemed to suggest that she was content with what she saw.

There was no time to think about it. He was taken out and guided down the marble steps to the drive. Joined by a third armed policeman, they crossed to the waiting vehicles. The rear door of the last car stood open and Day was put inside. One of the officers got in next to him, adjusting his holster as he sat down. Shouted orders were given and the cars all started their engines. From the window, Day saw Stelios being helped into the car in front and the police van being moved to the other side of the drive to allow the convoy of cars to pass.

His final glimpse of the Villa Myrsini was of Maria crying at the library window in Christina's arms.

On board the yacht *Alkyoni* the police action was methodical. From the shore, Andreas admired the professionalism with which his men took over the vessel, secured the contents and identified the crew. They met with no resistance. Akis Lianos, highly respected as the chief of security, still had the complete co-operation of everyone from the captain down, and ensured that the boarding party quickly accessed the lower decks and storage areas of the yacht. Noise was kept to a minimum, and nobody on shore noticed much beyond the arrival of the police launch. Andreas suspected that most, if not all, of the crew were ignorant of the activities of Pierre Ridgeway, and regarded Theodoros Kakouris as a benign employer.

He stood waiting impatiently for news. There was no point in going aboard, nor in pressing for an update. After a while, he sat down on one of the benches along the edge of the quay. He was rewarded after an hour when Akis Lianos crossed the gangway and sat down next to him.

'No trouble, but nothing significant so far. There are plenty of documents to go through; they may yet give us something. We've identified the man whose job was to supervise the crates that were brought on board and those leaving the ship, and he's willing to co-operate. The captain has offered to make a statement, so I'll have both of them taken to the local station. The rest of the crew live on board; they don't have anywhere else to go, so I suggest we leave them here, impound the boat pending further investigation, and place them under restrictions.'

Andreas nodded.

'Make sure a couple of our men remain on guard at all times,' he said. 'One other thing I want you to do for me. There's a block of marble on public display somewhere; it will be in some big showy place where they hold parties. Find it and make sure it isn't touched. It may be important. It's too heavy to move, of course, but put a guard on it till further notice. Understood? And good work, Liano. Very good.'

Andreas strode away from the harbour, well pleased. The leader of the police team from Athens would report to him shortly, after which he would call Tsountas. He wondered what the hell was happening at the Villa Myrsini. Day should have been nowhere near.

Andreas had a very bad feeling.

26

The police convoy took the direct route at speed along the Naxos-Apeiranthos road and reached the outskirts of Chora in about fifteen minutes. They slowed when they neared the town, and when they stopped at a junction by the Orthodox Church of Agios Nikodimos, they created a spectacle for the people who had just left its sacred precincts. They all paused to stare at the white police vehicles and tried to catch a glimpse of those inside. Day, forced to lean slightly forward on account of the handcuffs, found their scrutiny humiliating.

At last they reached the station and pulled up outside, once again becoming the object of curious attention as people shopping in the *plateia* turned to watch and others gazed from the café tables. A boy peered in at Day through the car window. When his turn came to be taken inside, he had to be helped from the back seat. A woman he knew slightly stared at him in astonishment from the opposite side of the road.

With the reinforced doors of the station secured behind them, his handcuffs were removed and he was told to empty his pockets onto the desk. His mobile, wallet and keys were placed in a bag which was put in a box, his name was written and his signature required. Instructions were given for his mobile to be examined. He saw no point in protesting, since Andreas would put everything right soon enough, but his anger was hard to control. Further down the room, Ridgeway was undergoing similar treatment; he too was doing as he was told, and then he was led away.

Day was taken to a room where a forensic officer asked him to remove his shirt. Samples were taken from beneath his nails, and the cuts and scratches on his hands and body were photographed while his shirt was cursorily examined. His shoes were sealed in a plastic evidence bag, and he realised they were to be taken away. In the circumstances, he thought, the police were only doing their job, so he did all that he was asked. He even allowed his mouth to be swabbed for DNA and his body to be lightly searched. Still buttoning up his shirt, and now barefoot, he was taken though the station and up a flight of stairs to the floor above, where he hoped he might find Andreas waiting for them. Unfortunately, that was not the case.

He had never given a thought to what a cell in the Naxos police station might be like, but had he done so he would have been wrong. Far from the windowless box he might have imagined, this was like a cage at the zoo, the front wall and door consisting only of bars. Through them the prisoner could see the corridor and could easily be seen himself. There was, of course, no privacy. From his enclosure he could also hear a lot of what was said downstairs in the station. That was how he learned that Stelios had been interviewed and released without charge, and that Captain John was thanked and allowed to leave. Theodoros made a big fuss until a lawyer arrived, and shortly afterwards Theodoros too was gone.

These things helped Day to bear the slow passage of time which would otherwise have been even harder. Hours passed. When he wanted the bathroom he was escorted. No food or drink had been offered, and he wanted none. At last, the noise level fell until all he could hear from below was the low hum of men's voices and the occasional command from Kyriakos. He had no idea what was going on, and the man whose job appeared to be to check on him periodically through the bars did not volunteer a word.

He wished he could sleep to alleviate the tedium. He sat on the narrow, steel-framed bed which was the only furniture in the cell, stretched and flexed his arms. There was no sound from Ridgeway, even though their cells were not far from each other. He wondered how long he could put up with this before demanding to speak to Andreas.

Then he heard the crisp footsteps of police-issue boots, footsteps which turned out to belong to Captain Skouros accompanied by a junior officer who carried a set of keys. Skouros ordered Day to remain at the back of the cell, and the young officer unlocked the door for him. Skouros came inside and the door was locked behind him. Day realised he was not about to be released.

The police captain held out a slim file.

'This is the warrant for your arrest and lists the charges against you,' he said in English. 'It explains your right to request a lawyer and an interpreter. As a foreign national, you are permitted to call your consulate, and you may telephone one member of your family or someone close to you to inform them of your situation. Do you have any questions?'

Day took the papers from him and shook his head.

'Please read the document at once and give us your decision on your options. You will be interviewed by Inspector Tsountas in a few hours, and you would be well advised to have a lawyer present.

As it is Sunday, it may not be easy for a lawyer to be found, so the sooner you ask for one, the better. Do you understand?'

'Yes, I understand.'

Skouros nodded and left. Day was once again swallowed up by the solitude of distant sounds. Some time later, he heard the same procedure being followed with Ridgeway.

The documents were in *katharevousa*, the formal language used in legal transactions, and Day was looking through them for the second or third time when Kyriakos appeared in the corridor and stood watching him through the bars. Kyriakos was smiling, a smile of grim satisfaction rather than friendliness or amusement. From the smell of him, he had just enjoyed one of his favourite cigarettes.

'*Kalispera*, Martin,' he said, placing an unpleasant emphasis on Day's name. 'I was so pleased to find you at the Villa Myrsini this morning. It saved us a lot of trouble. I shall speak to you again shortly, and I'm sure I'll find what you tell me very enlightening. You enjoy enlightening people, don't you, Martin?'

He scratched the side of his nose thoughtfully, never taking his eyes off Day, who said nothing.

'Rather than instructing the rest of us, perhaps it's time to give some thought to your own situation. How does it feel, being behind bars? It must be quite disconcerting for a man of your education. Perhaps you should get used to it.'

Still Day said nothing. Kyriakos was making no attempt now to conceal his personal animosity. When he pushed a large envelope through the bars so that it fell on the concrete floor of the cell, Day chose not to bend and pick it up. It lay on the ground between them like a gauntlet.

'You should read that,' said Kyriakos. 'I've just served you with the official allegations against you as authorised by the public prosecutor. You are now officially charged with the murder of Vassos Nikolopoulos. Other charges will be brought against you under Antiquities Law 3028-2002 for activities contravening the laws protecting the cultural heritage of Greece.'

'This is all ridiculous, Kyriako.'

Kyriakos Tsountas laughed in his face.

'I'd advise you not to take that tone with me, Martin, not in your position. Look around you - perhaps you should show some respect. And I hope your Greek is good enough to understand the charges, because no interpreter is available. I'll send for you in a few hours. Then we'll see how confident you feel.'

Kyriakos walked away and Day heard him telling someone to bring Ridgeway to the interview room in ten minutes. He later heard the order being obeyed. Pierre Ridgeway protested hotly as he was fetched from his cell, but soon they were all gone and a deeper stillness flooded back into the corridor.

'Oh God!' he thought, as he picked up the envelope. 'Oh God. Where are you, Andrea, and what on earth do you expect me to do now?'

Day read the charges several times, trying to work out the legal language before being questioned again by Kyriakos. As it turned out, there was no rush. He heard Ridgeway being returned to his cell after what seemed about an hour. After that, nothing happened at all. It felt like being in a small room backstage in a theatre, waiting to go on, with no sense of where the actors had reached in the drama, and no idea of your own lines. He was given a sandwich and a small plastic bottle of water, and was watched as he ate. He later required the bathroom, and a man was found to escort him. After that, there was once again the emptiness of his own company, with nothing whatever to do except think.

The light faded as evening arrived; finally, only the emergency bulbs gave a dim glow. He guessed it was late in the evening when he was told he was to be taken to the interview room. He was so tired by then that he felt sure the timing was deliberate. The same man who had taken him to the bathroom returned to fetch him. Having ordered him to move to the back of the cell, the young officer came in, handcuffed him and took him out. Day supposed that Yianni, too, had been handcuffed even within the police station, but there was no time to think of that now. Ridgeway stared at him from his cell as they passed.

He was taken to the ground-floor room where he had been interviewed before, after the deaths of Stefanos and Klairi. A muscular officer waiting inside pointed Day to one of the chairs at the table. He sat down obediently. The young policeman who had brought him from the cell removed his handcuffs and took up position beside the door.

For a while there was silence. The two guards watched him from either side of the room. Then Kyriakos arrived carrying a slim file and took the seat opposite him. He spoke into the recording machine in Greek, and continued in Greek for the rest of the interview. Day could understand well enough, not only the words, but the menace and personal antipathy that lay behind them.

Having repeated the charges for the benefit of the machine, Kyriakos looked at him for the first time and gave a malicious smile that just as quickly vanished.

'Martin Day. Or should that be Doctor, or perhaps Professor? *According to Greek law, you have the right to remain silent and it will not be held against you, although when you come to trial it may be asked why you did not mention any facts that might help your case.* This is much the same as in your country, I believe. So, let's begin by making one thing very clear: I'm not a man who tolerates my time being wasted. I expect you to answer my questions fully and accurately. It would save us both a lot of time if you made a complete confession.'

Day stared at him and said nothing.

'Nothing to say, Martin?'

'I don't believe you've asked me anything yet.'

'Let's begin, then, with the most serious charge against you: that you murdered Vassos Nikolopoulos on the night of Friday 22nd July.'

'I had nothing to do with that. I told you, I flew back from Athens that afternoon and spent the rest of the night at my house in Filoti.'

'Let's be clear, however. You have nobody to corroborate that, do you? You travelled alone and you spent the night alone. Basically, you have no alibi whatsoever.'

Day tightened his lips and said nothing.

'As I thought. Then let's consider the following morning, when the body of Nikolopoulos was discovered in the swimming pool at the Villa Myrsini. You were present when the body was retrieved from the water.'

'You know I was. I've already explained.'

'According to you, you arrived very early that morning to speak to Maria Ioannides about something which you say you cannot divulge, and of which she is completely unaware. Kyrie Kakouris, however, remembers you saying that you had come to speak to her father. You seem to have changed your story, Martin. That gives a very bad impression.'

He looked down at his papers.

'You were scratched, dishevelled and bleeding when found by the police, which you explained by saying you entered through thorny vegetation rather than coming through the front door. I find that strange, you see.'

'I heard Maria scream, the door was locked. It was the only way to reach her.'

Kyriakos gave a theatrical sigh and shook his head. He appeared to be rather enjoying himself. He suggested that Day had, in fact, attacked and killed the victim the previous night, having lured him into the garden on a pretext in order to do so.

'Having killed him and watched him sink to the bottom of the swimming pool, you ran away. You went through the junipers so you wouldn't be seen from the house, and that's how you first sustained the bloody scratches that we observed on you the next day.

'The following morning, you needed to return to the scene of your crime to make sure that your victim was truly dead. He was, as we know. Then you tried to convince the family that you, Martin Day, were a friend who only wished to offer your help and support.'

Day was silent.

'Still nothing to say? You'll be only too happy to talk when put under pressure by my colleagues on the mainland. I thought you might prefer to speak to me.'

'Get Andreas Nomikos. I'll only talk to him.'

Kyriakos scowled.

'You're being a fool. It won't help you to be stubborn.'

'I'm completely innocent of this murder, and I demand to speak to Andreas Nomikos.'

'I'm afraid you're in no position to demand anything. I see you haven't asked for a lawyer. Rather proud of your own abilities, are you?'

'No, I've nothing to hide,' said Day, who had assumed that Andreas would not want a lawyer involved, and that he would have no need of one.

'You're disappointing me, Martin,' muttered Kyriakos, and returned his attention to the file on the table.

'The other charge against you relates to your beloved archaeology. Here I must confess that I'm intrigued. Though carrying a lesser sentence than murder, this speaks to me of a highly duplicitous man. You seem to have convinced members of the Hellenic

Police that you are an *asset* in the retrieval of stolen antiquities, and yet it seems that you yourself are one of the criminals. More interested in your personal wealth, I assume. You may shake your head, but the evidence is convincing. According to your bank records, you received a large sum of money shortly after arrests were made in connection with the robbery of a private collection in the Peloponnese.'

'That was the reward offered by the owner for the return of the stolen goods,' protested Day angrily.

'Was it, though? Not all the artefacts were recovered. Some have never been traced. Nor was the entire gang apprehended; in particular, its leader was never caught. I suggest that your payment was for arranging that the key members of the syndicate remained at large with a proportion of the haul.'

'That's absurd. Check your facts, Kyriako. The money was paid by a firm of lawyers in New York.'

'Oh, and that means it's legitimate? Naturally it does! There are no corrupt lawyers in America.'

'Come on! You know me, we've worked together. Remember the discovery in Spedos Bay? I arranged its excavation by the proper authorities, and I asked you personally to place a guard on it. It's crazy to think I'd break the antiquities law.'

'I certainly do recollect the discovery in Spedos Bay, but you could hardly spirit that thing away unnoticed, could you?' said Kyriakos. 'More transportable and less readily identifiable items are easier to sell, I imagine.'

He consulted the documents in front of him again.

'Let's consider a few of your recent associates. It's all well-documented here: my predecessor has left excellent records.'

He lifted a sheet of paper from the table and held it ostentatiously in front of him, appearing to find it difficult to know where to start.

'You seem to have quite an extraordinary number of criminal acquaintances. For instance, there was the infamous Emil Gautier and his collaborator, Jim Grogan. Both these men were smuggling ancient artefacts out of Greece from Kalados Bay here on Naxos. The man who owned the boat which transported the objects for them was a man with whom you were at university. You used to socialise together, in fact - before his arrest, of course. Ah, and here's something interesting. Before you betrayed these men to the police in order to distract attention from yourself, you famously 'discovered' an ancient tomb near Melanes. This tomb, I see here, *appeared to have already been plundered*. I'm quoting the police report. Who might have plundered it, do you think? I suggest the answer is that you yourself were responsible for that, before cynically reporting your discovery to the authorities.'

Day maintained a contemptuous silence rather than give Kyriakos the pleasure of seeing his growing distress.

'There's a lot more here. Think back to the occasion when the police, led by your friend Nomikos, apprehended the thief Sotiris Artsanos, together with his haul of stolen antiquities. Artsanos was armed with a shotgun; you claimed that he would have killed you but for the timely arrival of the police. Yet he did *not* kill you, and subsequently you received the credit for the recovery of the stolen goods. Those that *were* recovered, that is. Perhaps you had found time to help yourself to them? Tell me about your relationship with Sotiris Artsanos.'

When he received no reply, Kyriakos slammed his fist on the table.

'You will only be given so many chances to co-operate!' he shouted.

Again, silence. When he next spoke, Kyriakos did so very quietly.

'Trust me, Martin, you *will* confess, sooner or later.'

'Get me Andreas Nomikos. This is a farce!'

'Who is Jacques Avian?'

'A colleague. A highly respected historian.'

'He poses as a lecturer in art history, or some such, at the Sorbonne,' continued Kyriakos. 'He also knows a great deal about the Parisian black market in antiquities, an interesting sideline. Your friend Jacques is *intimate*, in fact, with the underground world in which ancient artefacts change hands. He seems to be operating barely within the law. And yet you've kept up a close friendship with him over the years. Why is that?'

'I like to communicate with people who know what they're talking about,' Day snapped. His dislike of Kyriakos Tsountas had become a slow-burning rage that he hoped he could continue to control.

'Jacques Avian is an extremely suspicious individual, and your association with him puts you in a very bad light. Come on now, you need to take a reality check, Martin. You're in more trouble than even you can imagine.'

He allowed another silence to fall, never taking his eyes off Day.

'I was interested to learn of your recent visit to the yacht *Alkyoni*. Kyrie Kakouris has given us some very helpful information concerning your behaviour on that occasion. He told me that you showed a strong interest in some kind of ancient vase. You also availed yourself of the opportunity to search the boat for precious artefacts; the vessel's captain corroborated this only a few hours ago. Kyrie Kakouris admits that he was afraid to challenge you at the time, because he had to consider the safety of the women on board. He felt that you could turn violent.'

Day shook his head at his own stupidity. Andreas had even warned him: *Nothing Kakouris does is likely to be without purpose*. Kakouris's invitation to drinks on the yacht had been no more than a piece of strategy. He had shown Day the reproduction vase in front of witnesses who would put whatever slant on the story he told them to. Should there arise a need to misdirect the police from his own activities, he could then point them towards Day, and it had only cost him a cocktail.

'You see, things are looking rather bad for you, aren't they? Now we come to the best part: your fellow Brit, Pierre Ridgeway. The proof of his illegal trading is substantial and his conviction is inevitable. In addition to the evidence already acquired by the IAFA, Kyrie Kakouris has made a sworn statement concerning Ridgeway's criminal activities. And we understand that you and Ridgeway have been working together for several years. Don't look so shocked; surely you knew? Actually, I don't even need you to admit it, since Ridgeway has already given me a very damning account of your collaboration in the hope of a more lenient sentence.'

'No!' shouted Day. 'I'd never heard of Ridgeway until two weeks ago.'

He knew he was flushed with anger and on the verge of panic. Kakouris had abandoned Ridgeway, who had seen a way to pass the blame onto Day in his own interests.

'Control yourself, Martin. Your friend Ridgeway is trying to help you. He's actually asserting that the death of Nikolopoulos was an accident. Amusing, isn't it? One has to admire loyalty among thieves. Do you know what an anakritis is, Martin? In our legal system, the anakritis is the investigative judge with responsibility for preparing the case for trial. Be in no doubt, the anakritis will prove that you and Ridgeway are criminal associates, and that you murdered Nikolopoulos to protect your illegal activities.'

It was more than Day could take. He stood up in a rage and slammed his hands hard on the table in front of Kyriakos. He may have let out a shout. Alarmed by his own emotions, he knocked over his chair as he flung himself back to avoid doing something he would regret. He was forced to regret it anyway. The muscular arm of the Naxos police restrained him at once. Breathless, he was held there in front of Kyriakos.

He was furious to see that Kyriakos Tsountas was smiling.

'I want to see Andreas Nomikos,' he shouted, much louder than he intended.

'That's enough. It's I who decide who you see and do not see. Nomikos will not be sympathetic to your profiteering interest in antiquities, I suspect. And he is not in charge of this murder investigation; I am.'

Kyriakos folded his arms and stared up at Day. He seemed to be deciding how to proceed. His look was vindictive, but calculating. Day tensed, fearing violence against which he would be helpless.

'In accordance with the law,' said Kyriakos finally, 'you'll be brought before the anakritis within five days of your arrest. At this point you may present your defence. The anakritis has the power to order your continued detention until the trial. As you're a foreign national, considered in law to be a flight risk, and as you're charged with premeditated murder, that will most certainly be his decision. Thereafter, you should expect to remain in custody pending trial for a period of up to twelve months, possibly longer. You'll be held in a mainland prison and cross-examined. You will not, I promise you, enjoy that at all.'

Kyriakos ended the interrogation with a few cursory words into the recorder. With a sideways motion of the chin, he ordered his officer to return Day to his cell.

Day's night was one of the worst he could remember.

He was stiff and sore. He had tripped and fallen on the concrete staircase leading back to his cell, an apparent accident in which he had landed hard on the steps and against the wall. He had been unable to save himself because once again he had been handcuffed.

He had felt a hand on his back as he went down, and suspected that this was a punishment for his outburst.

He lay down on the bed in his cell with his knees in the air because he was too tall to fit. He had two blankets, one beneath him and one over him, but neither made him comfortable. The pillow stank of other men's hair and some less recognisable odours. He had been given a final pre-packaged sandwich and told there would be nobody to take him to the bathroom till morning.

The man who told him this did so with a semblance of sympathy as he wished him goodnight. Day thought he recognised the man from his former visits to the Naxos police. Those had been good times, times when he and Andreas had discovered a shared passion for the fight against antiquity crime, and when the now-retired Inspector Cristopoulos had visited him at his house to ask his opinion.

The lights went out, leaving Day to think about his situation until he was able to sleep. He tried to persuade himself that Andreas must be working on the case against Ridgeway and Kakouris, and that he would come and put matters right in the morning. Nevertheless, with no distraction but the sound of Ridgeway snoring further down the corridor, it was hard to be positive when he thought back to the interrogation. Months in prison on the mainland. Cross-examination techniques that he had no wish to experience. Most chilling of all, the ambitious Kyriakos determined to see him convicted of murder.

The following day, Monday, he spent almost entirely alone in his cell. He was told, when he decided to ask for one, that no lawyer would be available. His time was punctuated by meals and bathroom visits, and the occasional indistinct conversation from downstairs. He heard no familiar voice as he listened in vain for Andreas. At one point, Ridgeway lost control and had a bout of shouting, but it got him nowhere and he was left to vent his feelings alone.

He wondered whether Yianni had been kept in this same cell, and where he was now. It was all a far cry from the usual drunk, or petty thief, who might normally find himself here, quickly dealt with and as quickly released. One or two policemen had come to stare at him; perhaps one day they would tell their grandchildren that they had once detained two men in the same month on charges of premeditated murder. Day could feel their contempt.

He began to slip into depression. The gravity of his situation was undeniable, and his agreement with Andreas had begun to feel unreal. The prospect of the struggle that lay ahead of him made his chest constrict. Would he be able to fight this? He was accused of trading in the ancient heritage of Greece, and of killing to save himself from discovery. He felt a strange kind of guilt, even though he had done nothing of which he was accused, and if he was beginning to believe it himself, perhaps everyone else would too. Why would they not, especially if he was brought to trial and convicted? He himself had begun to suspect Fabrizio, after all, something he now deeply regretted. In the same way, he thought, his friends would eventually believe that he was truly capable of murder and had betrayed the heritage that he cared more about than anything in the world except Helen.

The thought of Helen brought panic shooting to the surface, yet the more he fought against it, the more desperate he felt. Oh God! She was on her way to Naxos. He cursed himself for sending the email that had made her decide to fly back to Greece. Perhaps she had been calling him and received no reply. His request to use the single phone call he was permitted had not been denied, but neither had it been granted. He needed to get word to Helen, and only Andreas could do that now.

On the few occasions that he saw someone, whether they had come to stare at him or were simply passing down the corridor, Day begged to see Chief Inspector Nomikos. A few of the policemen shrugged regretfully, most ignored him. One suggested he was mad. As the light grew dim again with the onset of the second night, Day admitted to himself that he was afraid. According to Andreas, Kyriakos was ruthless, ambitious and unprincipled; he would not be the first casualty of Kyriakos's ambition.

Why was Andreas not showing his hand to get him out of there? Only that same slow-burning anger that had kindled in the interview room sustained Day in any small way through the second long, uncomfortable night.

27

Andreas ended the video call with Dimitris Delimbaris, the anakritis who would be dealing with the prosecution of Pierre Ridgeway. The most recent discussion had lasted almost an hour, and it was their third call of the day. Andreas had been working on the current charge against Ridgeway since the arrests the day before, because the case against him had to be in place before the legal deadline. It needed to be water-tight, given the man's international reputation as one of the most trustworthy and scrupulous dealers in art and antiquities. As with many of Andreas's antiquity fraud investigations, tthe complexity of the matter was phenomenal, and he would have much more work to do over the coming months. In the case of Pierre Ridgeway, the trail went back over a decade, and every aspect had to be transparent before the case reached the courts. Only when Judge Delimbaris declared himself satisfied did Andreas allow himself to sit back in the chair with a sigh of relief.

'Excellent work, Nomiko, I wish they were all like you,' the anakritis had said just before disappearing from the screen.

Andreas wondered whether Delimbaris's last comment, delivered with dry sarcasm, had anything to do with a certain chief of police who was currently in charge of a murder case. He would put money on the anakritis not having received a competent submission from Tsountas in the case against Martin Day, and looked forward to having the opportunity to read it for himself.

That would have to wait, unfortunately. He forced himself to open another folder on his computer, the one containing his work on Theodoros Kakouris. For an hour or more, as the sun set over Naxos far from the window of Andreas's rented room, he checked every detail, every report and every statement for what he feared would be the last time. Finally, he shook his head and closed the laptop with as much restraint as he could, given the degree of his frustration. He had to face the fact that he simply had insufficient evidence on which to authorise any further investigation into the millionaire's activities. Whatever objects of beauty and history Kakouris may have acquired on his recent trip round the Aegean, stopping at islands just long enough to transact an interesting piece of business at each one, they were not to be found on the boat. Nor had they turned up at the Villa Myrsini. Nothing had been found anywhere near the magnate to indicate an ulterior motive to the summer cruise of the *Alkyoni*.

He would have to go out soon, find something to eat, stretch his legs. His eyes were red and sore from too long in front of a screen, and he was in need of food. A beer would be welcome too. From below, he could hear the children of the house being given their dinner. He had one last thing to do, and he had better do it first, distasteful though it was.

'Inspector Tsountas, please. This is Chief Inspector Nomikos.'

'Yes, sir. One moment.'

When he was put through, he wasted no time on civilities. He required, he said, an update on the previous day's search of the Villa Myrsini.

'You can start with why you initiated the raid two hours earlier than I instructed,' he told Tsountas coldly.

'Well, sir, I had reason to believe that the suspects had become aware of the proposed action, and a surprise arrival by our team would prevent the destruction of evidence.'

'You can put the details in your report, which I want in my hands tomorrow morning. Include, please, the reason behind your failure to consult me, as operation commander, before acting unilaterally.'

He was slightly mollified to hear a less arrogant tone when Tsountas acknowledged this order.

'So, what did you find during the search of the villa?' he continued.

'We opened the safe, where we found the vase that you mentioned, Chief Inspector. There was also some money, and an artist's sketchbook which appears to be old and which Stelios Ioannides states belongs to him. Some documents, including a copy of the owner's will and the title deeds to the estate. I have everything safely here at the station. Elsewhere in the villa we found art works and sculptures, all modern, which I ordered to be photographed and recorded, and those were left at the property.'

'And Stelios Ioannides? He was brought in?'

'He was. After questioning, he signed a statement and was released without charge. His daughter and niece came to fetch him as he's practically disabled. I was satisfied that he had nothing to do with the criminal activities of those around him. I managed to get the story of the vase out of him. It belonged to the man who was killed, the one who ran the wine festival.'

'Stefanos Patelis?'

'Yes, that's right, sir. Apparently, Patelis felt in debt to Ioannides, who had used his influence to arrange the immediate performance of an operation on Patelis's wife which probably saved her life. Patelis made him a present of the old vase.'

'By 'old vase' you mean the valuable lekythos in the safe?'

'Yes, sir. Old man Ioannides claims he told Patelis that he couldn't accept the gift, and that it must be handed in to the state authorities because it looked like a valuable old piece of antiquity and that was the law. Patelis agreed in the end, but wanted a bit of time to explain to his wife because the vase had belonged to her father and had sentimental value for her. Ioannides agreed to keep the vase in his safe for a while, and then Patelis and his wife were killed. After that, he tried to find out more about it. He showed it to both Ridgeway and Day.'

'Did he?' said Andreas, surprised for the first time.

'Well, it makes sense: Day an archaeologist and Ridgeway a dealer in antiquities. He swears he was going to call the Greek Archaeological Service, but he was curious about the old thing. He likes that kind of stuff, apparently.'

'Kyrie Ioannides specifically told you that he showed the artefact to Ridgeway?'

'Yes, sir. It remains to be seen whether Ridgeway and Day were acting together, but that is my belief. Ioannides has signed a statement confirming all that I've told you, which will form part of the evidence against both the suspects.'

Andreas let this pass, despite a strong urge to bruise the man's insufferable arrogance. That satisfaction would, he hoped, ultimately be granted to him.

'Next, Theodoros Kakouris, please. Status?'

'Released under caution yesterday. I've never seen a lawyer appear so fast, sir, and it was Sunday too. There was nothing to incriminate Kakouris at the villa, and your man Lianos found nothing on the yacht either. We can hold the boat another twenty-four hours, but I don't expect we'll find anything now. Probably tipped off.'

'Release the yacht,' said Andreas, suppressing a sigh. 'We can't detain it any longer. If the old vase, as you call it, had turned out to belong to Kakouris, we would have had him, but without that we have nothing. Return their passports to Kakouris and the two women immediately and let them leave the island if they wish. The crew too. I assume you took statements from the boat captain and the crewman that Lianos sent to you?'

'Yes, sir. The crewman's testimony confirms Ridgeway's responsibility for the crates of artefacts that were sent to Paris and London in his name, and the captain confirms showing Day round the ship, and his curiosity about everything.'

'I expect you and I would also show signs of curiosity in a luxury yacht,' growled Andreas. 'The captain and the crewman, where are they now?'

'Back on the yacht at their posts.'

'Right. Pierre Ridgeway and Martin Day. They were both arrested at the villa and remain in custody, I assume? I've spent most of today discussing the evidence against Ridgeway with the anakritis, Judge Delimbaris. He's satisfied with the details of the charges, to which should be added the statement from the crewman. You can start to make arrangements for Ridgeway's transportation to the mainland. The authorisation is on its way to you. You've got a lawyer for him? An interpreter?'

'Both, sir. I understand Ridgeway has been advised by his lawyer to make a confession in exchange for lenient treatment.'

'A confession? Well, we'll see. Now, Martin Day. Tell me about him.'

'Refusing to co-operate.' Tsountas laughed drily and not without pleasure. 'He's been charged with the murder of Nikolopoulos, and I've prepared the evidence for the anakritis accordingly. I also questioned him about the antiquity trading offences which you'll be dealing with, and prepared a document for your inspection.'

Andreas grunted.

'I interrogated Day last night, told him what he was facing and advised him to talk, but he's an arrogant one. He'll change his mind when he finds himself in Korydallos.'

Andreas clamped his jaws tightly. The name of Greece's most inhumane prison was anathema to all right-thinking Greeks.

'I believe he's been asking to speak to me?' he said at last, thanks to one of the junior officers in Tsountas's command.

'He may have said that.'

'I shall come to the station tomorrow at ten in the morning. Kindly arrange the interview room for me. I'll require your presence during the interrogation, of course.'

'Thank you, sir. Everything will be ready.'

Ten minutes after the phone call, Andreas was sitting at a nearby bar with a beer. He needed to wash a very bad taste out of his mouth.

He also needed to think, so he forced himself to drink slowly. He had lost Kakouris, that was for sure, but at least he had put an end to the activities of the pernicious Pierre Ridgeway. In Athens, his colleagues were even now investigating Ridgeway's international network of contacts and clients. There was no end to this business, and Andreas was quite sure that he would still be pursuing the criminals who traded in Greek cultural heritage when the time came for him to retire.

Nothing was ever simple, however, and he would never be able to convince himself that his involvement of Martin Day had been justified by the outcome. Or should that be 'outcomes'? He was beginning to look forward to the interrogation session the following morning with Kyriakos Tsountas at his side. He ordered another beer from the bar and a plate of food. He told them to bring whatever they liked and a salad to go with it. With a slight inclination of the head and a courteous smile, the proprietor left with his order and Andreas settled down to make his detailed plan for the next morning.

His mobile rang in his pocket and he tried to ignore it. The ringing stopped and began again almost at once. Reluctantly, he reached for the phone and looked at the name of the caller.

It was Helen Aitchison.

28

Andreas sat alone in the interview room at Naxos police station, two documents in front of him. He chose to begin with Tsountas's report on the raid at the Villa Myrsini, which had been made available to him on arrival as he had instructed. The second folder contained the charges against Martin Day. He would come to that next.

He read carefully, only occasionally shifting his position or emitting a grunt when he needed to relieve his feelings. There was nothing in the report of the raid beyond what he already knew, and no evidence to support Tsountas's decision to disobey his orders. Not only that, but they could anticipate trouble from Kakouris's lawyers. He blamed himself to some extent for not sharing with Tsountas the disparity in the strength of evidence against Ridgeway and the millionaire. At least the man had stopped short of arresting Kakouris.

He opened the other file, which contained Tsountas's notes on Day's supposed antiquities offences. He read the inspector's enthusiastic overview with incredulity and contempt. He then moved on to the official murder charge and had to read it a second time. It made uncomfortable reading and had already been given the initial approval of the public prosecutor. The evidence was largely circumstantial, but even so it left Day in an unenviable position. Andreas imagined that his friend must by now be very worried.

He closed the file and sat back, running his fingers through his mane of fair hair and then resting his hands firmly on the arms of his chair. His face was impassive, but his mind was busy. Occasionally he sniffed, a decision made, an approach formulated. He allowed his eyes to wander round the blank walls of the windowless interview room, but they were registering nothing. He reached inside his jacket and brought out his phone, checked it, nodded, replaced it.

'*Elate!*' he called.

The door opened and the young officer who had been standing outside in the corridor entered at once.

'Please tell Inspector Tsountas that I'd like to begin now,' Andreas said.

The officer nodded smartly and closed the door again. His footsteps receded as he went to obey the instruction. Several minutes passed before Kyriakos let himself into the room and shook hands with Andreas. Taking the seat next to him, he asked what role the chief inspector wished him to take in the interrogation.

'Perhaps you would begin. I shall take over when I'm ready.'

There was a rap at the door and it was opened by the same young officer as before, who came inside and took up a position at the side of the room. He was followed by Day and Skouros. Day was given the chair opposite Andreas and the handcuffs were not removed. No lawyer or interpreter took the chair next to him.

Day had not slept well on the second night of his detention. He had refused food and taken only a little water since waking. He had convinced himself during the hours of darkness that nothing would happen until the end of the five days during which he could legally be kept in the police station, at which point Kyriakos would do whatever he wanted with him. He feared that would be to send him somewhere a great deal worse than here. He had given up hope of Andreas.

Captain Skouros and a junior officer had appeared outside his cell about half way through the morning, and again he was told to move to the back wall. He had already begun to do so. The young policeman unlocked the door and Skouros came in, preparing the handcuffs. Day offered his wrists.

The sight of Andreas in the interview room brought no surge of relief. Andreas was expressionless, his chin slightly raised, his hands clenched on the table. Day was made to sit opposite him. Kyriakos, who sat proudly on Andreas's right, casually switched on the recorder.

'Chief Inspector Andreas Nomikos of the IAFA, and Inspector Kyriakos Tsountas of Naxos police, interviewing Martin Day,' he announced into the machine, adding the date and time, and addressed himself coldly to Day.

'Martin, you are charged with the murder of Vassos Nikolopoulos on the night of Friday 22nd July at the Villa Myrsini. The victim was known to you as a friend of Stelios Ioannides, by whom you had been employed to give two talks on Greek antiquity. Correct?'

'Yes.'

'You failed to admit, when first interviewed, that the last time you saw Nikolopoulos alive was when he and Kyrie Ioannides showed you an ancient object they kept in the safe. Why did you lie about that?'

Day simply shook his head.

'Was it because this was when you decided to acquire the object for yourself, by whatever means necessary?'

Day shook his head again, with a glance at Andreas.

'If you failed to persuade him to sell it to you,' went on Kyriakos, 'which no doubt you hoped to do for a fraction of its true value, you were confident that there would be other ways to get hold of it, weren't you? This would be all the easier since only the two old men knew of its existence.'

'Rubbish! I merely examined the lekythos and gave my cautious opinion that it might be genuine.'

'Genuine? I'm told it's a great deal more important than that.'

'Yes, it is. I wasn't qualified to assume so at the time.'

'Is that so? Whatever the truth of it, soon after you suggested to its owner that he should let you have the artefact, Vassos Nikolopoulos interfered with your plan. Come on now, Martin, you might as well give us the truth. He told you to think again, that he'd recognised you for the con-man you are and would stop you getting your hands on the vase. That must have been an unwelcome blow for you, Martin. Perhaps not a complete surprise, though? You were already prepared to do something about it. So, tell me, what exactly *did* you do?'

He waited in vain for Day to respond, and resumed with undisguised malevolence.

'Let me tell you, then. You invited Nikolopoulos to meet you alone in the garden. I expect you assured him your intentions were honest, that you would explain everything. You hoped to persuade him to withdraw his objections. Perhaps you would have tried a bribe, as the man had no money. And if all else failed, Martin, you were prepared to kill him. Exactly when you made the decision to kill him will be for the anakritis to establish.'

Kyriakos got up from the table and walked round to stand behind Day's chair. Day tensed.

'You met by the swimming pool some time after midnight,' continued Kyriakos from behind him, 'once everyone else had retired to their rooms. It was not as easy as you'd hoped, was it? Nikolopoulos refused to back down, and you had to act decisively. Again I ask you, what did you do?'

'Nothing. I wasn't there.'

Kyriakos's face appeared suddenly next to Day's right eye, and he shouted into Day's ear.

'You knocked him unconscious and pushed him into the pool. That's what you did. Then you left him there, motionless in the water, to die. And then what happened? Something caught your eye from the house, and you thought someone had seen you.'

'This is bloody madness!'

Kyriakos gave a short derisive laugh and returned to his place at the table. He stood leaning on his hands, his face close to Day's.

'You were now terrified of discovery and capture. You are basically a coward. You fled towards the darkest part of the garden and forced your way out through the thorny vegetation. Your car must have been hidden out of sight down the road, and you managed to sneak back to it under cover of the trees. You'd made it! There was nothing now to connect you with the murder. Providing, of course, that nobody had seen you.'

Day remained tight-lipped. He could no longer bear to look at Kyriakos's gloating face, nor at Andreas's blank expression and cold eyes. He stared instead at the hands clipped together in his lap and tried to wait out the interview.

'Ah, Martin. Should we feel sorry for you? Did you hope that Yianni Ioannides would be blamed for your cowardly attack on Nikolopoulos? That would have been convenient for you. Unfortunately, it was never going to happen. Yianni Ioannides, guilty though he was of a double murder, had an alibi for the killing at the pool that night. Unlike yourself.'

Day looked up sharply, but there was nothing he wanted to say.

'Wouldn't you like to know who saw you from the window of the villa when you killed the old man? Could it have been the beautiful Maria? What must she think of you now?'

He thrust his face closer to Day's, his breath chilling the sweat on Day's skin.

'I think you're ready to confess, Martin,' he purred. 'It would make everything so much easier, you know. You'd feel so much better.'

He waited for Day's resistance to break, and went on with contempt in his voice when the confession he wanted showed no sign of coming.

'The next day, you were desperate to find out if you'd been seen. You also needed to make quite sure that your victim was dead. You wanted to stand over the body and know your way forward was clear. Perhaps you'd get a chance to comfort your friend Stelios and cheer him up by suggesting you'd take his priceless vase to be authenticated. Who knows what went on in your mind, but you were clever enough to return to the garden that morning through the thicket to give yourself fresh scratches to disguise the ones you sustained the previous night.'

'You're barking mad!' shouted Day, suddenly overwhelmed by anger. He glared at both Kyriakos and Andreas, and pounded his handcuffed hands on the table in exasperation. 'I demand a lawyer!'

He seemed unable to stop drumming his fists.

Skouros made a move towards him, but drew back when Andreas raised his right hand in silent command. Andreas reached towards the recorder, his finger hovering over the button as he announced into it that he and Inspector Tsountas were about to leave the room, giving the time when the interview was suspended. He switched off the machine and pointed to the door. Kyriakos followed him out and the door closed behind them.

In the interview room, Day focused on regaining self-control. Behind him, Skouros was breathing noisily as if his air passages were blocked. The younger man stood stiffly at the door, ready to open it at the return of the senior officers. Day sensed that both men were expecting trouble from him, and that Skouros at least was likely to react violently. He made every attempt not to move a muscle.

The door opened again, and Andreas and Kyriakos resumed their seats. Slowly and carefully, Day raised his interlaced fingers to wipe a drip of sweat from his eye.

'Hello, Martin,' said Andreas, looking directly at him for the first time with a certain sadness.

Andreas did not reactivate the recording machine, but turned instead, with professional courtesy, to his colleague.

'Inspector Tsountas, would you please dismiss your men from the room? I have something to say in private.'

Surprised, Tsountas nodded to Skouros and both men left.

'I'd like to give you some information which I've felt unable to share before now,' said Andreas, when the door was closed. 'Martin Day is a co-opted member of my own team, supporting my investigation into the suspected illegal activities on board the yacht *Alkyoni*. He was recruited on 12th July, and has been under constant surveillance by members of my unit since that date, for his own protection. In my opinion, as a civilian he was entitled to that. I can therefore disillusion you regarding his involvement in the death of Vassos Nikolopoulos on the night of 22nd July. He was nowhere near the Villa Myrsini; he was at his home in Filoti, where my men were observing his movements.'

Kyriakos looked at him in shock; Day was no less amazed.

'My officers also accompanied him to Athens,' Andreas continued quietly, with a look at Day, 'although I don't suppose he realised they were there. They're extremely good.'

'Why didn't you tell me this before?' said Kyriakos, rather too loudly.

'I'll come to that. I need hardly say that the charge of murder against Martin is null and void. Intriguing idea about the scratches, but I'm afraid they were sustained exactly as he explained. So we'll need to start again from the beginning with your murder case. Do you have any other suspects?'

Kyriakos found nothing to say, though his expression suggested that there was a great deal he would like to say that would be far from advisable.

'The charge that he's involved in antiquity trading will also have to be dropped. Your case against him is uncorroborated and would certainly not stand up to the scrutiny of Judge Delimbaris, should we permit it to reach his office. There is simply no solid evidence. Let's consider the law itself. Martin has not imported, exported, bought or sold a single item of cultural significance. He has not made an illegal excavation, nor has he defaced or destroyed an immovable monument. He does not have in his possession any illegally-acquired artefacts, although I find it curious that you have not proposed a search of his property. He has not conspired with others, nor acted independently, to loot items of cultural significance from their original locations within Greece. He has not been involved in the trading of objects looted by others. In short, he has not infringed any part of the law protecting cultural heritage. Or am I mistaken?'

'We'll see about that,' snapped Kyriakos.

'I don't think so, Inspector. The investigation is under my direction, and you overstepped your duty in sending a draft to the public prosecutor without my permission.'

Kyriakos Tsountas snapped shut the folder on the table in front of him with exasperation, his face red with anger. Andreas had not finished.

'You asked why I didn't speak of this before. The answer will not, I'm afraid, make easy listening. It involves the circumstances surrounding your posting to Naxos last year. Unfortunately, my observations have confirmed the misgivings of our superiors: you do seem in danger of repeating the mistakes that resulted in your transfer here.

'I was part of the official investigation into the disastrous raid on the *Lady Warrior*. You had recently applied for promotion, but your superiors had reservations about your readiness for higher rank. The decision was made to give you responsibility for the biggest operation of your career, one in which you could demonstrate your capabilities. This was the *Lady Warrior*, a freight vessel sailing from Istanbul to Cairo under the flag of Malta, which was rumoured to be carrying an illegal cargo of narcotics, military uniforms and currency; you were to lead the raid on this ship.

'It was brutal. A man died. You also disobeyed a direct order in the conduct of the affair, adding gross insubordination to the complaints against you. You survived the internal enquiry, despite the protests of several of the panel, but there was no place for you any more with the Volos force. You were posted here, and the scandal was buried. It was not, however, forgotten.'

Tsountas found nothing to say and barely managed to remain seated.

'I'm required to report to our superiors on my findings, Tsountas, including your conduct of the operation against the Villa Myrsini, your investigation into the murder of Nikolopoulos, and your treatment of the detainees in your custody.' He sighed, and his tone became slightly more gentle. 'Perhaps a leave of absence would be beneficial, and some serious thought on the subject of your future career.'

With the angry departure of the chief of police, Captain Skouros re-entered the interview room. He stood to attention, his eyes on Andreas.

'Remove the handcuffs and leave us, please,' instructed Andreas.

When the captain had obeyed and the door was closed, Andreas gave Day a sincere and unreserved apology.

29

.

'That's it?' said Day grimly. 'All over?'

'It should be.'

'I find that less than reassuring. You owe me an explanation.'

'You're right, I do, and you shall have one. I suggest we get out of here first. There will be formalities, but it shouldn't take long.'

'I need you to contact Helen. She might be on Naxos already and she won't know where I am. They took my phone.'

'I know, and we've been in touch. She understands why she couldn't reach you and she knows she'll see you back at Filoti later.'

'How did she sound?'

'Impressively calm. Relieved you'd be all right. She has a lot of questions, but she's keeping them for you. Come on, let's get going.'

They went to the front desk where Day's belongings were returned to him in exchange for his signature. When he put on his shoes it felt oddly as if they belonged to somebody else. The young man on duty outside the main door stiffened respectfully as he emerged ahead of Andreas onto the sunny square and looked around. Café Seferis was full of customers sitting at the pavement tables and the road was busy with the usual comings and goings. The shock that he felt at seeing the life of the *plateia* in full swing in front of him made him realise how much he had been affected by his arrest. Perhaps he had already begun to feel that he would not see this lively scene again. He wondered whether he would ever tell Andreas that, in his cell inside the Naxos police station, he had come to doubt his chances of release.

Andreas was checking his watch.

'My car's round the corner,' he said. 'You have a choice. I can take you straight home to Helen. Or you can let me buy you a beer and something decent to eat, and tell you everything I can. After that I can either take you to Filoti, or you can pick up your car, which surprisingly is still at Villa Myrsini.'

'I'm going to call Helen,' Day said. 'Then I'll take the explanation.'

Andreas nodded and they walked to his car. As Andreas got into the driving seat, Day found a private spot and called Helen's mobile. They spoke for several minutes, during which her voice sounded small and tight. She told him to make sure that Andreas answered all his questions so that he could tell her later. He promised to do so with a determination that nobody could fail to understand.

Andreas drove out of town to a quiet beach taverna favoured by tourists rather than locals. Day looked exhausted, his clothes were crushed and his hair was matted. He would want to avoid anyone he knew, and he had said as much. They chose a table on the sand away from other people and moved it still further, so that they could talk without being overheard. Andreas noticed Day sat with his back to the taverna.

When the woman who owned the place gave them the menus and asked what they would like to drink, Andreas had to answer for them both. He ordered two large beers and two plates of lamb with *patates tyganites*. Day was actively ignoring everything and staring at the sea.

'That okay, Martin?'

'Thanks.'

The drinks arrived first, large glasses of Mythos beer with condensation pooling from their sleek sides. Day laughed suddenly.

'It's only been a couple of days, but I feel … It hardly seems real to be sitting here.'

He picked up his glass and savoured his first sip, before steadily drinking a third of the contents.

'Cheers,' he said belatedly as he put it down. 'That's a lot better. So, what were you doing while I was enjoying our friend's hospitality?'

'Interviews with Ridgeway on three separate occasions, four video calls to Dimitris Delimbaris, the anakritis, and several long virtual meetings with my group in Athens about Kakouris. These are influential men with friends in extremely high places; we had to get it right. But I know that what you really want to know is why I left you so long. May I start at the very beginning?'

As Andreas laboured through his story and Day listened quietly, they ate the lamb stew and crisp, salty chips which constituted Day's first hot meal in three days. He tried not to interrupt, but to understand and to remember the alternative version of the events in which he had taken part. He would repeat them to Helen later, and gradually, he thought, they might make sense to him. His anger towards Andreas had disappeared by the end of the meal. He declined another beer, but drank a great deal of the bottled water on the table. Occasionally he asked a question.

'Did you really put people to watch me, like you told Kyriakos?'

'Yes, of course. At a distance. Did you imagine I would lie?'

'Probably best if I don't answer that,' said Day. 'I can't believe I didn't notice them. Anyway, I have reason to be very grateful to them. I'll try to think back to what they might have seen.'

'If you mean the attractive young lady who visited you late one particular night, you can rely on our discretion.'

'It wasn't like that, Andrea!'

'Really?' Andreas's eyes twinkled briefly, but he looked relieved. 'What else do you want to know?'

'I understand it took time to complete the case against Ridgeway, but not why it was necessary for me to be arrested at all. You were pretty sure I'd be charged with the murder, weren't you? You could have prevented it. Why didn't you?'

'Getting evidence to convict Ridgeway was only one of my concerns at the start of this case. It was the one that offered the greatest chance of success, but even that was far from certain. Another objective was to investigate Theodoros Kakouris, one of the most well-connected but little-known men of power in Greece. Of those two matters I had no difficulty talking to you openly, and I did so. In the case of Ridgeway we were successful, and my colleagues are already investigating people connected to him. Kakouris has probably moved beyond my reach again. I haven't, of course, answered your question. Your arrest, I'm afraid, was necessary if I was to succeed in my third objective.'

'Which was, it seems, Kyriakos himself?'

'That's right. I told you some of it a few days ago, and you heard what I said in the interview room. The story goes back a long way. Before I transferred to the Antiquities Fraud Agency, I was on the official police review board looking into the raid on the *Lady Warrior*, the cargo ship searched by the Volos police. Tsountas was in charge, and it really was an unmitigated disaster. You remember I said he was accused of gross insubordination? It was a particularly appalling example of hubris, unacceptable at any level in the police force. It led directly to the crewman's death, which was aggravated suicide, and Tsountas's superior officer took early retirement. The review dragged its feet. It was still in progress when I moved to my new job, but I kept in touch through former colleagues in Athens HQ. When the whole thing, including the suicide, was quietly made to disappear, and Tsountas was promoted and sent to Naxos, I couldn't let it go.'

He stopped speaking and seemed to be reviewing his memories with grim distaste. Suddenly, Day understood.

'You needed him to show his hand, make another big mistake. You gave me to him deliberately, didn't you? You knew he had something against me, that he'd reveal his vicious side when he had me in his power, and you could make sure this time he didn't get away with it. Thanks a lot. The last guy on the receiving end of that man's brutality killed himself.'

'Look, Martin, I'm really sorry about what happened to you. I was keeping a close eye on it all the time.'

'I certainly didn't notice.'

He drained the last of his water and sat back. He could hear the voices of other people in the taverna behind him, and was surprised not to have been aware of them before. It was like emerging from an altered state, from the cloud of otherness that had clung round him since leaving the interview room.

'I think I will have another beer,' he said. 'Just a small one.'

Andreas waved to the proprietor and asked for two small glasses of Mythos. While they waited, Day picked a piece of bread from the basket on the table and threw small pieces to a sparrow that was hopping round his feet. The repetition of it seemed to soothe him.

'You have nothing on Kakouris, you said?'

'Nothing. The yacht and the villa were both clean.'

'Well, I may have something for you. My friend at the Epigraphic Museum called me back about the inscription on the *Alkyoni*. It's only a theory; she hasn't even seen a photograph, so it's educated guesswork at best.'

'Understood. What did she say?'

Day told him. As he listened, Andreas began to smile. Not only could he see a possible way forward in his pursuit of Kakouris, but Day was talking to him in his normal manner at last, and the old spirit had returned to his voice.

Andreas picked up the bill for lunch and they returned to his car. Their talk was of historical cases of vandalism in which parts of monuments had been removed from Greece and turned up in places as far flung as Alexandria and Istanbul. It was good to think of other things for a while, and it occupied Day's mind until they reached their destination, the Villa Myrsini. They pulled up by the Fiat.

'Thanks for speaking to Helen,' said Day. 'Let me know how things go with Kakouris.'

'Certainly. And believe me, I'm deeply sorry for what you were put through.'

'Means to an end, it seems,' Day said without conviction.

He got out and shut the door. Andreas turned the car and drove away.

It was only then that Day became keen to avoid being seen, especially by Maria. He strode over to the Fiat, which showed signs of having been searched, hoping to get away unobserved. He was not in luck. When the front door opened and Maria called his name, he had no choice but to go to her. He passed his fingers through his hair as he walked, but there was little he could do about his general appearance.

'My God!' she said, and held him in her arms to look at him. 'What on earth has happened to you? Oh, Martin! Come inside.'

'I'd rather not, Maria.'

'I expect you don't want to be seen like that, but don't worry, Papa's asleep and Christina's out walking. Come on, what do you need? A shower? A *tsipouro*? Whisky?'

He laughed. He could not help but be charmed by her.

'Thank you, but I really do have to go. Have you had any word from Yianni?'

'No, but he has a lawyer now and she's spoken to Papa. Christina and I feel so guilty, Martin. We should have helped him.'

Day's face must have been more expressive than words, but Maria was not expecting an answer.

'Poor Christina,' she continued, as they walked slowly to his car. 'Not only did she have to put up with that awful Pierre Ridgeway, but she had to tell the police that she could give Yianni an alibi for the night Vasso died. It wasn't how they wanted Papa to hear of their relationship.'

'Their relationship?'

'Yes. When Yianni went to Kalamata to work in the restaurant, he lived with Christina's family, and that was when they fell in love. They kept it a secret, and had to slip off together to be alone. They're first cousins, you see. Christina's parents would have disapproved. By the time Yianni left Kalamata they'd decided she would follow him to New York and they'd get married.

'Soon after he left, though, Christina found out she was pregnant. Yianni was ecstatic. They brought forward their plans and arranged to have the baby in America. Christina's parents took it quite well, and Yianni was about to book Christina's flight when she had her accident.'

'What happened?'

'She was hit by a motorbike, hit and run; that's how she got the scar on her face. She was taken to hospital but she lost the baby. It was a little boy. Poor Yianni was broken-hearted, but then he made one of the biggest mistakes of his life: he didn't go to Kalamata to be with her. I think he just couldn't handle it.

'Christina couldn't forgive him, of course. They didn't even write to each other after that. Nobody was allowed to even mention it to Yianni.

'Then last year Christina wrote to Papa asking if she could come and visit. Of course, he was delighted. He knew nothing about the relationship between them, but he adores Christina. She and Yianni are together again, and she's like a sister to me. Oh God, Martin, if only I hadn't looked for Paraskevi!'

'You're not to blame for any of this, Maria. What's Christina going to do now?'

'She's going home to Kalamata in a few days. She wanted to see Yianni, but she hasn't been allowed to. When the police told us what he'd done, she went to pieces; she stayed in her room for a long time and wouldn't speak to anyone. She thinks that Yianni's anger against Stefanos was all part of his grief at losing their child. Stefanos seemed to have thrown away his chance to be a parent, a chance Yianni would have given anything to have.'

There seemed nothing Day could say in the face of so much loss and misunderstanding. Maria had turned to face him and was looking at him again anxiously.

'You really do look awful, Martin. What happened to you? It was so terrible when you were arrested and taken away like that. Have they really let you go? You're free?'

'Yes, I'm free.'

It was time to tell her the truth. In one important respect, he was not free. He had not made a confession to the police, but he was about to make one now. He took her hand.

'If I was a better man, Maria, the kind of man you have every reason to want at your side, I would have found the courage to say this before. I'm not going to have a relationship with you. I can't be what you want me to be, I can't be a partner for you, because I'm already involved with someone else. She and I have been apart for a little while, and I suppose I've been working it out, but I'm going to do everything I can to put it right with her. I should have been more honest with you, I'm sorry. I hope you can eventually forgive me.'

She nodded slowly, her eyes on the ground. He waited for her anger, but when she looked up again it was with a sad but indulgent smile, the kind that a parent might give a naughty child. He wondered whether she had even been truly surprised.

She leaned across and kissed him lightly on the lips.

'*Adio*, Martin,' she said. 'I think we'll meet again. I hope so.'

He watched her until she disappeared inside the villa, then thoughtfully got into his car.

30

Silence, but for the smallest of sounds. The susurration of the long yellow grasses in the intermittent breeze. The hum of purple bees gathering nectar from late-flowering plants on the hillside. Partridges calling after the heat of the day had passed, the song of a lark, and the distant cry of a gull out at sea. Goat bells and faint bleats from fields far away. The tiny noises of flies, and of the wings of doves. The rattle of a loose shutter moving against its neighbour in the gentle stirring of the air.

It was the half-closed shutters of the bedroom window that were rattling, making a faint protest as they allowed the scents of the valley to enter along strips of warm afternoon light. The rest had been a dream. Day surfaced with a frisson of sadness, as if he had just been ejected from Paradise.

His cheek was resting comfortably on a soft cotton pillow, and Helen's closed eyes were only inches from his face. Her hair was gold in the light that slid between the louvres. For a moment, he was surprised to find himself on her side of the bed; then he remembered how he had got there.

He was thinking in images and feelings, but if words had been available at that moment, he might have reassured himself that by waking up he had not left Paradise.

Day was enjoying his second shower since arriving home that afternoon. The first had been a necessity to restore him to himself and make him acceptable to Helen, and cleanliness had never felt so good. It had made falling into bed together afterwards even more delicious. The current shower was still more sweet because they were sharing it together. He should really have installed a power shower by now, but at the moment he was enjoying how the lazy warm water trickled gently down her body.

'Let me wash your back,' he murmured, preparing his hands with soap and starting on her shoulders as she turned her back to him. He then blamed the small size of the cubicle for the misdirection of his hands, and drew her against him.

Eventually they dried each other and put on towelling wraps before going out to the balcony and sitting close together.

'We're completely private here,' she said in a mischievous tone that he had not heard before. He was very happy to match it.

'We could do anything; nobody would see us.'

She laughed, put her bare feet on another chair, and took his hand. Her familiar fingers in his own gave him a pleasure far greater than he expected.

'Let's go somewhere special for dinner tonight,' he said. 'Anywhere you want.'

'That's a good idea. I'd like to go to O Thanasis, please. I know that isn't what you meant, but we don't need to go into Chora and find somewhere new. We should do the things that are part of our life here. Do you understand? In fact, would you make us a G&T, the way you used to?'

He went willingly inside to do as she asked. As he fetched the ice tray from the freezer, he thought how it seemed a very long time since they had last sat together on the balcony to watch the evening take over from the day. She had been away barely two months, but it felt longer. He emptied the ice into the glasses and halved the lemon that had been ageing in the fridge. He squeezed one half over the ice and threw the skin into the sink before licking the juice from his fingers. The zesty spray reached his nostrils as he cut the rest into slices. His tastebuds tingled. His senses seemed oddly heightened, either from his recent days as a prisoner of the Hellenic Police or from the last few hours as another kind of prisoner altogether. It was the same when he opened the gin and savoured its strong citrus aroma followed by its floral and fruity sweetness. It was as if a layer of clothing had been removed from his sense of smell. The bright, spicy bite of the tonic as tiny drops sprang into the air was irresistible: he took a quick sip from his own drink before adding a slice of lemon and a squeeze of juice to both glasses. He checked again. Finally satisfied, he carried them to the balcony.

Helen was staring at the fading light above the distant peak of Mount Zas which, as the evening temperature dropped, was appearing more clearly with each passing moment. He gave her a glass and sat down beside her.

'Welcome home, Helen. This house was an empty place without you.'

'It's good to be back,' she said, clinking glasses and taking a first sip. 'Oh, I see you haven't lost your touch!'

'Thank you, very kind of you to say so,' he laughed, looking at her longingly and deliberating exactly how private the balcony might be.

It was almost dark by the time they walked down to the village. His senses still heightened, Day walked with a spring in his step, deeply happy at the reversal in his fortunes. They decided to walk the length of the main road before going to the taverna for dinner.

The main street of Filoti was surprisingly lively, buzzing with people enjoying the warmth of the evening. Even though it was Tuesday and a working day, both visitors and locals seemed to be in festive mood. Everyone was dressed up, every light in the town was blazing, and they passed a local celebrity enjoying a glass of ouzo at a pavement café, chatting to the proprietor. It reflected their mood perfectly.

Outside Taverna O Thanasis they stopped in surprise. The outside tables were all occupied, and even the interior of the restaurant was full.

'I don't remember ever seeing that before,' said Helen. 'Not one empty table.'

They were just turning away when Thanasis came hurrying out, his eyes sparkling and his arms wide open, a picture of *filoxenia*, the famed Greek hospitality.

'La Belle Hélène!' he cried. 'She is back, and more lovely than before! It's good to see you again at our *tavernaki*, Kyria Helen. Come inside! I will find you a table. Sit at the bar, enjoy a little ouzo first.'

'Why is it so busy tonight, Thanasi?' asked Day, as they accepted his invitation.

'Tonight there is to be a concert! That is why all the people are here in the town. It is in honour of our most famous son, Iakovos Kambanellis. You know about him? His name is very respected on Naxos. He was a wonderful poet, he wrote many plays, and the words for more than a hundred songs. Tonight some of his songs will be performed in our outdoor stadium, at the other end of the town.'

He placed two glasses of ouzo, a little bucket of ice and a bottle of water on the bar next to them, and an anxious expression came over his face.

'I think there may be some tickets left, if you would rather go to the concert? You should not miss it. I will get them for you.'

'That's very kind, Thanasi, but we'd prefer to stay here,' said Helen, much to the big man's delight. He nodded and left them to enjoy their drinks.

Within twenty minutes, people began to walk past the taverna towards the open-air venue, and a table near the window became free. Having cleared it and covered it with a fresh chequered cloth, Thanasis brought them menus, bread, cutlery and two small glasses, and went away to welcome more customers.

'I'd forgotten what it's like living with you, Martin,' said Helen. 'I feel rather drunk already.'

'Is that the ouzo or my intoxicating personality?'

'The ouzo. And the gin.'

'Then we'd better order some food. What would you like?'

'The traditional cuisine of Naxos,' replied Helen without hesitation. 'The more traditional, the better.'

When Thanasis had seated his latest arrivals, a large group of tourists from Chora, they had a chance to ask him what was cooking in the kitchen.

'We have veal with artichokes, sea bream, and *paidakia*. I remember the little chops are one of your favourites, Martin. Also, in honour of the concert tonight, there is a shrimp *saganaki* made with a very special Naxian cheese.'

He bent down to them and almost whispered in his enthusiasm.

'I recommend that you begin with a small portion of this cheese, perhaps with a few other little *mezedes* and another ouzo. My good friend Dimitris is the cheese-maker. He is renowned on Naxos and his cheeses are highly admired throughout the Cyclades. We sometimes call this one 'black cheese', because of the dark colour of the outside … what is the English word?'

'Rind.'

'That's it. This cheese is yellow and salty and delicious! I find it slightly spicy. Excellent for cooking, but also quite delicious to eat on its own.'

He leaned in slightly towards Day.

'Its name, *arseniko*, means 'male', Martin. So it must be good for us men, no?'

He winked, and Day glanced over at Helen, who was doing her best not to laugh.

'We'd better have some *arseniko* then,' he smiled. 'A portion of fava, of course, because it's Helen's favourite. What about the *paidakia*, darling? Or would you prefer something else?'

'The chops will be perfect. And some vegetables, please. I need vegetables. More than just chips, Martin.'

'Okay, I think we're done, then. Can we leave it to you, Thanasi?'

'Of course!' the big man grinned. 'Some wine?'

'Of course!' Day echoed. 'A *misokilo kokkino*, please.'

Thanasis departed for the kitchen and Day smiled at Helen. For a while he felt no need to say anything.

'It's good to have you back,' he said finally. 'Do you want to talk about it?'

'Yes, but later,' she said. 'First, you have to tell me more about what's been happening to you while I've been away.'

Exceptional circumstances can modify even the most sacrosanct of principles, even one as important as enjoying good food without distraction. Helen wanted to hear everything, more than just the bare bones of the story that she knew already from his late-night message, from Andreas, and from what he had told her on arriving home. They declined Thanasis's offer of more ouzo, but when the jug of wine arrived, Day poured a small amount into each glass and they drank it as they ate the piquant *arseniko* cheese. He described the people at the villa and his early visits there, told her about his talks, and about Vassos, Stefanos and Klairi.

As various film producers had found, he had a gift for story-telling. His afternoon with Helen had restored much of his equilibrium, and distanced him to some extent from the emotions of the recent past, so to his own ears it was as if his experiences might have happened to somebody else. He was largely unaware that he was being selective in what he described.

Their *mezedes* were taken away, their main dish was brought, and still he talked. From time to time he refreshed his throat with water, sipped his wine, or enjoyed the crisp edges of a grilled lamb chop. Luckily, nothing seemed to have spoiled his appetite. The vegetable dish that Thanasis had brought them was a *briam*, baked aubergines and Mediterranean vegetables, and naturally he was enjoying the freshly-cooked Naxian chips.

He told her about the wine festival and about Fabrizio, and then about Fotini and the situation that Fabrizio had been forced to accept. He recounted the story of his visit to Athens and the lekythos. Helen listened without interrupting until he had run out of words, but she still had some questions.

'The art dealer - what was he really like?' she said. 'I need to understand these people.'

'Pierre Ridgeway? In appearance he was quite good-looking, I suppose. Small, about my age, looked rather like Tom Cruise but with none of Tom's appealing openness. He also had a bad habit of flirting with younger women in front of his wife.'

'Mmm,' she said, scooping up the last of the fava dip with a piece of crusty bread. 'Not my kind.'

'No. He's a hard man, a man of few words, with sharp eyes and a persuasive kind of charm, and clever.'

'Not clever enough, it seems,' she murmured. 'What about Theodoros Kakouris?'

'He's quite different, a big personality, and rather likeable until he throws his weight around. Larger than life, outwardly very friendly. He showed another side when he was taken to the police station. And he's devious. I found that out rather late.'

'How old is he?'

'Late sixties, maybe. No idea.'

'You're not very good at ages, are you, Martin?'

'Not at all. Age doesn't matter to me.'

'That's not what you said when you were turning forty, I remember.'

Day laughed and finished the wine in his glass.

'So, why would a man like Kakouris, who has enough money to buy anything he wants, risk breaking the law just to acquire antiquities for his collection?'

Day shrugged. The antiquities trade was abhorrent to him, and involvement in it almost inexplicable. He poured a little more wine into her glass and then his own. He was beginning to feel reluctant to talk any more. It was over, Helen was back, and he wanted to move forward, but he owed her an answer to all her questions.

'There'll be some artefacts that can only be acquired outside the law,' he said. 'Things that have been looted or illegally traded for centuries and have no provenance. If Kakouris coveted such a thing, he would have no choice but to acquire it on the quiet.'

'I see. Is there no way to involve the authorities and buy such an object legally?'

Day sighed. 'I don't know. Perhaps.'

Helen stroked his fingers on the blue and white tablecloth.

'I know you don't really want to talk about it any more,' she said. 'Just one more thing, please. I understand why Andreas thought you could help him, but I don't understand the rest of it. Why did he let you be arrested and charged with murder? It's incredible. He should have got you out of there.'

Day forced a smile. He had managed to give her no details at all about the time he was under arrest; that much had been completely deliberate.

'He gave me his reasons.'

'Well, can you explain them to me, please? Andreas was our friend.'

'He still is. When he took on the investigation into Kakouris and Ridgeway, there was something else he wanted to achieve. He told me from the start about his suspicions of the illegal trading, but nothing about the other man he was going after. In the end, there was a role for me in achieving that objective too.'

He paused thoughtfully.

'I have a lot of respect for the Greek police, Helen, you know that. Unfortunately, there are always individuals who let the rest down, and it seems that Kyriakos Tsountas is one of them. Andreas knew this first-hand and was determined to sort it out. He needed to make Kyriakos give himself away, on record, and face the consequences.'

'Kyriakos?' Helen sat back in surprise. 'The man I met last summer? I know you and he didn't get on too well, but I thought he was just socially awkward. What on earth has he done?'

Day told her about the *Lady Warrior*, reluctant though he was to go through it all again. Helen frowned. She took a small sip of wine and looked at him thoughtfully.

'How did Andreas mean to do it?'

'As part of his current investigation into Ridgeway and Kakouris, Andreas needed the local force to raid the villa at the same time as his own team raided the yacht. It wasn't ideal, but it also gave him the chance to put Kyriakos to the test. Kyriakos went in too early and too hard, but this wasn't enough for Andreas. When

I was in his power and charged with murder, Kyriakos revealed himself as the kind of policeman who gets a conviction by any means at his disposal, even if he has the wrong man. He doesn't follow procedure, he isn't too fussy about evidence, he just relies on extracting a confession.'

'What do you mean?' she said, her eyes reflecting her concern as one thought led to another. 'Were you ill-treated?'

Noticing that she had stopped stroking his hand, Day covered her fingers with his own and looked steadily into her eyes.

'It's honestly nothing to worry about, darling. I'm fine. Andreas was always in control, and he was successful in the end. I expect this island will soon have a new chief of police.'

Vangelis came to ask if he could clear the table, for which Day was grateful. A wave of tiredness had just come over him. He asked for the bill, but Vangelis returned instead with a complimentary plate of fresh fruit and placed it between them on the table. Day looked at it sadly and finished the last of his wine. Helen politely pierced a piece of orange with her fork and regarded him thoughtfully without eating it.

'It's not over yet, is it?' she said. 'Who killed the old man in the swimming pool?'

'You mean, if it wasn't me?'

'Hey, that's not what I meant. Don't you want to know who it was?'

'Sorry, but can we go home?'

Helen put down her fork and nodded. They paid Thanasis at the bar and wished the family goodnight. Day was suddenly desperate for fresh air and headed outside. Behind him, Thanasis embraced Helen in a moment of gratitude and affection.

'He's your number one admirer!' said Day without turning round when she caught up with him.

Helen said nothing until they reached their front door and Day had his key in the lock.

'Did you really say that *Thanasis* is my number one admirer?'

Day sighed and shook his head. They went into the wood-scented front room without switching on the light, and he turned to her as soon as the door was closed again.

'I'm sorry, Helen. I'm … I don't know. Worn out. This morning it looked like I could be in prison for the rest of my life. This afternoon you were here and I was in heaven.' He put his hands on her shoulders. 'Are you going to stay with me?'

She did not reply. Taking his hand, she led him to the bedroom, where she took off her clothes without turning on the light. There was no excitement, and he even wondered whether this would be the last time he would watch her do this. He undressed next to her and they got into bed. She nestled against him under the single sheet and he left his arm under her shoulders. He could smell the soapy scent of their shower on her body and felt the weight of her hand on his chest. The room was still hot from the heat of the day, the warm night air of the valley still wafting in through the open window. The woven curtain that kept out the insects allowed in the cry of an owl, the high-pitched little owl of Athena.

'Shall I tell you why I stayed away so long?' she asked.

'Yes, please.'

'There were the book-signings and things, but there was another reason I didn't come back. And you're right, it was to do with you.'

He was suddenly not exhausted any more, but full of dread. He managed a little noise to show he was listening, but said nothing.

'You know me better than anybody, Martin, or I believe you do. You know about all the years I spent determined not to be vulnerable ever again, after the break-up with Zissis. Even after his death I turned down any chance of a new relationship. You were a good friend to me.

'Then, last year, you asked me for a different kind of relationship, and I decided to give it a chance. It was a good decision, and I've been very, very happy with you.

'I don't know when that changed for me. It might have been when you went into that underwater cave last year, while I was stuck on the boat not knowing what was happening to you. I felt exposed, and I didn't like it. That's how it is with you, you know: you're unpredictable, you enjoy risk-taking, it's not easy loving you. There came a point - I was afraid, Martin, to tell the truth. Being afraid is a wake-up call, but I don't expect you to understand that. I don't think you've ever been afraid in your life.'

Day remembered the hours in the police station being afraid in a way he had never been before. He understood what she was telling him, but he was glad that she didn't know that on this point she was wrong.

As he had not found anything to say, they lay in silence for several minutes.

'I did a lot of thinking in London,' she went on. 'I didn't want to come back to Naxos because I felt I couldn't talk to you about it. What could I have said? You might have given me the answer I didn't want to hear. You like your independence, you're happy with your own company, you're fine living alone, without responsibilities. Well, I want something else now.'

He turned on his side so that their faces were close. Her eyes showed none of the vulnerability he had expected to see in them, only a kind of defiance.

'I'm not sure I understand, Helen. Please just tell me.'

He probably held his breath until she told him what she wanted. He would never afterwards be sure.

31

Helen had been looking forward to meeting the artist on Paros who had chosen Andreas over the attractive Fabrizio Mirano.

Although she had only met Fabrizio once, some years ago in London, the memory of him made her smile. However, he had always been married to his work, and sadly he had made the mistake of putting his personal life on the back burner. Fotini must have given up waiting for him, which had worked very much in Andreas's favour.

Andreas was equally devoted to his work, but he always made time for the important things in life. After working on the Ridgeway-Kakouris prosecutions for many weeks, he had just enjoyed some leave with Fotini on Paros and was now about to return to Athens, taking her with him this time.

He had suggested meeting Helen and Day for dinner on Naxos on the evening before their return to the mainland. The chosen restaurant was called Zambelis, where Andreas had eaten once before. It was hidden away in the old town near the Kastro of Naxos, and had an excellent reputation. A memorable dinner, Andreas said, was the least he could do, and he would be paying.

Day was in high spirits that evening, quite irrepressible. As the Greeks would say, he had found his *kefi* again, that extremely buoyant mood and enthusiasm for life that characterises our best of times. As he showered and changed for the dinner at Zambelis, he reflected that the last six weeks, since Helen had explained how she felt, had been among the happiest of his life.

He opened his wardrobe and wondered what to wear. Helen had just gone to the spare room, where she kept some of her more dressy clothes in an empty old wardrobe that had come with the house. This would be a special occasion, and they had agreed that from now on they would live every day to the full. With that in mind, he pulled out a pair of dark blue trousers that were clean and crease-free, and then a shirt that he had not worn very much, perhaps because it was white, long-sleeved and had a button-down collar. It was, however, freshly ironed, and as he put it on he liked the quality of the cotton. The weather was warm for September, so he wouldn't bother with a jacket. He might even roll up the sleeves of the shirt after a glass or two of wine.

He wandered to the balcony to wait for Helen. It was the time when small birds flocked together to begin the nightly roost, and they had gathered in the plane tree in the neighbour's garden. It was tall, like the palm trees near Diogenes where the same evening ritual took place. He listened to the natural music of the birds' chattering as they squabbled among the branches, and watched as a single bird would occasionally emerge from the foliage and pop back in at a different point.

He turned round as Helen arrived. Despite her weeks in England, her skin was tanned and her honey-coloured hair had lightened again in the Aegean sun. She looked happy and well, and had dressed for a celebration. Her trousers were silky and flowing, topped by a low-cut fitted jacket in a matching material. She was holding a chain on which hung a delicate tapering spiral, the necklace he had given to her last year. She gave it to him and turned round, lifting her hair so that Day could fasten the clasp. He fastened it and kissed her neck.

'Time to go?' he said.

'Yes, I'm ready. Nice shirt, by the way.'

'Thanks, I've not worn it for a long time. I've never been sure about the collar. This is an Oxford shirt, you know. Would you believe it? I now use both the Oxford comma and the Oxford collar, despite being a Cambridge man.'

'Idiot!' she laughed.

He locked the balcony doors and caught up with her in the front room.

'You look lovely, Mrs Day,' he said quietly, and unlatched the front door from behind her. He so liked the sound of that.

They drove through the village and out into the countryside. At Halki, an old man with a donkey was holding up the traffic, though nobody seemed to care. The straight road after Halki offered the chance to speed up, but Day disliked driving fast. There had never seemed much point for someone whose worldview extended thousands of years. They passed through the olive-growing area of the Tragea, where the low sun was turning the trees into richly-dressed dancers in green and grey with touches of black lace, and the sky had taken on the pinks and yellows of the forthcoming sunset.

Chora was busy, and they were lucky to find a parking space behind the Kastro. The spectacular heatwave of July and August had extended Naxos's tourist season, encouraging a fresh wave of visitors to enjoy the more mellow heat of September. Six weeks before, when Helen had arrived back from England, the more popular beaches had been crowded, but now the children had returned to school and by late October the islanders would begin to plan for the quiet winter ahead.

The footpath from the car park into Chora led through the labyrinth of lanes that had been constructed centuries ago to protect the castle from pirate attack. It was still quite challenging today to find the best way through it, as there was minimal signage and the lighting was subtle and sporadic, but Day loved the place. They strolled together uphill and round corners created by buildings that seemed to have grown into one another, with staircases rising to first-floor doorways, and flowerpots at every corner, balanced on steps and ledges. Voices could be heard faintly from within some of the buildings, but there were few people walking in the lanes. They chatted quietly, as the atmosphere of the Kastro seemed to require.

The tranquillity was shattered by the abrupt demand of Day's phone. He pulled it from his pocket and saw that the caller was his friend, Nick Kiloziglou. He stifled the insistent ringing and grinned at Helen.

'G'day, Mr Kiloziglou,' he said, over-doing Nick's Greek-Australian accent. 'What news?'

'G'day, mate!' said Nick, playing along. 'Mother and daughter still both doing well. We're wondering if you guys would like to come over soon? You need to meet the newest member of the family.'

'We'd love to. Have you decided what to call her yet?'

'Yeah, she's called Alexandra. It was my mother's name.'

'Alexandra Kiloziglou. Very nice. Is Nestoras enjoying having a sister?'

'Ah well, yes, but he's pretty sure she's his baby and he knows best what she wants. It's a lot of fun. Anyway, we just wanted to tell you that it's now officially safe to visit us, everything is under control …'

Day heard laughter in the background and presumed it was coming from Nick's wife, Deppi.

'As I was saying, Nesto has everything under control and would like to see you. I think he wants someone to kick a football with him.'

'Me?' said Day, pleased. He rarely considered sport. 'Really?'

'Just joking, mate.'

Ah. I see. Right, we'll give you a ring back and fix up something. When were you thinking of receiving visitors?'

'Whenever you like. Orestis is looking after the business for me; he's coping just fine. Make it soon.'

'Will do, with pleasure. Love from us both, love to Deppi.'

He put his phone away and took Helen's hand again.

'Did you get most of that? Nestoras wants to show us his new baby. We could go over there next week, couldn't we?'

'Yes, let's go soon. Her name's Alexandra? I like that. Isn't it funny, there have been so many babies recently? You know, in your stories about the people at the villa. At least little Alexandra's story is a happy one.'

Day nodded. He wondered if she had ever thought about children, especially in the years after her Greek husband had walked away from the marriage. It was something he had never asked her. Before he could decide whether now was the time, she had moved on.

'Do you remember how you used to feel about Deppi?' she teased.

'Of course. And let's not forget that you had a few dates with Andreas!'

'Mmm. Funny, isn't it?' she laughed. 'You and I did some clever footwork around each other for a very long time.'

They were still recalling strange little snippets from their past when they arrived at Estiatorio Zambelis, where they were to meet Andreas. The white-painted wall of the restaurant bordered the narrow lane, and over the arched entrance was an ornate ironwork decoration featuring the letter Z. They ignored the menu displayed in the lectern and went straight inside. The interior courtyard basked beneath a ceiling hung with golden lighting. Andreas and Fotini were sitting at a table in the corner. Andreas stood up.

'Wonderful to see you again, Helen,' he said, kissing her on both cheeks affectionately. He introduced Fotini, and Helen sat down next to her. Day took the remaining chair, aware of a particularly large smile that would not leave his face.

Helen and Fotini were soon deep in conversation, and Andreas was looking on contentedly. He bore little resemblance tonight to the authoritative chief inspector; he wore a linen suit and an uncharacteristically benign expression. It was hard to believe he was the same man who had dominated the interview room in the Naxos police station. Day congratulated him on his choice of restaurant.

'Impressive, isn't it?' said Andreas. 'I first came here a few years ago with a lawyer friend of mine. I've told you about him before, I think. It was on one of my occasional trips to Naxos to get his advice. He only liked the best places, and this was his favourite.'

'A very good friend to have. Does he still live on Naxos?'

'I'm afraid he's not with us any more,' said Andreas. 'Perhaps we should order the wine so we can drink a toast to him.'

As if she had heard him, a woman dressed as beautifully as any of her guests appeared at his side. She introduced herself as the owner of the restaurant and invited them to call her Anna. Day suspected she might have chosen the name with her multinational guests in mind. He had heard her using many languages as she passed round the tables, putting people at their ease and answering whatever question they had about the food and the wine in their own language.

By general agreement, they spoke with her in Greek. She gave them menus and a wine list, and offered to explain anything on the menu in detail. Day had no trouble believing she knew exactly how everything was cooked. Having asked if she could bring them a small aperitif on the house, she smiled and glided away.

Soon they were all studying the menu with glasses of an unidentifiable but delicious drink that most resembled a fortified wine served on a great deal of ice.

'First and second course,' instructed Andreas, 'and, as I said before, you're my guests tonight. I shall have a steak, and probably the mussels to start. How about you, Martin? The steaks are very good here.'

Day chose the same as Andreas because it sounded exceptional. The mussels were cooked with spicy local sausage and ouzo, and the steak with mushrooms, cream and bacon. Bacon in Greece? How could he resist? He put his menu down on the table and sat back with a happy smile. He did not even feel the need to mention chips.

'Helen, what will you have?' asked Andreas. 'The lobster, perhaps? Come on, we're celebrating your homecoming.'

'I'd like to start with this carpaccio of sea bass, please, prepared with Kitron liqueur. Sounds delicious. Then the grilled prawns, I think. Thank you, Andrea.'

'It's my pleasure,' replied Andreas, regarding her fondly. Day saw the look and grinned at him. 'And Fotini *mou*, what about you?'

Fotini had noticed a fillet of *tsipoura* cooked with oregano, cumin and paprika, with orange-flavoured couscous.

'What a mad combination,' she laughed. 'I have to try it. A small salad first would be fine. I like the sound of this one with chicory leaves, *xynotyri* cheese and pomegranate seeds.'

'Excellent,' said Andreas. 'Would a Mavrotragano from Ambrosia Wine be a good choice tonight, do you think, Martin?'

'Absolutely.'

When the wine came, they raised their glasses to Stefanos and Klairi Patelis, as well as to Andreas's lawyer friend. With his first swallow, Day also privately toasted Vassos, whom he had liked. The wine was rich and oaked, with red-fruit and earthy flavours. It was about as far as it was possible to get from Day's beloved barrel wine, and reminded him of the night of the wine festival and his final conversation with Stefanos.

Helen, meanwhile, was asking Fotini how she had come to live and work on Paros.

'I was born in Thessaly, but I always wanted to travel and particularly to live near the sea. I love its moods and the shifting light on the water. When I finished school, I applied to the Artemis Pantrakis Bequest for funding to support my first year at art college, which meant I could move to Thessaloniki for my training. After I graduated, they gave me a bursary to live in the Cyclades for a year. I chose Paros because there are many fine artists living on the island. It has worked out well.' She glanced over at Andreas. 'I think Andreas said that you paint, too?'

'Oh, occasionally, just for pleasure. Actually, I haven't done any painting for months. It's been a bit of an unusual summer.'

'You've been in the UK?' prompted Andreas.

'Yes. Martin has probably told you that I had to do some book promotion for my publishers.'

'I hope you'll be staying here for a while now?'

'Yes, we'll be here as much as we can.'

She smiled at him but gave no details. Fotini asked about her books and the conversation went in another direction, but Andreas was looking intrigued. He was, after all, a detective.

'What's been happening, Martin?' he said, quietly enough so as not to be overheard. 'Good news?'

'The best.'

Andreas nodded and understood that he should say no more. He changed the subject.

'Did you hear? Stelios Ioannides gave the lekythos to the Greek Archaeological Service, and they've invited your friend Professor Stilgoe to work on it. They were very interested in his theory, and welcomed the chance of such a prestigious collaboration.'

'Thank you, Andrea. I'm sure we have you to thank for that.'

Andreas smiled modestly. 'I did almost nothing. The lekythos is extremely important; its history is astonishing. Anyway, it has helped me a great deal.'

'It has? In what way?'

Andreas hesitated, then asked Fotini and Helen if they would excuse them for just a few minutes. Once outside the restaurant, he felt able to continue. They walked a little way as they talked.

'Stelios Ioannides and I had a long conversation. I knew he he had shown the lekythos to Ridgeway as well as yourself, and I asked him why. He said he'd appreciated your advice, but thought a second opinion would be a good idea. He quickly regretted it. Ridgeway told him nothing about its importance, history or value, but wanted to buy it from him. He kept up the pressure and made a real nuisance of himself. Ioannides took a great dislike to Ridgeway and refused absolutely to let him have the lekythos. He wanted to wait for you to tell him more about it; he knew you wouldn't let him down, he said. After that, he intended to hand it over to the proper authorities.

'I found this all very interesting, and went back to question Ridgeway on several occasions. In the end, it paid off. It was he who killed Nikolopoulos.'

'What? That never occurred to me. Ridgeway was trying to resuscitate him!'

Andreas smiled grimly.

'Yes. I must admit that turns my stomach. I like to think nothing shocks me any more, but performing CPR on the dead body of your victim is particularly revolting.'

He lowered his voice still further as a couple approached from a nearby bar.

'Once the facts began to emerge, including pretty conclusive forensic evidence, Ridgeway's lawyer advised him that an admission of guilt was in his best interest.'

'He admitted to *murder*? I thought they threw away the key.'

'You're right, murder carries a life sentence in Greece. Ridgeway confessed to manslaughter.'

'So what actually happened?'

'Nikolopoulos challenged him about his behaviour towards Ioannides, much as Tsountas assumed. Ridgeway claims that he felt threatened by him to the extent of being afraid for his own safety.'

'I'd put money on Vassos being incapable of that,' said Day.

'You may be right, Martin, we'll never know. Anyway, they agreed to meet and discuss things calmly. Ridgeway admits that it was he who lost his temper, but that he was provoked. He hit out at Nikolopoulos, making the man lose his balance and fall into the pool. Then he stormed off, leaving the old man in the water. Later, seeing the need to put himself in a better light, he changed this story and said he watched Nikolopoulos getting safely out before he went back to his bedroom in the villa.'

'Do you think that's the truth?' said Day.

'Very little of it, in my opinion. Ridgeway swears he only gave Nikolopoulos a slap in the face, but the pathologist found no sign of a blow to the victim's face, and there was a serious wound to the back of his head. The object used to inflict this injury has just been found: a piece of decorative marble from the garden which had been replaced after the murder. The forensic report has confirmed it was the murder weapon, and Ridgeway's DNA was found on it.'

Day let out a long breath. He had just had something of a flashback to Elodie Ridgeway, and the smile that had suggested she was content to see Day under arrest.

'Have you questioned Ridgeway's wife? Didn't she give him an alibi?'

'She said she never realised her husband wasn't with her that night, because she was asleep. She also told us she knew nothing about her husband's business affairs.'

'I find that hard to believe. Well, she presumably won't see much of him for a while. Ridgeway has a lot more to worry about now than a charge of illegal antiquity trading.'

'Indeed he has. On that subject, it's not only Ridgeway who's been taken out of action. His associates in London have been arrested for receiving the goods, and in time we'll find plenty of others like them. There'll be more like Ridgeway, and traders at both ends of the chain, and we should even get to some of the collectors who turn a blind eye to where their acquisitions come from.'

Day smiled; he enjoyed it when Andreas used colloquial English expressions.

'Will that include Theodoros?'

'Kakouris? Ah yes, we had a breakthrough there too. A crew member from the *Alkyoni* had been told to submit a false customs declaration for Kakouris relating to a shipment sent from Naxos to a private address on the mainland. The shipment was meant to contain several crates of fine wine bought at the festival, reasonable enough in the circumstances, but the actual content turned out to be antiquities. The subterfuge of the shipping method suggests they have no legal provenance and the authorities have been called in. If I'm right, it will turn out that the artefacts originated in the various ports of call made by the *Alkyoni* in the past few weeks.'

'Well done. You really achieved what you set out to achieve.'

'You must take some of the credit, my friend,' said Andreas, stopping as they arrived back at the entrance to the restaurant. 'It was your inscription that gave us the authority to bring the crew back in for questioning, re-examine the export documentation and open those shipments.'

They arrived back at the table just in time for the first course. The mussels were steaming with a fragrant aroma of ouzo, the delicate pieces of raw tuna were softened and cured in a light dressing of the local citrus liqueur, and Fotini's salad was piquant with bitter chicory and the pungent sweet-and-sour *xynotyri* cheese.

They talked of other things during the meal. Fotini was looking forward to the next few weeks in Athens, meeting old friends, going to galleries and seeing Andreas when he was off duty. After that they planned to return to Paros for a long weekend, before Andreas went back to the capital and Fotini stayed on the island. The storms and colours of Paros in winter, she said, would be inspiring for her seascapes. Day said nothing, remembering the rain, the winds and the grey days of a Cycladic winter. Helen and he would be spending Christmas in England this year, and it promised to be a very memorable one.

The main dishes were no less delicious than the first course. Day and Andreas were unable to think when they had eaten better steak, and Day was gratified when the food arrived with a side portion of fried potatoes. He caught an amused glance from Helen, who was expertly opening her prawns in a far more delicate manner than he had ever managed. The most beautiful dish, however, was Fotini's. The fillet of *tsipoura* with its piquant sauce and orange-scented couscous looked like something from a Michelin-starred restaurant.

'So, what's next for you, Martin?' asked Andreas, after everything had been enjoyed and the table cleared.

Day looked at Helen, but she was absorbed in something that Fotini was saying.

'We'll be going to London in a couple of weeks and probably stay there over the winter. I spoke to my agent yesterday and we're going ahead with a new proposal for the History Channel, contract to be signed before Christmas.'

Fotini and Helen had now finished their conversation and Fotini asked him for details of the project.

'We'll be making a television series in which we talk about current excavation sites in Greece and describe their importance. A small team of us will write the episodes, and each one will be filmed on location at a dig.'

'Martin will present the programmes,' Andreas added helpfully.

'One of the excavation sites will be on Crete, where our friend Fabrizio is part of a team making a breakthrough,' added Day with a smile to Fotini.

She returned his smile.

'I'm also hopeful that we might include the opening of a new dig here on Naxos,' he continued. 'It's not confirmed yet, but I've heard a whisper that the Ephorate of Antiquities is hoping to begin next year.'

'It will all keep Martin very busy,' said Helen, 'and hopefully out of trouble. He'll be back doing what he loves most.'

'Good,' said Andreas, and glanced meaningfully across at Day. 'I look forward to hearing all about it.'

'You will,' promised Helen. 'We'd also like you to be the first to hear our good news.'

The digestif of Kitron liqueur which Anna had already brought for them made a perfectly acceptable alternative to champagne. It was the yellow variety, the least sweet, and Day's favourite. Andreas, delighted to have had his suspicions confirmed, used it to propose a congratulatory toast.

'To Helen and Martin!' he said, raising his glass. 'May you be very happy!'

The time to bring the evening to an end came all too soon. Andreas went to pay Anna for the meal, and rejoined them in the lane outside the restaurant in high spirits.

'I really like this place,' he said. 'Let's have a post-wedding celebration here when you're back from England.'

'Actually, we're going to arrange a party,' said Day. 'You must come! It will be a feast of Greek food in some wonderful romantic location.'

'Of course, we wouldn't want to miss that,' said Andreas. 'Will it be in England or in Greece?'

'Oh, it will be here on Naxos, though we haven't decided on the venue yet. We want a really quiet wedding ceremony, you see, just ourselves and a couple of witnesses, so we thought we'd try to persuade our friends in England to come here for a party in May next year; they could even make a holiday of it. We can provide quite a bit of free accommodation in the Elias House. Do you think it will work?'

'Yes, that sounds a very good idea,' said Fotini. 'Why would anyone not want to come to Naxos?'

Andreas grinned.

'Well, we'll see you when you get back,' he said, kissing Helen on both cheeks. 'And thanks again, Martin. I mean that.'

They went their separate ways from the restaurant. Helen slipped her arm round Day's waist as they headed back towards the car, talking quietly about the evening they had just enjoyed.

They emerged from the labyrinthine old town quite near to the Portara. It was illuminated, and shone in the dark like an ethereal gateway at the end of the causeway that jutted out into the sea. Small waves were rippling gently against the dark sea wall in the imperceptible off-shore breeze. At the statue of Ariadne they stopped and kissed. When they drew apart, Helen gave a little laugh.

Day looked at her in surprise.

'Sorry. I was just thinking how much I'm looking forward to you turning back into your old self now.'

'I see,' he said, though in fact he did not.

'You've had some bad experiences recently, Martin. I can tell you're trying to make light of what happened, but I can imagine for myself. I was worried it might have changed you. Perhaps it will have done, a little bit. That's why I think that you really must leave all that behind, forget the police and leave them to do their job without your help. Even Andreas.'

'You sound like Fabrizio.'

'Think about it, Martin. The new TV series will mean a lot of travelling, but it's going to be sensational, and I'm sure you'll enjoy yourself. You know, I'd like to see you when you're filming. Would you mind?'

'No, I'd like that.'

They left Ariadne to her solitary contemplation of the sea and sauntered on, talking about the exciting times ahead and the friends they planned to see in London. When they reached the car, just as Day was opening the door for her, Helen became serious again.

'From now on, let's not dwell in the past, darling. Our own past, I mean. Let's live together in the moment, and live life well. You know, seize the day.'

He touched her lips gently with his own, believing that she had just told him that she could leave behind the bad memories of her first marriage. At the time he did not apply her advice to himself, because a pun had sprung into his mind that exactly matched his mood.

'I agree,' he said, 'and you're welcome to *seize the Day* as often as you like. I'm looking forward to it.'

Day and Helen's party will be the subject of a short story,
A Greek Feast on Naxos, which will also contain recipes for Greek dishes.

Many of the characters from *The Naxos Mysteries* will be at the feast, and an
outstanding question will be answered.

A Greek Feast on Naxos

A short story with recipes and notes on Greek cuisine,
with contributions from Greek cooks Aglaia Kremezi, Yiannis Vassilas,
and the author's friends in Greece.

www.thenaxosmysteries.co.uk

Printed in Great Britain
by Amazon